THE LAST BOOK

Further Confessions of Felix Krull, Confidence Man

BY

NOWICK GRAY

COUGAR WEBWORKS * VICTORIA, BC

© Copyright 2017 by Nowick Gray
All rights reserved.

Published by: Cougar WebWorks – CougarWebWorks.com

Cover Design: SelfPubBookCovers.com/FrinaArt

Picaresque metafictional mashup, metaphysical literary fantasy, dystopian magic realism... *The Last Book* goes beyond fan fiction, propelling Thomas Mann's romantic hero Felix Krull into the speculative waters of reincarnation, time travel, and alternative history. He meets his match in Sophie Vaughan: first woman president, astral traveler, and avatar of lost Lemuria.

ISBN: 978-1976084478

ACKNOWLEDGEMENTS

Great appreciation to Samantha Sabovitch, Avi Sirlin, and Matthew Jackson, generous in their close reading and astute in their feedback; along with valuable input from the rest of my Victoria writers group: Kate Howell, Nancy Issenman, and paulo da costa.

To the baby Nashira for her forbearance, patiently swinging in her cradle in the predawn hours while I typed away at an early draft.

And last but not least, the incomparable Thomas Mann, as elaborated in the prefatory confession. In particular, I must credit Mann's original work (trans. Denver Lindley; Knopf, 1955) for Felix's re-audited speech to King Carlos I of Portugal, beginning, *"By his very existence the beggar, huddled in rags..."*

People who proclaim the end of the book just haven't read their literary history. I mean, the first novel, *Don Quixote*, is about the end of the book. That is the premise of literature.

—Tom McCarthy

TABLE OF CONTENTS

PREFATORY CONFESSION 9

PART I – HIGHER CALLING 13

PART II – LIMBO 127

PART III – THE FIRST WOMAN PRESIDENT 223

EPILOGUE: FROM SUCH A REMOVE 373

PREFATORY CONFESSION

"It is not without a certain meager trepidation that I set out to record, for the reader's considered benefit, the events that have occurred since that fateful scene in the living room of the Villa Kuckuck, on the Rua João de Castilhos..."—or so the original Felix Krull may have expressed it, had the pages of Thomas Mann's last, unfinished novel continued.

From such a remove in time and space as I currently enjoy, I can only attempt to recount the denouement of my adventurous pilgrimage in the spirit of Felix's native manner of speech, with the characteristic flavor of that epoch. For this undertaking I ask the reader's indulgence, as I will endeavor to make amends by way of a more contemporary delivery. Meanwhile I make no excuses as I confess to a certain lingering tendency, in a more advanced age, to dawdle and divert, to digress and speculate; for the old Felix has remained a part of me through the progress of time.

I have often wondered if it was worth the effort to delve back into the easily forgotten past, back to a story of an old, lost world. In essence it is the rudeness of the interruption of our story by Death on his pale horse that motivates me to take up the authorial mantle—out of spite, as it were; to exercise a playful revenge. And so, lest the reader be tempted to disbelieve my providential transference across the several planes of life, let me offer the confidence that I have, in the process, exposed the masquerade of that spectral impostor.

I remain indebted to Thomas Mann, with his account of my early life and career entitled *Confessions of Felix Krull, Confidence Man,* for the basis of my tale—no, let us admit, for the entire recorded substance of it up to the point at which the present chronicle begins. Born Felix Krull, I was the favored son of a locally prominent, thoroughly bourgeois German family. Quick of wit and tongue, I was loath to remain in the social mold into which I was born. My predilection for flattery and deceit landed me, via a series of youthful escapades, in the shoes of a reluctant marquis who, like me, wanted no part of the role assigned him so arbitrarily by fate and family. Having switched identities, we parted company in Paris. The ex-marquis went incognito with his lover; while I set out on a world tour which had been arranged to take the marquis first to Lisbon, then onward by steamer to Argentina.

On the train to Lisbon, I made the acquaintance of a professor, Dom Antonio José Kuckuck, who invited me to call at his villa and meet his family. In the course of my visits I became enamored with the daughter, Zouzou. The first complication was her expected marriage to a colleague of Professor Kuckuck. Then, with my ship due to sail in a matter of days, I found myself in the embrace of Zouzou's mother, Dona Maria Pia. At this point in the story, we are left hanging by Thomas Mann, or rather by that gaunt interloper who whisked the writer away before he could relate another word.

As I take up my own pen, in my leisure at the end of it all, to recommence the tale held so long in abeyance, I would ask to establish a compact with the reader concerning the credibility of the subsequent events that unfolded. For presently we must become acquainted with the estimable Sophie Tucker Vaughan, the first woman president of the United States of America, who demonstrated more than earthly powers to make my acquaintance and enlist me to her service.

To any familiar with my previous exploits, it should come as no surprise that I would consort with one of such rank; I merely need mention the long congenial meeting I enjoyed with King Carlos I, monarch of Portugal. Indeed that fortunate encounter would serve to flag my resumé as a "person of interest" to a higher power.

Enough said about the journey to come, offering a redemption of my crude, if flamboyant, rogue's quest. In its scope, however, I must add that the very notion of history itself must be re-examined. As a number of possible futures become apparent, must we not also admit the preponderance of alternative pasts? Clearly I can provoke no argument in stating that time is all of a piece, comprising past, present, and future; and in that summation it presents no singularity, rather an infinite multiplicity.

To take but one most pertinent example: who exactly was, is, or will be "the first woman president"; and what scenario best describes her attainment of that office? This witness—both observer and participant—undertakes to offer here one such history, alongside my own serial misadventures. Now let us return to that divine moment, at the node between past and future, what was and what might have been.

PART I

HIGHER CALLING

The principle which gives the thought the dynamic power to correlate with its object, and therefore to master every adverse human experience, is the law of attraction, which is another name for love. This is an eternal and fundamental principle, inherent in all things, in every system of Philosophy, in every Religion, and in every Science. There is no getting away from the law of love. It is feeling that imparts vitality to thought. Feeling is desire, and desire is love. Thought impregnated with love becomes invincible.

—Charles F. Haanel

CHAPTER I

In that expansive moment of our embrace, both unexpected and inevitable, I could imagine Maria and I were destined for some private measure of greatness. Yet I was haunted by doubt. Smothered in her bosomy grasp, challenged to taste of the deep well of mature love, I felt the realization of a more primal and boyish yearning for maternal comfort given without reserve. And what of my newly flowering love affair (as I chose to think of it) with the daughter, Zouzou?

Neither Maria nor I had any thought of her husband, the good Professor Kuckuck, as an obstacle to our union. His attentions appeared well occupied with his beloved museum, his speculations on cosmic and earthly mysteries too far or fine for such common domestic dramas. Nor could I have foreseen my own removal to a theatre of action so far exalted from this minor stage as to reveal my immediate ambitions as the two-bit fantasies of a *fin-de-siècle* punk—to borrow a term from that distant shore.

What caused the momentary heat to pass so quickly was no such specific premonition on my part; rather, a more familiar and generalized trait: a characteristic detachment, an instinctive reluctance to give myself over to any sort of romantic entanglement. Behind me lay my brief career amid the naive bellboys, brass-handled doors and elegantly tiled baths of the Paris hotels. On life's table before me were arrayed the *ragouts fins*, charred steaks and chocolate soufflés which fed my current life of pretense among the all too hospitable upper crust in this charming city of Lisbon. Ahead of me... ah, knowing what I now know, would I have chosen differently?

How useless to speculate! How tempting to revise one's life, when it's too late. No, let's leave awhile what might have been, for the easeful dreams of a more advanced old age. For now I will confine myself to what I was. With my soft fair hair, my blue-gray eyes, my golden brown skin—and my record of successes to date, both material and romantic—I considered myself fate's darling. But to what end, what sustaining purpose?

It was not that I was ungrateful for the genuine friendship of Professor Kuckuck, his wife Maria, and their lovely daughter Susanna, so charmingly nicknamed Zouzou. Rather, I lacked a vision of the course of events that my fortuitously arranged life was to take. It was all very well for a part-time bellboy (never mind small-time jewel thief and widow's delight) to step into the shoes of Armand, the Marquis de Venosta, about to embark on a world tour. The reluctant marquis had found his own anonymity in a Paris suburb with his illicit heartthrob, Zaza. (You see, even our peach-bloom consorts, so similar in name as well as appearance, were matched by destiny!). He had provided me with an itinerary, contacts, a generous letter of credit. What I missed in the transition was the overriding nobility of purpose which would have made such a tour a significant formative influence. I sensed I was just a part-timer, playing at life. I was spoiled by fate, which had granted me the talent of spontaneous improvisation of languages I barely knew; the talent of acting on faith that my field of social intercourse was unlimited; the talent... well, the bare fact was, I began (even with Maria's hand drifting down my back) to question if such talents were of any real use to me; and if so, for what?

The opulent brocaded settee beckoned, as if to receive us bodily where we nearly toppled in our unsteady embrace. Would Zouzou find us thus entwined, and turn the scene back on itself? I did register an impulse to carry the grande dame through to the privacy of her inner chamber. But then what, after the mutual conquest?

The settee, the other chairs facing me with their lustre of

entitlement, the closed bedroom door, all in concert mocked me with my indecision. It seemed as if I could truly have in this generous world whatever I would desire. Who and what, then, remained deserving of my devotion? The memory of Zouzou's feverish kiss, stolen twenty minutes ago amid the oleanders, still buzzed on my lips.

Maria must have sensed my peculiar reticence, for she seized the moment for her own slightly mysterious purposes: "Felix, I want you to stay with me."

I cringed at the mention of my true name, the collapse of my assumed identity as the Marquis de Venosta. I could only assume it had to do with Professor Kuckuck's distant acquaintance with my purported family, which he had once noted in passing.

Maria leaned away, holding me back at arms' length, and glared with huge black eyes into mine. Her fleshy nose and lips quivered in contrast to the taut tension of her aristocratic cheekbones. Her anger dampened my attraction to her, which now seemed ill-advised in all respects. For once in my life, I was tongue-tied.

"What's my pretty boy to say for himself? Should I send him back to his Godfather Schimmelpreester?" (I cringed again. *How in heaven's name—?*) "Or should he perhaps attempt to recoup his tarnished image by, say, dueling with Dom Miguel Hurtado for the forbidden hand of my, yes she is, luscious daughter? Hmmm? You understand, of course, that about Susanna I'm making an unsavory joke. Concerning my own desires I'm deadly serious. Your hesitation disturbs me in no small measure."

"Please, Maria, understand: it's just the shock and shame of my exposure to you as who I really am. It's taken me so much by surprise that I... I don't know what to say. Of course, your reference to my godfather, and, without question the duel with Senhor Hurtado which you understandably offer in cutting jest... no, it's out of the question for me to carry on any longer with my ridiculous charade, my selfish wanderlust, and especially my duplicity in matters of the heart. How can I begin to tell you what you've come to mean to me? If you can find the wherewithal to see through my boyish errors, my thoroughly deceitful character, to the real Felix, the whole person I mean to be if..."

A vision of Zouzou's pert lips, infused with the lush, intoxicating aroma of our garden tryst, clouded my thought and caused my speech to falter.

Maria, her bounty of hair piled high and pinned tight, her brow stormy, her hands on hips, blew out a snort of exasperation. "If what? Is it yes or no!"

"If I could only, by the grace of your patience, reach the maturity you hold out for me, then, my Maria, I cannot refuse you."

Even as we embraced once more, however, I sought a way out, a way to arrange the next assignation with Zouzou.

Again Maria with her perspicacity must have seen through my outward desires to an inner destiny bound elsewhere, for again she pulled her little trigger. "I'm overjoyed, my dear Felix. But I trust you understand, that should you even *consider*, let me emphasize the very forethought of attempting to cultivate any further this romantic 'friendship' with my Zouzou, then you'll be finished, exposed to your own shameless relatives as well as to the Venostas, who have served as your unwitting sponsors until now. I'd only give you undeserved honor to add that the better families of Europe will know you for what you are—"

"Maria, I can appreciate your sentiments. Let us not dwell on past misunderstandings. If I am to 'stay with you,' whatever you have in mind for that to mean, naturally I will do so with utter devotion. And naturally I realize the folly of attempting an affair of any sort with your admittedly lovely, yet thoroughly inaccessible—"

"That's quite enough! It's impertinent of you even to discuss my daughter's availability in such a way, in view of her engagement to Senhor Hurtado. I will hear no more of it. I forbid you to speak of her in my presence!"

Maria's countenance had taken on a dark, elemental beauty during this close exchange, colored by the rising blood of her unreleased passion. Offsetting this magnetism I felt an unwelcome sense of her cowish bulk, accompanied by the acrid scent of her sweat. In the balance, though I had truly, with some primal necessity, desired her as well, I could not help but convey now a blithe calmness—this also despite my fresh unmasking, my precipitous commitment to her, and my impossible love for her daughter.

Maria scowled to watch the signal-lights of my silent eyes. She clearly didn't know what to make of me, how to move me irrevocably toward her. Finally she turned in a huff and retired through the very door she'd closed so purposefully before, looking back with lowered eyelids and a spiteful, provocative bounce of her matronly hips.

No sooner had Maria gone than a voice chirped in my ear from behind, where the arched dining room doorway had previously stood vacant. "What's it to do now, *mon cheri*?"

I whirled. My anger and hurt mingled with delight and discovery; my eyes brimmed. From Zouzou's eyes and upon her smiling lips danced childish mirth. She had certainly regained her spirits from the humiliating scene earlier, our intimacy on the dappled garden bench so rudely breached by the imperious mother. Zouzou beckoned me quickly back outside, then boldly led me to the secluded bower, the very spot from which her jealous mother had so vehemently banished us. The autumn air hummed, its multitudinous bees and birds applauding our return. Zouzou sat us down firmly on the pretty bench. There she held my hands, in hers, upon her white-skirted knees.

"So you're giving up on me that easily, Marquis? I cannot imagine what you hope to gain by your intimacies with *her*. Especially given this unmasking of your subterfuge. Who are you, really?" Her turquoise eyes, so bright and vast were tinged with a trace of hurt. She inquired further: "Do you yourself know?"

What a time to answer that ageless riddle! I wouldn't even attempt it.

I took the more direct approach to the issue at hand: "Do you think I love your mother? You said before, you believed as I did that love was a vital potion, a fresh spirit infusing nature, living everywhere nature lives, in everyone whose body is not a statue, whose mind is not a closed box. Do you think there is that spirit between your mother and me?"

Zouzou appeared thoughtful... kicking at the pebbles in the walk with her dainty foot, heedless of the odd bits of paper that still lay on the ground—the remains of my sketches which had so embarrassed her and yet at the same time had prompted her to reveal such depths of affection. As I waited for her response I became entranced with her long, fine black curls which wavered delicately in the breath of the fresh October air. Finally she put my hands aside.

"No," she said carefully, "I don't think you love her. And I don't think she really loves you, either; though she may think she does. I know her. I can see it's a way for her to enjoy a kind of power, through independence from my father. Ever since he became chief curator of the museum, he's been gone from her orbit, preoccupied with his work. So she's needed someone else to control. Before you, it was Hurtado."

I was taken aback. Did she mean Hurtado had preceded my entry into this charmed triangle? What she said next bolstered that suspicion:

"Now, it seems she wants to leave Dom Miguel to me, which of course is all for the best as far as my father is concerned. Who knows—if the picture wasn't clouded by

Hurtado as my father's 'worthy assistant,' he would just as likely favor matching me with you."

Zouzou sat straight and still as she spoke, looking at me with her eyes round, honest, knowing, yet innocent: the compelling paradox of the debutante. I felt an almost overpowering impulse to seize her, to love her with freshness and also with strength, with graceful force, with mutual bodily desire.

I held back, arrested by her childlike purity. I wondered if she was as innocent as she appeared. What was she trying to accomplish—if anything? How could I discover who *she* really was?

Then she took my left hand, with a hint of hesitation, and brought it briefly to her lips. She looked into my eyes and said, "I shouldn't tell you this, but I'm not marrying that strutting goose Hurtado."

My heart flew up with a flurry of wings. Zouzou blushed as she squeezed my hand; then she scurried off toward the house and the shadow of her mother. I looked up, and to my dismay, saw the grim face of Maria clouding a second-story window. Focusing more clearly, I discerned with relief that it was only the tight-lipped servant, Mardou. She quickly drew the shade.

I had to walk somewhere, alone with my thoughts. I slipped past the house and out to the street, then wandered down to the tennis club. No one was there. I paced around the grass courts at least half a dozen times, eyes on the white line. My mind was in a turmoil; my steps slow, measured, meditative.

I had perhaps become too complacent with my initial, larger-than-life success in this newfound social environment. The grand tour, true to form, would include hobnobbing with royalty, fleeting romantic liaisons, and stimulating conversation with the cognoscenti of the day. I had become enamored with the naive belief that after such a promising beginning I was bound to rise to infinitely greater heights. The very uncertainty of the future at the other end of the world tour had only elevated my youthful hopes—for I was not yet twenty-one.

At the same time, I thought, one should not assume that beneath all the show and pomp there can't be a reflective sense as well, a balance provided by gracious humility. Indeed, the encounter with Maria had revealed my most defenseless position, had exposed me to myself as well as to her knowing, womanly gaze. It was this naked, vulnerable self that the precocious seventeen-year-old also was on the verge of discovering.

I was faced with an agonizing decision. I could attempt to salvage what was left of my transatlantic itinerary, already jeopardized by my unmasking. Or I could grasp the slim chance of entering further into Zouzou's good graces—and face then the Scylla and Charybdis of the betrayed Maria and the spurned Hurtado. It would mean pushing my luck beyond the bounds of normal reason, canceling my berth for tomorrow's sailing of the *Cap Arcona,* and reserving it for the next voyage six weeks hence. Alternatively, I could try for the *Amphitrite* in two weeks. In such deliberation, I felt myself under a sort of spell, an aura of anonymous mystery which overshadowed the spurious pretense of my social persona, as the shaping force of my fortunes. Dare I call it love?

I sat abed, late that night, back in the comfortable haven of my hotel room, pen in hand. I dawdled with it in practical consideration of my dilemma: should I approach Schimmelpreester directly about this matter of Maria's recognition of my true identity? Could I reasonably assume he was to blame? Did it even matter, now? Perhaps it would be wisest to retreat to the Paris suburb of Sèvres... to search for the real Marquis de Venosta on the rue Brancas, Seine-et-Oise, and cancel our unwieldy enterprise. Or should I try to contact him first by mail, or telegraph? Could I simply forget Zouzou and Maria and depart for more familiar—or less familiar—pastures? My elegant hand luggage stood unpacked but waiting in the half-opened closet, mocking my indecision.

I regarded the splendor around me in this second-floor suite at the justly named Savoy Palace, and felt it all passing away, dissolving before my misty eyes. I was not allowed to shed any actual tears over my predicament, for at that moment came a knock at my outer door—jarring, at this hour. Hardly imagining either Maria or Zouzou would venture such a bold visit, I nevertheless bade the visitor enter. From where I sat I had a narrow view of the outer room through the open bedchamber doorway.

It was Mardou, the Kuckucks' maidservant, with a slim letter in hand. She must have convinced the night clerk—a somber fellow of grave demeanor and a Moorish cast similar to her own dusky complexion—of the urgency, or intimate character, of her mission. Visions of a midnight rendezvous with a desperate Zouzou now danced in my head in earnest. The messenger swiftly, with lowered eyes and silent tread, crossed my threshold and deposited her weighty cargo on the foot of my bed, failing to meet my steady glance until the last moment as she twirled back to the bedchamber doorway and shot me a dark dart of undeserved reproach.

"The letter came for you today after you left," she said in hoarse Portuguese through lips that scarcely moved. "Senhor thought you should have it before you leave tomorrow."

I thanked her politely, if absently, as she disappeared through the outer chamber and main suite door. Feeling an ironic comfort that *someone* knew what I was to do, or at least believed in my stated plans, I reached for the envelope. How was it that for the professor I was a departing guest, while for his wife I was a prize yet to be enjoyed?

The letter came from none other than my Godfather Schimmelpreester, postmarked in Cologne and addressed to the "Marquis de Venosta" in the care of Professor Kuckuck. Taking the cheese knife handy by my bed, I quickly slit open the top of the envelope.

COLOGNE, 22 SEPTEMBER, 1895

My dear Felix:

I'm hoping to catch you before you depart for Argentina. You see, I learned of your novel situation through correspondence with a certain old acquaintance of mine from the University in Cologne, now a professor, who turns out to be host to a guest of such remarkable similarity to you, that I knew you'd been up to some interesting business of your own devising. I must say I was impressed, if not too surprised, by your assumed title, knowing your gift for camouflage.

When I tried to reach you at the Saint-James and Albany, my friend Herr Stürzli had a good report of your efforts as a waiter there. I can well guess that such an occupation, however helpful to you at your stage in life, was simply no match for your considerable talents. So I'm not offended that it didn't work out. Besides, look at you now!

At any rate, to get to the point: in recent months I've been cajoled by my younger brother Axel, the sausage-maker, to abandon the sign-maker's trade and go off in his service to the New World. He figured me for a good German stereotype to drum up new export connections. My new place of residence there is, of all insults to God's good earth, Albuquerque, New Mexico, USA. I shall spare you the details of such squalid and naked pursuit of wealth as passes for human normality there, only to assure you of the possibility of a cultured intransigence under the otherwise degenerate influence of one's mundane surroundings. I must say, the sausages are moving well already: my sales charts are the envy of Cologne!—where I have happily returned, for a short time, to settle my affairs.

Enough of my doings. My intent is to lure you from

whatever roguery you have up your sleeve, to come join me in this growing business. This is the same family sausage you used to enjoy so. I know you can speak well for it, and I'm convinced of your capability to make the most of the vast market America represents.

Well—I'll let you decide for yourself. Don't be too disillusioned by my prejudiced distaste for the country. It's large and full of opportunity for a young rake such as yourself. I will, however, counsel you to make the best of your Krull talents in a solid and expansive enterprise like this sausage trade. Do let me know soon, as I'll be traveling back again in a month's time.

With fond regards,
your Godfather Schimmelpreester

Only when I folded the letter and slid it back into the envelope, did I notice the neat cut in the overleaf beside the wax seal. Someone had peeked into it and then carefully pasted the envelope back together—and then still made sure I received the message. Who?

I could not countenance, at this juncture, either Maria or Zouzou having a change of heart and wanting me gone. I still didn't know if my godfather had informed Kuckuck directly about my true identity at this point, but if so, I felt sure the professor would understand. His cosmic perspective would include and forgive my part in this masquerade in which all energy goes by the name of matter—and for which the particular, arbitrary names matter not.

I was stuck, however; I had to pick one face to wear, one place to stand in the friendly company of fellow sentient beings.

As often happens in such situations, the cornered mind searches frantically for an escape route. Or it lashes out at whatever stands before it as a threat.

Or, it calmly accepts the full dimensions of its fate.

I chose a favorite approach: I would come to a firm, if arbitrary, decision and then sleep on it. That way I could at least enjoy my necessary rest; and in the morning I'd know how I stood with that ultimately tentative decision in the light of the unconscious—the unacknowledged arbiter of our destinies.

So I rode on my spinning schemes down the corridors of sleep where the doors to dreamland stood ajar. The hat I carried on the top of my head contained ten gallons of sausage meat. I was bound for Albuquerque...

I heard the sounds of an orchestra tuning up, and saw a bit of light through one half-opened door. As I approached I could distinguish the dark heads of spectators in what appeared to be the top rows of an auditorium. Upon entering, I found the room instead to be a sort of beer hall, with live music on the main floor and tables situated on the mezzanines.

The place was a hubbub of droning voices. I sat at a table where I recognized Stephen Prutedalus, an old school chum, with some friends of his. They were aesthetes talking on and on (hardly recognizing my presence) about double exposures and improvised harmony, about boldness and caution in paint...

The concert beginning below, unseen, was a welcome distraction from their pompous talk. The opening strains of the new *Scheherazade* suite by Rimsky-Korssakoff drifted barely distinguishable through the rumbling conversation, scraping of bench legs on floor, and clanking of beer mugs on the heavy wood tables.

Our party on the mezzanine was fortunate in having a soloist come up from the orchestra (this was a new, delightful twist) to play next to our table. Possessed of a graceful figure and striking brown eyes, she was holding her shimmering flute amid swaying strands of chestnut-colored hair, looking directly at me, playing without inhibition as she stood by the beer-parlor wall. I was intrigued by her delicate handling of the subtle variations of tone. What was more, I perceived the sound weaving visually, in the form of the strangely flexible flute—as if the instrument of the snake-charmer had become one with the snake.

Finally recognizing the most poignant melody of the piece, with this enchanting soloist rendering it with living affection, I could no longer contain my own feeling.

I rose out of my chair, emulating her floating notes with my best fluting whistle. Childish as this effort might sound when merely reported, in the live air of the moment my part blended in with a surprisingly pleasing effect, and the flautist flashed her surprised bright eyes at me as she played. The impromptu accompaniment spurred a noticeable power and verve on her part, as we matched tone for tone. I could not stand still as she did, but wove back and forth in front of her with the dancing sound. As the solo part drew to its end, I eased back away from her, until the very last note, holding it higher and stronger than I believed possible... and she followed right along with it, breath lasting longer than the symphony called for, and she knew it but didn't care, with the crowd hushed and wondering, listening, waiting, until finally I stopped and she stopped exactly as one.

Breathless, beaming, this lovely companion in melody walked up to me, then hesitated. I drew her close in a melting warm embrace, a full-feeling meeting of moist lips, softer than sound... and asked her name.

"Sophie," she murmured.

And then she was gone.

CHAPTER II

Morning entered through curtains of violet gossamer. My first thought was of the two o'clock sailing of the *Cap Arcona*. I reached over to the charming cherry table by the bedside for my gold pocket watch (I say "my" loosely, as the reader understands that the watch, like everything else I carried with me at the time, bore the initials "L.d.V.": Louis de Venosta). It was only seven thirty-five. I had time to pack my steamer trunk and hand luggage and have them sent to the dock; to hop down to the Café Borgia for breakfast, first accomplishing a small errand of exchange; to stop by the museum for a departing chat with Professor Kuckuck, in lieu of a final visit to the female members of his family; and to catch the cable car to the quay.

I found the Café Borgia alive with brisk morning chatter in the sunlight. Comforting my pocket was a fat wad of cash, from the humble pawnbroker, sufficient to stake my upcoming sessions at the onboard gaming tables. It had been one of Maria's innumerable and indistinguishable diamond necklaces (old money); she would never miss it. After enjoying a quick coddled egg, toast and marmalade, and a cup of the excellent *café Viennois* of which I was so fond for its exquisite preparation in that cosmopolitan establishment, I headed along the bird-embroidered Avenida da Liberdade toward the Museu Sciências Naturaes. It was only then, amid the remarkable whistling of the autumn thrushes, that I was able to recall the dream I'd had.

What a remarkable creature—Sophie—appearing to me as if from the world beyond. Her regal bearing, her charming ability to shine as a virtuoso while embracing my humble contribution, the unspoken yet unmistakable invitation to further intimacies... Had my very soul confirmed, by her manifestation, that my destiny need not be chained to such lesser lights as Zouzou, or indeed her huffing maternal counterpart? By this time it was too late for analysis; I'd already set my course onward, quite naturally, and had slipped into a carefree mood.

Passing the narrow Rua do Príncipe, which led to the great Rossio, I recalled fondly that first acquaintance I'd made, quite unawares, of the two Kuckuck ladies, mother and daughter, beneath the bronze fountain. And I started to falter in my steps.

That vision, as I proceeded onward to the Rua Augusta, coaxed me to bypass the museum and continue one block further, to the Rua João de Castilhos. Yet at the junction of the Rua da Prata another force, of a subtler yet more insistent vibration, acted to steer me true to my intended course.

My feet leaden and my brain benumbed by the turmoil of these warring impulses, I mounted the marble steps of the museum and entered. The door to the director's office was partly open. I knocked anyway and walked in at Professor Kuckuck's chipper response.

"Why, hello, Marquis. What a pleasant surprise to see you here, when I've just been thinking of you."

"And a good morning to you, Professor. I trust your thoughts of me were kind?" I was wary of his censure, given the possible disclosure of my identity by his old acquaintance, my Godfather Schimmelpreester.

"Oh yes, yes. In particular I've been reflecting on your uncanny aptitude for the principles of species development, of universal evolution, of... well, I won't go on about your qualifications; the point is... here, here, sit down and be comfortable."

The mahogany paneling of the museum director's office ceased swirling and resolved into minute focus. I admired its fine grain, its rich hue, its oiled finish, and settled into the red leather chair.

"It is indeed fortunate that you dropped in," Kuckuck continued. "I was wondering how I might find you before you boarded that ship. You're scheduled to cast off in a matter of hours, is that right?"

"That's right. I wanted to drop by and pay my respects..." My voice faltered; my hand went to my brow.

"You look a little wave-weary already, Marquis. I want to know if you're determined to go off on this jaunt of yours, leaving us without the further pleasure of your company; and in the case of the museum here..."

I sensed what was coming: an offer to stay on at the museum, as the director's assistant. Surely the professor didn't fathom the complication of my pact with Maria—or did he? I began to suspect that Maria had somehow wheedled her obtuse husband into shoring up the walls she was already erecting around her capricious "marquis," neglecting to apprise him of my duplicity.

Forget about her, I decided. If the director intended to install me in Hurtado's position here, perhaps he favored me as a match for his intriguing creature of a daughter. At that moment a vision of Sophie swept over me, an aura of persuasive charm surpassing both mother and daughter. I wished it away: *Sophie, indeed. A phantom!* If indeed the professor eyed me as a suitor for Zouzou, how could I possibly refuse?

"I'm really, as you correctly labeled me once, a sea-lily, professor. I float with the currents and sway with the tides. Though I'm bound even now for the New World, I could countenance a change of heart, given the opportunity as a suitor for—"

"A suitor!" he exclaimed. My dear marquis. I'm shocked that you would even think to countermand our wishes for the marriage of our daughter to Senhor Hurtado. Especially as I have come to understand, by correspondence with a certain acquaintance of mine, that your pedigree is a sham."

So the game was up. I sagged in my chair, a scolded boy. Patience was never a virtue of youth; but had I hoped to play out the string of pretense and win the right to woo the daughter over time, Maria would have unmasked me anyway. Best to have all cards on the table, and walk away if I must.

Kuckuck continued: "You see, our maidservant has taken care to inform me of your godfather's correspondence, though he doubtless had wished more discretion. I intended to counter his offer with a better one, accounting for your innately nobler prospects. What's in a name, or indeed a given title? I care simply that you're willing to abide by our decision for this matter of Susanna's marriage which, to be blunt, concerns you not in the least."

Though Kuckuck had properly shamed me back to my senses, I endeavored to make amends. If I could buy time, mollifying Maria and using my position as leverage with Zouzou, who had already confessed her distaste for the pompous Hurtado...

I stood and bowed contritely. "Professor, I beg your forgiveness. Indeed I am flattered by your trust in me, and your willingness to overlook both my boyish impulses, and the subterfuge by which I meant no harm, rather only service, to yourself. I don't know what has come over me this morning. Perhaps I am seasick already."

My stance was unsteady; I leaned forward, placing my hands upon the desk. I feared slipping into the dream of the magic flute, wavering before it, and the vision of its lovely—

"Here, let me help you."

Kuckuck had risen from his desk and now he was easing me back into the red leather chair. I accepted the refreshment of a goblet of mineral water, poured from a crystal decanter.

He stood sucking contemplatively at the edges of his mustache as I drank; then, satisfied at my renewed composure, he returned to his chair and fished out his pipe. Seeing him raise his eyes for approval, I nodded, and he applied a match before resuming his speech.

"My offer of a position here at the museum stands," Kuckuck said. "I would wish you to grace the institution with your proven facilities, assisting me in this lifework dedicated to the ennobling of the spirit of human unfoldment in the midst of nature's varied and beautiful forms."

He puffed on his pipe, waiting for my response which was not forthcoming. I held a few more cards close to the vest.

"In any event, whether you accept or prefer to leave our circle, I trust you will refrain from further disruption of our familial symphony—or small concerto, be that as it may."

He had made himself quite clear. My fantasy dissolved, senses restored and options thus delimited, I stood once more to declare the position guiding me from the day's outset: "Professor, I fear your estimation of my aptitude, as you called it, in the service of your museum is overgenerous. Senhor Hurtado, for instance, has far greater qualifications in such a capacity; while my own true talents are as yet undiscovered even by myself. It would be inappropriate and truly, sir, out of my place to accept such a responsibility when my life is, to be frank, orientated westward, almost beyond the direction of my own will. So despite my gratitude for your gracious hospitality, as well as for your present offer, I must respectfully decline, in the interests of my own as yet unknown but imperatively independent destiny."

Kuckuck nodded, as though unsurprised by my response. "I see your mind is quite made up. I confess disappointment that our marriage of professional talents is not to be. I trust it will turn out for the best this way."

The professor, I thought, looked deflated, yet also unburdened; as if he'd fulfilled an obligation, and escaped suffering any lasting consequences. I felt more convinced that Maria had sought external means to hold me, her loosely bridled stud, in sway. I wondered if on top of this simple stratagem she'd gone so far as to reason that a resentful Hurtado, bypassed for the museum position, would balk at the marriage to Zouzou; that my perception of the daughter's availability would thereby increase; and thus, I would have all the more motivation to stay with her.

I thought of poor Hurtado left to his own devices in such a situation—potentially dangerous in the event of his insight into Maria's manipulations. I could well become the object of his misdirected rage, were I to play the role Maria had scripted for me.

It would have been well to take my leave at that point; but another tack occurred to me in the shifting winds of fate and choice. "There is one more small thing."

"Yes, what's that?" A glint of suspicion, almost fear, shone in the professor's starlike eyes.

"Your wife. If she hasn't made it clear to you, let me in all humility confide in you in the open spirit of our friendship. She and Dom Miguel Hurtado... well, suffice it to say, the marriage of your daughter is highly questionable in my view, in light of Dona Maria Pia's concern for him as, as..."

Professor Kuckuck, his eyes cast down, blanched and sighed with one inbreathing, choked sob. "Enough, I will not hear it! I've suspected as much for months, I tell you. I myself was afraid to admit what my worst fears indicated. To tell you the truth, I wouldn't have believed Maria would go along with Zouzou's marriage to Hurtado just so that... to keep him close by, for her own—" Kuckuck broke down with a cascade of hoarse, dry cries.

I felt genuinely sorry for the man, as I left him there in his office; yet I could not help but enjoy this indirect revenge on Maria, for her attempted entrapment of me. It seemed, further in my defense (leaving aside the spontaneous and involuntary nature of my disclosure), that all was not well in the first place between Antonio José and Maria Pia. I merely supplied the broom to poke into the interwoven cobwebs of their suspicion, power and jealousy, and to sweep away the last remaining obstacle, if I were lucky and kept my wits about me, to Zouzou's hand and heart.

I left the professor in his office and went out into the street. Under a gaslamp which would later shine forth its contribution to the golden-gray sunset over the city, I lit a cigar and pondered my as yet undetermined fate. As I leaned against the post, watching the passersby traveling on foot and by carriage, I felt a tugging at my trouser leg.

A stray puppy?

It was a man: or rather, a half-man, shelved legless, in ragged clothes, upon a small wheeled platform. Gazing up at me with face bewhiskered, gray eyes pleading, hand outstretched.

Hardly the "picturesque" beggar I had proposed, in my fondly remembered conversation with the king of this realm, as somehow content with his station in life. I fingered the roll of bills in my pocket and considered these were needed for the voyage ahead—provided I found it necessary to keep to that plan. Inspired by an alternative to monetary alms close at hand, I reached down with my cigar, still mostly unused, and offered it to the man's filthy fingers. He grasped it and eyed it, and me, curiously, having perhaps never had the pleasure. He made a comical figure indeed, now; but not wanting to offend this unfortunate, I stifled a chuckle as I strode away, bound for more pressing matters.

Without yet needing to join my luggage at the quay, I took a mule bus back across town to the café. Navigating the decayed streets of old Lisbon the roundabout way, I passed the tennis club before reaching the Villa Kuckuck, and there found

Zouzou at tennis with Dom Miguel Hurtado. I felt put off, seeing her entertaining herself with her greasy-haired fiancé. Hadn't she told me she was through with him?

Rapt in their concentration, they failed to notice my arrival until an admirable devil-may-care backhand by Zouzou skipped off the top of the net toward my inconspicuous vantage point beside the small grandstand. Despite her shortness of breath, she greeted me in her characteristically cool manner.

"Why... hello, Marquis." I felt annoyed, even with Hurtado there, that she was keeping up appearances. "I'd decided you were not coming by, after all, to say goodbye. You are still planning to leave on the ship this afternoon?"

The breeze fondled her hair in precisely the same manner as it had the previous day in the garden.

"Oh yes," I had to say, "I'm still planning to leave. And I wouldn't have missed the opportunity to pay you and your mother my last respects."

Hurtado looked at me sharply.

I added: "As well as your lucky companion, whom I did not expect to have the pleasure of encountering again."

Now the vain sculptor smiled in that sickly way of his.

I prattled on: "Besides, I thought, as I considered how I might spend a couple of idle hours—what more pleasant place to take my last stroll in your charming city, but along the Rua João de Castilhos? Forgive me if I've interrupted your game."

My eyes must have given away something of a deeper nature than my banter, for the spectacled Hurtado, done with his unpleasant smile, merely nodded curtly. He flipped his long hair about, motioning with his racquet and a fresh ball that he was ready to pick up the game. "Forty-love," he stated in a cracked voice.

I climbed to a bench halfway up the grandstand, where I sat for the remainder of the set, cheering vocally for both players as the quality of the shot demanded. They didn't seem to mind my good-natured whistles and raves, and when he had finished her off, Hurtado invited me down to the court.

He put his arm around me and, as Zouzou put her racquet in its case and changed her shoes, he walked me slowly down the sideline. I wondered at this apparent change of affection, until he spoke with a patronizing air: "Marquis, I've an idea, a little plot I've hatched, and I wonder if you might consider being an accomplice." His teeth gleamed and his eyes sparkled merrily.

I wouldn't commit easily to such an invitation, and so kept my tongue until he divulged more.

"I'm going to the Praça do Comércio on a special and, let us say, a sacred errand. You see, these wedding arrangements have left me with barely time enough—time which all the same I've managed to squander at a silly game of tennis—even for a most important detail: to buy for Zouzou her engagement ring."

My heart tasted venom for my rival but I kept my composure. If there was a new role for me, I might yet play it to my advantage.

Hurtado carried on: "I was lucky to be granted a holiday of sorts when Professor Kuckuck was too ill to work and suggested I take the day off as well. I saw the most stunning gem in a jeweler's shop on my way here, and after consideration of its expense, have decided to go back and buy it. I wonder if you have an hour to spare—When does your ship leave? Two o'clock, did I hear?—if you'll be good enough to divert the bride with another game of tennis, so she won't be tempted to tag along with me. Can you do that?"

Though I resented the sculptor's condescending attitude, I was cheered by his presumption of my innocence—or his confidence, at least, in my imminent departure, presumably forever. In the spirit of good sportsmanship I agreed to do as he'd asked.

"Zouzou," Hurtado crowed, "you'd better change those shoes again, and get out your racquet. Our friend the marquis would like to challenge you now to test your true skill, to see if that last set wasn't decided by the ill luck of the wind, which must have been just fickle enough to counteract the benefits of his partisan support." He winked at me.

Zouzou cheerfully accepted: "I'll be glad to see if the marquis' talents include endurance and consistency as well as strong first impressions"—an obvious reference to my previous appearance on the tennis courts. Or, was she referring to my brush with nobility, my friendship with the king? Or, rather, would she be thinking of our encounter yesterday on the garden bench?

Her fiancé laughed. "Splendid. So, I'll be off on some business I have to do. I want an accurate account of the score on my return."

Zouzou played a dispirited match, swatting ball after ball into the net or over my head into the screening beyond. At its quick and merciful conclusion, I met her at midcourt and guided her back to her strapped sandals and racquet case, where I sat beside her. The sun shone a dappled pattern on the smooth green carpet of grass. My heart pounded up in the lengthening silence, finally throbbing out of the stillness as two robins flew in a flurry before us. "Zouzou, I'm going to have to leave, but I cannot bear to do so without you. Come to America with me."

Her eyes widened. "To America! But, but..." She sat down quickly on the bench, put down the tennis shoe she had been holding, and composed herself. Then with admirable alacrity she gathered her thoughts and spoke what had evidently been waiting inside her before I'd inserted my golden key.

"I have been thinking a lot about you, Felix. Especially since yesterday... and despite the fact that Mama has moved up the date of the wedding to a week from Thursday. It's all happening so fast, and there's been so little opportunity to really get to know you, deep down. So little chance for... for intimate contact."

"Then I could cancel my berth on today's sailing. There's another ship in two weeks' time, or a month after that. As for funds, I could arrange the ticket for you."

Her eyes were becoming moist. I sat down beside her and took her trembling hand in mine. She bravely continued her rebuttal: "I'm still held back by this question in my mind: Who are you? Your name or title means nothing to me. Your philosophy of love and beauty I've heard, and argued with, and have been forced to recognize as somewhat valid. And yet I still wonder—or part of me does—how much of the real you is presenting this philosophy of love, and why? I still wonder if your 'love-potion' theory of nature isn't just a pretty icing on a much more common cake. In short, I mean to ask, are you sure you know what love is?"

I wasn't ready for that pointed a query. But I prided myself as a master in the art of quick repartee, and so the familiar theme of love wasn't entirely daunting. I answered: "Zouzou, I was immediately attracted to you, I confess, by your beautiful outward nature, your physical appeal, your face, your lips. How could I do otherwise? That was all I knew of you at first. I won't dwell on the importance to me of first impressions—I trust them. Then, in time's natural course, I proceeded to collect further impressions of your character, which only deepened the soundness of my initial appraisal—fanning a spark to a steady flame, as it were. It doesn't always work that way, as you can guess. You've been to enough salon affairs, balls and other haunts of the beautiful people of high society, who masquerade as gods and goddesses while their lives are petty, deceitful, conniving, pretentious, and self-serving. In your case I perceived a true ray of inner light, by which to inspire and illuminate my growing knowledge of this being called Zouzou."

Her eyes shone at mine, fluttered with lashes and then cast a gaze at the ground in demure modesty, while I carried on: "Look, I have my own life to concern me. You realize I can't stay here. Meanwhile I've been fortunate to be offered a chance to carry out a sensitive diplomatic mission abroad, not as a marquis but as myself, Felix Krull. If you can in turn trust your own natural sensibilities to believe in me, I'm trusting my instincts to ask you to accompany me."

I waited for her response, wondering if the word "instincts" was badly chosen. And cognizant that my plan of action had only the flimsiest hope of success. Unmasked by Maria, I figured the world would just have to live with two Felix Krulls. Schimmelpreester I could notify later from America, if...

"It's all too sudden, Felix. I need more time to know you. And in these circumstances, with the wedding planned... no, it's impossible."

I pivoted on the bench to embrace her, an impulse that meant either a final goodbye, or a last appeal to her affections.

As if on cue, Maria appeared on the scene. "I hope you two have finished sweating through this hard-fought game of yours. Because I'm afraid it's over." She was huffing and puffing, red-faced from the fury of her own exertion, the short walk uphill from the Villa Kuckuck. "Susanna, I want you back in the house this instant: the gown fitter's arrived, no doubt charging by the minute for her time. As for you, my royal guest—" and she waited until Zouzou's banishment was complete.

"I think you have but one slim choice remaining. You can stay here with me as I asked previously, and will ask now for the last time. Or you can leave under your own power, but stripped of any title, or for that matter any shred of assumed respectability. Have you forgotten your recent pledge to me?"

I felt futility on every side. Walled in by Zouzou's

reticence, by Hurtado coming back soon with a fortune invested in one dire ring, by Kuckuck on his wretched warpath now, by the ex-marquis no doubt happy as a lark and in no way willing to give up his freedom or borrowed identity in France, by Godfather Sausages bound for his commercial enterprise in the otherwise alluring New World... I even felt a pang over my insubstantial seduction by an imaginary flute player named Sophie.

"While you're searching your memory, I might add that I would sincerely like to trust your motives in this latest tête-à-tête with my daughter. I won't accuse you now of anything more insidious than catering to the last-gasp flirtations of a rebellious, yet still firmly engaged, adolescent."

I kept my composure, despite realizing that Maria was still expecting a response. I could only wonder how I had until yesterday felt such compelling attraction for her. In this exhibit of her spiteful jealousy she had lost whatever noble charm she had once possessed.

She waited, then spoke with a final exasperation: "If it's such a matter of life and death, I'll add one more spice to the recipe. Senhor Hurtado once killed a man who played light with his honor. It was an honorable duel—and there was considerably less than a marriage at stake. Just be aware of the prospects before you, *mon galant*."

CHAPTER III

"Zouzou, I must say, that is an absolutely stunning ring."

She beamed, directly across the table from me. I heaped it on. "In fact, I believe it's the most charming adornment of natural beauty that I've ever laid eyes on."

Her eyes flashed, not just from my flattery but with what I read as a threefold challenge: first, to know my intention; secondly, to warn me not to persist; and lastly, to dare me to go on.

I sensed in Maria, seated to my left, a huff of irritation before she cast an agreeable smile in her daughter's direction. Professor Kuckuck looked at me askance from the far end of the breakfast table before glancing to the kitchen, where could be heard a clatter of trays and serving utensils. Dom Miguel Hurtado, seated opposite Maria, simply swelled with pride.

Then, as Zouzou held her tongue, Hurtado responded: "It makes me proud to hear your compliments, Marquis. I feel certain that before long you, too, will deserve a prize as lovely as that which I have the fortune to anticipate... or which Zouzou has to contemplate on her hand." His gaze fell contentedly on the stone. The diamond truly dazzled.

Mardou came in with sausages, zwieback and black currant jam. She distributed the viands from her silver platter, hesitating when she, too, was arrested by the shimmer of diamond-day. Then, as had become her custom, she left sending me a dark, inscrutable message from her black eyes and tight mouth. I had learned to disregard such looks as her habitual countenance. This grimace, however, outwardly no different, struck me at the time with a kind of cautionary disparagement which I took to heart.

I still wasn't sure enough of my own designs, to press my flirtatious luck. Yet I felt charmed, in one way or another, in my oddly chosen course of decision making. Was that why I'd arranged through an exchange of messages to come for this late breakfast, after a lonesome night in the small, ordinary room at the Savoy Palace that I was forced to take because I'd already checked out of my luxurious suite—to make fast my commitment?

I'd arrived at the quay on schedule, still uncertain whether to proceed, only to find the *Cap Arcona* undergoing engine repairs. The boarding officer informed me that she'd be ready to steam out on Thursday, two days hence.

I wondered how I might best take advantage of being granted an unasked-for reprieve. Perhaps this wrinkle of fate was the signal I needed to succumb fully to Maria's final invitation. But did I really envision sharing Maria's bed? I didn't even know if she and her husband still slept together.

That I retained a measure of sensible reserve was evidenced by the fact that I kept my steamer trunk and most of the smaller bags ready in dockside storage, even as I showed up on the Kuckucks' doorstep with my single crocodile valise in hand.

"Oh, yes, I'll pick up the rest of it later," I told Maria as she'd graciously greeted me in the living room, scene of our first climactic embrace. "It would seem an impropriety on my part to appear at your door with such an auspicious pile of baggage, don't you think?" I felt flushed, standing there alone with her, even to recall it again, that divine moment. Playful fancies of unripe fruit were one thing; the heady aroma of a fully-formed feast close at hand, quite another. "How are we going to work this out, anyway?" I said this in a low tone near her ear, as the others were close by in the dining room.

She hushed me and sent the valise up to the guest room in

the care of Mardou, then ushered me into the dining room. The salient fact that emerged from the mealtime conversation was the fixed date of the wedding, a mere nine days away. Maria asked if I'd had any trouble canceling my berth. I said I hadn't. At my reply she looked secretly troubled. I wondered if I should mention the delay in the ship's departure, or simply maintain the pretense of a change of plans based on a change of heart, an "overpowering remorse at the thought of leaving my dearest friends, indeed newfound family." I decided to risk being thought less than honest for not bringing up the subject of the ship's repairs in the event one of them caught wind of it from another source.

"What are your plans, now, Marquis, if I may ask?" Kuckuck inquired.

How odd that empty title sounded; yet I was grateful for the implicit respect it signified, a reputation still unsullied. "Concerning...?"

"Oh, you know—employment, diversion, study. Since you've decided to stay, and I'm sure you're welcome here for an indeterminate amount of time"—he looked at Maria—"how do you plan to occupy yourself in our fair city?"

"To begin with, there's this famous wedding afoot, which I'm very much looking forward to attending." At this remark, Hurtado muffled an audible smirk with his napkin. I noted too that Zouzou made an inscrutable face, her rosebud lips pursed. "Then a long list of historical sites—I feel I've barely scratched the surface, the uppermost strata, over the depths of historical research one could carry on here. The botanical gardens, meanwhile, I find an inexhaustible source of stimulation."

"Felix," Zouzou intruded, disdaining the paternal pretense and eliciting a gasp from Maria, "we must get you acquainted with some of the young people in society here. There'll be the ball of the season in about a month's time. If we can't get you matched up before then, well, it'll be a perfect occasion—"

Maria cut her daughter short: "Zouzou, how boldly and impolitely you're behaving for our guest, once again. I must ask you to desist from this childish prattle. The marquis has better things to do than to consort with your idle friends, who themselves have nothing better to do than to play tennis, gossip, read romantic novels, and heaven knows what else."

Hurtado snickered and pushed his delicate wire-rimmed spectacles up on his long nose. I guessed by this insipid reaction that he also had by now been informed of my unmasking. So why the continued pretense on the part of Maria and her husband? Perhaps they had given him to understand that "Felix" was a pet name, a shade more intimate than the more official "Louis." Whatever the degree of his knowledge, he didn't seem to care much, as he proceeded to divert the company with tales of his own uninteresting teenage years, tedious accounts which extended for the better part of the breakfast.

I was able to remain silent until the last of the black currant jam disappeared from my lips. By that time the discussion had been given over to the topic of wedding arrangements, a conversation made paradoxical by the reversal of roles: Maria gesticulating with the ebullience of a new bride; Zouzou sullen, displaying the dour submission of an aging mother.

During this exchange, Hurtado was consulted on the carriages to be arranged, the list of honored guests. Professor Kuckuck appeared lost in abstraction. Mardou came in to clear away the dishes, leaving without so much as a glance at me. I needed time alone to think.

I eased my chair away from the table and began by addressing myself to no one in particular: "I'm afraid I must beg off from the flower show this morning. The air is calling me outdoors, and I feel I must go walking where wildflowers grow. Maria, you've told me of cliffs along the shore not far away. Can you direct me there?"

"Certainly, Marquis, if you insist that's what you must do. But I beg you to reconsider coming with us to the flower show. You could exercise your considerable aesthetic sensibilities for the sake of gracing our wedding in the utmost beauty." I flinched at the words, "our wedding."

"No," I said with conviction, "I really must leave such preparations to those more intimately involved." I nodded toward Hurtado and Zouzou on the other side of the table.

"Very well," she assented. "Let us go out straightaway, and I'll point you in the right direction." She threw down her napkin with agitation bordering on excitement, rose to her feet and escorted me out the patio doors.

The patio was alive with Moorish patterns in gaily colored gravels, sparkling in the sun. The sky had an infinite turquoise reach to it today, with a fresh breeze lifting spirits upward and outward. We walked side by side on the path behind the house, past the garden with its hidden bower. We came to what in the closer environs of the city would have been called an alley; here it was more of an overgrown cart-track, leading off beyond the cluster of villas at the top of the Rua João de Castilhos and winding out of sight toward the cliffs. "There you are," said Maria, waving her arm down the deserted lane. "Enjoy yourself."

I remained standing, sensing the occasion for a moment of truth; she likewise could not bring herself to leave.

"Felix, aren't you happy for our Zouzou?"

It irked me how she so quickly dropped the pretense of my nobility in private.

She pressed the point, her advantage. "Don't you feel it's a wonderful occasion for Lisbon society?"

"That may be," I stated flatly. "I really can't say I have much feeling for the match, however well suited it might be to your wider purposes as a family."

"Do I infer correctly from your tone a hint of jealousy?"

"Maria, why are you baiting me like this? Isn't it enough that I did as you asked, and came back to you? I would be interested to know at this point how we are to continue our liaison in the very household of your good husband—"

She stopped me abruptly, nostrils flaring. "Leave that to me."

I could tell she was burning with some inner passion, yet my coolness deterred her from acting upon it. I stood still before her, arms straight at my sides, a soldier awaiting his orders from above.

Maria wore an expression of puzzlement. "Felix, when I asked you the day before yesterday to stay with me, you gave me to believe that you would, wholeheartedly. The second time, yesterday, you had even less time for a well-considered choice; yet here you are again, still..."

"*Encore.*"

"*Vraiment.*" She smiled. "So let me ask you: over this past month, you have come to share this same desire, have you not?"

Her hot breath came to me as a warning: this jaunt to the cliffs was fraught with more possibility than I meant to entertain. Another breath, the freshness of the sea, washed over me and I felt the urgency to go.

One answer alone would give Maria satisfaction, so I uttered it blindly, to secure my escape. "Yes, of course I wanted you."

Ah, what a turn of the dagger is a simple shift of tense.

Whatever the actual shape of my desires, during those lonely hotel nights, was immaterial now. My frail hatchling of a plan—to play out my two days of grace on the strength of Maria's desire, for the sake of my slim gambit to lure Zouzou away—seemed imprudent at best. Venturing back to this lioness's lair had been a mistake.

"I'm off now, Maria, and you have important business to attend to."

"Indeed I do," she said, her voice hoarse with emotion. She closed her eyes and heaved a huge breath. I saw that queenly bosom rising like an ocean swell. I hesitated... and then Maria, with a husky half sob, turned and faded back to her villa.

I knew, or at least thought I knew, that by Thursday I, too, would have made up my mind: to have escaped with Zouzou, or escaped alone. In effect, I'd already decided. Rather, it was decided for me, all along—such is the fate of those noble of birth. Within sight was the time when future events would conspire with those past to whittle my hypothetical choice down to one certain option.

My thoughts ran free out on the ragged bluffs above the River Tagus that lovely autumn day. The mild air carried the slightest hint of salt upriver from the ocean, along with the fresh crispness of fall. I can't say I was totally unoccupied with the schemes of my life; that I didn't gaze with some expectancy, albeit vainly, along the far bank's horizon in an attempt to envision the Atlantic and all it could represent in the way of adventures in distant continents. But I was— unaccountably—at relative peace with myself. Thus I could meander almost childishly in the windblown grasses, the stolid rocks, the unjudging clarity of the sunshine.

At length I tired from the brisk air and exercise. I'd seen no one at all out here, so close to the great port city. As I gauged it was getting on into the afternoon, yet had no inclination to return to the conundrums of my adopted family circle, I sought a soft resting place in the relative shelter of rocks where I could nap for a while.

I drifted down in sleep amid wildflowers, in a profusion of pale colors—a botanical array the particulars of which the professor would be better qualified to cite. I hasten to add that their floral properties could scarcely explain the remarkable encounter I had, in the dream state, with a woman who introduced herself as Sophie Tucker Vaughan. As if we had not previously met—but we had.

I held the limp hand she extended, standing before me as before a dance at a ball—though we stood alone against a backdrop of wild and glorious nature—and I recognized her as the very same chestnut-haired beauty who had so bewitched me with her flute, in my dream of two nights past.

She tossed her head. "Good to see you again, Felix."

Was this to be just another romantic encounter such as I have enjoyed in dreams, as in life, so often as to surely bore the higher-minded reader?

I played along: "The pleasure is mine... Sophie. And to what gracious fortune do I owe this repeat performance?"

She sniffed haughtily. "It's time we had a little chat. And you can dispense with the classist formalities, by the way. You're in my place now, my time. Plain talk will do. I gather you're adept at mastering new lingo." And she flashed a mischievous, disarming smile.

"Okaaay," I replied, as easily as an American teen. "So what's up, chick?" *Now where did that come from?*

She laughed. "Nice one. Native intuition shows promise. A bit misapplied, for a woman over forty, though. For now, let's just say I wanted to get better acquainted. It's a good window for me, between jobs, so to speak, and I gather you're in a bit of a bind, yourself. Two birds in hand, and no bush to hide behind."

I gave a snort of appreciation. "Something like that."

"I know what you must be thinking: 'This is all very well, this dream vision of a woman by a lake, but it doesn't mean anything, it's only a dream.' Am I right?"

Indeed the reasonable soul reading this account can be heard to sigh: *Another dream, is it? Of what consequence is a mere dream—a phantasm, an illusion, not to be believed...!*

Yet from within that dream, Sophie's discussion of the matter of dreaming itself served as a trigger to burst the illusion and bring me to lucid awareness.

I am confident that the modern reader will bear at least a passing acquaintance with the mystic art of lucid dreaming, in which I dabbled from a young age. I had taught myself, by diligent practice of certain tokens and techniques, to observe the dreaming self from a safe distance, unperturbed even in the throes of the most fiendish nightmares; or, if I wished, unencumbered by any limitation to the panoply of sensate desires. When properly nestled in that zone of consciousness, I could even initiate flight, not far but buoyant, propelled by pressure of the insistent will alone—or, to be fair, as a sail well rigged to catch the astral wind.

Even so, I had never before encountered such a personage as Sophie, unknown to me in the waking world, making a repeat visit to my own dream country. She was dressed informally, in a loose pink velour shirt, and well-fitted denim pants which I took to be ordinary for outdoor fashion in her time and locale. Her lips were full and naturally red. Her rich brown eyes as she looked into mine were round and large, and shone like deep pools, emanating a palpable, energetic power. "Over forty" notwithstanding, I found her attractive with a subtle depth even more alluring than the superficial beauty of the young woman, which I might add, she still possessed.

She invited me to sit beside her, on the shore of a lake which glittered jewel-like in the midst of a sylvan scene... a remote corner, she informed me, of a future North America. The year, to be exact, was 1994. This precise information I accepted not with the all-embracing nonchalance intrinsic in the province of dreams; rather, it served as a signal that a future reality, on a sliver of factual light, had inserted itself into my world, as a kind of bridge.

Yet that nonchalance remained close at hand, so that I

took my ease lounging in the soft grass beside her. Her shoulder-length, ruddy-hued hair hung casually into the grass. She had none of Maria's overbearing hauteur, none of Zouzou's childish, pouting impudence.

I noticed myself wearing similar attire; denim pants and casual flannel shirt, woolen socks in svelte hiking boots of rich burgundy. We talked easily, in her simpler, unadorned argot, across the gulf of personal and collective histories and geographies. Instead of becoming mired in the mundane details of the intervening century of change, we spoke of matters of enduring public interest: the equal rights of men and women; the disproportionate power of machinery, technology, statistics; the duties of good governance.

Having, in my own recent history, consorted with royalty, I observed that "rulers too often seem unaware that theirs is but a grandiose exercise of playacting."

"Are they unaware?" was her rejoinder. "Or is your typical politician really smarter than meets the eye? A glorified confidence man..."

That smarted. I volleyed: "Or woman."

"Touché."

My latent curiosity about our first encounter on the dream plane, itself so romantic in flavor, was put aside for this more worldly meeting of the minds.

As we talked, a white Persian cat emerged from behind Sophie and approached me for a vigorous rubbing of its head. Its name was Beri, Sophie said. Its opal eyes, I noticed, were the very color of the water in the lake.

The cat padded to the shore and bent to drink.

Sophie followed her pet with an enameled cup, which she dipped into the water and raised to her lips, then offered to me.

I drank, and immediately fell into a deeper dream—or corner of coexistent reality, as the case proved to be.

This time my presence was evident only as co-auditor, along with Sophie, of a certain speech with which I had impressed His Majesty, King Carlos I, upon my entry into Portuguese society:

> *"By his very existence the beggar, huddled in rags, makes as great a contribution to the colorful picture of the world as the proud gentleman who drops alms in his humbly outstretched hand, carefully avoiding, of course, any contact with it. And, Your Majesty, the beggar knows it; he is aware of the special dignity that the order of the world has allotted to him, and in the depths of his heart he does not wish things otherwise. It takes the instigation to rebellion by men of ill will to make him discontented with his picturesque role and to put into his head the contumacious notion that men must be equal."*

Soft cat fur nuzzled my cheek, gently shunting me back to the lakeshore. I sat up. Sophie was sitting beside me, this time sipping tea.

"What was that all about?" I said. "Those were my exact words, as I recall. As if recorded somehow..."

"Indeed." She put her tea down, took both my hands in hers and looked into my eyes. "That hypothetical beggar was *picturesque*, you said."

"I see you have an appreciation of irony."

"So did you mean it? You don't believe in equality? Or were you just sucking up to the king?"

"Ahem." I recalled with discomfort that my act of charity to the actual beggar outside the museum, the day before, might also appear in a less than favorable light, if viewed from afar. I resorted to a defensive posture. "'All men are created equal.' Isn't that what your American doctrine sets out to prove? Then explain to me how your Southern states were built upon that detestable institution known as the slave trade?"

"Not so politic with me, are you? Never heard of our Civil War?"

I became aggravated with her turn to animosity. "Why should I care what you think of me?" I wished to bring the issue to a personal head.

Sophie replied, "All right, fair enough. I have to say I was impressed with how you smooth-talked your way into that royal's good graces. It's an invaluable skill, in diplomatic circles."

I preened with the compliment.

As if reading my mind, she added:

"The petty thefts, the gigolo gig, not so much."

"What's a gigolo? Never mind, I can guess."

She gave a short laugh, and I became fixated on the shape of her mouth. Then she tossed that romantic fancy aside with the sober pronouncement, "You may as well know, I'm considering running for president of the United States."

At this point my stake in Sophie's affairs, and hers in mine, came to clarity as a burning question. Who were we to each other? Passing shades in a stageplay of illusion? Yet she had conveyed an intent, an arrangement of this meeting, for which I still could divine no definite purpose, nor clear connection with my waking life. I could not even form words to voice my query. Underneath it all, I felt a pang of desire, recalling the spontaneous conclusion of our first meeting, that luscious, uncompromising kiss.

Sensing my discomfort as it burned on my boyish cheeks, Sophie tilted her head at me, cooing. "It's all right, Felix. I trust in you, in your innate talents and integrity of heart, and I feel certain you'll be of help and comfort to me when the time is right."

"I'm flattered, truly. But I still don't understand. What are you suggesting I do? And how, when—"

"I'm working on it. Trying to structure a deal. I needed to

check you out firsthand, and give you a heads-up." She turned and stared out onto the lake. Then she said, placing a hand on my foot and looking me in the eye, "A lot depends on you."

Like a schoolboy I persisted, "Okay, but what do you want—"

"You don't need to complicate your petty schemes or tawdry love affairs for my sake. I don't even expect you to take this meeting between us as a bona fide reality. So I will tell you now, in advance, that when you wake up, you will encounter that little tart Zouzou, who has just broken up with her betrothed and will attempt to seduce you. She's approaching as we speak, so I'll leave you to it for now. Catch you later."

CHAPTER IV

A cooling afternoon breeze from the River Tagus stirred me awake to the Portuguese day, in my own familiar, if rapidly waning century. I found it not in the least comforting. The character of my just concluded altered state impressed me with the proximity of another plane of existence, remote in worldly terms and yet intimately compelling. I ran the dream over and over in my memory, the better to preserve its undulating vividness. I could hardly consider it an ordinary dream, given its unique qualities: the purposeful reacquaintance with Sophie; her insistence on a narrative both entwined with my own history and tied to a palpable future; and the utter lucidity of the experience on both our accounts.

Yet like any dream the vision had vanished. I lay stranded, a beached fish on the dry Iberian shore. My uncaring company remained: the wild pears, the shapely cork and live oaks, the carobs, stone pines and various evergreen species not found elsewhere on the Continent.

Until now I had considered myself the master of my own destiny, and to a demonstrably greater degree than the mass of humanity. Sophie had shown me, by her very appearance as a conscious voyager on the astral plane, and by her direct communication concerning my own character, that my life at present was a clumsy sideshow.

I felt the pang of her disparaging comment about my current flings: *tawdry*, was it? The truth stung.

I could take pride, as a consolation, that a few of my attributes had impressed her, that I could sniff the halls of power a world away, that I was bound for adventures far beyond my ken. The imbalance in both ages and aptitudes humbled me, yet piqued a hunger to fulfill the greater calling she had proposed.

The shimmering waters of the river brought home to me once more the primacy of this world, the sweet prize closer at hand—if I dared imagine its likelihood, in its own right.

What Sophie had told me about Zouzou was predictable enough—but if true, how would I respond?

Pash, no, it was outlandish. The ill-fated wedding was a fait accompli. How would this self-proclaimed avatar of the distant future presume to know—or even care about—the drama of a fickle Portuguese maiden?

Indeed, again I must confess, I fear all the foregoing consideration of a so-called dream, as somehow real, rings of absurdity to the hardheaded reader weaned in a materialist age which gives short shrift to psychic phenomena.

So I will leave the matter to be decided, as I had to then, by the unfolding of events.

I picked my way along the rocky bluffs above the river, homeward to the villas of Lisbon proper, until a path took shape under my feet. In due course a lone figure appeared swaying before me, a gray waif outlined hazily against the bluffs. As we approached I saw that this new apparition was none other than Zouzou—just as Sophie had foretold.

Zouzou looked heartbroken, petals falling from her shoulders and hair. "Felix, oh Felix," she cried, "we've broken it off, it was so silly—" and then she began to laugh, giggling in her tears, before continuing—"He wouldn't listen, and didn't care at all. I loved those pink gardenias, and the yellowish-gold ones; he said they were horrid together, and he wanted blue ones and red ones. Oh, but they clashed so, not at all proper for a wedding, and... I know what you're thinking, with your sad understanding eyes which are in fact unconcerned: What a stupid, trivial argument to break up an engagement. And you're right, of course. Mama too could hardly bear it. She didn't like either kind of flowers anyway, and she started to scold herself for letting us choose them together. That part was dreadfully funny!" And Zouzou howled and sobbed, nearly shrieking, as she fell into my arms.

Even in her weeping, she shone radiantly of the sun brimming big on the western waves, beyond the mouth of the river. And as the orb settled into darkness, leaving its image larger than life on the horizon, so Zouzou's radiance lingered before me, as she cried on my shoulder in diminishing heaves.

I tried to comfort her. "I know, Zouzou, it was silly, and tragic—that is, in the eyes of the world. Given what you have shared with me of your true heart, though, I must say I feel not so much sympathy as love—in the confidence this turn of events may prove the blessing you and I have asked for."

At that she pulled back; her wet round eyes gazed at me in confusion. "Me?" she said, her voice sounding of false indignation. "Did I ever lead you on to such a notion? What were you thinking, changing your plans and saying you would stay in Lisbon, even as a guest at our house, as I was about to wed Hurtado?"

"You told me you would never agree to the marriage. And now you've made good on your promise. I trusted you... and you performed admirably."

Zouzou pouted, silent, and twisted about, as though in search of a palatable exit. Finding none, she gave herself back to my embrace.

I had come to expect such fickle behavior from this fey creature; and adding to its neutralizing effect on my natural longing, I found myself distracted by thoughts of another time, another destiny. "I don't expect your mother will warm to our friendship anytime soon. More likely she'll try to patch things up between you and—"

Zouzou made a gagging sound which quashed that theory. "Tell me," she said, looking up into my eyes. "When you speak of your love for me, is it real, or something you imagine, that you wish for but don't yet possess?"

"It's as real as the sensation in my fingers when I hold you like this." *Tawdry*, I heard in my mind.

"Pfui!" Zouzou scoffed, reverting to her favorite expletive, which she no doubt found appealing for its adolescent force. "Skin deep—is that the scope of your love, your reality?" She danced away, then faced me with eyes alight. "I thought you were going to say something to comfort me. Do you understand what's happened to me today, what I've done? My life is nothing now: dead flowers in the wind. And here we stand, together on this path which goes nowhere—which I followed by instinct because my eyes were clouded with grief and wild, childish hopes—"

"And now I don't understand you. What were you hoping? You told me you weren't ready to come to America with me. And if you ask me, your stubborn stance on physical affection is rather... childish."

"I didn't ask you." She burst into tears.

I restrained myself this time from grasping her tender shoulders as they shook. I merely tilted my head down to look in her eyes, waiting.

"What I would like to know," Zouzou began again, "is..."

"Is..."

"Do you want me or not? Am I grown up enough for you?"

I didn't know how seriously to take these words, so unexpectedly did they come from the quivering mouth which before this encounter had offered such strenuous arguments against love. I had tried my best to console the poor girl. I could understand how vulnerable she must have felt after the episode with the flowers—how alone and perhaps even dependent on me. Had she really cast herself adrift from Hurtado for my sake? I could scarcely believe it.

My own situation now felt changed as well. I wished

Zouzou could know the impact of reality my dream had had on me, and to understand with my own dawning comprehension that her vision of a life with me was itself an ephemeral dream. The reality closer at hand—the web of resentment and intrigue sure to intensify concerning both Maria and Hurtado, meanwhile presaged no practical solution.

"You know I love you," I said. At this she looked startled. I continued: "You also know it's impossible for us here, in your household and in your family's society. And the rest of my life beckons—"

"Does it include me, this life of yours?"

Sophie, real or not, had become the voice of my conscience, my better self. I believed in the possibility of a richer life, one of public scope, of destiny both personal and global—the one presented to me as if in gold lettering as an invitation from an angel—because I wanted to believe. Yet I could not give voice to such, to this young lady so much in need of my comfort and reassurance.

"Zouzou, come, let's sort our thoughts while we walk together." With my arm on her waist I thought to steer us back on the path to the Rua João de Castilhos.

She resisted, like a reluctant goat of the region tugging back at its tether.

"No? I thought you wanted to go home."

"I know Mama will be furious, and worried. And Dom Miguel—no, let's walk the other way." And to my astonishment she turned, took my hand in hers, and started us on the path away from the city.

In silence we settled into a steady walk, with eyes on the dim path before us. Leaving her question aside, I felt a flush of confidence in being with her in such innocent intimacy. I knew she still needed reassurance; in that regard I had somehow fallen short. And so I wished to make amends; to give fuller account to her desires, if she was so determined to exercise them.

Zouzou stumbled on the darkening path. As she lost her balance, my arm tightened to steady her, and under her arm my hand caught a half grasp of her own charming breast—a charm with such power as was imputed to the "magic potion" from our customary cerebral sparring.

Now I was convinced we needed a change of scene. If I had had any qualms about the propriety of stopping in the little shed which had loomed into view out of the evening's shrouds, they faded behind a growing clarity.

I continued to hold Zouzou in my arms, and the longer I did so the more I began to ache with my own present desire. And then she kissed me. A kiss which opened my eyes to a wholly new aspect of this enigmatic creature called Zouzou. Her pert lips were relaxed, yet urgent as with a silent hunger. I could not hold back, in fact had no ready reason to, and so gave myself freely to her, responding in kind.

Then with both arms locked firmly at the small of my back, she said, "Felix, I don't know how long you're planning to stay with us: another day, a month, a year... At this moment it means nothing to me. I only want you to know that I love you, and I want you tonight. I want you right now."

My head swam. Her words, in clarifying her intent, served only to deter me. It was what I had yearned for, had forced myself again and again to apprehend was beyond the bounds of possibility. Yet Zouzou's offer was not clear-cut. She had not said she would marry me. Would I give in to her impulse, regardless of the dire consequences? Or would I refuse what every cell in my body cried out to accept?

I tossed my head in the direction of the shed. "Come on," I said, "let's look in this bit of shelter over there."

It wasn't the Ritz, this quaint old feed shed. Yet it beckoned with benign peace from its tilted perch on the hill alongside the path. Three walls held up a decrepit but intact shed roof which angled up to the ever darkening sky. Its shape formed a living shadow, open arms which called in the dimness for love.

Zouzou was mute, wan, pensive. She still possessed a hint of hesitancy, as she always had at times alone with me, save for the episode on the garden bench, where she'd paid for her impulsiveness with shame in the sight of her mother. As I thought back to that breakthrough in our formal relations, I wondered if once again Dona Maria Pia would appear on the scene to wreak her singular brand of havoc. Certainly she'd known the direction I had followed on my foray along the cliffs. And hadn't Zouzou left a trail of petals strewn behind her—perhaps knowingly?

It was now quite dark out, and the prospect of a lantern-swinging or torch-bearing search party struck me as uncouth, unbefitting the dignity of the noble family who had so graciously hosted me, and therefore unrealistic. On the other hand, when I thought of how our dual absence would be perceived back at the Villa Kuckuck, I felt not so very confident of my position. I shuddered at the prospect of our inevitable return, likely put off until morning.

Still hand in hand, we entered the dark shed with tentative steps, until we could discern that it was largely filled with a heap of dry, but still soft and fragrant hay. It took no thought at all to find ourselves quickly tumbling down together on the yielding bed. Zouzou's hands and lips were all over me. My mouth was drawn to encompass hers, as if I were a predatory snake about to swallow her whole. Alas, my jaws were not so hinged; and if my mind was fast becoming unhinged, I yet was reserved in a portion of my ardor, so that I held Zouzou at breath's length, standing, or rather sprawling, at my last line of defense.

I knew if this had been my first such experience, I would have seen it through to its inevitable and speedy conclusion. But it wasn't, and my fresh temptation was tempered by the consideration that Zouzou's judgment in such matters might not be relied upon—that in the light of day, our private adventure would be remembered only as a potent dream, and discarded for the required reconciliation with Hurtado. Which result would leave me in such a state of misery that I might then be prompted to make a drastic appointment with my rival at the figurative gates of Paris.

Still, that face before me, with its soft lips parted and panting with desire, drew me once more into melting union. The lithe body, of a girl even now become woman, asserted its firm and vibrant heat. How could I further resist?

When I closed my eyes and felt in the dark Zouzou's breasts spilling out of her half-opened blouse (whose strings had in our tussling come undone) the face that filled my inner vision was that of Sophie, wearing an expression neither pleased, nor offended; her chestnut hair, straight and silky, replacing Zouzou's black curls; the full and broad lips instead of the girlish pucker; the long-lined nose, not the upturned button which pressed urgently into my cheek. It was Sophie, however distant in her time and space, who held me in her power; and this nubile waif in my arms was powerless to erase her presence in my soul. I owed it to this girl now to try to explain.

"Zouzou," I began, but she'd already sensed the life go out of me.

"Hmmpf," she said with a sniff. "Is it my mother you're thinking about?"

I took the easy way out. "Yes, but not in the way you think. I'm worried, about her reaction. She will make it impossible for you, for me, for us. And in the measure of our momentary bliss, we will reap regret, and torment, and disappointment."

She drew away from me with a deep, poignant sigh and put her attention to retying the strings of her blouse. Then she got up to leave.

I reached out and grabbed onto her skirt. "Zouzou, wait—" My words were halfhearted, perfunctory.

She snatched the bit of cloth out of my flaccid fingers.

And then, without another word, she was gone.

CHAPTER V

With an incongruous mixture of feelings I lay there on that pile of hay, listening to Zouzou's footsteps and then the empty wind. Despite my sobering sense of having pricked the balloon of my earlier fantasy—not to mention the discomfort of desire denied—I felt calm. The vision of Sophie's face, modeling just such a countenance of sublime neutrality, stayed with me until I fell into sleep... where I was entertained more vividly yet, by a return of her image as she'd appeared in the afternoon's dream, sitting by the same jeweled lake, beside me.

"Well," she said matter-of-factly, "do you want to hear more?"

She was dressed the same as before, in denim and pink velour, but this time I wore my own more formal attire, the silk vest, the shoes of Italian leather. I took this variation from the previous scene here simply as more proof that in the realm of dreams, as in our more familiar domain, all is malleable, the details of stage set and costume at the whim of the director.

Of course I wanted to understand everything at once. Foremost was the question I blurted, "Why me?"

With my immediate direction hanging in a state of limbo, I needed more clarification as to her mysterious purposes. If I were to be completely honest I might admit that with my blunt question I was also pressing her for praise.

She laughed and then, in her irresistible husky voice, told me she liked my "profile," and had decided to find out if I were "major-league material, or simply bush league."

"You are referring to your American game of baseball, I presume, of which I am familiar, in case that information did not find its way into my 'profile.' Baltimore Orioles, Cleveland

Spiders. I follow the sport from the international edition of the *Herald-Tribune*. I might say that Wee Willie Keeler serves as a role model for me, with his sage motto, 'Hit 'em where they ain't.'"

She nodded, impressed. "Knowledge of baseball, or the lack thereof, used to be the litmus test for outing foreign spies during the War. This interest of yours could come in handy."

"So now you're asking me to be a spy?"

I didn't like that half-moment's hesitation before she replied, laughing a little too lightly: "Oh, not really, not at all. More consultatory, special envoy kind of thing. Shadow diplomatic corps. Or what they used to call 'kitchen cabinet.'"

"That's cute. Anyway, you have my interest. What salary do you propose..."

The more lucid part of me watched somewhat appalled at my haughty strategy, playing hard to get. As if this were an equal negotiation. I did, I feel, wield that essential lever giving the whole interchange weight—my belief; and the power to withdraw it if the prospects were not to my liking.

Sophie caught my drift and gave a sniff of disdain. "Playing hard to get? I saw what happened earlier this evening, with your trollop Zouzou. I know you're serious about this." She gave me a level gaze, and all our costumery fell away—figuratively speaking. Then she thrust:

"I must say, you're one self-centered, chauvinist—okay, I won't indulge in name-calling. But it's true."

I stared at the lake, at a loss for words. The emptiness around me was appalling. What if she left me stranded amid such barren, inhospitable beauty? Was the surrounding forest as endless as it appeared, the lake as cold? I had no choice but to engage further in this one-sided exchange.

"What do you want from me, then? Why didn't you leave me peacefully sleeping in the hay, or on those rocks on the cliffs?"

"Poor boy."

"I'm not a—"

She brushed my lips closed with a gentle finger. Now I was ready to listen.

"Okay—you're a handsome and charming young man who doesn't know where he's going in the world, or in life. Who's got so much talent he doesn't know how to use it. Who's so concerned about living it up and taking advantage of people on his scam of a world tour that he'll be blind along the way to real love, affection, understanding."

"You're trying to tell me I should stay with Zouzou—assuming I get rid of Hurtado first, oh yes and the father, and the mother—or was it Dona Maria Pia you had lined up for me? Is that what I'm missing by leaving Lisbon to try my luck elsewhere, 'young man' that I am, who's—you're right—not willing yet to settle down to a future of unknown worth? Why then did you barge into my life and ruin it all?"

Despite my hurt feelings I took a measure of pride in my handling of the English language, neglected since my school days. I found myself, in fact, as fluent in it as if it were my native tongue.

Sophie took no notice of my powers of speech, only my wounded tone of voice. "My, my. Such anger, such self-justification. To be truthful—as I told you before, I've been watching you for some time—"

"What are you talking about? Who are you, anyway? Or should I say, what are you?"

"So harsh a vibration, and I only mean to help you. I'd have to say you were wavering pretty wildly of late, regarding the prospect of your precious freedom abroad. I've been rooting for you all the way, hon, but you keep coming so close to blowing it, that I figure, I'm not gonna leave this kid to chance."

"No? Why not?" I took a closer interest in those long legs

clad in tight blue denim. "What's in it for you?"

That gave her pause. Moment by moment—as if by a trick of that magical boreal light—I began to soften to her, to think of her not as a tormentor but simply as a mentor. Or perhaps, not so simply...

"All of this you'll learn in time. But I guess you do deserve to know something more of my motives." And she looked directly into my eyes, with an openness I could only associate with love. She took my hands and held them warmly in hers. "Mine too is a solitary life, when it comes down to what matters: real companionship, with one who understands me, who can relate to this concept of ambition, success, power, without getting carried away with it. It's hard to find people who don't get hardened to the softer realities of life. To gentleness, honesty, openness, trust."

"Then what would you want with an unrepentant scoundrel like myself?"

"Ah, I guess that gets down to my real motive. I should add to my list of epithets that you're kind of cute. All in all, I find it a challenge. Like you trying to seduce all these women."

"Seduce? How about accommodate? Surely if you've been watching me—"

"All right. I'll give you the benefit of the doubt on that one. Likewise, I'm not really trying to seduce you."

"Then, what, exactly, are you doing?"

"Oh, getting to know you, up close. Isn't that what you tell them?"

With Zouzou I felt I had a sparring partner, at least. With Sophie I felt she was toying with me, cat with mouse. Yet her teasing innuendos held deeper promise, stated faith and qualified respect, even nascent affection. My heart beat resonantly within the drum of my chest, my very being, its rhythm dancing toward a job with the president, or a place in her bed?

I won't presume to dissect that particular emotion; for it quickly gave way to the annulling cognizance that all was transpiring in the context of a dream, and was therefore as worthless as chaff. I consciously wished to awaken, to be rid of the useless enticements conjured by this temptress, and to recover from the blows she had so mercilessly delivered to my self-esteem.

My hands still lay nestled in hers; the lake still rippled with the reflections of a multitude of trees; the cat still purred at her side. I thought, okay (Sophie's slang already taking root), if I can't leave at will, I'll stay with this blooming dream and see what comes of it. Why restrict myself to the pleasures of the mundane, terrestrial plane that usually goes by the name of civilized society?

There remained a more fundamental question, then, to address:

"What I'd like to know is, are you some kind of witch?"

She giggled as if at a private joke. "All in good time, all in good time. For now, let's just say the short answer is no. The next version goes like this: I'm what you might call astral-wise. You have a passing understanding of the ancient art of lucid dreaming, yourself. So you can appreciate that one such as I, gifted in psychic capacity for, well, longer than you can imagine; and studious of advanced techniques perfected by DARPA in the 1980s—"

"DARPA?"

"Right. Too much information. I'll catch you up to speed when it matters, dear. Come, let's have a swim."

And in the twinkling of an eye she'd pulled her pink velour shirt over her head, without apparent thought to exposing her bare breasts, so beautifully unbound, to a stranger. I guessed that meant we weren't strangers any longer. I rose and followed suit, removing my vest and tailored shirt. I waited when I got to the trousers, watching her long lithesome legs pull with utmost grace from hers, and from the final trifle of silk. Never, I must say, had I seen such legs emerge from a pair of pants.

I hesitated still.

"C'mon, silly," she cajoled me, and so I stripped down, too, looking in vain at the curtain of trees for surreptitious witnesses. She plunged in screaming to the frigid waters. I kept my icy decorum as I waded in after her, lips turning bluer by the step.

When my head went under, I found myself in another dream.

A hundred cities fall, their teeming millions screaming, strangled, dying, plunging into the abyss. The great ravine, its walls a midnight blue, shudder with the tumult of the falling cities. Limbs and cries scatter in the dark; while above, atop the canyon walls, the deep firred forest sleeps. Moon clouds roam silent in the smoky sky; the dimming stars drift far from sight; and the hundred cities die, with a dusty, gasping heave, on the soft unknown of the canyon floor.

I surfaced, still panting, and saw Sophie's gleaming body as she walked out of the lake. A few quick strokes and I was shivering beside her, berating her for attempted murder and reproaching her for not bringing towels. She looked at me as if I were mad—and took me in her arms to rub me vigorously and warm me with her own body heat.

My childish anger was thus soothed in short order—in proportion, I might say, as my all-forgiving manliness was aroused. Then Sophie left me to fend for myself in the brisk air, turning away with a broad, self-satisfied smile to reclothe her magnificent anatomy.

"Pears?" she said, bending over the rucksack which lay beside her clothes.

"I beg your pardon?"

"Do you like pears? I brought some along." As I dressed she reached into the rucksack with one hand and with the other, stroked the cat, stoic as a rough-hewn sculpture gazing out over the lake.

"That friggin' cat," I observed—adopting again a phrase alien to my ear, yet comfortable on my tongue—"gives me the creeps. And as for the ritualistic ordeal..."

She simply smiled, holding her tongue for the moment. I accepted a pear to help slake my sudden hunger. Once freshly clothed, we sat down together on the shore, as we had begun; this time munching on the ripe fruit.

Sophie faced me, crossing her legs in the manner of a fakir. "You were saying?"

"Why the pain and suffering? You could have just told me about whatever you wanted me to see, from the comfort of, say, a nice campfire here. Was the ice-cold lake really necessary? The visions of death and dismemberment, the disorientation—"

"Whoa, wait a sec. You chose to go swimming with me. As for the rest of it, sure; but as I learned in teacher training, you can't simply lecture, you have to use audio-visual aids."

"Audio-visual, right. But the doom of civilization? Is that your prophecy of the future, the future you're inviting me to be part of? I may choose to rest content here with the Sino-Japanese war, the eruption of Krakatoa."

"Think of it as a cautionary parable. A future you may choose, with my help, to circumvent."

"That's not a trivial burden to bear. By my own paltry efforts, to perhaps forestall—"

"Ah, there's the nub: *perhaps*. The so-called future, I suspect you realize already, is not fixed, but malleable by forces not entirely in our control—and thus not wholly knowable. Yet by gauging the signs and portents—and factoring in a healthy dose of history—one can catch the probable drift of events, even of whole empires, civilizations. I can tell you with confidence, since you've asked, that two years from now—that is, in 1996—I will be in the White House. And if you run true to form, you will join me there."

"Really. At the spry age of 120? Or will this feat, of causing a century to vanish in an eyeblink, be accomplished as you have done it, by some Hindoo magic of astral projection?"

"I told you before, I'm working on a deal. But it's not so simple. You'll notice I only appear to you in dreams. To be able to operate in this world as you do, will require, they tell me, further software development. And the reverse holds true as well, to bring you bodily into my time. But there is another way... if you agree."

The vision of the silent apocalypse returned. "A Faustian bargain? Carrying the stench of decay, the price of everlasting light and power?"

Her eyes grew large and black, as if exposed in the dark light of truth. Then she recovered her game face and said, "I should tell you more about me, so you'll know what you're getting into. Are you still hungry? I hope so, because I am."

Sophie's rucksack provided, following the pears, a more substantial repast of smoked meats, cheeses, baguette, tapenade; even a small leather flask of red wine. She informed me about the nature of that ubiquitous and versatile packaging substance, plastic. Then, while we enjoyed this rustic yet eminently civilized picnic, Sophie shared some details of her past, relevant to her current policy considerations.

Raised in a middle-class, suburban family, she had trained as a teacher, and found a post in the Arctic; then she had gone on to enroll in an Aboriginal Studies program in Canada. There she plunged into Native American history, nursing the seeds of what she envisaged as a pan-continental policy, which would grant all land north of the fifty-second parallel to Aboriginal nations to administer, develop and maintain as they wished. The lands below that boundary would incorporate the ninety percent of the Canadian population who resided there, mostly urban and white, into the enlarged melting pot of the United States and Provinces of Continental America.

It was all beyond my grasp. I still couldn't quite believe—even while dreaming—that Sophie was real, that she was living a real human life somewhere. So I asked her to tell me more about her background, where she grew up, where she went after university.

"I was born in Indianapolis. 1950. A baby-boom baby—conceived in that extended flush of victory after the War..."

War again. I started to ask about it, then thought better of my curiosity. There would be too much for her to explain, and I'd be better off keeping my mouth shut and just listening.

Sophie no doubt sensed both my impulse to ask questions and my conclusion not to. She went on with her story: "My family moved to Gary, Indiana when I was eight. My dad got a good job with a steel mill there; he was an accountant. I grew up fast, taller than the boys, grew breasts, all the rest. What would you like to know about?"

"You're doing fine."

She gave me an engaging smile. "I learned how to kiss, and how not to. I became a cheerleader. My favorite sport to cheer for was basketball. I played a little field hockey, then gave that up to play the flute in the school orchestra."

"Ah the flute. And a beautiful one, I might add."

Sophie paused with a sigh. I took in the resonance of her last statement. She nibbled on a crust of bread. Leaning for a long time back on my hands, they prickled with grass. I plucked a stem, touched it to my tongue. Sophie coughed, took a squirt of wine from the flask. The moment passed.

"So what drew you into politics?" I asked.

"Depends on what you mean by politics," she said. "For grad school I did a practicum in Central America. And that was in the late seventies, when the civil wars were heating up, death squads, liberation theology. So yeah, I got politicized then, on top of the indigenous history of North America I had already assimilated. About the dark underbelly of American empire. Of course that topic is off limits in conventional politics in the good old USA. I ended up teaching back in New Mexico, first in a Navaho school and then a junior high school, in Albuquerque. I served a term as a school board trustee, then chief administrator. In 1990 I campaigned for Congress on a platform touting traditional values: education, sustained economic growth in harmony with the environment, and care of the aged. I won. And then I was reelected to the House of Representatives in 1992. This year I'm running for the House again, and I've decided the time is right to look ahead to a run on the presidency in '96."

I felt, hearing this account, a personal identification with Sophie's life—foreign as it was to mine in the details of outward circumstance. I was particularly fascinated by her swift rise to power. Not that I had such ambitions myself, exactly. But I sensed that the ingredients of her success, if I could recognize them clearly, would serve as well to spice my own taste for worldly fortune.

I hasten to qualify that temptation by reminding the casual reader of my true spiritual intention—my desire not for mere riches and status, but rather for the sheer delight of participating fully in creation. In putting my case forward for all to judge, I would plead independence from the more jaded motives of the larger portion of society's hierarchic aspirants, be they the social-climbers or the power-wielders. Yet I am also moved to plead humility; for at the stage in question of my continual evolution, I knew my place as a neophyte. I was eager to soak up knowledge and experience from this clearly superior being who had by the grace of the ages seen fit to contact me, to nurture me along in the folds of higher truth than I could yet call my own.

I sought more clarity. "And so if I am to imagine myself, as you would have me believe, transported through the intervening void both temporal and geographic—not to mention, cultural and technological—it will involve a form of astral travel?"

A cloud passed across the back of her eyes. "Yes, you could say that."

"Then I suppose we'll need to be meeting like this regularly, for my training?"

"Not necessarily. There are certain shortcuts, and if conditions are right, you don't need to do or know anything. It will just happen."

"In your case, I gather you have invested much intention and would it be fair to say, technique, into this mystic art?"

"That's correct. You possess the rudiments already. You have to stay with it, the steady breath, the focus of attention. Cultivating patience, a subtle energy matching that of the object, the destination, the desired state. It's a matter of empathy, harmony and correspondence. Which gets into, I don't mind sharing, the secret of my success in politics. Identifying with the constituency, voicing their concerns for them. You see, it's easy when you start from the right place."

When she brought politics into such a light, my life of pretense by comparison seemed a sham, a low con-game perpetrated on unwitting subjects for my own self-gratification. And yet I too had been a success in my own way; witness my friendship with the king. I had to admit my prospects were decidedly shaky of late, however. I wondered if I indeed held a measure of correspondence with Sophie's approach to life—if the method was the same, only the motives different. I understood her intention as purer, more divorced from self-serving power. And she, perhaps for that very reason, seemed infinitely more assured of success than me in my shallow cockiness.

There we were, half reclining on the soft grass, facing each other...

"So," I said to her, "do you feel I'm starting in the right place, for you?"

She looked a trifle embarrassed by my question. "Here we are now, Felix. It's the place of my choosing."

Misunderstanding, I moved closer to her, put an arm around her shoulders, leaned in to kiss her.

She pecked me on the mouth and brusquely rolled away. Leaning up on her elbows, she shot me a stern sideways glance through tousled hair. "Wait till we get to where we're going," she cajoled.

"Where are we going?"

"You'll find out when we get there."

"When are we going?"

"You'll know when the time comes. Not now."

And one man, I believe the saying goes, *left on base*.

"But you need to tell me now: are you in or out?"

Casting all trepidation aside, I had no choice. "Why not."

She merely nodded, as to the formality accomplished, and started buckling up her rucksack. "Should have brought my fishing rod," she muttered. "Oh well, next time. C'mon, Beri." She shouldered her pack and, with her pet trotting past her, walked quickly into the curtain of trees.

I leapt to my feet. "Sophie, wait! You can't leave me like this! Sophie!"

Abandoned to that desolate place alone, to fend for myself like a wounded moose—

It's only a dream, a voice called from the far edge of my awareness.

I didn't pay it any heed. No more than I was able to take

any solace in a promised future rendezvous with Sophie, with her departure so painfully present.

I ran into the forest where she and the cat had so quickly disappeared. The trail I hoped to find there was nowhere to be seen.

Then, it was as if someone had turned the lights out. I was surrounded by darkness, filled with darkness. There was nothing around me; I myself was nothing. In such a place which was no place at all, even my pain was gone, my frantic frustration, my very desire. I did have a sensation of falling— yet no sense of a direction to fall. Movement in void: that was all.

My eyes were tickled awake by the pale Iberian dawn. I felt the comforting nest of hay around me with some relief, mingled with a sense of wonderment at all that had passed in the night. I was not as nonplussed as I might have been, were I not practiced already in the art of belonging out of my element— which amounts to enjoying an element of my own—*plastic*, as it were, a portable and infinitely flexible element of my own making, as I made my way chameleon-like through the jumbled strata of society.

I still didn't know what to make of this spirit-woman, Sophie, who claimed an existence in a future world ostensibly outside of my dream state, yet had such power to orchestrate it. Was she running her own confidence game, of a different order altogether?

The Theosophists of my own century, with their celebrated Madame Blavatsky and her tribe of psychic enthusiasts, had popularized the notion of a spirit body able to detach itself from the sleeper and venture forth across ordinary barriers of time and space—to the next room, a distant city, even a past or future destination. What had once struck me as intriguing but airy nonsense now carried a more palpable weight.

Beside me in the straw there was nothing but a memory, where Zouzou had lain. Had I dreamed that sordid episode with her here, too? Painfully, almost wistfully, I knew I hadn't.

I hoped that for the sake of the poor girl's good standing at home, she'd managed to slip in unnoticed under her mother's enveloping wings. If not, I was done for. But then, given a certain cheerful stoicism...

I looked out past the old feed shed's entrance, laced in so picturesque a fashion with a lush and vagrant grape vine, to face the sparkling vista to the west. With a fond tap of my hand on the weathered boards, I set off with a spring in my step. Along the path I plucked a perfectly ripe wild pear from a gnarled tree, and fixed my sights once more on the Rua João de Castilhos.

CHAPTER VI

Coming in disheveled from my night on the cliffs, and apprehensive about the suspicion aroused by Zouzou's own untimely arrival home, I was surprised to be greeted by Maria with any civility at all, let alone the offer of a hot meal.

I found her sitting heavily down to table, before a steaming platter of golden cutlets. She looked as if she hadn't slept all night. Her usually tight-drawn hair fell in unkempt wisps about her face; her cheeks sagged and tugged at dark circles under reddened eyes. Pitch-black coffee, half finished, sat in a couple of china demitasses left in the middle of the table.

I put on a cheerful face and told Maria that I'd been out on the bluffs all night, taking such shelter as presented itself to me.

"Oh, in that musty old shed? Gracious. Sit down, 'marquis'! We have more pork chops. Mardou!" When Mardou arrived, Maria snapped: "Let's have a breakfast laid for our rustic guest. And get rid of these coffee cups!"

Mardou showed me her familiar look of contempt; though in this instance, I couldn't help but reflect a glimmer of shared indignation over Maria's harsh tone.

I proceeded to gloss, for Maria, in the most general terms, a dream I had had about a bright future in the Americas—in the face of an abstracted indifference on her part, as she dissected her chops.

"Monsieur le marquis," she broke in with a snort of a laugh, "you may be interested to know that Senhor Hurtado is no longer eligible for the hand of my daughter."

Her curious twisting of events, backward to a time when she had maintained some control of the situation, amused me.

"He is, by the way, to take over, instead, my husband's

position as chief curator of the museum."

"Oh? And why is that?"

"Dom Antonio José has taken ill. He had to leave, suddenly, last evening. He thought it best to spend a period of relaxation away from the rigors of his profession, at a Swiss sanatorium."

Even though I had witnessed Kuckuck's breakdown—what was evidently the precursor to a more serious emotional collapse—in his office only a day ago, I immediately suspected Maria of a heinous crime. My fears arose from the intuition that she had harbored ambitions for Hurtado—who now was available as never before. How well the turn of events was working out for Maria's secret designs (excepting that portion of them concerning me); indeed, how well prepared she was, despite her apparent distress along the way, to benefit from whatever course fate laid out for her. I felt a twinge of admiration for her, of respect for that quality that I shared with her, of making the best of opportunities that lay hidden in the unfolding patterns of our lives. No, I decided, she didn't need to resort to murder. She could find an opening in circumstances through which to pursue her desires, without forcing matters in so crude and silly a fashion.

She went on to remind me, lest I take it into my head to revive my own ambitions in the new field of possibilities, that I remained neither eligible nor fit to take court of her daughter. "I find it reprehensible," she finally said, "that you've managed to complete your self-destruction at the expense of Zouzou's, and our family's honor."

"What are you talking about?"

"Oh, come now, Felix. I saw Zouzou when she came in last night. She didn't have to spell it out for me. I saw the bits of hay all over her hair, her clothes in disarray, her tears. No, don't tell me what you didn't do. It doesn't even matter now." Finally she sat silent, brooding, one eye wandering.

"As for your daughter," I responded, "I am compelled to tell you, with complete honesty, of my wholly innocent behavior toward her. She was in a piteous state, it is true: both before and after our encounter out there on the cliffs. I sought only to comfort her in a compassionate, which is also to say, a dispassionate manner. At the same time I was preoccupied, as I have already described to you, with thoughts of my own, wholly independent future. Believe me or not as you wish." I did not feel it necessary to defend myself further by describing Zouzou's behavior toward me.

As Maria hovered over her plate, expecting me to say more, perhaps to reveal what I had already deemed unnecessary to reveal, I continued toward the more basic conclusion: "I don't know that it matters to you anymore, but I have decided to take leave of you today. The *Cap Arcona*, as I might have informed you but did not because I feared your hasty intervention, had been delayed for engine repairs. Now my destiny is clear to me, and I can see that I am to venture on to the New World."

There. I'd finally said it. I would leave her and her European machinations behind forever, leave her to her lover and hope that the professor would have found the primal instincts necessary for surviving whatever affliction had befallen him... and I would try to forget about Zouzou.

I searched Maria's eyes for the impact of my finale. One eye, the left, quivered slightly. She managed a nervous smile, taut lips stretched too wide over gapped teeth.

In my mind I heard myself whistling a few bars of "Dixie." Dixie was a long way from Argentina, I thought; but then, I had all the time in the world. Humming quietly, I sucked the bone of the last of the excellent grilled pork chops, and glanced up to see Maria staring at me again with her baleful and wounded eyes. Patting my mouth with my linen napkin, I rose to leave the table.

"So that's how it's come to be," Maria stated, and I sought

neither to argue with her nor to agree to the bald truth, and went upstairs to retrieve my traveling case from the guest room in which I'd not even set foot. As I first reached the carpeted steps I heard her saying again, as if speaking for me, "Yes, that's how it's come to be." Another couple of steps, nearly to the landing, and her voice turned shrill: "Would you like me to show you to your room, Marquis?" Then the good madam's voice broke into a mad cackle. I was almost out of her sight, but not out of earshot, as she continued, louder: "Or would you prefer I direct you to the boudoir of a certain young lady? Ah, a tender one she is, I'm sure you'd..." and then instead of a cackle her self-mockery turned into a bawling lament.

Wondering how seriously she may have played her contemptible madam's game with Dom Miguel Hurtado, I had no sympathy either for her humor or her grief. I wondered, in particular, if the night's insomnia were due, not to her fretting over Zouzou and me, but rather to her consolation of the rejected bridegroom. When I heard the front door slam I imagined she had gone to find him.

I found Zouzou standing barefoot, holding a dressing gown around her, leaning casually against a wall in the upstairs hallway. She had been listening to every word that passed between her mother and me. As soon as I approached, she pulled me next to her and whispered in my ear: "That was very kind of you, Felix, not to put the blame on me for what happened last night."

The tender creature took my hand and led me to her room, where we sat side by side on her bed. Outside the house could be heard indistinct sounds of clatter, epithets, moans, as Maria vented her rage to the elements. I wondered whether she would flee to Hurtado, or find a more immediate instrument of attack.

Zouzou faced me, still holding my hand, and said, "I owe

you an apology for my behavior last night. It was unbecoming of a young lady, as my mother would put it; and worse, it was inconsistent and unfair on my part to open up like that and then desert you so abruptly, just because you remembered a face of some woman who wasn't even real." Her brow knitted and she began to cry. "Now Mama has got what she wants."

The raging outside argued otherwise.

Zouzou whimpered, "And I'm left with nothing, nothing."

She looked at me, waiting for me to save her from her fate. Her cheeks were awash with salt water, running freely. Black, wispy hair fell gently across her eyes. I had no words to console her. We'd been through enough discussions of love on its philosophic levels, and life with its infinitely debatable options. She still possessed a radiant allure, but that was overshadowed by the dark clouds which tossed about the stormy, dominating presence of her mother, and by the subversive influence of a rival force I could not resist any longer.

"Zouzou," I had to say at last, "fond as I am of you—yes, if you will permit me to say so, even as much as I love you—I must tell you that I believe everything has happened for the best. That includes your behavior of last night, all of it. I appreciate your openness of feeling as well as your later change of heart. I don't blame you one bit. I wish I could tell you what you'd like to hear, and do for you what before yesterday I would have given anything to do. I still don't fully understand what's in store for me, but I'm convinced that I have to leave on that ship this afternoon, to go to America to find out."

She sat with eyes closed, and rested a hand on my thigh. My whole being tingled. I tightened an arm around her waist. The flesh yielded, almost imperceptibly: a *subtle body*, indeed.

I was inspired on the instant to imagine: Maybe if Zouzou went along to keep me company, until such time as Sophie chose to manifest in the flesh... Why not? What had Sophie told me?

No complications for her sake. Nothing, in any event, that I had to do...

The racket from Maria's ravings had abated. I touched Zouzou's cheek softly with my palm. I kissed her lips lightly. "Will you come with me, then?"

She stopped breathing. Then she shook her head slowly, and a faint smile appeared on her face. "It's funny, how like tennis it is. Now the ball's back in my court. Two days ago, when I faced this same question, I told you I needed more time to get to know you, or some such schoolgirl's excuse; and I told myself later that night that I might even find a way to do it. I almost had the courage to carry out my resolution, last night. I don't know if I can find that courage anymore."

"Not even right now?"

"Certainly not. Do you know what Mama would do if she found out? It's unthinkable. She'd, she'd disown me, she'd—"

"Tear your eyes out? Really, what can she do?"

"Oh Felix, it's too late. You cannot stay; you must leave. And I have no ticket, nothing packed... it's just not possible."

"I told you before, I can cancel my berth. There's another sailing—"

Zouzou shook her darling black curls too vigorously, side to side. She sighed heavily and said, "It's not meant to be, Marquis—I mean, Felix." Small tears appeared on her cheeks.

I let out my own sigh of resignation. "What are you you going to do, then? Patch things up with Dom Miguel?"

"I do believe now Mama is counting on me staying here unattached so as to keep that repulsive Hurtado around. He didn't waste any time latching on to her, I noticed. I almost feel like, no matter what happens, my mother's planned it that way. Do you know what I mean?"

"She's a perceptive and strong-willed woman. But come," I said, firing my last arrow from Cupid's quiver; "surely we can think of a way—"

We heard the front door slam shut. "Susanna!" echoed through the house, a royal shout. Maria was back. There was time for one last kiss, Zouzou holding her lips tight to stifle her despair. Then I dashed to an open door down the hall where I found my valise, still sitting unopened in the empty guest room. I gave a final glance behind me, through the open door of Maria's room where her jewelry case sat in its customary place on her dresser, and paused with a pang of longing—not for more jewels (*tawdry*), but for my former jackanapes self; now cut loose and unsure of what was to come.

When I passed Zouzou's room for the last time, I saw she had fallen over on her side and was gently sobbing. There was no help for it.

Down the staircase, I avoided Maria by great good fortune as she disappeared into the kitchen, and made my exit, fairly skipping down the Rua João de Castilhos toward the harbor. My timing was fortunate in respect to the imminent departure of the *Cap Arcona*. Reaching the commercial district, I hailed an approaching mule bus bound for the quay, but as I prepared to mount its steps, my leg was arrested by a now familiar tug.

It was the half-man, who smiled up at me in recognition. He puckered his lips, in the suggestion of a desire for another cigar. I had none. But I did feel suffused, of a sudden, with a warming presence, a pang of genuine compassion. I bade the driver wait one moment; and from the inner vest pocket where I had sequestered my earlier gains, I extracted half the wad of bills, and handed them to the man at my feet.

"Thank 'ee," he said. "Godspeed."

CHAPTER VII

As I stood at the railing of the *Cap Arcona*, I flattered myself to imagine, in the throng at the pier, mother and daughter in tearful embrace. A tender mirage, certainly. Was their brief dalliance with me, like my visons of Sophie, but a passing dream? Freed from their web, where was I next bound?

The fading canvas showed pale stucco against the hills, the neighborhoods of the rich, where I had been, in the end, an ungrateful guest. As that picture in its turn receded into fog-blue mist, it became clear how my juvenile infatuation with Zouzou had deluded me into forgetfulness of my avowed progress in the world.

I had once undertaken as my supreme, even sacred mission to refuse all entanglements offered in whatever appealing garb of partial or temporary happiness, even when these apparent successes were the objects of my own desires. Thus in my most recent masquerade I had sought, ultimately, not deception and its small rewards but escape to greater halls of wonder and possibility.

I still had in my possession the marquis' letter of credit, a boon I relied upon; though I couldn't be sure that Maria in her spite wouldn't contact the Venostas as she'd once threatened, to spoil the whole affair. If I never saw the Meyer-Novaros who were supposed to greet me as welcoming hosts in Buenos Aires, or, for that matter, my Godfather Schimmelpreester in the cultural wasteland to the north, I would still have my native resources on which to rely. I could assume a wholly new persona, as yet untried.

I cared not even to foretell the exact nature of my future successes. While Sophie had charged me with a certain undefined responsibility—"A lot depends on you"—I would have to throw the challenge back to her, in whatever realm she truly dwelt, and in the meantime trust my instincts.

Lingering at the deck railing as land sank from view, I imagined seeing bubbles rising from my silently opened mouth, and I felt my place in the Great Chain of Being, as a creature descended from the primeval organisms scuttling to this day across the oceanic slime. Yet, encouraged by Sophie's evaluation of my character, I felt too my uniqueness, which in a colder light cast me in a condition apart. I was essentially different from Professor Kuckuck with his vast and relevant knowledge of the secrets of the Earth and stars; from the ruler of the country I was leaving forever with his hobbyist's interest in oceanographic lore; yes even, as the perceptive reader no doubt has intimated from time to time in my naive narrative, from the bright-eyed and optimistic, naturally gifted social success that had so convincingly come to be my role before and during my enjoyment of the title, "Marquis de Venosta." As my friend the marquis had observed, my most basically distinguishing characteristic was a capacity to hold back my innermost identity, as if there was a secret behind even my own name from the beginning.

I looked to either side of me. The *Cap Arcona*'s deck was strewn with the flotsam of Western civilization. On one side was a shriveled dowager with her nose in a book, accompanied by a petrified professor in tweeds; on the other, a middle-aged, middle-class couple, both of ample girth, alongside a bored-looking debutante who held her hair against the sea-breeze, and a waif of ten who stood with a sour expression, manacled by his mother's grip to the lounge-chair's armrest.

Sporadic voices from this collection of ostensibly intelligent beings were muffled under the wind. Their eyes—and perhaps mine, as well—were glazed in the glare of the salt-rimed air. Their movements were sparse and choppy. I nodded back to my own world of thought. A twinge of loneliness struck me: I was not so free yet as I might have liked to think. No, I was merely adrift on the wide oceanic bosom... and the heartbeat I imagined I heard therein was merely the throbbing of the ship's engines.

More heavily now I heard the ship's engines groan. My own viscera felt a slight grinding vibration. As the disquieting iron noise faded into the stiff wind, I wondered what was to befall a perfectly endowed prince who had lost his only realm, the rich reserves of his confident personage. Yet I knew that my whole life up to this moment had without deviation led precisely and necessarily here, in its own proper stage of development.

I accepted my current course with a surpassing calm, as if I were proceeding onward into the Nothingness that lay above as well as below. I became apprehensive with a sense behind sense, as the azure of the afternoon sky gave way to a mass of billowing dark clouds, and my nostrils tingled with the acrid ozone of an impending storm. The ship tossed, my head lolled onto my chest, and I slept... succumbing to murky visions of the depths over which the ship passed, wherein it was reputed that Plato's fabled lost continent of Atlantis lay, slumbering in eternity.

I awoke abruptly when my dormant senses were disturbed by a whiff of fresh coffee. I pictured the marquis approaching, with serving tray in hand, ready to bow with respectful gaze lowered, his princely finery exchanged for the smart trim of the hotel waiter's uniform.

The young man repeated his question. "Would the marquis desire a café-au-port, our liner's own creation, before the meal? I am sorry if I disturbed the marquis' rest."

He was, of course, an ordinary waiter, if offering an unusual drink. I inquired as to the arrangements for dinner, thanked him politely, and turned with steaming glass cup in hand to face the last strands of light still dancing atop the iron waves.

I sat alone now, the neighboring passengers having already

retreated indoors, and my brief nap and the subsequent refresher serving to restore me to my habitual state of mind. I could not help but wonder what noble family would entertain me this night, or for the duration of the voyage; what fascinating individual would first engage me in long nocturnal conversation...

Alas, these habitual preoccupations struck me at once as trivial; as purposeless as the ship's pennants snapping from their guy lines. Again my thoughts turned to Sophie. Whoever, whatever she was, she had changed me. My coming adventure as the Marquis de Venosta I now perceived as an empty sham, and I wished for nothing more from this long sea passage than a fresh glimmer of greater hope from that disembodied intelligence, whom I intuited already as a mentor.

Dinner in the grand ballroom of the *Cap Arcona*, while presenting the sumptuous gustatory experience I expected, roused in me no particular inspiration as a social affair. The baroque décor was elegant enough, with its gilt embellishments sculpted into the corners of the ceiling, its vast crystalline chandeliers and its rich brocaded tapestries. The courses of food, in contrast, were arranged on a series of long tables clad with plain white tablecloths, and served buffet-style for the free perusal of the patrons. I sampled everything: Parisian pea soup, American turkey, Black Forest ham with sauerkraut, mashed potatoes, sweet potatoes, paella, jellied crab salad, crown roast of Argentine beef, broccoli with hollandaise sauce, Russian perogies with sour cream, cranberries, pickles and condiments of every description.

Everyone milled about the serving dishes and sat at the eating tables in a random fashion. It was disconcerting if one expected an orderly etiquette. Arriving after most, I found a seat at a table with three ample ladies, powdered and rouged, and two portly, brown-suited husbands. The attentions of the fifth wheel, apparent at once by her eyes watching my every bite, proved disconcerting, but there was no help for it. My comments upon the "sumptuous gustatory experience" provoked an exchange of raised eyebrows from the others, and a coughed bite of perogi from my admirer. I engaged my tongue with more satisfying pursuits and let them prattle to one another about the sights of Lisbon, the outfitting of the staterooms, and the heroic but ill-fated sailing exploits of the third, now sadly departed husband. Was I meant to be impressed, or challenged to rise to the occasion?

Stuffed to the gills, I vacated my seat and retreated to the serving tables to sample—dipping a fork here, a spoon there—the desserts: Lady Baltimore cake, plum pudding flambé with hard sauce, raspberry almond ice cream, Bavarian cream pie, gingerbread, pineapple cheese cake, mandarin oranges. Without the taste to engage further with either old money or nouveau riche, bourgeois or aristocrat, professor, dowager or debutante, I stood with my last plate of cake, near the entrance to the bustling hall, beside a ship's lieutenant.

The mustachioed Spaniard, by the name of Reynaldo, explained that this new, open format was part of the ship line's attempt to appeal to a middle class of clientele, and to introduce a semblance of the informal style of the New World. Our conversation, in its turn, quickly trending to the banal, my mood turned desultory and I felt disinclined to extend the evening much further. As the ballroom was cleared of leftovers, and smaller cabaret tables replaced the long ones of the banquet, I excused myself to retire early.

Making my way down the passageway toward my stateroom, I passed the gaming room exuding its smoky hubbub, and could not resist a try at the tables. As if to purge myself of those ill-gotten gains at Maria's expense, I bet and lost the entire remnant of cash from the pawnbroker, on three throws of the fickle dice. I walked away feeling hollow and bitter at squandering a stake which might have abundantly sustained the half-man to whom I'd already surrendered an equal sum. Yet I would sleep consoled, that in that uncharacteristic act of charity I had at least prevented the waste of the entire windfall on a doomed game of chance.

Thereafter I would dine and retire peacefully to my quarters, with neither temptation by the opposite sex, nor entrapment in the gambler's vice. So, in fact, passed six more days and nights across the incognizant face of the ocean, without notable event or intercourse germane to what I vaguely came to think of as "my mission." Therefore let us hasten without further delay to matters of graver import.

On the seventh day when I first awoke in my private stateroom, with the gray sunlight muffling the one round window, I intuited an impending death of an abstract and generalized sort: the death of Western culture and European manners, and the fall of the neatly ordered shelves of useful phrases in four languages in my own memory. Even as I ordered scrambled eggs for breakfast on the deck in the open air, flanked by the same fellow passengers in their customary deck chairs, I imagined the filtering down from a new sky of an ashy, obliterating manna, by which alone I would have to be fed. This morning, my monogrammed stationery and pen and my letter of credit of twenty thousand francs (all courtesy of Louis, Marquis de Venosta) comforted me not at all in their habitual way, as they hung inside the coat pocket close to my heart.

Again that night, after the usual rich buffet, I sensed something in the air, an intangible energy that gave me more than the usual interest in partaking of the ship's social life. I stayed around for the cabaret, seeking out my friendly officer for company while the musicians set up for the evening's performance. Lieutenant Reynaldo informed me as to all the fun I had been missing. There was one young lady in particular, quite the gay dancer, he said.

"I suppose you're right," I told him, trying to guess the one he meant. "I seem to be dreaming my life away."

"The ocean has that effect on some people. Ah well. It won't be too much longer. I myself may take a vacation from these interminable crossings. Run my own little cruise boat, around Cuba, say. Have you ever been there? Charming island. With your command of Spanish, you could have a good time there."

Then he nudged me with an elbow in the ribs: "Hey, see that one over there just coming in. She's the one I was telling you about. Tonight, my friend, I will allow you the honor of the first dance with her."

I nodded my thanks and smiled, but I can't say that I was much interested. Though I had guessed correctly, she appeared on closer inspection as no prize. Her arms, I noticed, were rather plump. Her hair, piled all to one side of her head, was a dingy dark brown color and reminded me of a species of mammal who might have been nesting there. Her round cheeks, framing a vacant smile, glowed with too much rouge.

Nevertheless I agreed to dance with her—a Polish girl named Rosa—after being introduced by Reynaldo. Then he broke in and I sat down and watched them for a couple of numbers, until Reynaldo's attention was diverted to a more recent arrival in the room. I relieved him in turn, but in short order I tired of Rosa's dance spirit, more haphazard than gay, and myself looked to the relief of a new partner. I wondered where that shy debutante kept herself in the evenings. In the meantime no one I saw would do. It was no use.

The air was stifling in the gaslit cabaret room. Back at our table alone, I loosened the top two buttons of my shirt, following the Spaniard's example. The trio of women with whom I had shared a dinner table on the first evening were sitting at a neighboring table, with the dazzling crystal glow of gems ringed around their necks, all three now smiling at me luridly. I was becoming enveloped in nauseating clouds of cigar smoke, and more was puffing my way from the two thick-necked escorts of the ladies. It was time to leave. I drained the last of the dust-dry wine from my glass, rose from the table and headed for the door, muttering apologies to those I jostled on the way out.

Down the narrow corridor I made my way, catching a glimpse inside the gaming room, with its clatter of chips and its smoky, intent murmuring. I reached the exit door, climbed the several steps, and emerged onto the main deck. There I drank deeply of the moist, salty air that blew all around me and buffeted my face. I walked to the railing and looked out at the black waves and sky. Ever present, below the sounds of the churning waves and the steady rush of the breeze, was the deep, so deep as to be almost silent, throb of the ship's engines as it swayed onward in its course.

Without warning, the ship heaved up on its side with a thunderous blast. Unable to hold onto the railing, I was violently pitched out into the night, and could then only try my best at a clean entry into the slate-black water. My bearings were lost; the black of the sky and sea merged, and I lost consciousness as I smacked into the swallowing waves.

A blast of heat, throwing me against the wall of the train, as we careen into the tumbled riverbed. A storm of body parts, from other victims, splattering around me as my vision winks out, goes black. Sophie! Sophie, where are you? My consciousness floats above the scene, the very air crowded now with the lot of us, disembodied, stunned yet grateful to endure yet as witness, yes even of the senseless carnage, framed in bloody seats and blackened metal, broken glass and the screams of those left to suffer. Sophie, not among us nor the dying. So there is a sense to it, this I know.

I am alone, lost, wandering through a nameless boreal forest. Sophie is far away—where I began and where I am headed, but lost, circling, spiraling down. I meander more and more desperately, in the waning light of an autumn day, through endless bog, without any hope of recovery. I thrash, I trip, I wrestle my way through interminable thickets of prickly brush. My feet are soaked, slogging with ever slower steps through the muck of the marsh. Panic gives way to exhaustion, as I pant with heaves and wheezes of my dandified chest...

CHAPTER VIII

When I came to, I was lying prone on the floor of the lifeboat which smelled of salt and vomitus, surrounded by eight wet souls exclaiming over my miraculous recovery. I raised my head to glimpse over the bulwark the moonlit bubbles swirling on the waves over the sunken liner. In my unconsciousness I'd missed whatever dramatic clamor had accompanied the calamity of the ship going down. There were no other lifeboats in view, in the choppy darkness. It was with a disquieting mixture of sadness and gratitude that I found myself among the only survivors.

The silence of the dark sea settled around our craft like a shroud, and the excitement of this modest rescue effort gave way to a wave of grief for those lost to all time. Vocal mourning begat more immediately painful moaning over various bruises suffered in the incommodious transition from luxury liner to wooden lifeboat. I looked into each pair of frightened eyes, crouched in the haggard frame of a face, but recognized no one. The death of the elusive debutante struck me in a momentary pique as the most lamentable loss of the hundreds unaccounted for. I tested with wondering fingers the solidity of my own flesh and bones and knew, as though for the first time, the miracle of inhabiting this human form.

"You had a close call there," said the young man hunched beside me. "When we pulled you out of there, I was sure we'd be throwing you back."

I shuddered at the thought. "I'm infinitely grateful for your efforts."

I felt an instant affinity with the lad. He appeared about my age, with the soft features and innocent eyes of youth, and a swatch of coarse, sandy-colored hair waving over his forehead. He had spoken to me in Portuguese, with a German accent. "You know," I went on, switching to German, "I myself thought I had died. But of course, in the thinking of it, lay the contradiction—which, however, didn't occur to me at the time."

"Yes, yes, that's interesting, isn't it? The same thing happened to me once several years ago when I was thrown from a horse, and got knocked on the head. Then in the end, after you've accepted your own death, you wake up."

I looked into those clear gray eyes, so conscious, so alive, and knew I'd found a friend. "What's your name?" I asked.

"Seppl. What's yours?"

I was momentarily stumped. Then, at first with only a glimmer, and finally with full if dim recognition, I was able to recall my name. "Felix," I told him.

Still, I was mystified. Then my hand instinctively groped into my inside coat pocket. I felt a pad of stationery, a pen and gold cigarette case—this was encouraging. Folded behind the pad was a soggy document. I fished it out for a look and with difficulty in the poor light discovered that my actual name was Louis, Marquis de Venosta. In the dank recesses of my brain, more rusty bells began to clang.

Seppl was regarding me curiously.

"Oh," I explained, "for a moment there I thought I'd lost the paper that will allow me to draw the funds I need when we reach port. If we reach port. God, I wonder what happened."

While the seven other passengers were engaged in their own conversations, in Portuguese and Spanish, on the same topic foremost in our minds, Seppl proceeded to give me an accounting of the catastrophe.

"Following the explosion, the ship's crew didn't have the presence of mind to launch the available lifeboats. It was as if they, and the sleep-walking passengers, accepted their fate, or even wished to die with the sinking hulk. 'Come on!' I urged a bunch of them standing on the top deck. 'Let's get the lifeboats into the water!' Nobody moved. So I found the nearest lifeboat chained up over the edge of the deck, and lowered it into the water. I mounted the rail, held my nose, and jumped. Only a few of that crowd on the deck came after me, though—these folks you see here. No sooner had we gone over the rail, and the second explosion hit, sending the whole thing over the other way, and everyone else with it. I don't know where you came from, but there you were, already in the water."

"I only heard one explosion, and I was thrown overboard with it. No one else was on deck at the time."

"There were plenty on deck after that, but precious few with any clue as to what to do. Luckily we at least survived it. It didn't take long after the second blast before she sank to the bottom."

"How long?"

"Not more than a couple of minutes. I wonder what caused it."

"Indeed," I said, "and more pertinent now, what is to be our fate in this wretched dinghy."

"It's not the dinghy that's wretched," he corrected. "But the fact that we have no provisions: no food, no water, no blankets, no signaling apparatus..."

No hope? I dared not voice the logical conclusion. As one, our group huddled into a reflective prayer, tinged with despair as we bobbed in the darkness, cold and wet with the spray of brine, while the uncaring waves slapped our bulwarks. Even if we had possessed oars, there was nowhere to go, in the mid-Atlantic.

Clearly there was no point in such abject pessimism, I came to realize. Else we might as well have perished in the first instance, and not bothered with this exercise in fortitude. Or else we might, in the light of such precarious reprieve, decide to end the charade now and dive to our expedient graves at the bottom.

So I took up the conversation again with my newfound acquaintance, and asked to hear more of Seppl's life. By what confluence of fate had our paths, both starting out in Germany, crossed on a ship to Argentina? Or rather, not even there, but on this craft of prospective salvation?

Seppl twisted his mouth, showing more grief than he'd exhibited in the tale of the shipwreck. "I was studying guitar," he said. He smeared his damp hair to one side.

"Oh. And it's smashed to pieces now, or—" I looked out across the black waves, strewn here and there with odd bits of floating wreckage.

"I left it locked in the stateroom."

"Too bad."

"Yes, it is too bad," he said with a wince. "I was studying in Barcelona. I took a brief vacation in Portugal, and in conversation with some musicians I met, got the ridiculous idea in my head that I should go to South America, for a lark. So—"

"That's a rather ambitious journey for such a young man as yourself to take on, so impulsively. Your family must be wealthy."

"My parents are both dead. They left me enough funds to travel on. I figured, you're only young once; why not enjoy it?"

"Well said," I remarked. "But where are these funds now? Did you not lose everything on the ship?"

"Ah, fortunately I wired a large sum ahead to Buenos Aires. These fellows I ran into said I'd enjoy the Latin American music. Not to mention the scenery, the pretty girls. What about you?"

"Do you mean my background, my plans?" It all struck me as so irrelevant now, both past and future.

He chuckled darkly. "It appears we need set no limits on the scope of our discourse."

Inspired at least to reciprocate after what Seppl had divulged, I told him I was going to see the country a bit myself and then perhaps venture north to the States, sightseeing along the way. My godfather had given me resources to travel with and I thought I'd take advantage of the chance to venture out of the old countries while I was, like my compatriot, still young enough to enjoy such liberty.

In our conversation we paid scant attention to the presence of the seven other passengers, who by this time had exhausted the current store of speculations about our survival. Seppl and I prattled on merrily as if we'd just met on the Champs d'Elyssés. We agreed to meet for a bona fide planning session over a proper collection of maps, upon reaching port by whatever provident means, and at last settled more appropriately into the general plight. A huddled mass of blind hope, we spent a long, restless night on calm waters, enjoying but intermittent moments of sleep in recovery from our shared disaster.

I forgot whatever dreams I might have had by the time I came fully awake in the pale twilight, to the monotonous sound of lapping waves and what sounded like a distant, dull roar carried on the cheerless salt breeze. My thoughts turned to Sophie. I remembered her still, with utter clarity—Sophie Tucker Vaughan and her future world, awaiting my entrance, whether grand or subtle; this New World with its commonplace air travel she had told me about, the advances in remote communications stemming from the first attempts using Hertzian "radio" waves in my native era, and myriad other marvels of technology. More remote than ever, now, was the prospect I might ever arrive to fulfill any predestined purpose there. I had simply been deluding myself into believing a silly fantasy.

Then I thought I heard that low, distant hum again, and my heart responded with its own resonant frequency. Sophie, if I were to grant her an independent existence, had led me to expect I would come to meet her not only in her realm but in her time. As the droning sound approached our bobbing lifeboat once again, it occurred to me, with a surge of irrational confidence, that we were to be saved; Sophie had found some providential means to bring me forward in time to arrive in that promised future.

Then I thought I could discern, through the wispy and partial overcast, a long metallic object the shape of a cigar, coinciding with what now I perceived as a definite roar of engines—or by any account, a sound of unnatural origin. The other passengers had begun stirring, and a few eyes opened, but too late to see the glimpse of good fortune which had been granted me.

"What was that noise?" Seppl said beside me, stifling a yawn, as the sound again diminished into oblivion.

How could I voice my answer, so foreign to his worldview and that of our fellow passengers? Maybe it was wisest to tell the crazy truth, as I saw it then, or a version of it, and be done with it.

"Oh, that's the aircraft which my guardian angel has sent to deliver us from the depths. It's flying back to Atlantis to report our sighting, so we should be rescued in no time. Not to worry, my friend; you can go back to sleep."

He sneered at me and rolled over.

Within two hours we were steaming toward New Orleans on the David Livingstone, out of Cape Town. The grand ocean liner had appeared in the morning haze, half a mile away. The mirage loomed more improbable as it approached our bobbing craft. Its towering white hull, sleek lines and pristine, curved surfaces gave it a sleek, futuristic quality which I intuitively associated with Sophie's world. Had I entered a dream state unnoticed, nodding off in the gently rocking lifeboat? If so, the dinghy and its clutch of other passengers had come along for the ride.

Our company included a distraught couple from Madrid who had lost their six-year-old girl; a middle-aged man and wife from Herzegovina who took a cruise every year and had already determined this would be the last; a singer in the ship's cabaret who sobbed for her lover and singing partner, Sybil; and a couple of bearded businessmen, bitter with losses too ponderous to fully calculate. At the sight of the giant gleaming angel of a ship slowing to pull alongside, drawn by invisible command to our anonymous location, I shook my head, befuddled. In fact we all were rendered speechless, like the copper-age denizens of the Americas who first caught sight of explorers' sails.

This oceangoing vessel carried neither sails nor masts; only posts atop which twirled what looked like sentient machinery, on spider strands of wire. Only I, at least, had the advantage of foretaste, of secretly exhilarating recognition. Still my thoughts raced, seeking to comprehend. Had my astral witch caused an entire contemporary ocean liner, along with its passengers and crew, to bridge back a century to effect our rescue? Or had my co-survivors been granted a group pass, in a leap across that chasm in time, to facilitate my own priority-status transfer?

The presence of that theoretical airplane became further evidence of our forward jump in time. I surmised that its pilot had spotted us and radioed for help. That conjecture led back to the lost *Cap Arcona*, and the mystery of its sinking, a few hours before. That is, ninety-nine years plus a few hours before...

The others on the lifeboat gaped in open-mouthed awe at the wonder of it all—as, for that matter, did the line of passengers who hung over the railing to gawk at us, in the din of the grinding cables which had been looped under our boat from above. With the final crack of the winch came shouts of approval from the waiting crowd.

The scene on deck, I must confess, disturbed me even with my prior hint of its implausible manifestation. Certainly it was becoming clear to the others that all of us on the lifeboat looked like a museum exhibit in the midst of the large milling crowd of the liner. Though we sported a variety of fashionable oceangoing attire, we now appeared homogeneous. The muffled colors and prints, the browns, grays and dark greens, the subdued russets, the twill and tweed and herring-bone, all looked quaintly dated. For around us on the vast new deck were dazzling colors and fabrics such as we'd never seen before. So too were the cuts of the fashions outlandish, in our eyes. Collars which splayed out clear to the shoulders, shiny plastic boots, stars and stripes and spangles and satiny scarves, and everywhere bare limbs... one thinks of a carnival, a circus of clowns. Faces adorned with huge round darkened glasses, and glasses which curved around to the ears, bowls of frizzed hair or bleached hair chopped short and straight, bright globular earrings, white painted lips... and so, I guess, were they entitled to gawk over us. Amidst it all bleated a tinny cacophony, though I saw no performing musicians on deck. Hearing the words "New Orleans" repeatedly, I inferred our destination.

I approached a certain middle-aged, rather conservatively dressed woman who had been looking at me vacantly through large, tortoise-shell glasses, holding her arm loosely around a teenaged boy, neither of them knowing what to make of me or my ebullient companions.

When the youth saw me peering fascinated at the small machine he held, from which issued that harsh semblance of music, he touched a control to lower the volume, and with further encouragement from his mother, switched the infernal device off altogether.

I brought out my best English greeting; for the moment blotting out the existence of such technology, yet seeking confirmation of the truth.

"How do you do, madam, young sir. I surely appreciate your intervention in our unhappy fate."

"Yes," the woman said, "isn't it wonderful that our liner was so nearby to where your... your accident took place. I'm so sorry. All those lives."

I mirrored her downcast eyes. She looked up again.

"But you're safe, aren't you. For that we can thank God."

Or Sophie, I thought. "Indeed we can, madam."

I thought her to be around fifty years of age, and not unattractive, with the roundness of her face accentuated by the curled hairdo and small hat, and with her soft, gentle bearing. She hugged the gangly youth to her side more tightly. He gave me a sheepish half smile. He wore heavy horn-rimmed glasses and his light brown bangs covered his entire forehead. His hair in the back crept down onto his collar in an unsavory fashion that reminded me of someone... the animal sculptor, by the name of—Hutardo, was it?—no, Hurtado. By either name, the goose.

After a short reflective silence, the woman perked up and said, "I'm Margaret Smith; and this is my son Devon."

"Felix Krull," I said as I lightly shook her hand. It sounded out of place, not quite right, but it would have to do.

"'Cruel'?" said the youth.

"Devon!" his mother chided him.

"Wha-att?"

"An understandable interpretation," I said with a smile. "Actually, it may help to think more of the confection you call a cruller."

"Oh, like one of those twisty donuts?" Devon said.

Margaret hastened to bring the conversation back on track. "Were you traveling to the States in your boat... I mean, the ship that went down?"

"No, actually, we were headed for Argentina. But such is

life. I was considering traveling up to America at the first opportunity. And so this turn of events, however unfortunate, has simply compressed my itinerary, as I gather we are bound for the charming port of New Orleans."

She gave me a cold, concerned look.

My merry countenance sagged and I hastened to add: "Forgive my lightheadedness. We are all in a profound state of shock at this disaster which has claimed so many innocent lives. Now madam, if you could be so kind... I wanted to ask—"

"Yes, it's so tragic, isn't it. I mean, what about their families?" Her brow knitted and her mouth puckered, deepening previously faint wrinkles.

"Yes, quite true," I said, "an unspeakable tragedy for all concerned."

In this sentiment I was sincere. Especially heart-rending was the pitiable state of the surviving couple missing their daughter, and the singer whose beloved Sybil was no more. As for the dead, they were beyond help now. So at this point the collective grief was overshadowed by the mystery—both common and personal.

"Mrs. Smith, can you, and you must excuse me, but I think my senses have become a bit skewed from the experience; can you—"

"Please, call me Margaret."

"All right: Margaret." I made a slight bow.

"I can only imagine what you've been through. I mean when I hear of these jetliners crashing with hundreds aboard... of course there no one, or hardly anyone, ever survives, and I suppose that's really for the best, or—I shouldn't say that. But surely you know what I mean. On the other hand, you've just—"

"What I'm wondering is, what year is it?"

"What do you mean?"

"What year are we in, right now?" I was trying to keep my

voice low.

"Why, 1975, of course. That is, if I'm not too senile yet to remember correctly; the years do fly by." The boy had commenced to giggling with the falsetto overtone of the adolescent. His mother wore an expression of extreme puzzlement. "Yes, nearly 1976. That's a peculiar question. Why do you ask, so very politely? You look so worried. Is something the matter? Do you have amnesia, from your trauma?"

Once elated by my dawning fate, I now deflated, a fish out of water landing with a flap on a hard wooden deck. There must have been a slight mistake—if the matter of being thrust into an era two decades short of my hoped-for reunion with Sophie could be considered slight.

When my informant said that it was 1975, the three survivors closest to us had perked up their ears, cocking their heads and looking closely at us, from her to me and back to her again.

Seppl was one of them. He stepped forward and asked her, "Did you say the year was 1975?"

"Yes, of course. Why, I don't understand you people. Is it the language? Here, one, nine, seven, five," she said while showing each number of fingers, to the amusement of her son, who mimicked the display.

"So that's it!" Seppl shouted. "That's why everything looks and feels so different! We've come somehow forward in time. We're... that's... we're eighty years in the future? Did you hear that? Do you realize? Ahaha, ha ha ha ha ha ha!"

At his manic laughter the tension of the crowd broke and everyone erupted in loud guffaws, or nervous, high-pitched giggles, depending on one's status in time. That is, we newcomers found ourselves, like Seppl, reeling from the inanity of our apparent position, or juxtaposition; while the rescuers as a body hooted loud and long at his (which was also our) evident dementia. Margaret Smith remained silent, as if respecting me for—strange twist—being the genuine article.

CHAPTER IX

As it transpired, there had indeed been a contemporary shipwreck, a tragedy claiming all on board the maiden voyage of the *Carthage Star*. It happened that an anachronistic wooden lifeboat with eight, then nine castaways appeared floating in that very spot, surviving a similar disaster eighty years past. Because the distress signal from the floundering *Carthage Star* was monitored and relayed to a spotter plane, we, the survivors of the *Cap Arcona*, were rescued as if we'd been the lucky few to endure the wreck of the modern vessel.

Thus did the officers as well as the passengers of the *David Livingstone* persist in the basic premise of their interrogations, whether formal or casual. The quaint wooden lifeboat was seen in the end as evidence of the shoddy, irresponsible outfitting of the downed liner, causing speculation as to the questionable quality of her more vital parts. Our story that our ship was the *Cap Arcona*, out of Lisbon in October of 1895, was simply discounted as a troubling but ridiculous hallucination cooked up in our addled brains as a result of our trauma—a collective delusion. And well rehearsed we were, with our universal wonderment at the fuel-less electric lights, the ubiquitous phenomenon of plastic, the gadgetry such as Devon's portable music player. None of us castaways had the luck to have brought our passports or any other dated evidence along for our swim in the deep, excepting me and my letter of credit. And while its smeared ink could still be construed in one place to read *1895*, I was loath to bring it forward to the officers' attention when it would have been most effective in proving our case. What would have been the point, in establishing in these otherwise rational beings the basis of an unsolvable mystery?

As for the question of our dress, I suppose in their rationalizations the disbelievers could see our garment styles as a kind of cultish nostalgia. They were quick to organize a collection of their spare clothing with which we castaways could clothe ourselves, discarding our salt-sodden garments in a bizarre ceremony which saw the lot tossed overboard amid a tumult of wild shouts and cheers.

Even with our clothing as evidence of our eerie journey through time thus disposed of, I imagine that among our benefactors there had to remain some questioning, or wonder, or suspension of judgment, or nagging desire to believe Seppl with his mad outburst, in the days and even years that followed this initial circus. But being most comfortable in their habitual illusions, these people of the twentieth century were not unlike my contemporaries: indeed, if I was to carry on in my charades as a poseur, I thought I would be as assured as ever of success.

In the resulting collective masquerade, we managed to blend in without raising further controversy over our true origin. Accommodations were found for all: the two couples among our survivors were given unoccupied staterooms, as was the pair of businessmen, who found common cause in their disposition and agreed to the arrangement. A volunteer, an older woman aboard the rescuing liner, offered the extra bed in her room to the tear-streaked singer. And Seppl and I accepted the invitation to share the quarters of a gentleman by the name of Paulo Weismann.

Paulo was a lean, leathery old geezer paying first-class passage. Following our first night of genial but cursory introductions, I found him reclining outside on the upper deck wrapped in his plaid sea blanket, sipping hot bouillon and squinting into the haze at a gray morning sun. I took the presumption of seating myself upon the chaise lounge next to him, to strike up a conversation. I found him a willing talker, as many elders are, seeking to reclaim, in the recounting, the experience of their bygone years. As if to repeat is to validate, etching stories into the brain so it cannot forget; and to share audibly, to imprint others with that same template of lived adventure—thus conferring meaning, shape, an existential stamp, upon lives which otherwise would scatter into fragments, leaves in the autumn wind.

Having lived precisely eighty years himself, the man intrigued me as a human repository of the unaccountably lapsed history since the demise of the *Cap Arcona*. And I could glean from it with minimal risk of exposing my true past, since, at four times my age, this elder took the prerogative of having his say, foremost. Encouraged by my willingness to listen, he spoke, in a wheezy voice and with a vacant gaze out to sea, of his first inklings of self-reflection, a sense he had come from another place, condensing from sea foam or volcanic mist, into the shape of a boy.

Hearing this gave me a prickling of recognition, as of a shadow in forest foliage.

He went on to speak of his upbringing in Portugal, in a German expat family settled in Evora. At times he would fix me with a disconcerting stare, letting the words sink in, or gauging their effect. Little black mirrors, his pupils appeared. Like looking into one's own soul, or to the innocent black hole at the heart of one's life.

"I was nineteen when the war came," he said. "I had come to Cologne the year before to visit relatives after my schooling. A bad idea. I should have stayed in Portugal, should have seen where the world was headed. Instead I got taken into the army, sent to the trenches on the Western front. Nineteen fifteen was hell on earth. I survived, barely."

So the looming European war, which so many in my native Germany had talked about, did arrive, with no one to prevent it. I had been even luckier than this old gentleman, in being granted a free ride over the intervening years. The cold dread of such a conflagration had an impact still in the listening.

"There but for the grace of God," I told him.

"That is God's truth. Watching a poor sod next to me lean back for a nap after handing me a cigarette, and his helmet falls off momentarily, I tell him the gunners are finding their range, and the next one screams in and a chunk of steaming lead comes flying into the trench, embeds itself in the fellow's head, spraying brains all over... Sorry. Where was I?"

"You survived, thank the Fates. After the war, did you make it back to Portugal?"

"No, I went to Prague to study linguistics at the university. I became an academic. A short marriage, no children, divorce, and I continued my life with books. Much tidier than the nasty real world, with its brutish wars, its corrupt politicians, its hucksters and frauds."

"True. But tell me this, did you ever put authors in the same boat? I mean, novelists, after all, are nothing if not confidence artists. Even science, I might venture, is built upon an edifice of assumption: unwavering belief in the primacy of rational mind, the logical order of Creation, and the reliability of our perceptions. I confess I find these pillars no less made of papier maché, a charade of artifice, in the face of the unknowable void."

"Yes, well, we come to the same dilemma in linguistics, in philosophy, do we not? The Hindus, I rather think, had it right when they pinned the epithet *maya* on this realm of shifting phenomena: a grand illusion."

"Yes and no," I said, leaning back at greater ease on the steamer chair.

The middle-aged couple from the lifeboat passed us on their rounds, huddling against the breeze in overcoats and their conjoined arms. Once again, as whenever I would spot one or more of the other survivors among the general passengers, our eyes would meet only briefly, exchanging a dark look of recognition and denial, before turning away.

The linguist peered at me with those points of light, or infinite darkness.

"That is," I continued, "we can say everything is an illusion, compared to ultimate truth. In the meantime, it's what we have to work with."

The old man nodded. "Indeed. Which is why, by 1937, I could tell that even Prague was too dangerous. Though I had a comfortable position as curator of rare books for the university library, I gave it up and moved to Switzerland." He gave a chuckle. "I wound up dusting books for an antique shop in Zurich. The next war, in its turn, passed, far less traumatic for me personally this time around—though of course the horrific holocaust raged all around that pristine domain of banks and alpine peaks—and I took early retirement in 1955, at sixty. Now look at me, going off to listen to Dixieland jazz in New Orleans, with my new girlfriend, Janie, who is there waiting for me."

Remarkable it was to hear such a condensed history of the twentieth century (at least the first half of it; and now three quarters gone!) through the single lens of a man's life. How constant are the themes when reduced to such basics: birth, marriage, death; war and peace; the world of books, and the world... as it is.

Just then Seppl wandered by, bowed and shook Paulo's hand, but declined to join us. Instead he enticed me to join him for billiards, a new favorite pastime of ours. I bade the old gentleman goodbye.

At dinner that evening, a steward informed us that he had passed away. Saddened by this capricious loss (*Poor Janie!*) I took heart that Paulo at least had lived a fully allotted lifespan. And I was inspired by the gaiety of his outlook, even at eighty, letting go of the weight of the past and relishing the prospects ahead. I would, in a manner of speaking, be carrying the torch he had passed to me.

New Orleans, indeed: legendary melting pot of all the Americas, heat and rhythm and spice... a sensuous splendor, I imagined, to soothe the aches of unfulfilled destiny, of smashed itineraries, of abstract fantasies and lost loves.

As for poor Janie... it dawned on me that perhaps she was Paulo's fiction, his fond dream, or momentary muse, and never existed at all.

My original visions of Sophie were still as clear to me, when I chose to think about them, as if they had happened yesterday. Despite her intervention on my behalf (I could only assume she was the midwife responsible for dragging me through this etheric portal), I had to chide her for my delivery so achingly premature. But she was, sad to say, far out of earshot.

In Seppl I felt I could at last confide my tall tale about Sophie, and air my grievance. One evening we stood at the deck railing, smoking cigarillos, two rakes on a cruise. His eyes lit up at the point where he understood Sophie's role as an active agent of our future.

"So what do you make of it?" he asked. "How come it's not 1994 like she said?"

"Precisely," I said, flicking ash.

"Do you think she somehow arranged the wreck of the *Cap Arcona* so as to extract you bodily and whisk you away to her time, but then she dropped you by mistake along the way?"

"Hmm. Like a stork delivering a baby, and a knot comes loose, and down I go..."

"Except," Seppl interrupted, "it wasn't just you she dropped. What about the rest of us, the whole lifeboat, for that matter? And mother of God, if that was her scheme, it also meant the drowning of all of those other innocent people."

It was an unconscionable assumption, even given my default self-esteem, overinflated as the sensitive reader might confirm. Perhaps Seppl and the rest of our select few were all "special" in their own way, some with more pressing missions to complete in this interim time period. Still, the tradeoff was hardly fair. While I had cultivated no special affection for any of those unfortunate fellow passengers who perished, life is always sacred, its loss a canker on the lip of our creator.

"I can't believe the Sophie I know would be so callous," I told Seppl.

"She is a politician, right?"

"Good point." I stared glumly at the gray, lifeless waves, the steely horizon.

"But let's give her the benefit of the doubt," he said, as though to cheer me. "Maybe it really was an accident, and we should be grateful she did what she could to rescue us. Maybe she's not so all-powerful as you make her out to be."

Seppl's humanizing of Sophie lit up in my brain, like the flashbulbs of the passenger's miniature cameras, a thought that at once was logical and impossible. If Sophie indeed lived as a real woman in 1994, of early middle age, then the younger Sophie lived somewhere coterminous with us, Seppl and me, as we leaned against the railing pondering such riddles.

"Something went wrong, at any rate," I told Seppl. "But listen, what if I went to find Sophie, in *this* time? You could come with me, to vouch for my story. From what she told me of her life, she's probably twenty or twenty-five, now. She said she attended university in New Mexico; taught for a few years in Alaska; went back to school in Canada; worked in Central America. At least, I think it was in that order."

"Sounds like quite the pilgrimage, Don Quixote. I'll have to put on a few pounds to fill my role adequately."

"Very funny. But no, we could make inquiries. We could use the telephone system. We could fly..."

"Okay, fine," said Seppl. "And what if we do manage to track her down. She won't know you from Adam."

"She managed to convince me. Without even showing up

in the flesh."

"Right. You still have to convince her, not only that you came from the distant past, but that you've glimpsed her own future."

That insight caused me to draw in my breath, choking on tobacco smoke, with a further realization, a conundrum: Could that younger Sophie, and the maturer version traveling the ages at will, even coexist?

I had no clue; but in such a manner we delved into further speculation about Sophie's plans for us. Would she put us back in the nineteenth century again, after a brief vacation? Would we find ourselves, by some unaccountable adjustment, in 1994 when we reached New Orleans? In the absence of a clear personal manifestation on her part, we were left without enough evidence to construct a convincing scenario.

Our discussion had a quieting effect on Seppl. He grew accustomed to our incredible status as time-travelers, concluding, "Then time as we know it has no meaning. In essence, there is no time."

I flicked the butt of my cigarillo away, its ash grown cold. "A commendable observation, my sagacious friend."

I was left genuinely eager for the challenge of testing the temper of an unfamiliar place and time. It was my forté, after all. Indeed, while at sea, our entire contingent had settled into an ostensible normalcy that was both psychological and social—compelled, by the impulse of conformity, to resign ourselves to the majority belief in our delusion, and willing the eighty vanished years to sink beneath the waves.

By the day land first appeared, I was able to say hello to Margaret Smith again and join her and her son for luncheon. Until now I had avoided her and the uncomfortable truth she carried of my situation. The safe topic of conversation, now that we faced the end of our connection here, was life back home for them in Topeka, Kansas.

Margaret told me she had two other children besides Devon, her present companion who complained in a cracking voice, "Mom, we're not children anymore." There was Terry, twenty-six and moved out; nineteen-year-old Sharon who was still living at home while attending a community college in nearby Kansas City, and Devon, fifteen. Her husband, Mervin, had died two years ago of a heart attack at the premature age of fifty-five.

It wasn't as if he was under any great stress like the men who sold their souls to the big corporations, she lamented. He'd enjoyed a nice stable position with Topeka Feed and Fodder for over twenty years. One day he'd just dropped dead. It made her think about life in a new way, she said—that life is short and precious and therefore not to be wasted.

When the money Mervin had been saving for his retirement passed to her, she decided to use part of it for something special, and to give a portion to each of the three children. Terry had used it to cover tuition for flying school; Sharon had put it into an account to finance schooling for a career as a nurse; and Devon had bugged her unceasingly—at this Devon wore a large grin—to take him to Africa.

As Margaret felt vaguely fearful all the black people, from years of news reports about violence and crime in the big Eastern cities back home, and didn't really know any because you didn't see many in Topeka, they'd compromised and settled on South Africa. What she'd seen there, the poverty and discrimination, had caused her to consider personally the concerns for social justice held by a Quaker friend with whom she played bridge.

"Now, Felix, tell me something about yourself—" Mrs. Smith stopped short. "That is, I don't want to pry. You're a pleasant young man, though. May I ask how old... no, that's all right. Goodness. The food here is delicious, isn't it?"

And she thereby let both of us off the hook, the

uncomfortable subject of the mystery that had thrown our fates together. We passed the remainder of the luncheon time with harmless small talk, which featured an innocuous description on my part of the picturesque port of Lisbon, as if I'd been there yesterday, and which ended with a panegyric by Devon on the Kansas City Royals baseball club, which had fallen short of the championship playoffs in 1975 but was endowed, by his estimation, with great potential for taking the flag the following year. Although Margaret said not another word about the incongruous nature of my arrival on the *David Livingstone*, I sensed that the question lived on in the form of a sad and searching flicker in the depths of her eyes.

CHAPTER X

I was on my own in the milling crowd set to disembark, shortly before noon. Seppl and I had made vague plans to rendezvous that night in the Vieux Carré. The noisy bustle of the modern port city meanwhile excited me with a heady sense of anticipation; I sensed New Orleans to be palpably alive, ready to offer up its riches of new experience.

As I waited, I took stock of my personal appearance, gathered my sense of self-possession. I felt respectably attired in my second-hand pea-coat, navy mohair sweater and designer bluejeans; I'd managed to hang onto my old saltwatered shoes which still fit like kid gloves. As well as outfitting the destitute survivors of the *Cap Arcona* with suitable clothing, the patrons of the *David Livingstone* had had the charitable goodwill to take up a collection of money for us, so that when it was distributed equally we each carried in our pockets over four hundred American dollars—a small fortune by our previous reckoning. In addition I still had the marquis' seal ring, the gold cigarette case and watch, the packet of stationery, and that document for which I still held out the fantastic hope of useful conversion to hard currency: the letter of credit. In a small donated suitcase I carried a change of clothes: a smart checked long-sleeved shirt, a Shetland sweater, dark brown dress pants only a little too large; also spare underwear and the bottom portion of a pair of pajamas. I thought I might first check into a modest hotel and then see about clearing funds through the First National Bank of Louisiana, referenced on the credit voucher.

Thus prepared, I walked the gangplank down to the dock and began my new life. First stop was Customs, manned by an ebony-colored agent of the United States Immigration and

Naturalization Service. The officers of the *David Livingstone* had seen to it that the nine castaways were issued with temporary documentation detailing our names and countries of origin (I chose my most practical and expendable identity, that of the marquis) and the circumstances of our passage (the mandatory story, our rescue at sea following the unfortunate sinking of the *Carthage Star*). Then they washed their hands of us. We dispersed as nine impostors—living ghosts of nine nameless corpses feeding fish by the sunken *Star*.

Whatever his responsibilities and suspicions, the agent was persuaded, after some minutes of consultation with a superior, to let me pass freely into his country, under a six-month travel visa.

Or did I wish instead to apply for a work visa? "Yuh cain't work without one. Legally that is."

"No, thank you, kind sir. I have enough funds, represented by this letter of credit, which you can see—"

"Oh, yeah... mm-hm... what's this date, heah?"

"1975, of course. It got a little wet in the ocean."

"Mm-hm. Oh, yes, I see, twenty thousand francs, is it? How much is that worth in real money?"

"I haven't kept abreast with the rates of exchange while at sea."

"Oh, hmm, course not. Well, sounds like a lot. Do enjoy your stay, sah."

I walked off swinging my suitcase gaily—and quickly despaired at the very real possibility of actually having to work to make my living in this giant, mechanized monster of a land. Honking metal-clad vehicles of every color and shape, from the sleek motorized carriage to the ponderous engine-drawn lorry, filled the streets.

The trucks I gave the widest berth. A countryman, Karl Benz, had created a stir the very year of my departure abroad, with his chuttering invention, the *Lastkraftwagen*, for the hauling of goods; and I could see now that if I had bought stock... but never mind.

There was not a horse in sight except under a policeman. A pistol was still a pistol, I noted.

I was not prepared for the rate at which my donated pocket money would disappear, beginning with the nightly hotel rate of $22.50, plus tax. That was for what I considered modest accommodations—a small room with attached bath, large and well-made double bed, full carpeting. I supposed the presence of a color television, electric air conditioning unit, and telephone—appliances described as such in the handy About Your Room card—were responsible for the exorbitant fee.

The television itself provided what promised, at first, a vast wonderland. On three different channels were streams of lifelike moving pictures with sound, with all manner of entertainment and news. I thought if I spent a week here in front of it I would know everything I had missed learning about this modern world. Sampling the afternoon fare, however, proved uninspiring, with a live courtroom proceeding, an inane quiz show awarding thousands of dollars in cash prizes, and a sappy romantic drama. Each show was interrupted by pitches and pleas for more of those same dollars. It seemed *money* was on everyone's lips. My Godfather Schimmelpreester was right.

And where was he now, eighty years later? His great-grandson—or great-granddaughter—running the sausage trade, no doubt.

I turned off the glowing tube and went out to settle the question of redeeming a portion of that theoretical credit in my officially assumed name.

The marquis' letter, representing twenty thousand francs drawn on the Banque de France, listed the banking institutions I would contact in my principal ports of call. The First National Bank of Louisiana was among them, here in the lovely old city of New Orleans. But when I found myself at the address given in the letter, I stood before a small glass-walled storefront. *Established 1968*, said the small white lettering on the glass, under *Louisiana Savings and Loan*.

I was merely hoping for the best, then, as I entered and asked for an appointment with the credit manager, seaworn document in hand. When I confronted that pink-faced man he shook his shaven jowls with bemusement, looking at me as if I were some kind of carnival freak when I tried to tell him I was the Marquis de Venosta, great-grandson and heir of the financial estate of my forebear.

I had been so confident, that sunny day at sea when I'd found out that the rescuing ship's destination was listed on the marquis' itinerary; so confident in my fortunes being overseen by providence, I hadn't seriously considered that the time lapse might thwart the smooth operation of my established destiny. Now my obsolete charms were wasted on the efficient little man in the credit office, who spoke in a drawl so heavy I could barely understand it even though it was slow as molasses.

"That ole bankin' institution that this here letter of so-called credit wants to draw its accounts from is buried right here under ouah feet, young man. It wasn't even operatin' as a bank after '29. Turned into a vaudeville house. Then it became a tax office, and after the wah, a landfill and reconstruction—uh, pardon me—urban renewal project. Then, until about, uh, seven years ago, it was a heritage museum. In any event, here we are now. And this paper says, if ah'm readin' it correct, eighteen ninety-five. Ah guess you jes' inherited this ole letter, or found it in somebody's attic."

"Yes, that's right. That's what I'm trying to tell you. I inherited it from my great-grandfather, when my grandfather died recently. It was never used, you see, and—"

"If it makes you feel any better, even if this was the First National Bank of Louisiana—which you could still go to across town in their new building, by the way, if you don't believe me—this Bank de France here couldn't possibly honah an account so far out of date. No sah, this li'l document may as well be made out to the Marquis de Canasta. It isn't worth a French kiss from a View Car-ee hoah."

He offered me back the letter, taking care as he did so not to handle any more of it than was necessary. It hung from his fingers limp as an old handkerchief. I took it from him and folded it back into my pocket—for what, I didn't know.

He rose from his chair. I hesitated in my own seat, not knowing where I would go, what I would do when I got up. I asked him for the address of the new bank, even knowing that when I arrived there I would find no better luck. He complied with my request, then sighed and said, "Good luck and good day to you, uh, sah."

I too finally rose. I smiled lamely through a halfhearted handshake. Then with stinging eyes fixed on the marble tiles, I walked out to lead the life of an independent pauper. I wasn't looking forward to it. Feeling jilted, I wished that if Sophie had an agenda in store for me she would just come forward with it and get this monkey business over with.

In such a mood I proceeded, grumpier still over the exorbitant taxi fare, to the First National Bank. Mr. Pink's prognosis proving correct, I walked the money-driven streets until nightfall, and then sought out Seppl in the Bourbon Street bars for commiseration. I thought we might make exciting new plans for adventures together, finances be damned. But he never appeared in the ever shifting crowds, the ceaseless and manic mélange of pasty white tourists, Carib-black dudes in green hats, slinky dancers and sullen drinkers.

Of the latter I had been reduced to one, brooding beside a slumping frat boy on one side and a slurring, blowsy babe on the other, both down on their luck. The female wanted to talk so I listened, out of one ear. The frat boy perked up with more interest than I could muster, and responded to her complaints with some sophomoric advice about sucking it up and moving on.

Maybe these two will make a good pair if I disappear, I thought, rising to go.

Walking the bleary streets back to the hotel, I reflected again on the intriguing prospect of encountering a real live Sophie, young and innocent. I was nothing to her now, of course. Not yet. I would have to polish my natural charm for the occasion.

And if I failed to navigate the chartless territories, to find my Dulcinea, what then? Was I fated to walk these intervening two decades on my own primitive momentum, step by step, to no certain reunion?

After spending the night in the hotel room that I'd already paid for under the name of the Marquis de Venosta, I secured cheaper accommodations, under the more personal name of Felix Krull, so as to stretch my meager assets. When those funds ran out, I sold for hock the marquis' watch, cigarette case and seal ring, seriously devalued from their bath in the brine, and kept the cash on my person, fearful of robbery and protected only by my increasingly disheveled appearance. I took to sleeping in harbor nooks with an old blanket, which I inherited from a nameless predecessor and stashed daytimes in a little chain and anchor shed.

Now I really had to come to terms with my economic survival. How cocky I'd been in refusing to apply for a work visa! Was it arrogance, the lingering sentiment that I was too good for menial chores, too intelligent for honest work? Or was the truth a more basic verdict on my evolution—that I was simply unfit for survival in this new, unfamiliar environment?

In these few dreary weeks I had come to exist as the bums did, by panhandling and turning the proceeds, as the saying went, into liquid assets (and in my case, by indulging also in a few cheap if comically oversized cigars). My prospects appeared dim at best. I felt ill at ease with the constant throb of machinery, indoors and out, more pervasive even than the background sound of chugging engines during the ocean voyage. Here the sky, the land, the interior spaces all were clogged with the constant din of gears, motors, friction of moving parts, hum of electric current, whine of pistons and scream of brakes.

I took refuge in that palace of imaginative technology, the motion picture theatre. I had, it is true, already been introduced to the medium on a small and unimpressive scale, the hotel room's television. Now I was treated to the show of magic with full stereophonic sound, wide screens, butter-drenched popcorn and the hushed company of the rapt and youthful audience. The sheer impact of the experience on the senses pushed me back in my seat, at first, in fear that the characters and action were rushing out from the screen in a flood, a tsunami of life and death, larger and closer than both. Once I caught my breath and stilled my heart, I was able to watch, as from a distance, the scenes possessed of a certain flat superficiality, an impressionistic wash of color, like a rushing river with its rapids and ripples, its dancing foam and sparkling motes of light. And then I became entrained with the rest of the audience, drawn into the story lines, the character arcs.

My favorite film, it may be prudent to note, was neither the panoramic nor the grotesque, neither *Satyricon* nor *The Exorcist*, but the artful intrigue of *The Sting*. I saw it twice, rationalizing the extra expenditure as an investment of sorts.

Then it was back out to the light of day, the harsh glare of reality, the land of the automobile. I couldn't believe how much of this city was given over to it: whether for gasoline, parking, repairs, sales, rentals, pavement... I wondered about the extent to which the country at large had been taken over by this slick new beast of burden, this mechanical horse with the power of hundreds of living horses. I had seen a few city parks, yes; and I had to wonder if there still might be a few such nature preserves remaining after another hundred, or even fifty years further down the road. Was this gaseous sprawl the fault of technology, or simply an inherent drive of humanity as an organism, freed by space and wealth to so develop and expand?

With neither *a job*—callous epithet of humanity's downfall—nor funding for recreation beyond the low-priced matinees, I wandered the streets of New Orleans that rainy autumn essentially alone, but for the memories and visions of Zouzou, Maria, Sophie, and the Marquis de Venosta more and more obsessively swimming before me. Among all my nightly dreams in this period, however, Sophie made no overt appearance.

Late one night roaming the city, I swore I encountered my Godfather Schimmelpreester in the guise of a derelict passed out on Bourbon Street. When I shook the poor bum by the shoulders, he responded by calling out groggily in a hoarse whisper to a miserable little dog named Fitchie, who trotted over to lick his ruddy face.

I walked away, more disgusted with myself than with these unfortunates, and sought out Lou's Cabane, a lounge with a good German lager on draft. I entered the bitter-breathed darkness and found an empty corner. The place was a third full and I was glad to have a relatively private haven for my own thoughts.

A newspaper lay before me:

"Halloween Massacre": Ford Cabinet Shakeup

> *Washington.* In a final blow to the Nixon era following the Watergate scandal, President Ford today replaced several key

members of the Cabinet. Donald Rumsfeld becomes Secretary of Defense. Filling his post as Chief of Staff is deputy Richard Cheney, while George H. W. Bush will head the Central Intelligence Agency.

I knew nothing of this den of knaves, except to imagine their machinations in the heart of what I gathered had become the successor to Britain as the preeminent global empire. Considering my own lowly state at the moment, it struck me as the height of folly to believe I might one day have access to such corridors of worldly power. And if I did, by some sleight of celestial politics, arrive at such a station, what then would I even deign to prescribe for the expectant populace, those multitudes in constant need and strife?

Such lofty speculations failed to distract me from my immediate plight. I caught a vision of Maria in the face of the middle-aged cocktail waitress who took my order for a boilermaker. Her dirty-blonde hair was no match, but the reminder prompted me to take out my monogrammed stationery and pen, which along with the worthless letter of credit I kept as a mementos of a glorious past.

Boilermaker in hand, I opened the stained sheaf of stationery and felt the urge to write a letter to Zouzou, then thought the exercise silly. She was practically a centenarian by now, if she still lived at all. I had folded and reinserted the letter of credit behind the leaves of stationery, and a corner of it caught my eye. I took it out and gazed at it again. I thought of my laughable efforts to redeem it that first, hopeful day here in this alien land.

Sophie's land. If I gave credence to her existence at all, she would be close to my own age now, somewhere on this vast continent.

What would I say to her, if we could speak?

I took up my pen and wrote:

NEW ORLEANS, 4 November, 1975

Dearest Sophie,

Let me write to you not as an anguished soul, nor as an unfulfilled body, although I may suffer these things; but rather as a humble effort to overcome our separation, all the more momentous with our current proximity in time.

Is it too outlandish to wish simply to meet, in an indeterminate place, to whisper common talk, to know each other as consenting humans?

I cannot see you anymore in my dreams, but I still know you. If you were with me now, in this room, we could talk, perhaps, of love—but chances are, we would stumble, grope in the darkness for words, finally put on our hats, and part in the winter drizzle, smiling coyly of more distant dreams.

And if it turned out to be more lasting, deeper, and free, what then? Would our future you once ordained be altered irrevocably by my hand? Instead of politicking for the might of empire, or even the greater good, would we learn to dream as one, walk the sands of the city beach, share gossip, drink brandy, pick flowers, read Shakespeare, stroll babies, hide from angry clouds, watch clocks, attend funerals, daydream, dance, touch tongues, try to fill the half moon?

We would ignore the revolutions, make fun of status seekers. Our irony would grow like old ivy. Our drowsy eyes would twinkle like fading stars over the Sunday comics. We would console our aching feet with long, slow evening walks.

In the all-forgiving passage of time, our children would redeem us, like art. Through them we would be creatively fulfilled. They'd give our lives continuance and meaning. They would complete our shortcomings...

Enough! I rose in the fumes of stale whiskey, quickly folded and stuffed the unfinished but clearly degenerating letter into my baggy pea-coat pocket along with the rest of the dog-eared stationery, and strode out onto the queasy cobblestones. Across the street I saw a giant fish carcass which gleamed on the moonlit dock and yawned bloodily where its head should have been. I lurched over to examine it and saw at once the easiest way to dispose of the detritus of my past—my delusions of grandeur, a privileged freedom, a great love. Grinning with drunken inspiration, I fished out letter, stationery, and worthless letter of credit, rolled them together in a gigantic cigar, and plugged it into what remained of the piscean gullet. I applied a flame, then lit a proper cigar of my own, and set out to inspect the restless American night.

PART II

LIMBO

Death is the sanction of everything that the storyteller can tell. He has borrowed his authority from death.

—Walter Benjamin

CHAPTER I

It didn't take me long to land in jail on a vagrancy charge. I strayed too far from the district where most of the wharf rats hung out; and in the waning daylight of the fifth of December, 1975, as I sat with outstretched hand on a curb by a parking lot in a more upscale quarter of New Orleans, I had the misfortune (or poor judgment, which amounts to the same thing) of encountering an off-duty policeman, who promptly ran me in.

At least now I would have a decent residence. Clean, disinfected walls. En suite plumbing. Meals served punctually. Congenial neighbors...

My ears rang as the cell door clanged shut.

"Hey, lookit what we have here. Looks like a dandy." The sneer on the lean one's face, from the top bunk, was most unpleasant.

"I don't know about that," said the other. "Smells like he's down on his luck." As if he could tell, still lying on his bottom bunk, halfway across the room from me. "And the duds don't look so hot, neither."

"Evening, gentlemen," I said with a straight face. "I take it I can have my choice of the other bunks?"

They looked at each other. The fat one snickered. "It's your first time, ain't it?"

I sat down nonchalantly on the bottom bunk of the empty bed across the small cell from them.

"Yes, as a matter of fact, it is."

The lean one started to speak to me—"Say, bud..."

His friend cut him off: "Now Jake, I know what you're thinkin'. Remember the rules. We don't want to get too personal on him yet. It'll come."

"But Jim, this one's different. Can't ya see it? I'm dyin' to know—"

Jumbo Jim heaved a melodramatic sigh. "Oh, all right then, go ahead and ast him. What's rules except to be broken?"

Jake looked at me then, with kinder eyes. "Say bud, what'd ya do?"

"Vagrancy, the officer told me. Begging money, is actually what I was about."

"German, are you?"

"Why, yes. At least I was. I plan on staying in this country awhile, however. And you gentlemen: what unfortunate circumstances led you to this state of affairs?"

"'State of affairs?'—Listen to 'im, Jim. Where'd you learn yer English, kid, England?"

"No," I said, miffed at the evident diminishment of my accustomed powers in adopting the local inflection and vernacular. "As a matter of fact I only had an elementary instruction in your formidable language during my school days—a long time ago."

"For that, then, you do a pretty fine job," said Jim.

I nodded in appreciation, then sought to take up the thread of my inquiry. "And so—"

"Ah, the question. The one every first-timer begins with. It's against the rules of the profession, don't ya know. But who gives a shit anyways." He glanced up at Jake, who merely gave a shrug of assent; a traded favor. Jim proceeded to tell the tale: "This time it was disorderly conduct. The bouncer at the Lion's Gate had a little trouble convincing me the other night—was it last night, Jake?" (Jake nodded) "—to go in a certain direction, like out the door."

"I tried to come to his rescue," added Jake of the leathery face, and half the big man's size. Jake had a large nose which was bent in the middle, and next to it on one side he sported a blue-black bruise, which he nursed from time to time with tender fingertips. "And got cold-cocked for my trouble."

"At least you got to come along wit' me for company, though, hey slugger?"

"One big happy family. All two—"

"Three of us," said Jim with a smile toward me. I felt better. I must be doing something right; perhaps simply being there constituted an initiation into their fraternity.

"Say, what you do for work?" asked Jake. "When you work, that is." I regarded his worn leather vest, studded with rivets, and idly wondered what sort of obscenity I might see on the back of it.

"I can't say I've found any lately," I said. "Have you got any ideas?"

Jake looked at Jim, then back at me. "That depends. Is it what they call honest labor yer after, or something a tad more—"

"Creative," Jim finished.

"Yeah, that's it. You seem to have a certain kind of talent, though I don't know's I could put my finger on exactly what it might be. Makes me think you might be a good joe to have along on a night when we're—"

"Long gone from this goddam tank," Jim put in.

"I've done a bit of this and a bit of that," I offered. "I can't say, in all honesty, that I've held down any job for long. But as you correctly intuit, Jake, I have discovered a certain, well, knack for being in the right place at the right time." I thought with fond nostalgia of Diane Philibert and her jewels.

"'Cept when you got picked up and hauled in here," Jim added with a chuckle.

"Hey, we haven't even ast him the second question yet. What's yer name, kid?" This from a guy no more than three years older than me.

"Felix," I said, and shook both their hands. I wondered what Sophie's opinion would be—or was, in the moment, if she had a front-row seat—of this jailhouse alliance. Fuck it, as my new friends might say. A guy has to do what he has to do; and anyways, she'd given me carte blanche, right?

This wasn't the first time Mssrs. J and J had been in jail, nor would it be the last. They favored rooming together, and the local authorities indulged them in that respect. They were well known and liked by the guards, and evidently by the jailhouse caterer, judging by the amount of cake Jim was given, after the evening meal, to satisfy an inordinate craving.

Over that cardboard-tasting supper, punctuated by burnt coffee, and accompanied by harsh white light from the buzzing tube overhead, I found out that Jake Rubino was twenty-four, son of a Czech mother and Spanish itinerant factory worker. They had come over to America in 1955. In this country Jake had a rough youth growing up in reform schools, as his father was killed in an accident in a steelyard, and he was removed from the custody of his mother when she took up prostitution. Jim was more close-mouthed about his past and I didn't press him.

We would all three be released from the New Orleans City Jail after a single night there. Jake and Jim offered me space in their run-down shack beside the railroad yard, and as I had no other prospects before me, I accepted. The vague yet pervasive smell of rat piss was a small price to pay for a dependable shelter and a sociable introduction to the trappings of modern civilization.

It was under the tutelage of these companions that I got my first real introduction to refrigerators, telephones, electric razors, and so on—such items having come into their possession by means I didn't question. Not that any of these gadgets took much intelligence to operate. In contrast, the airplanes that soared overhead were a continual source of amazement and fascination for me; and I often recalled with a pang of gratitude the intervention of the aerial deus ex machina that had initiated the rescue at sea of my lifeboat and its company of castaways.

I felt an obligation to pay my way with Jake and Jim, who bought the groceries that first week without complaint; and so I took on the job they offered me in their landscaping business. It meant riding in the back of Jake's beat-up white van with the tools rattling beside me, but I could not complain, for I had begun my progress toward what my mentors fondly referred to as the American Dream. In the evenings Jim gave me instruction in the operation of the automobile, his metallic green, '64 Mercury Comet. On its last legs, Jim said, so he wouldn't renew the insurance coming up; for now it served me to chutter around the vacant lot by the tracks, practicing maneuvers.

During my second week with my hosts, I discovered the shady underside of J&J Landscaping. It was a one-day contract. The old lady pulled away around mid-morning with a set of golf clubs in the trunk of her Buick. In no time Jim was parking his wheelbarrow full of old leaves close to the house and looking in the windows. He tried to look nonchalant, as we were in partial view of the neighboring suburban estates through the mimosas and weeping willows which ringed the property. It became obvious to me that he was "scoping the place out." This was a phrase I'd heard him use with Jake recently; now I could see what it meant.

At lunch when the talk of my two co-workers turned to jewels and bureau drawers, silverware and china, I tried to ignore it. Then, in the afternoon, Jim disappeared around the side of the house with a ladder while Jake was weeding flower beds and I was pruning lilacs.

Big Jim reappeared a short time later behind the wheelbarrow full of burlap sacks, smiling broadly. He whistled and Jake came walking over at a good clip. I followed suit. Jim gave us peeks at his cargo: silver tea service, china plates wrapped in fine linen, boxes of silverware, and hints of blue velvet which I knew signified jewelry. "Time to kick off work," Jake said. "Let's go home and celebrate."

Celebrate spending the rest of my life with these guys behind bars, is what I thought, all the way home in the back of the van with the tools and the loot. *Best get out of this mess, and quickly.*

When the old lady got home, the law was one phone call away from our doorstep. Maybe Jake and Jim did have a rational plan up their sleeve. I didn't mean to stick around with them to find out.

I volunteered to take the Comet and shop for steaks and wine while they sorted out their booty. It was a risk driving without a license, but Jim had been favorably impressed with my new skill, so he handed me the keys and a fifty-spot. On Howard Avenue I turned left and kept on going till I reached the interstate. My heart was pounding as I waited for the light at the entrance ramp to change. I told myself I had nothing to lose by taking this plunge—provided I could handle a highway cruising speed twice what I so far was used to—and everything to lose by staying. The light turned green.

I eased the accelerator up to thirty, forty and kept pushing as I eyed a break in the lane of streaking vehicles. This was no arena for the timid. Gunning the balky engine, I managed to enter the flow of traffic and leveled off at a cruising speed of fifty, prudently below the limit. Once underway, driving at highway speed wasn't so hard as I'd feared, as long as I stayed in the slow lane and was content to ride where the road led. It was a breeze compared to city driving, with its multitude of intersections, bicycles, driveways, pedestrians, turning lanes, bus stops. I turned on the radio and leaned my elbow out the open window, thumped on the steering wheel to keep time with the music.

The road was smooth, the night endless. This was, I

realized, what American life had become, in essence: sitting back with fingertip control as your mechanical servant carried you wherever you wished—to the next city, the next state, even clear across the continent. Why, I could even continue to Argentina this way, if I were so inclined—as the kings of old, and perhaps the very gods, might have dreamed—propelled by the magic of internal combustion over the buoyant asphalt forever.

CHAPTER II

The capricious destination "Mobile, Alabama" had a certain ring to it, so I exited the interstate there. I'd been careful to observe the highway regulations so as not to get pulled over for a license and registration check. I doubted if Jim, under the present circumstances, would feel inclined to report a stolen car to the police. But there was no margin for error. Besides having no driver's license, I'd forgot my travel visa back in the house in New Orleans, and I carried no other means of identification. My incarceration in that clammy jail cell, brief as it was, still lay close in my memory.

I stopped at a food mart first thing in Mobile for a late, take-out supper, to be paid for out of the fifty-dollar bill Jim had given me for shopping. The Comet needed gas as well, and so when I got back on the road, I would have thirty dollars and nowhere to go.

I pulled into a parking spot to eat my hamburger and fries. Out of curiosity I took a look at the vehicle registration, so I'd be minimally prepared if I did get stopped for anything. The Comet was registered in the name of Charles Ready. Was this their friend Chuck whom Jake and Jim had referenced on occasion, the same "Fuckin' Chuck" who'd walked drunk off the pier when his wife had run out on him? I figured that was the case; that Jim had, so to speak, inherited Chuck's car and, in turn, passed it on to me.

Breathing easier, I went back into the store and bought a city map. Would I be Charles Ready now, late of New Orleans, ready to take up a new life in Mobile, Alabama?

No, upon consideration, the association was too sordid for my liking. Let the law suppose what it might; I would remain, as far as I or anyone else was concerned, Felix Krull.

On the map my eyes happened upon an amusement park, and I thought that would be a fitting location in which to muse about an unformed future—a future defined, for the moment, as the segment of time for which thirty dollars would last. When that was gone... would I have to pray for a free lift on Sophie's Tilt-a-Whirl?

I wandered among the scaffolded machinery, the sideshows and arcades, watching the kids in the kiddie cars, the couples gliding through the tunnel of love in their small rowboats, the families walking hand in hand. I avoided the haunted cave, because it reminded me too much of my nightmare in jail. I watched the Ferris wheel for a long time. After the allotted number of revolutions, the attendant brought the wheel to a stop to let each car empty. I looked at the people in the top car patiently waiting to come around to the bottom. That was me as I had been, I thought: riding high, without a thought for the bottom. Now here I was on the ground, and I couldn't see any way to get back up to the top. Oh, sure, I could buy a ticket and ride the damned wheel for a few minutes; but when the ride was over I'd be back on the ground again.

"My God!" I wanted to shout. "What am I doing here? Sophie, where are you? And what do you want from me? What do you want me to do? Come on, this is your turf, isn't it? The world, your amusement park?"

Too depressed to go on any of the rides, I walked around for a while longer and then retreated to the parking lot. I pondered the fate of a sailor who has disappeared over the horizon's edge. Back in the comforting womb of the car, I closed my eyes and felt myself fast growing old. I opened my eyes again, only to shrink from the sight of the human manikins stalking my now desperate solitude.

Tempting as it was to blame all my troubles on that stuck-up woman president, there was no help for it now. I had to take consolation in the modest prospects before me in the more immediate future. "I'll get a job, buy a new car, find a girl," I promised myself, brightening. "I'll even sell sausages at the corner deli. Shine shoes, anything. It doesn't matter where I start. I'll rise to the top with effort, style, a watchful eye, a careful turn of phrase at the appropriate moment..."

Just then I heard a gay song humming past the car window. I lifted my shaggy head to see an attractive young woman carrying a packet of french fries from the snack bar. She opened the passenger door of the small blue pickup truck parked next to the Comet. On the seat were two bags of groceries. She pulled out a can of root beer, popped open the top and took a swig, turning finally to look at me. I felt self-conscious in my baggy pea-coat, my dirty work clothes, my indolent slouch. I'd been too long on the bum, I realized. And too long without women.

I rose up in my seat, ran a hand across my forehead to push the hair away, and rolled down the window. I didn't know what to say. I'd lost my charm, my easy social grace. The best I could do was to strike a casual pose by resting my elbow in the open window, and smile at her. Words aren't the only way to a woman's heart; I still knew that much.

My practiced charm, appearing oftentimes, if I may say so, as an innocent intelligence in the eyes, must have still been serviceable.

"Hi," she said, after waiting for me to make the first move and then realizing it was up to her. "Wanna fry?"

"Why not?" I said, plucking a couple of fries from the open packet and sampling them. "Yum. Tasty."

I was reminded of Zouzou as I admired her black curly hair, though it was cut short to a trim bob. She had wide round cheeks, a small, delicately upturned nose, and glittering black eyes. She had the kind of active, slightly puckered lips that led me to guess she was fond of that characteristic American abomination, chewing gum; though at the moment her mouth was merely working on a bite of fried potato. Her tiny chin rounded to a point under wide cheeks.

"They make the best ones here," she said. "Sometimes I stop by on my way home from work if I have the munchies and don't wanna wait for supper."

I savored her mild, pleasing Southern accent, and wanted to encourage her to speak more. But still self-conscious of my appearance, and indeed unsure of my provisional identity, I fumbled for the appropriate idiom. "Yeah, I know what you mean."

She took another sip of root beer, eyeing me as she tipped the can back.

"So you came a long ways. Did you know about these french fries, too?" She gave a little laugh.

"How did you know—"

"Your license plates."

"Hmm, of course. Uh, yeah, just drove in, to, ah... actually I'm in transit. Looking for a new place, I mean work, you know, and a place to stay. Do you know of any hot tips for me?" I couldn't help thinking, after I said that, of the hard red nipples on her soft small breasts, which at the moment coyly hid behind a bulky cable-knit sweater.

She eyed me a moment longer, as I put on my best expression of boyish innocence. "Well... yeah, actually. There might be something. I waitress at the Riviera—it's a pizza and steak house downtown. They might need a dishwasher soon. I think Darren's about to quit. You might come in and talk to the manager, check it out."

I nodded enthusiastically. "Oh, great. That sounds wonderful. I'll do that—first thing tomorrow."

"As for places to rent, let me see... I don't know of anything offhand. There's lots of listings in the paper though. You'll just have to try that, I guess."

"Yeah, I guess so," I said in a dejected tone.

"You like getting high?" she asked.

I'd heard about recreational drug use, but hadn't yet found the occasion to try it. The riffraff I'd hung out with so far were strictly boozers. I was ready for a change. "Yeah, sure," I said.

She opened the glove compartment of the pickup and took out a plastic bag and rolling papers, put them into the purse hanging from her arm, and said, "Your car or mine?"

It seemed she'd already chosen mine. "Here, hop in," I said, motioning to the empty seat beside me.

"So why'd you come to Mobile?" she asked while rolling a slim marijuana cigarette.

"I liked the name."

"What part of Louisiana are you from?"

"I'm not really from there, exactly, but—New Orleans."

"Yeah, you have a kind of accent. Almost, what, Spanish?"

"Actually I did come over from Portugal, a little more than a month ago."

"Flew?" she asked before licking the paper and twisting it tight.

"I wish. No, I came by boat."

"Oh wow! You mean one of those ocean liners?" She took out a book of matches and lit up.

"No, a reed dory. The *Cap Arcona*, under Atlantean registry."

A cloud of smoke erupted from her mouth as she laughed and coughed at the same time. She drew another inhalation and held it in this time as she passed the funny cigarette to me.

I followed her example. By the time the joint, as she called it, had burned down to her fingertips, we both were giggling uncontrollably over some nonsense I cannot, for the life of me, remember. I do know that before she returned to her vehicle, I told her my name was Felix; she said her name was Sandy, and I was welcome to follow her to her house and to crash on the floor there. She had a foam mat and sleeping bag I could use.

The drive to Sandy's house transpired in slow motion, as I followed the hypnotic lead of her tail lights. I began whistling a slow jazz-blues rendition of "Dixie," putting aside any thoughts of conquest, or seduction, or expectation of any kind. *Sophie*, I thought, *in that regard you are teaching me well. So far.*

Arriving at a drab gray house on Jackson Street, I followed Sandy up the stairs to her apartment. We were both tired from the long day and the soporific smoke. She laid out my makeshift bed for me in the living room, muttering about what the landlady downstairs would say when she saw me leave in the morning. A light hand on my arm and a brief good-night, and the young lady was gone to her bedroom to sleep alone. Just as well, I thought as I undressed. Better not to rush into anything. She's merely being hospitable. If I simply have a little more patience...

In the morning I awoke late to the aroma of coffee and bacon. I dressed, rolled up the sleeping bag and mat, ran my fingers through my hair and went into the bathroom off the hall. I looked a mess. My clothes had become no cleaner overnight. My hair, which should have presented to the world its fair softness, was in need of washing; my blue-gray eyes were bloodshot. I tried to grin at the mirror. My teeth were yellow. Who'd want to kiss a seedy-looking character like that? I'd have to change my image, pronto. I began by enlisting the help of a hot shower, along with a toothbrush, comb, and pink safety razor I found in the bathroom.

"Morning," Sandy greeted me as I walked into the kitchen. "Did you have a good sleep? Wow, you're all spruced up."

"I took the liberty. I hope it's all right."

"Yeah, sure, no problem."

"You're most kind. As for sleep, I was, as they say, dead to the world. I don't even remember dreaming. For me that's unusual, as I take pride in my capacity for vivid recollection, cultivated along with a lucid self-awareness in the dream state itself."

She looked at me askance while lifting the bacon out of the pan with a fork. "Mmm, right," she said.

I seemed to have put her off, having lapsed in my self-awareness in the waking state, and reverting to my habitual, rather formal, manner of speech. I appreciated her direct, unpretentious manner, and her casual appearance: clothed loosely in her nightgown and bathrobe, hair still teased by sleep. Informality, for better or worse, was the American way.

"What about you?" I asked. "Do you have vivid dreams?"

"No, as a matter of fact, I have a hard time remembering them at all. I think it's the pot. You watch all your cartoons while you're awake, stoned, and then the dream machine shuts down for the night. That's my theory anyway. Do you want toast, coffee? The bacon's ready. Help yourself." She sat down at the breakfast table, forcing a smile.

I took a seat in the light-blue plastic-upholstered chair opposite her and sipped coffee. In a flash of insight I saw this fledgling relationship in the most banal light. I took bacon and toast from the serving tray onto a plate, and buttered my toast, not knowing what to say next.

Sandy sipped her coffee testily and said, "So, you still want to come to work with me today and tell the manager you're interested in that job if it opens up? Or if you want, I could mention to him that I know someone who's interested."

"No, no, I'll go in person. I've found that to represent oneself directly, with the force of commitment behind one's desires, is by far the more effective approach when dealing with business people."

"I'm sure." There I'd gone and shut her up again. She nibbled at her toast, reached once more for her coffee cup and tipped it over. "Oh, look what I've done."

I was up in an instant, grabbing a dishtowel from a rack

beside the sink and mopping up the puddle.

"Not with the dishtowel, you idiot!" She grabbed it out of my hand and tossed it into the sink, getting the dishrag instead to swab the mess off the plastic tablecloth. The spilled liquid had done it no harm at all. Meanwhile I'd backed off toward the kitchen doorway.

"Hey, I'm sorry," she said, wringing the rag out in the sink. "I don't know what got into me. The stupid dishtowel's not that important. And there's plenty of coffee; I'll pour another cup. Please sit down, finish your breakfast." She sat back down and brooded over a fresh cup of coffee.

"All right," I said calmly. We finished eating in silence. Then I tried to break the ice that had formed between us. "Is this your chosen career, this job as a waitress? I worked as a waiter once myself."

"No, not really. The money's not bad, with tips and all. But I couldn't hack it for too long."

"So what else would you like to do?"

She put down her cup and held her chin in her hands. She gazed into space, or at least to a point behind me high on the wall over the door. "Oh, I've been thinking of going up North, to Alaska or the coast of Washington, maybe go fishing for a living, or sailing for an adventure, or just hang out in the rocks and tide pools, or on the glaciers. Watch icebergs and whales, you know. I think it'd be fun."

Wanna come with me? I wanted her to say. But she didn't. At least not yet, anyway. The stars in her eyes faded to the shimmering haze of the northern lights, curtains wavering over her inner thoughts.

I imagined Zouzou scoffing at me from eighty years and more than an ocean away. *Scoff all you want*, I silently answered her. *You didn't have enough faith in love to come away with me.*

To Sandy I responded, "If I may offer a small contribution

to your considerations, I hope you're not planning to go on your solitary adventures before I have the pleasure of enjoying more of your acquaintance."

She wrinkled her brow at me. "Say what?"

Chastised again. Feeling vulnerable and nervous, I'd resorted to speech tailored for the polite society of Europe. It had served me well there, to talk myself into and out of situations as required. Now with this simple Southern girl I'd painted myself into a corner, and instinctively endeavored to paint myself out, using the same brush. "Forgive me if I've offended you. I meant not to be so forward as merely to indicate my humble appreciation of your friendship."

"Man, this is bizarre. Are you putting me on, or what?"

I took a deep breath, facing a moment of truth. How to come clean, as the vernacular would have it, without giving my whole story away?

I retreated to the casual, clipped American speech I'd learned from the bums. "Oh, I'm really sorry, Sandy. You're right—I got carried away. I studied Shakespeare once, y'see. Played a few roles on stage with that kind of jive. Sometimes it just comes back."

She tilted her head, gauging this frequency switch in her audio reception. "Ohh-kayy. I was wondering, is this guy weird, or what? Shakespeare, huh? Was that in high school?"

"High school? No, I didn't finish school at the upper level. This was... with a theatre troupe in... Munich."

"You mean they do Shakespeare in Germany?"

"Oh, you bet. It was very popular. In translation, of course."

"Mmm, interesting. So you're German, are you?"

"Originally, yes. I prefer to think of myself as American, now."

"That's nice. Look, Felix, I have to get dressed and go downtown pretty quick to do a few errands before work. You can tag along—we can have lunch together, and you can go in to work with me later on." She'd risen from the table and began clearing dishes away. "You could check out a newspaper, for rentals, or other jobs, though I wouldn't expect much there. You're welcome to stay here another night if you like, until you find something."

One night at a time, was it?—or did I just hear an open invitation? Probably a noncommittal mixture of both.

"I really appreciate your hospitality, Sandy." She shyly kept her eyes averted, arranging dishes on the counter. Pressing my luck with a touch of comic relief, I stood swelling my chest and raised my voice to a near-bombastic pitch: "Certainly, I accept most humbly. My financial status, it is true, dictates an imminent return to the positive side of the ledger. I shall indeed look forward to furthering our as yet nascent acquaintance *au déjeuner, et jusque ce soir.*"

"Hey, that's French," Sandy said with a giggle. "I thought you said you were German."

"Ah, I am many things," said the booming voice of wisdom.

"I'll bet. Now tell me, what's 'nascent' mean?"

"Ah, it is indeed significant that you should ask. A propitious word to serve as the key to a hidden doorway of a deeper level of inquiry—"

"Hold on," Sandy said. "I think I need to get high before I hear any more of this. My poor brain's too small right now. It needs enlarging. Wanna help?"

She led us into the living room, took an oriental water pipe out of a cabinet, and filled the bowl with green hemp from a lacquered box. "Not the best weed in the world," she said, "but it'll do." She sat beside me on the couch.

When the smoldering bowl was finished I returned to the explanation of *nascent*. "It means emerging, coming into being. Like the opening of the human perceptions and heart to the floodtides of the cosmos. With our infinite capacity for self-discovery and sharing of our inner resources and spiritual gifts, we give birth to a new dimension of being, extending the evolutionary impulse from mere Nothingness, through material Being and living Organism, to... to what? It is the eternal quest. Call it... love."

"And what play is that speech from?"

"Oh, a beggar's opera I saw in a dusty village in Portugal, many years ago. I'll tell you more about it sometime. But we should get going, right? To do your errands?" I sat upright, ready to stand.

Sandy held me firmly with her languid gaze. She was lounging back on the couch, far from thoughts of worldly responsibilities. Her bathrobe fell open at the chest. She reached for my hand.

I trust the savvy reader will forgive me for not wallowing at length in the graphic depiction of sexual desire and gratification—even in the case of this healthy young man and woman both too long in conditions of abstinence. For Sandy, that creature of the nineteen seventies, "too long" was a matter of weeks since her previous consort. For myself, suffice it to say I was not keen on waiting twenty more years for the esoteric pleasures of Sophie Tucker Vaughan. Life must go on.

Where Zouzou had represented a courtship of the most painstaking conventionality, Sandy's amorous invitation bespoke an epochal shift of sexual mores. Thus I could not lay claim to any special powers of seductive persuasion, in this instance. The humbling recognition of a more general trend came when, in the throes of passion, Sandy confided she was taking "the Pill." The effect was disquieting: momentarily I thrilled at the release of the burden of conscience over risking pregnancy; yet in the next breath I envisioned an entire generation of liberated women to choose from, among whom this random young specimen was hardly unique, or deserving of my lasting attentions. At last I lay content beside her, with a canned refrain, of tinny car radio timbre, echoing in my lust-washed brain: "Love the one you're with."

Needing more staff over Christmas, the restaurant hired me on as a dishwasher. My nights at the Riviera Pizza and Steak House were, if anything, tantalizing. I would stand over the great foaming sinks; Sandy would scurry about the dining room, and each time she popped into the kitchen, we would exchange loving glances—or, if the manager wasn't around, a quick embrace. "Oh, Felix," she'd invariably say, "keep your wet hands off the back of my dress. What will the customers think?" I learned to make do with a passing brush of our lips.

Without these brief flashes of romance, the job would have meant unutterable drudgery for me. If I could have been paid by the dish, it might have been a different story. I could have used my talents to devise an efficient system of operation so as to reap the maximum profit from the enterprise. Instead, I was just putting in time, and unevenly at that.

Which began to grate whenever I brooded more on this enigma called Sophie. I wondered if I would be judged for not trying to be more proactive, preparing for that greater future. Should I be enrolling in the study of political science, currying favor with ward chiefs and mayoral deputies? While scraping plates and stacking saucers, I tried reconstructing Sophie's resumé, devising strategies to track her down—if not beside a nameless frozen lake, then in a classroom, or back in Albuquerque on one of her jaunts there. This train of thought always ran in circles, putting me in mind of a lab rat in a maze—a mode of life which ran exactly counter to my nature. Better to milk the present, I concluded, for all it was worth. For further self-justification, I figured that was probably Sophie's intent in the first place: let this cocky schmuck apprentice his way up the ladder by his own fancy bootstraps.

Problem was, I found the disco club boring after the first half hour under the throbbing colored lights and jackhammer beat. I couldn't stand to watch the inane television fare with my love-pet, either, even while we fondled one another on her couch. Sandy's stereo provided more interesting ambience, especially enhanced by the effects of the drug we smoked together on a nightly basis. Soon that, too, became empty entertainment... as empty as our attempts at deeper intimacy over candlelight suppers, whether at a fancier restaurant or in Sandy's apartment. Something was missing, all along, and I was too thick to realize it. Once I did grasp the situation—if one can grasp an emptiness, like embracing a ghost—I didn't know what to do about it, so I continued pretending we were perfect lovers, made for each other. Even when she turned her back to me all night; even when she stopped coming by for kisses at the sink in the Riviera.

Sandy made the decisive move on Christmas Eve. It was nothing personal, she assured me. She'd been offered a better job, as head waitress at the Café Champignon, a restaurant in Montgomery that was owned by the same management as the Riviera's. I was not quite despondent as I sat beside her in her blue Mazda, outside the drab house at 12A Jackson Street at midnight, looking at her as she stared straight ahead through the windshield at the rainy night. But I was truly sad.

Why wasn't it working, I wanted to know. Why—when I'd said no problem, I'll come with you—had she said no? We'd been together less than two weeks.

That's the way it is, she told me. No big deal. It happens all the time.

Not to me, I told her.

Okay, she said, welcome to the new world. And she got out and slammed the truck door behind her.

I slept that night, or tried to, on the couch in the living room, staring at the ridiculous silver tree in the corner. When morning came I had to wonder what had become of Christmas.

Sandy was half apologetic. We tried to smile at one another as we exchanged the gifts we'd already bought for each other. We had a quiet breakfast and then spent the early part of the day walking around the neighborhood in a drizzling rain, trying to talk. I could keep the rental, Sandy suggested. Yeah, I agreed—with money to pay for it as long as I could stand to keep washing dishes, alone.

The Comet was falling apart, too; but I could afford at least a new muffler and rebuilt carburetor—the most pressing repairs, according to my understanding of the machine which I had gleaned from Jim's tutorial.

Nothing like car problems to get a man's mind off his other troubles.

By the first of the year Sandy had moved out.

The interminable boredom of the job at the Riviera finally proved untenable; I felt compelled to quit and take my chances with other employment. I managed to keep afloat by means of a series of fleeting odd jobs in the high-turnover professions: gas-pumping, car-washing, car-parking, more dishwashing. These jobs were relatively easy to come by—though my chances were reduced when a prospective employer would discover that I had no Social Security number, no work visa. Some, however, didn't mind a more informal arrangement, preferring to pay me in cash, at a reduced rate.

When I was down and out I thought of Jake and Jim, doubtless in jail again. I hoped they were all right, knew they would be. My present condition made me second-guess my accelerated departure from their company. In the balance I was glad I had left. Now I could (any day) start to experience fully that American ideal called *freedom*. Which came only after the acquisition, by whatever providential means, of *wealth*.

For those on the bottom of the economic heap, such as myself, freedom meant trading one subsistence job for another: like selecting boxes of empty calories from the supermarket shelf, each sporting a different color, a different brand name, to suggest there was a choice. The same could be said of any consumer item, or for that matter, voting ballot. In this election year of 1976, for example, a humble peanut farmer named Jimmy Carter had surfaced as the "people's choice," the new hope of the moribund Democratic Party, to run against the rather Neanderthal figure of the incumbent president, Gerald Ford. Would it matter, in the end, which hands held the reins of of the imperial chariot, galloping across this American century on its own power-crazed momentum? And what role could a transplanted dandy, now a working class peon, hope to play in such a high-stakes game?

The concept of freedom, I sensed, would have to be found within my own, more intimate country of self-determination. Yet I was not completely free, for I dwelled within this larger cultural arena, with its particular constraints. When success is measured in dollars and cents, personal freedom is compromised—reduced to basic needs, flights of fancy toward imagined futures, recollections of past exploits.

Thus resigned, I witnessed the passing of an uneventful spring, following the soggy footsteps of winter. Uneventful, that is, save for a certain prophetic dream I had one night late in May—the day, as it happened, that my long-gone travel visa expired.

In the dream I answered a ringing phone, handed to me by white-haired Sandy in a threadbare robe. "You are invited to a ball at midnight on the twenty-second in Albuquerque," the female voice sang. "The Silver and Turquoise Merchants' Association is hosting the gala event for all retailers from across the Southwest. Formal wear is not required; this is a costume ball, so let your imagination be your guide. Come, for example, as a white, whispering bear. See you there."

I finally recognized the voice as Sophie's. But by the time I blurted out, "Sophie, is that you? Where are you?" the line had clicked silent.

I took the hint, at least, to make a couple of calls of my own the next morning. Funds or no funds, it was time to sniff out Sophie's trail. First, however, directory assistance denied the existence of any such entity as the Silver and Turquoise Merchants' Association, at least for the city of Albuquerque and its surrounds. Next I called the administration office of the University of New Mexico in Albuquerque.

"Can you please tell me if you have a record of a student named Sophie Vaughan?"

"Sir, we can't give out that information."

By my recollection Sophie was born in the precise heart of the century, 1950, and following the sequence of conventional schooling would have graduated in or around 1972. I took the odds and pressed the point.

"I can appreciate your constraints, at least regarding the current student body," I told the functionary holding the other end of the wire, a thousand miles or more distant. "Perhaps you can still help me, though, by consulting the records for the year she graduated, 1972."

"You can always consult the yearbooks for past alumni. It's just not within our policy—"

"I understand, certainly. I'm sorry, I didn't catch your name."

"This is Sheila."

"Thanks, Sheila, for taking the time out of your busy day. I can tell you are a caring person who probably is looking forward to seeing your child at the end of his or her school day..."

"Yeah, actually. Third grade."

"That's sweet. A little girl?"

"Yes, how did you guess?"

"Well, if I must tell you, my little girl is none other than this Sophie I'm trying to reach. You see, her mother has had a difficult time recently, what with the accident and the surgeries, and we're trying to contact our Sophie to let her know..."

"Aw, I'm sorry to hear that, Mister... Vaughan, did you say?"

"Yes, Sheila, it would really mean a lot to her mother, with this next surgery coming up."

"Just a minute, please. I'm looking... I'm sorry. There is a Sophie Vaughan listed in the class of '72, but we don't have any forwarding address. Unless the student chooses to let us know their whereabouts... is there anything else I can do for you today?"

I sighed, my unlikely quest stalled at the first instance. "I thank you, and Mrs. Vaughan thanks you for your efforts. Take care of your little girl."

I set the receiver down in its blue plastic cradle on the wall, its umbilical cord dangling useless. Beyond that institution of higher learning Sophie had roamed to the wilds of the far North, and the jungles of Central America... expeditions too vast for me to contemplate, flying blind to catch a trail, and requiring more resources than I now possessed.

My faint hope, engendered by the false promise of yet another worthless dream, sloughed away, leaving me naked and without recourse—save for a methodical, comprehensive survey of school boards, graduate schools, internships... a daunting enterprise in its own right, with scant hope of success.

Without Seppl to back my impossible story, even if I managed to find Sophie I would certainly appear as a crazed stalker—whether on the phone or in person—since her younger self would likely be oblivious to her later acquaintance with me. That is, the me of eighty years before... You see the difficulty.

In such a quandary, I needed a new direction of my own

making. And for that to happen I would have to break out of this funk. Put polish on my suit of armor; find a trusty steed; practice on a few local windmills...

CHAPTER III

Mid-June, the summer heat in Mobile was already stifling—like the state of my life in general, going nowhere fast. I thought I might improve my lot by moving out of doors. First I paid a visit to the Army–Navy surplus store. I found a durable canvas rucksack on a wooden frame, a lightweight sleeping bag and bug net, a poncho that could double as a rain shelter, an all-purpose pocket knife, aluminum cookware and decent walking boots. Thus prepared, I quit my latest dishwashing job in Mobile, packed the camping gear with dried foods to get me through a month or so, abandoned the failing Comet with a farewell kiss on the hood ornament, hiked six blocks and stuck out my thumb on the highway to New Orleans.

No, not Albuquerque. Schimmelpreester's offer lay in the dusty past; and Sophie's recent calling card, if that's what it was, arrived tainted by the passage of future time, in the telltale emblem of Sandy's white hair, not to mention the imprecision of detail: fine, to invite me somewhere on the twenty-second, but what month, what year? I would have to bow to the common wisdom concerning such putative guidance: *It was only a dream.*

If pressed to answer for my impetuous leading to return to the port of my debarkation, I might confess a silly nostalgia for my first real home here in America. Aware of the risk one runs in returning to the scene of one's crime, I felt moved by a more symbolic, almost ritual urge to retrace my steps and start this whole exercise over again. False steps acknowledged, perhaps I had learned, along the way, to earn greater favor from whatever powers oversaw my progress this next time around. Otherwise I had no fixed plan to pursue; but to remain open, ever sensitive to opportunity in its dance with destiny.

I felt nervous at first. Jake and Jim had imparted to me, in my basic training for life in the land of highways, the admonition that it was unwise to pick anyone up, because you never knew what some mental case might spring on you. If such a fear was the common mindset of drivers, then I might be standing out there a long time—perhaps attracting undue interest from a law officer. My now-illegal status in the country didn't help my cause. But as I lacked any other means of personal identification, to pin me with an expired visa left in a house in New Orleans would be a judicious feat. In the balance, I felt that my appearance of boyish innocence, my hopeful expression and confidence would work in my favor.

I stood in the same spot for an hour and a half with no luck. I walked down the highway a half a mile to where another road brought more traffic into the westbound lane. Still I had no luck. I began to question my innate knack for influencing people to trust me. It's one thing to engage a person in conversation face to face, eye to eye; it's quite another to see them whizzing by at sixty miles an hour in their glass and metal enclosures, insulated from the finer and subtler essences of human interaction which had always been my stock in trade.

Nevertheless, a car did finally stop for me. A skinny man with checked coat, crew cut and horn-rimmed glasses, whose back seat was full of all kinds of brushes, said he could take me all the way to New Orleans. He made a space on the back seat for my pack; I jumped in the front; and we cruised away. He proceeded to talk nonstop for the next two hours, giving me his whole life story—which I will spare the reader from hearing, in the interest of proceeding with my own all-too-lengthy tale.

When we reached the harbor in New Orleans, I politely thanked my driver, refusing his offer of dinner together and a shared motel room. With a meek smile he thanked me for my company and slowly drove off. I ate in blessed anonymity at a hamburger stand, and retired that night in one of my old dockside nooks. I found there a dog-eared copy of Mark Twain's *Huckleberry Finn* and went to sleep dreaming of rafting up the Mississippi, then flying to Albuquerque—no plane, just arms gliding.

I took a walk down the tracks to a spot at a safe distance where I'd be able to see Jake and Jim's shack. It was gone, the whole area leveled and a chain link fence put up with a large sign advertising planned construction of a high-rise office building.

Another time warp? I wondered in the moment. *Have I dreamed my way to 1994?*

The rest of my surroundings in the city, the buildings and vehicles, the clothes of the citizens, even the by now familiar strains of popular music, remained contemporary. I had been gone over six months. This was simply the pace of change one had to expect in this nation on the move. Harking back to an earlier time, my own roots as well as those of this storied land, I shouldered my pack and walked on, to begin my journey by foot up the great river.

By the end of the first day I had left behind the urban sprawl and entered the timeless domain of nature, the lush wild growth of the riverbank. Redolent of leafy vegetation and water weeds; marked by tracks of muskrat, possum, raccoon; buzzing with clouds of gnats; the scene evoked the tramping journey of Huck Finn and his dusky companion. My skin slick with sweat, and weary from my determined pace in the sticky heat of the day, I set up a makeshift campsite, smoothing down a bed of long grass that would be sheltered by high overhanging brush from the morning sun. Too tired to bother with a campfire, I ate the one can of beans I'd brought along as a luxury for such an occasion, took a long drink of river water, and lay down to enjoy the cool and starry vista of night. I was too exhausted to sleep quickly; my legs ached too badly.

Accompanied by a lullaby of birds, I mused on the persistence of this Arcadian world alongside the breakneck pace of development: the rampant growth of cities and suburbs, highways and shopping centers; despoliation by logging, mining, drilling for oil; proliferation of plastics and unseen pollutants. Not that I wished a return to a bygone era, whether of Europe, or of this American South with its slaveholding and narrow provincialism. The cornucopia of foods and consumer goods of every description from global markets was not to be denied. Nor the drift to a national identity, with regional cultures remade in the image of the mass media.

Modernization, I gathered through my perusal of current events, came all of a piece. Space exploration, at the price of technocracy and exponential debt. Wonder drugs and miracle crops, amid spiraling rates of cancer and heart disease. Rapprochement with China, with jobs outsourced from a slumping domestic economy. Human rights championed at the UN, while the world teetered on the brink of nuclear annihilation.

Would my ready grasp of worldly issues prepare me one day to present cogent solutions as an advisor to a president? As gnats flurried about my tender ears, and ants burrowed between my toes, I had to scoff at the prospect. I was tramp on the run. Going where, I hardly knew; following my nose, trusting my instincts. If Sophie still saw fit to pluck me into her coterie, so be it. In the meantime, I took my Americana straight, raw and on the cheap.

Daylight dimming, the owls put lesser birds of fancy to flight, the jays retiring with caustic, futile rasps of protest. At last I sought refuge from the insistent chiggers, pulled the sleeping bag's bug net over my head and settled down to sleep. Letting out a long sigh, I felt, in the primal core of my being, *I have arrived. I belong here.*

The next day I came across a discarded spool of fishing line, which put me in a mind to try my luck at that most ancient of arts. I cut a long willow branch for a pole, tied on loops of the line to hold the length of it along the pole, and then bought a bobber and hooks at a roadside market. In the heat of the afternoon I stopped along the riverbank, and under a large flat stone found a good supply of grubs for bait. That day I only had bites, serving to nibble away the bait. But the following day I caught two plump catfish. I knew, from watching the dockside bums, that I would have to skin the ugly creatures. It was a difficult, slimy chore, which, lacking pliers, I had to use my teeth to accomplish. I was soon rewarded, however, with the tantalizing aroma of my catch roasting over the fire, and finally the unmatched taste of their creamy flesh.

Fish became the fresh staple of my diet, to supplement my portable store of almonds and raisins, granola, dried apples, and quick-cooking bulgur. I added to these foods what wild greens—chickweed, purslane, dandelion, chicory—I could recognize from experience on my native soil, as well as the occasional treat from a riverside garden: young carrots, lettuce, early tomatoes, strawberries.

I meandered with the river by day, fishing lazily during the hottest mid-afternoons, and eased into restful sleep each night, my dreams following also the curves and flows of the river. I found myself rising regularly to the pale dawn ruled by the morning star. Why was it called Lucifer, I wondered, if it also was Venus, the goddess of love?

In a couple of days I had my answer. A wandering missionary crossed my path, enjoining me to take up the ways of the Lord. I listened politely, watching his fervent gestures as he spoke. In his waving hands he held a tattered Bible. He spoke to me about the end of the world, the salvation of my soul in the coming times of tribulation. I told him I'd been through my fair share of tribulation already.

"Boy," he replied, "you hain't seen nothin' yet. Why, when

the Lord Jesus decides to move on this sorry world agin', we won't know what hit us. Unless we're prepared. I'd advise you to take seriously the word of the Lord and to take Jesus Christ as your personal savior." I remained calm and gave him no argument, though I wondered at the logical selfishness of taking Jesus for my very own. He stopped talking, finally, watching my line in the river silent and still in its passive search for fish. His slick black hair shone in the sun.

Finally he rose to leave. "Whew, it's hot as the blazes, i'n it?"

"That it is," I agreed.

"Here, boy, I'll leave this with you." He handed me his Bible.

"Oh, no," I protested. "You'll need it. I appreciate your generosity, though. You're a true Christian."

He stood there, immobile, the book held out to me.

"All right, if it makes you feel better, thank you, kind sir." I took the Bible and laid it down beside me.

I felt a tug on my line, looked to the water, and then it went slack again. I turned to the stranger and he was gone.

That night during catfish dinner I wondered again about the story of Lucifer, the fallen angel. But where in the vast book was the reference I wanted? No biblical scholar, I had no idea.

So before putting out my campfire I let the Bible fall open at random—to let, as it were, the voice of the universe speak. It opened to *Isaiah*, the fourteenth chapter. I didn't even have to read: the words "O Lucifer" jumped out at me from the sea of print.

In the back of my mind grew an uneasiness that had to do with Sophie. Was she responsible for this apparent coincidence? For the appearance of the itinerant preacher? Was she connected in some way, not with benevolent astral forces dedicated to my spiritual advancement, but rather with a sinister cult of the Devil? I read the text with a zeal to find out:

> Hell from beneath is moved for thee to meet thee at thy coming: it stirreth up the dead for thee, even all the chief ones of the earth; it hath raised up from their thrones all the kings of the nations.
>
> All they shall speak and say unto thee, art thou also become weak as we? art thou become like unto us?
>
> Thy pomp is brought down to the grave, and the noise of thy viols: the worm is spread under thee, and the worms cover thee.
>
> How art thou fallen from heaven, O Lucifer, son of the morning! how art thou cut down to the ground, which didst weaken the nations!
>
> For thou hast said in thine heart, I will ascend into heaven, I will exalt my throne above the stars of God: I will sit also upon the mount of the congregation, in the sides of the north:
>
> I will ascend above the heights of the clouds; I will be like the most High.
>
> Yet thou shalt be brought down to hell, to the sides of the pit.

Shuddering, I snapped the book shut. Was it a message for my own edification, a mirror held to remind me of the error of blind self-confidence, too-proud ambition? For an instant I imagined Sophie sitting opposite me, across the campfire with her sphinxlike cat.

That ephemeral vision of Sophie, on the heels of the Lucifer fable, got me wondering what I was really doing on this childish adventure. I had to answer with the attendant question, what difference does it make how I lead this present life, in the absence of any clearer direction from her?

In this ongoing internal dialogue of mine, which I was frankly getting sick of repeating over and over like an obnoxious pop song on AM radio, I was coming to the conclusion that I had best forget about this chimera called Sophie. I had dropped through a crack in the fabric of time, and had no choice but to get on with living my life in the manner to which I'd once been accustomed: burning through what options presented themselves.

Wasn't that the American way?

CHAPTER IV

One day about a week out of New Orleans, I hid my willow pole in the bushes and walked into a dusty town on whose post office was lettered the name *St. Francisville.* Charming name, that—and one I'd heard before from the lips of my old pals Jake and Jim. They'd spoken of it with a special fondness, as a place where they dreamed of retiring. After a short stroll through the town with its chair-rocking, straw-hatted octogenarians, I recalled it wasn't the town itself they had spoken of so wistfully, but rather, "the country around St. Francisville."

As a matter of fact, coming up from the south, I had not so far registered any particular attraction to the geography thereabouts, and the town impressed me not in the least. As I finished my cooling milkshake at the soda fountain next to two giggling teens and a couple of aged ex-farmers, I resolved, in the spirit of open-mindedness, to keep a fresh eye open for the special beauty of the countryside farther north.

The only traffic I had to dodge on my way out of town was a slow-motion police car. I waved good-naturedly to the dough-cheeked driver and received for my efforts a sour frown. I concluded that jaywalking was against custom, if not law, in St. Francisville; or perhaps the sheriff preferred my face without its week's growth of beard—what I had imagined until then as developing into a rather stylish goatee.

In any case, I again found no particular attraction for the countryside to the north: the same riverbank vegetation, lush though it was, that I'd encountered from the outset of my trip; the same gentle contours, the same silty earth sloping into the river. Before dusk I was far enough outside of town and its fenced-off parcels of shoreline to begin looking out for a suitable campsite. Just as I'd settled on a nicely cleared flat area, I noticed an old cabin half hidden in the woods.

I walked by for a closer look. The windows were intact, but showed darkness within. The front door was locked, since who knew how long ago. The yard, once defined as such within a fence, now half collapsed, was completely overgrown. So I returned to the clearing where I'd set down my pack, confident I could stay there unchallenged.

As I kicked my foot around in the long grass I hit a solid object and discovered, on closer inspection, an overgrown pile of railroad ties. Aha—just what I needed to make that raft, in homage to the venerable Huck Finn! With cedar trees at hand in the neighboring woods to supply bark strips for lashings, I'd be all set for my retrospective adventure.

I began pulling ties out of the disordered pile and laying them aside in a neat row for the next day's work. The space left in the grass would be a ready-made bed for the night.

The ground was not as smooth as I had hoped. I found a flat rock to scrape the high humps down. As I lifted the rock I remembered that I'd forgotten to retrieve my fishing pole from where I'd left it, in the bushes outside St. Francisville. I reproached myself for the lapse but had other things to occupy my attention at the moment. It was not, after all, a great material loss.

I proceeded with my task, leveling tool in hand. The dirt was surprisingly soft. Then, to my surprise, I found the edge of the rock scraping at a fold of burlap. Great, I thought, a campsite atop a refuse dump. With a final disgusted swipe of the rock, something clicked—something metallic inside the burlap.

I looked around to make sure I was alone and proceeded to excavate my find with new energy. The bags—there were three of them—contained silver tea service, china, wooden boxes of silverware, velvet jewelry boxes.

Long-distance thanks to Jake and Jim aside, the problem presented itself: what was I going to do with all these hot valuables? I could just imagine seeking out a pawnbroker back in St. Francisville, probably the local sheriff moonlighting.

Then I had it: the raft, of course. This bright idea faded as quickly as it had come, for the towns downriver could conceivably be on the alert for the stolen goods, and to float all the way back into the harbor of New Orleans with such cargo was out of the question. Nevertheless, I envisioned my abandoned niche in the old dock area, and reckoned a way might be found to unload and stash the bags, given a good moonless night and a bit of luck that the cop on his beat, or a welcoming party of the wise old wharf rats, wouldn't relieve me of my payload as soon as I touched land.

Then again, I could put the bags back in the ground here where I had found them, and wash my hands (as I once thought I had) of the whole dirty business. But hadn't fate—or Sophie—planted these valuables in my path again as a sign that they were meant for me?

Or was it, rather, a temptation to be overcome?

Darkness was not far off. I decided I was too tired and hungry to think straight. I would rebury the loot, cook a modest supper—no, better do without a fire tonight. I would eat trail mix and chew over my options while I did so, then lay out my bedding and, as the saying goes, sleep on it.

I was awakened, late in the night, by the sound of a car engine, tires crunching on gravel, and the flashing beam of headlights through the trees. Lying perfectly still—with my heart pounding, instantly wide awake—I heard a car door slam shut, footsteps on the cabin's porch, a man's muttered cursing, and finally the cabin door closing.

Now the question became, *Do I move on right away, or wait until morning?* It was likely late enough at night that this fellow would sleep in, allowing me time in the early morning... but I lay there looking up at the stars and listening to the crickets, thinking that I wasn't going to be able to get to sleep again anyway...

The next thing I knew, it was nearly light out and I was being soaked by a fine drizzle. A cloud bank thick as cotton wool had rolled in and I could barely see the cabin through the mist. I got up quickly, ate a few handfuls of trail mix and headed to the trees to collect strips of cedar bark. In a matter of minutes I had enough to work with and set about lashing the timbers together.

That job took me most of an hour; when I was done, there was still no sign of life from the cabin. I looked with pride on my simple craft, and then, with great effort lifting and sliding a corner at a time, managed to move it to the immediate riverbank and tilt one corner of it into the water. At that point it occurred to me that a long pole would be useful for navigation in the shallows. So I scouted in the woods again until I came up with a relatively straight and slender young cedar tree on the ground, about ten feet in length, which I trimmed with my knife. Still no stirrings from the cabin.

Lastly I set to work digging up and hauling out the burlap bags, carrying them one by one to the river. As I made a final trip to the clearing for my pack, I saw what I'd been dreading: a light on in the cabin, a wisp of smoke from its chimney. I hurried to my pack and ran with it to the riverbank. With a final look over my shoulder I saw a man's silhouette in the cabin's long window.

In a panic I pushed the raft fully into the water, trailing on the ground the long strip of bark intended for mooring. I balanced with one foot on the raft and one on the slippery, high bank as I reached for the first of the bags and brought it onto the raft. Naturally my lower foot had the effect of pushing the raft away from the shore, so I had to stop and tie the makeshift tether from a spike on the raft to a bush. I heard the slam of the cabin door and the sound of curses shouted toward me through the mist.

I just managed to finish loading and cast off, then looked up to see a shabby cracker standing on the bank pointing a squirrel-gun at me.

"Jes' what in the hell d'ye think yer doin' with all them bags, and them timbers I was savin'?"

"I... uh—"

"What, do I have to stay 'roun' day 'n night, not even go out for a few beers, and some squattin' bastard like you come along 'n think y'own the place?"

"Yes, sir, you're quite right, I have to agree. I can only plead ignorance, thinking that I'd stumbled on an old garbage dump, and—"

"What? I din't unnerstand ye. Where you from, boy?" He peered at me with the small red eyes of a pig. He had a salt-and-pepper bristle of a beard, a thick misshapen nose, and a splotched complexion which made him appear as if he'd walked through a fire. He held the ancient rifle aimed at my chest.

"I've been traveling upriver on my summer vacation; I'm a student, you see"—I motioned to my pack— "and now I'm heading back down—"

"You ain't headed nowhere with them there goods you dug up from my field. You jes' pole yerself right back in here to showre."

I had held the craft steady, eight feet out. Now I lifted the pole slowly off the bottom—or started to—then stopped, making out as if it were stuck. I pulled and pulled, grunting and straining.

"Ah, come on," said the cracker. "Fuckin' greenhorn. Yank on the damn thang."

I did. The end of the pole jerked clear out of the water, straight for the cracker. He backed out of the way, lost his balance on the mud, slipped and dropped his gun. It went off, aimed wildly. Birds screamed and scattered. I pushed off the bank with the pole. The cracker took up his gun again and reloaded, cursing all the while. The raft was too ponderous to make the distance I needed to get quickly out of his range. It was time to abandon ship.

I dove off the far side, tipping the raft as I went. Before entering the water I saw the heavy bags sliding into the water behind me. I swam underwater as far as my lungs could stand it. When I resurfaced, the cracker resighted but fired late as I kicked down under for another long stretch. I repeated this tactic, varying my course, until I'd reached the wooded bank of an island several hundred yards out in the river. I could still see the empty raft floating lazily away. It was tempting to think of swimming back out to retrieve it, but the cracker stood his ground on the far bank, firing until he ran out of ammunition. By the time he stalked away back to the cabin, the raft had vanished in the fog downriver.

It was not far to the other side of the island; from there I could see it was another long swim to reach the far shore of the river. I was not eager to repeat that exhausting feat right away. I also didn't know what to expect when I got to the western bank. Would the cracker have called the police—or worse, a gang of his friends—to meet me when I climbed ashore? There was no telling; and yet I also reckoned I could not remain long on the island before pursuit would arrive by boat.

Since the cracker had not come after me, and since I doubted he would dare to put the law on my tail, I felt safe enough to rest awhile in a bed of long grass.

My head spun over the predicament I was in. I had no change of clothes, no sleeping bag, no food. No fishing gear. I'd lost the raft, and along with it, the ambition to make another. I wouldn't cross back to the cracker's territory, couldn't stay on the island, didn't know where to go further west. At last fatigue got the best of my anxieties and I fell asleep, with a dry heat not of the Mississippi, but of New Mexico, burning through all these sodden feelings of despair.

I'm a clerk in an Indian craft store in Albuquerque, selling mostly cheap jewelry imported from Taiwan, along with Mexican and local Native American handiwork. An old Indian, a Navaho, comes into the store and asks to see what we have in medicine bracelets. I take out the appropriate tray from under the counter and let the customer see them. His wrinkled gaze rests on one particular item more tarnished in its silverwork than the others, with several chips gone out of the side of an ovoid centerpiece of otherwise exquisite turquoise. He reaches into his pocket and brings out a leathery palm containing several chips of turquoise. It dawns on me these are the missing pieces from the bracelet's stone. At that moment an iguana races past the doorway with a silvery snake in its mouth—and I can swear the snake's eyes are turquoise.

I awoke after maybe an hour, opening silver eyes to a turquoise sky... and then I turned and saw the muddy Mississippi. This fresh dream resonated in my memory with the earlier dream of the phone call about the silver and turquoise merchants' ball, the white bear... but I was damned if I could turn these clues, however vivid, into any program of action. Was Sophie toying with me, a lizard with a snake?

A brown turtle the size of a shoe slithered out of the weeds and into the water, unconcerned about such riddles. I rose to my feet and stood on the bank, stretching and taking in several deep breaths. There was nothing to do but take the inevitable plunge. I decided first, however, to peel off my clothing and tie it in a bundle, boots and all, around my back.

Unlike my simple amphibian friend, however, I was not in good swimming shape, and my arms and legs turned leaden after fifty yards. I briefly considered turning back; but I would still have that distance to reswim, and for all the effort I would gain no improvement in my situation. Fifty more ahead and I'd be the greater part of the way to the western bank. So I plodded on, slowing my frantic pace to a more sustainable crawl. Eventually, after a grueling eternity, my fingers touched mud, and I slithered onto the bank like some antediluvian creature carrying on its throbbing shoulders the entire weight of future evolution.

I lay there panting, feet still in the water, in a state of semiconscious exhaustion. I was not bothered by the close sound of traffic, as I was screened from view of the highway by a border of trees along the riverbank. I did, however, take notice when I heard the sound of a boat engine out of view around the south point of the island. I scrambled into my wet clothes in the shelter of the trees, then headed out to the road without waiting to see who it was that might be coming to look for me.

Fortunately the boat did not put ashore on my side. After cruising the bank slowly, it circled back toward the north around the island. This I could tell from my vantage point in the trees across the road, with glimpses not sufficient to identify clearly the boat's pilot.

I smelled police, though; time to get moving again. I groomed my hair with my fingers as best I could, tucked my shirt in neatly, and stepped out onto the road. My boots were still squishy, but respectable enough in appearance. My clothes, unfortunately, made me look like what I was—a fugitive. They dried out gradually in the mid-morning sun. I stood there watching occasional traffic go by for half an hour, until a farmer in an old truck picked me up. When he asked me where I was headed, I said, "West," then thought I'd better make it more specific—"Albuquerque."

The word had a weighty ring to it, in my mouth and ears, not unpleasing. I surprised myself by its definitive delivery, quite spontaneous.

The driver was going into the nearest town, called New Roads. When he let me out at the south edge of town he told me Route 1 continued south to US 190; there I could turn west to Opelousas, then south again toward New Iberia. I'd hit Interstate 10 and could take that west. I thanked him and watched him turn and drive back into town.

New Iberia had another tantalizing ring to it. Was that where I should be heading? Was there a modern Zouzou—or Maria—in wait for me there, if only I would take the hint and venture there with both eyes open, heart ready, freedom well tempered, spirit and flesh willing to entertain feminine good graces in a new context, here on American soil? I didn't know.

I did know the rogue's game was getting old. Sophie's words still stung: *The petty thefts, the gigolo gig, not so much...* Plus now, I knew what *gigolo* meant. Give identity a word, and it becomes a costume to try on and discard, in its turn.

Meanwhile I was starving to death, and if I got rides to Albuquerque at the present rate I'd arrive there a virtual skeleton. I had not even a solitary, soggy dollar bill, since I'd left my wallet in the drowned pack.

I didn't have to worry long about my plight, because inside of twenty minutes a police cruiser pulled to a stop beside me. On the door around the official crest were the words, "St. Francisville Sheriff's Dept." The all too familiar driver, with his doughy cheeks and sour frown, leaned over and said through the open passenger-side window, "Get in."

I childishly hoped the sheriff merely would give me a warning against hitchhiking. In a gesture of even more ill-founded self-confidence, I started to open the front passenger door—daring to hope that, having recognized me, the sheriff might have decided to offer me a ride. I was wrong, on both counts.

"What the hell you doing?" he exploded, reaching for his sawed-off shotgun. "Get in the back!"

I obeyed quickly. The locks on the rear doors clicked down by some remote control mechanism.

I wanted to complain to this officer of the law about the recent threat to my personal safety. Then I perceived how much he looked like a well-shaven, heftier version of the cracker who'd tried to kill me.

"You're under arrest," the sheriff informed me. "You enjoy your little swim?"

"Oh-ho," I managed to laugh. "You mean it's against the law to swim without clothes here, officer? I'm awfully sorry. If I had known—"

"Shut the fuck up," he snarled, cheeks bulging with his chaw.

He maneuvered the car around on the highway to go back in the direction from which he'd come. I was separated from the front seat by a sturdy wire screen. He spat tobacco juice out the window and continued talking to me out of the side of his mouth, keeping his eyes on me through the rear-view mirror.

"You have the right to remain silent," he said. "You have the right to a lawyer and when we get to the station to book you, you are allowed one phone call."

I certainly didn't want to remain silent. "Officer, sir, am I permitted to ask the nature of the offense with which I am to be charged?"

My captor laughed, in the process coughing up a wad of phlegm which he had to expel out the window. "I can see I'm gonna need a lawyer myself to interrogate you. Listen, buddy. You're in for high and low larceny, at least two counts. There's those bags you sent to the bottom which we are in the process of recovering, and the railroad ties you filched from my brother Lindy's field. That enough for ya? If you want we can tack on the hitchhiking, vagrancy, trespassing, disturbing the peace, ah, let's see—how 'bout we throw in the indecent bathing, for free?" I could see even from my limited view of his face that he was smiling broadly, enjoying himself.

That rankled, but I didn't respond. My mind was racing over a connection that cropped up in my memory from something he'd said. *Lindy*—I'd heard that name before, and as I thought about it I recalled I'd heard it from Jake and Jim's conversation in the van on the way home from their robbery that last day of work. Something fleeting, muted and vague, about "gettin' the stuff up to Lindy." Could I use that remembered bit of information—along with my previous peek at their loot—in my defense? Or would it strengthen the case against me? I didn't relish the prospect of blowing the whistle on my old friends. But it might come down to a matter of survival, them or me.

We'd turned right in New Roads and were quickly back at the river, rolling up a ramp onto a free highway ferry, which a sign said would land us back in good old St. Francisville. I kissed the West goodbye.

Part of me called out to the heavens: *Hey, Sophie—I suppose this, too, is your doing?*

Regardless, it was my mess to deal with now.

What about this Lindy, I thought. Couldn't I get off the hook by pinning the goods on him? Certainly his brother the sheriff would not take kindly to this stratagem. But then, the wheels in the machinery of justice would likely move me beyond his small sphere of influence before I could present my final case in court.

Indeed, I was only in St. Francisville overnight before finding myself on a plane to Chicago for indictment relating to a whole series of thefts over several states. So much for my dream of flying—stuck in an aisle seat while handcuffed to a joyless lawman. And so much for my faith in a so-called lawyer, a seedy rat-faced man in a checked suit who interviewed me for five minutes while I devoured a plate of fried potatoes and boiled beans in the St. Francisville jail. I never got a chance to plead my case before a jury; the lawyer said he had an associate in Chicago who would work out a deal for me with the judge.

Some deal. At the end of a six-day chain of holding pens and summary hearings, I was trundled along to a palatial cellblock in a federal penitentiary in Marion, Illinois to begin serving time: ten years with the possibility of probation after five.

How art thou fallen, indeed.

In the commons room, by way of celebrating America's Bicentennial, on that very Fourth of July, I saw desultory ranks of the underclass, largely of color ranging from black to red, glued to the tube, watching a figure reminiscent of Karloff's Frankenstein monster (that would be President Gerald Ford) droning platitudes before the robotically cheering masses in the nation's capital. These inmates saw through the empty rhetoric, tossing jibes and jeers until exiting the room with a noisy scraping and rattling of chairs.

Thus began my political education in America. And as the impassive guards led me in my gray and numbered togs to my gray and numbered cage, I saw the narrative arc of my life story, one might say in an expectant mood anticipating the years of leisure and solitude so conducive to the task of transcribing it. Serving the full sentence would land me back on the street with a decade to spare, to groom myself for Sophie's election campaign...

Alas! That writing project had to wait a goodly spell before I could turn my energies to its final accomplishment. To begin with, there was the immediate distraction of the riffraff who formed my present company—who cajoled me in the manner of all men kept together in segregation from their better halves; who chattered like drugged magpies, some with slurred speech and some with hyperactive frenzy, all the day and night; who leered at me, solicited indecent favors, and made increasingly violent threats upon my undefiled person.

Out of this brackish sea of outcast humanity bobbed one day an unexpected sight: Jake Rubino, eating alone and dejected across the vast cafeteria. A moment of fear, at his reprisal for my desertion, gave way to the realization that I could not hide here; and for my part, I harbored no animosity toward him. A moment of reflection more, and I was at his side, pumping his hand like the best of friends. No matter that it was his crime that had put me behind bars—he was a known entity, at least, in a place where to be without friends is to be a fox thrown in with dogs.

"Hey, Felix!" Jake said warmly, brightening instantly at my appearance. He pushed away his half-finished plate of cardboard meat and pasty potatoes and extended his hand. "What's a nice guy like you doing in a place like this?"

"Please," I said in a low voice, "call me Chuck." I shook his hand and sat down in the empty chair next to him. He had a puzzled expression on his face, but before he could protest I went on: "It's a long story, but I think you know most of it. In essence, I found your stash at Lindy's place, by accident—"

"Ah, come on, quit pullin' my leg."

"No, really," I said, and I told him what had happened.

Jake listened carefully, shaking his head from time to time. "Amazing, you guy. And I thought Lindy had it all together. Untouchable. With his brother the sheriff looking the other way, a lock. Just goes to show ya. But hey, what's this Chuck business? Ah, I know: that no-good tourist visa you left at the place. An exchange for Jim's car, we was wonderin'?"

"No hard feelings?"

"Like I said, it was Jim's car. Or Chuck's, God rest 'im. Anyways, I knowed you wasn't cut out for our kind of action, so, I could hardly blame ya. Look at the both of us now." He clapped me on the back and I felt his camaraderie to be genuine.

The guy across from us picked up his tray and left. I

lowered my voice and said, "I hope they never found the real Mr. Ready, by the way. It might make it awkward for there to be two of us around."

"No, kid, I think you'll be all right there. Even so, what'd you put down for the vital statistics? Wait, let me guess: Charles Ready, Jr., born, what, nineteen-fifty—"

"Five. In Mainz—"

"Germany, son of Sergeant Charles Ready of the US Army, and—"

"Genofeva Schimmelpreester."

"Not bad. They musta had fun writin' that down." Jake took up his fork and began toying with a congealed lump of potatoes.

"So then, what, if I may ask, are you doing here?"

Jake brightened. "Oh, you don't think we quit the game after that job, do ya? We hadn't even cashed in our chips yet. Had to make a livin' in the meanwhile, y'know."

"So where's Big Jim?"

Jake looked sad again, with downcast eyes and a thin-lipped frown. "Ah, they got him over'n New Mexico after he did a solo at some jewelry convention. I told him, I says, 'Jim, we don't do good separated like that, and I'm not comin' wit' ya to that job because it's too goddam risky.' Can you imagine the heat they had surroundin' that place? 'But the loot,' he says, stars in his big stupid eyes. 'Think of all that loot!' 'Yeah, you can think about it for the rest of your life in the New Mexico pen,' I says to him. Now look who's got the line on that one, huh? Anyways, I'm still hopin' we'll end up, through dumb luck, together again so's we can play out our days playin' crib together, like the old days, like a coupla old maids, I guess. Say, you play crib?"

To relate with telling detail the interesting but ultimately irrelevant entirety of my relatively brief stay in this higher institution of justice would be, frankly, somewhat humiliating. It may be pertinent to mention, however, that under Jake's tutelage I learned to play cribbage, and to beat him two out of every three. We played for cigarettes, which he greedily consumed on the spot if he won, and which I hoarded as favors to keep the cellblock bullies off my back. Having Jake on my side in the dog-eat-dog pecking order helped my cause also, to an immeasurable degree; for what he lacked in size and age he made up for in experience and rough intelligence. A Vietnam War veteran, he showed me once the scar on his right side where he'd been hit by shrapnel from a land mine.

And it was under that rib cage, twisted into his old wound, that Jake caught a knife thrust while interceding on my behalf against a gorilla-like aggressor, one otherwise uneventful afternoon while we toweled off in the shower room. The mixture of gratitude and distress with which I witnessed this noble sacrifice, and the subsequent carrying off of its groaning, blubbering victim is indescribable.

I was not allowed to see Jake after that, whether alive or dead—nor was I informed whether he was still in this world. Hearing through a cellmate that he'd been skewered in the liver, I assumed the worst. Four days I spent in mourning, with even the head gorilla and his henchmen keeping their respectful distance—not, I might add, under any evident disciplinary restraint on the part of the prison authorities. During this time I was brought around by grief, shock, horror and desperation to the conclusion that if I ever got out of this tank alive I would truly reform and leave behind forever any shady dealings that, no matter how innocently fallen into, could run me afoul of the law.

As if in answer to this unspoken pact between myself and my higher fate, I was soon released, redeemed in my insistent claim that the lawyer entering a guilty plea on my behalf had misled me. On the basis of new findings, all the charges had been dropped.

"By what providence," I inquired of my guard as he escorted me away, "am I being delivered to the land of the living once again?"

"Sheeit," he snickered, talking as if to an invisible third party. "Listen to this guy. Haven't they reamed his ass out of all that crap yet?"

Then he half turned to me and spoke more directly, though out of the side of his tobacco-bulged mouth in a way that reminded me of Sheriff Harper Elkin of St. Francisville, Louisiana.

"Y'know your friend's crony over New Mexico way? A Big Jim?"

"Yeah..."

"Scuttle has it that when he heard through the grapevine of your l'il sweetie's death—and his sweetie too for damn sure—he took pity on you and gave a statement. Said you had nothin' to do with any of their heists. You was just along for the ride. Plus, whereas the locals never scooped those stolen goods in the river, Jim tipped off the feds and they found them in this riverside barn, fella by the name of Lindy. Anyhoo, hope you enjoyed your vacation, sister. Come back and see us, y'heah?"

The bear of a guard tittered like a schoolgirl as he shuffled away back into the block.

I walked out into the care of another deputy of the state, who led me into the sickly fluorescence of an office cubicle to sign a series of documents, then to a room where I changed back into my mud-shined suit of civilian clothes. I was Charles Ready no more. I looked proudly down at my old self, then tried on a smile in the change-room mirror and wore it for the unsmiling secretary on my way out the door into the blazing light of day. I was a free man again—penniless, but free.

CHAPTER V

I was back on the road again, thumb out, headed for Albuquerque—for lack of a more meaningful destination. The intervening period of incarceration, nearly four months, had not changed my fundamental circumstance, of being adrift save the invisible lifeline to Sophie. If I was bound only for a touristic visit to the old sausage company, an updated Cinderella ball invitation delivered by hand, or a fate as yet undreamed of, didn't much matter. I had no other prospects to pursue, in what felt a vast, unwelcoming sea.

My second ride—in an air-conditioned semi which carried me as high above the road as a lord of Hannibal's elephant army—took me west from St. Louis toward Kansas, in what I thought it would be a minor detour from my southwesterly destination. When the driver dropped me off in Lawrence, Kansas, it was past midnight and still prairie-hot. I hadn't eaten a decent meal in months, and my mouth was puckered and dry from the salty potato chips the kind truck driver had shared with me on the way. I knew from his map that Lawrence, not far out of Kansas City, was but "a stone's throw" from Topeka. That still meant thirty-five miles of highway to cover, however, and at this hour my chances of getting a ride to anywhere but the nearest jail seemed slim.

I thought of calling Margaret Smith, collect. Surely she would remember me from the *David Livingstone* and give me shelter for the night—perhaps even a sample of her home-cooking.

After half a dozen rings of the phone, she answered in a sleepy, worried voice.

I spoke directly. "Hello, Mrs. Smith. This is Felix Krull. Remember, from the cruise ship?"

"Yes, yes, I remember."

"I'm very sorry to bother you at this time of night."

"No, that's all right. I'd barely gotten to sleep after watching a late movie on TV. Goodness, I thought something had happened to Terry."

"Please forgive me. The thing is, I'm in Lawrence. I've been hitchhiking, and I'm kind of stranded here, and—"

"You're certainly welcome to stay here. I could bring the station wagon out to get you if you like."

"I know this is quite presumptuous of me to ask."

"Not at all. When a person's in trouble, to help as one is able is the only thing."

"I really appreciate it, Mrs. Smith."

"Please, it's Margaret. Think nothing of it. I'll be out there in, oh, forty-five minutes. Where are you exactly?"

In that forty-five minutes I was filled with the renewed glow of friendship with this kind woman. My intentions, to be candid, were neither carnal nor romantic. I wanted rather the simple comfort of real human contact, a home for a night. Sitting on a curb outside the Seven-Eleven, I drew in the sweet aroma of alfalfa and ripening corn. The dust of the day had settled, the clouds of gnats giving way to lightning bugs and the chirp of crickets and frogs.

Margaret pulled up in a white station wagon, got out and greeted me with a warm squeeze of her delicate hand. I paused, unsure if I should give her a hug; the moment passed and our hands dropped. I noticed she'd lost weight since I'd last seen her, nearly a year ago; her hair was also different, straighter and cut short. She wore a blue, flowered print, cotton dress, and low-heeled, brushed leather shoes.

"It's so good to see you again, Felix."

On the drive home she asked how I'd been enjoying my stay in her country. I thought it best not to tell her yet that I'd spent my most recent chunk of it behind bars, and a good part of the rest on the bum. I also resisted my old temptation to embellish the truth with fancy rhetoric about the quaint charms of the Vieux Carré, the pleasant grandeur of the Mississippi, the marvel of the interstate highway system, and so on. Yet there I sat, dirty, hungry and broke, and I had to say something. So I started at the beginning.

"I decided early on that to truly appreciate this 'land of opportunity,' as it is justifiably known abroad, I should work shoulder to shoulder with its common people—both to know them and to find the natural avenue for whatever talents I proved to possess..."

No, no, this approach was all wrong; it didn't suit my listener. Margaret was looking at me with quick sideways glances, brows knitted as Sandy's had when I'd come on to her with my highfaluting nonsense. I tried another tack:

"So I worked at this and that, y'know: washed dishes here, pumped gas there, parked cars. It wasn't too bad. I was making a living, anyway. This was in Mobile, Alabama. Then after a while I got bored with mindless jobs for low pay, took what little money I'd managed to save and embarked on a camping trip up the Mississippi."

"Oh, that sounds interesting. Our family used to take camping trips in the fall; Mervin was quite fond of fishing."

"Yes, well, my particular foray into the wilderness didn't work out so well. You see, I found this pile of railroad ties, perfect for building the raft I'd dreamed of since reading that classic of your early literature, *Huckleberry Finn*."

Margaret said with a laugh, "Oh, how fascinating. I remember that character. Wasn't he in the movie about Tom Sawyer?"

"I wouldn't be surprised. The trouble was, under these railroad ties..." and I proceeded to relate to her the whole sad tale. I concluded by stating the half truth that I was bound for Albuquerque to look up a relative who might be able to offer me a job.

Evidently on hearing my litany of missteps, she thought none the worse of me. On the contrary, upon arrival at her modest yet ample suburban house, she fetched a leftover pot roast from the refrigerator and warmed a goodly chunk of it, along with the accompaniments, in the countertop electric oven. Though it was getting on two o'clock in the morning, we both properly accepted my need for a nourishing meal before the night's sleep. "Pot roast was Mervin's favorite dish," my hostess said.

Margaret buttered bread for me and poured a tall glass of milk while the rest of the meal was heating. Then she sat across the kitchen table from me while I ate, telling me of her doings in the past year, and those of her family. She'd regaled her bridge-playing friends with the story of the rescue at sea—without, I presume, painting the whole picture. Following her exposure to apartheid in South Africa, she'd been led to join the local Quaker meeting, where she found a solid sense of connection with others of like mind, and a new sense of peacefulness in her own life. She got along better than ever with Devon, for instance; even though, at sixteen, he was still in the stage of rebelling, no doubt missing the stabilizing influence of his father. Terry was doing fine as always. In fact he'd become such a skillful pilot that he'd started a barnstorming act at the state fairgrounds, flying "loop-de-loops and that kind of thing" in an old-fashioned biplane which had Margaret scared to death. She would never dare go watch him perform. And of course he stubbornly refused to listen to her complaints about such a dangerous career. Terry had his own mind—always had—like his father. Margaret looked sad again, her watering eyes magnified by the large lenses of her glasses at each mention of her departed husband.

This time, my lovely meal finished, I reached my hand across the quarter of the table which separated us and took her hand. At my touch a tide of tears was unloosed, but without any great noise, because, as Margaret managed to splutter, she didn't want to wake Devon or Sharon. She pulled me toward her with a gentle pressure. I leaned toward her in my chair, then stood and walked to her side, where I stooped, then kneeled, and comforted her with an arm around her shoulder. She lay her head against my chest and quietly sobbed, still holding my left arm tightly to her.

It was apparent to me I was fulfilling a role that none of her children had adequately managed, to allow Margaret to release her grief. It was also becoming evident, through the warm contact of my arm against the poor woman's breast, that there had been, since her husband's death, a particularly poignant void in her life. For my part, I was aware of reawakening feelings, notably a kind of filial attraction which was by now familiar through my relationships with Maria, Diane Philibert the toilet merchant's wife, even the Krull housemaid Genofeva, or—for those who care to trace such impulses to infancy—my nursemaid. In that potentially profane moment I resolved firmly to maintain a dignified sense of self-possession with this woman, whatever the nature of her need.

She stood, we both stood, embracing in the stillness of the night. She looked up at me, and sniffling, said, "I'm sorry, Felix, if I've embarrassed you."

"No, you haven't. It's all right. I don't mind at all."

She rested her head against my chest again and breathed deeply.

"Come," she said finally, taking my hand. "I'll show you where you can sleep."

We crept upstairs silently, passed two closed bedroom doors and came to two open doors at the end of the hall.

"This is Terry's old room." She pointed to the right. "If you like, I can pack you some old clothes of his to take when you leave. But Felix—" and I knew what was coming—"will you to stay with me tonight?"

If she'd let me answer then, I would probably have refused. But she added, still whispering, "Don't think badly of me. I'm not an immoral woman. I would just like to have you by my side. Would you do that?"

"Yes," I whispered.

We undressed in the dark. Margaret put on a nightgown. I had no such luxury, and plunged under the light covers nude beside her. There I entered into the most exquisite experience of intimacy I had yet experienced—without the usual fiery splendor of the sexual drama. We simply lay side by side, clasped in one another's languid arms, even feeling, in a casual and utterly marvelous manner, the tenderer parts of our respective anatomies upon occasion, with neither an undue upsurge of passion nor skittish withdrawal of the soothing touch. I wondered if Margaret had ever experienced such bliss in all her years of making love to Mervin Smith, and could only doubt it. I wondered if I would again, and somehow knew that until I did, I would aspire to it. But not here, not in Margaret's, Mervin's bed again, not in Topeka, Kansas. All the same, I fell asleep contented as a newborn babe, with Margaret beside me softly sighing, lightly kissing, then drifting off in silent and pure repose.

In the morning Margaret left me sleeping while she got up at the sound of the alarm to make breakfast for Devon and Sharon, both of whom rushed off to catch buses for school. She stayed up making a package of sandwiches, cookies and blueberry pie for me to take with me on the road, in a small frameless backpack containing also a change of clothes. She knew I would leave, without any need for us to discuss a change in plans.

When I got up I noticed that Margaret had had the sense of propriety to close the guest room door.

"Devon was sorry he missed you," she told me over a hearty breakfast of pancakes and scrambled eggs. "He wanted to tell you his predictions for the baseball season this year. You may remember how crazy he is about the Royals. Well, he said to tell you they're going to win the pennant this year."

"That's great. You tell him for me that I hope they beat the Yanks in the playoffs."

"I didn't know you followed baseball."

"Oh, not really. I kind of go by the names of the teams, more than anything else."

"Also it would have been nice for you to meet my daughter Sharon. I knew you needed your sleep, though. Here, I'll show you her picture."

Margaret went to the living room and retrieved a color portrait of Sharon, taken with cap and gown signifying her graduation from high school, and brushed with the skillful strokes of the touch-up artist. She appeared too milky for my taste, her plumped bodice underpinning a rather vacant smile. Her mother ventured, "Of course, if I could convince you to stay another night, you'd have a chance to meet her—and catch a playoff game on TV if you're so inclined." The latter option was offered I thought too artificially, as if to couch the former in innocence—but then maybe I was being unfair, my perceptions colored by reminiscence of a past complication.

"No, really, Margaret, you've been too kind to me." I fingered the backpack parked by my chair, leaning against the pale blue flowered wallpaper.

"You know you're welcome to stay," she went on, "another day... or longer if you like."

"Thank you, Margaret."

"Felix, about last night..."

"It was absolutely exquisite."

"Yes, it was, my dear young man. I have to thank you. I wish I could tell you what you've given me."

"I know. I feel the same, Mrs.—ah, Margaret. I think we may have shared something, well, if not unique, certainly divine."

"It will be unique in my life," she said with a wistful expression, half sad. There followed some moments of peaceful reflection; then she brightly said, "Tell me, are you really determined to go on to Albuquerque, of all places?"

I laughed, out of nervous uncertainty. She had caught me at a moment of truth, as I was no longer inclined to pursue the false excuse of a relative with a possible job there. I'd already lived out that story in one form (my bellhop's job in Paris), and was eighty years too late to take advantage of Schimmelpreester's second offer.

A homespun alternative presented itself, right here in the dusty heart of America. The predictable future collapsed in an instant, and I contemplated myself on this very threshold, twenty years on, saying goodbye to my aging Margaret as I set out to meet Sophie in Albuquerque. By then, arriving in 1994 by the slow lane, I would encounter the candidate when she was about to embark on her presidential campaign, fresh from her astral adventures and able to recognize me, greeting me with open arms when I showed up on her doorstep...

That whole prospect appeared untenable on a number of counts, to a young man footloose in an era still infatuated with the folksy ethic, "On the Road." That romantic quest may have had no object but Freedom itself; and yet, were I ever to culminate my journey with an entry into American politics, what more appropriate banner to march under?

Cast adrift, indeed like many of Sophie's generation—those of my ostensible age, without persuasive purpose in this decadent, bourgeois society—I would follow the script to the end of the road: California.

Yet I could not bring myself to offer such a dissolute change of plans to this staid Margaret, awaiting my answer. *Behold Felix Krull—a genuine Bohemian!*

So I stuck to my story, and rose to leave, backpack in hand.

Tears welled in her eyes. "Forgive me," she said. "I feel as I did when Terry left to go to that dreadful flying school."

I touched her arm tenderly. "Not to worry, on that account. I will stick to the land routes."

"Are you sure you wouldn't be more comfortable riding the bus?"

I discerned, in her creased brow, an unspoken fear of dangerous outcomes from hitching rides with drivers of unknown character and deviant motives.

As for the more secure mode of transport, I recalled with distaste my ride in the third-class carriage from my own German home to Paris, to accept the position my godfather had arranged in the hotel. I had vowed never again to subject myself to such conveyance, with its dispiriting mélange of the sad underclass of humanity.

"No, Margaret, I find the freedom of the open road more appealing; and also I must conserve my most limited funds until I can find secure paying work."

With a newfound sparkle in her countenance, she stepped across the room to rummage at her desk and brought out a small envelope.

"Here," she said, "Take this. You may find yourself stranded somewhere again, or need to tide yourself over to your first paycheck."

Folded inside the paper were five crisp hundred dollar bills.

"Oh my goodness, you—"

She stopped my lips with a finger and a smile. I bowed my head in gratitude, and rose to leave.

"You've been very good to me, Margaret. I will remember you, and this time together, always. Who knows, perhaps someday fate will bring me to your door again."

"Or me to yours."
"You never know."
"No."
"Goodbye, Margaret."
"Goodbye."

I held no rancor for the close-shorn farmers in their pickup trucks, the housewives bound for the grocery store, the long-haul drivers with their eyes fixed on the horizon, as they passed me by that day. All morning I stood, and by turns walked, with thumb out, along the dusty highway in the Indian summer heat, without success in catching a ride. Understandable, I supposed, in the conservative heartland of America, that a lank drifter such as myself would be left to his own devices. With the sun at its height and my senses drowsy from the nightlong sensual buzz, I sat beneath a shady elm and ate both chicken salad sandwiches, then lay down to nap on a bed of bent alfalfa upon the Kansas dirt, full of cornflower-blue memories of Margaret and her feathery bed.

A snuffling sound, amid the flitter of gnats, brought me back to harsh daylight in the midafternoon. I turned to see an ancient English setter wagging his hairy tail and drooling from ample red gums.

"Hi, pooch. Nice doggy. Aww..."

I sat up and petted him as he whined with affection for his newfound friend. I smiled and the dog seemed to smile back, his tongue beating like a heart as it lolled amid the shiny canine teeth. At length he rested his head on his front paws and continued to gaze at me fondly, expectantly.

I rummaged in the pack for Margaret's oatmeal-raisin cookies, happy to share in the spirit of generosity that had graced my time of need. With a prudent eye to the unknown future, I kept in reserve the plastic carton of blueberry pie, and set out on the trek once again, this time with the tongue-wagging escort at my side. He hesitated at the first farm driveway we passed, and I considered shooing him home; but I chose to honor instead that spirit of freedom which guided my own steps forward. So the dog continued on with me, tail waving as carefree as ever.

With the air alive with grasshoppers and warm breezes, and sparse traffic paying us no heed, the day marched apace into the afternoon. Thunderheads built on the horizon. I almost forgot my life of petty crime, and the absence of prospects before me, as the cadence of my steps and the good nature of my companion lulled me into a sense of open-ended emptiness.

I whistled snatches of "We're Off to See the Wizard," until I thought of Sophie behind her invisible curtain pulling levers, and my mood turned sullen again. Sandy and I had watched Dorothy's saga on TV—a yearly ritual of hers—and here in the flatland of the Kansas prairie I felt myself a composite of that questing troop in the land of Oz: the tinman heartless, the lion a coward, the strawman a brainless simpleton. Was I making Sophie a strawman for my own deficiencies? Regardless of the mechanism or motive behind my transplantation through time, the world brooked no excuses for lack of success. Especially this mute land, with its featureless horizons stretching in every direction under the vast uncaring sky, demanded a fundamental integrity of human will. A grain silo, a church steeple, a flagpole represented for many, in these parts, that assertion of pride, a dare against irrelevancy.

But I was no farmer, no pew-sitter, nor patriot. What claim had I, then, in the mirror of this inertia, to stand up and be recognized, even to recognize my own face as a being with purpose, a vision to follow? Lacking answers, I knew only the urge to continue, and did so with the solace of another being who, in that same dogged faith, put one paw in front of another.

I had a terrible thirst by the time our pilgrimage brought

us to the outskirts of a town. A roadside tavern promised the relief of a cooling brew. As I swung the screen door open with a tinkling of bells, the bartender with his hanging jowls looked at me and said, "No dogs allowed." He pointed over his shoulder to a sign on the wall stating the same.

My Toto frowned and curled up on the concrete outside the door. I found an empty flower pot there and a water tap, so satisfied the panting dog first, before patting his head and walking in. The TV on the wall carried the drone of a baseball announcer's voice into the room.

"That's Friedrickson's dog," a man in a green John Deere cap said to me. He was sitting on the bar stool closest to the door. The very smell of cold beer was intoxicating. I walked past the man without responding and sat next to him at the bar. He turned to me again and asked brusquely, "What's he doing with you?"

"I'll have a draft," I said quickly to the bartender, glad for the gift of cash from Margaret.

To my neighbor sitting at the bar I said, "The dog? I don't know. He followed me into town."

"Into town? You mean you was on foot? Where were you at then, when you started?"

"That, my good man, is a long story." I sipped the cold beer, nectar from heaven. He finished his glass and asked for another. From his girth I guessed he did so with fair regularity.

"I don't have time for a long story, the Royals is comin' to bat. You ain't a Yankee fan, I hope. Where'd you say you was from?"

"Mobile, Alabama, last. Since then I've been on the road, oh, I guess—"

"Sshh... let's go, George, baby!"

I sat at the bar and watched the ninth inning end. The American Revolution, a rerun: the Royals had lost to the Yankees, amid much grumbling to either side of me. The man in the green hat looked as if all the beer he'd drunk could well reemerge in the form of tears. The bartender changed the channel to election coverage.

"Oh great," said another man watching from his barstool, his voice insinuating sarcasm. "The Joe and Jerry Show." Former St. Louis Cardinal ballplayer and network announcer Joe Garagiola was interviewing President Ford, who had won his party's nomination that summer in Kansas City, over a rival who had been a cowboy actor.

The campaigning incumbent spoke haltingly, even, I would say, grudgingly, of matters foreign and domestic. Slick-domed Joe pressed that very point, querying the candidate as to his reluctance to run for a second term. Ford mouthed platitudes about "the will of the people" and his "duty to continue leading this great nation in a time of economic challenges and grave threats abroad."

Could I do better, I thought? In my heart of hearts I knew I could, given the opportunity and circumstances to allow my talents to so flourish. (I could hardly do worse.) At the moment I was far from such circumstances. I was just another guy with a beer in his hand, a few steps aside from a more uncertain destination, the open road.

The bar closed and all the sad-eyed men filed out, paying me no mind. I was the last to leave. The bartender said, to no one in particular, "Maybe next year, huh?"

Outside the bar the dog was gone. Friend for a day—a man alone can live with that. I considered the pooch's disappearance, and trusted his instincts to retrace his steps home, to a welcome dinner and a reassuring hand. My own fate, by contrast, was wholly unsettled. What would tomorrow bring?

The night was filled with fireflies and stars, but neither gave me cheer. Despondent, not over the fate of the local baseball club, nor at the state of the union, but at my own extenuated demise, I walked down the road as the sparse traffic dwindled to silence, and curled up for the night in a ditch.

The image of President Ford haunted me into sleep. Seething, I compared that hulking head of state, not with his populist rival Jimmy Carter, but with the scintillating charm and intellect of Sophie Tucker Vaughan. And when it came to speechwriting, or policy advice, I knew I could offer more of both style and substance than the current regime could boast.

Yet here I remained, my shoulders pressing against stones and clods of dirt—as in an early grave—as far as could be imagined from any gold-brick road to the White House. To close that existential gap would require a vital transformation, on the order of my resurrection from the briny depths. Would I have to pray next for a tornado?

CHAPTER VI

All roads in America lead to California. At every junction there is a choice, of course. I now looked askance at my dream-tainted leanings to head southwest, especially since, by my reckoning, Sophie in the fall of 1976 would have moved on to parts unknown in Alaska, Canada, Central America. I was prompted—as I told myself Sophie herself would have wished—to find my own way across the fabric of space and time; pushing past despair to new horizons, fueled by a primal, not to say desperate, self-confidence. What better locale for a fresh start and a healthy lifestyle, than the golden hills of California? So it was that I rose with my shoes the ochre of Kansas clay and, shaking the hayseeds out of my hair, had the luck to hitch a ride with a friendly trucker going all the way to Oakland.

A couple of months passed in what is so provincially known by that generic term, the Bay Area, where I enjoyed a dry sunny fall without incident of either notable success or trouble. I worked at odd jobs and befriended those with whom I could share temporary housing. Lack of engaging prospects or inspirations there had me moving on again, and I settled in for the winter in Arcata, a cozy coastal community in the north, complete with a cheap hotel room and a job in the health food store. I felt I had learned to forget what might have been, in favor of what was.

Arcata was shrouded in coastal fog, those winter mornings: heavy and gray, cold with the Pacific air masses piling in from Siberia and Alaska. The hairy folk in town glided from their pickup trucks to Natty's Café, bundled in hand-woven caftans of coarse wool, hair matted in long locks like felt, steeped in aromas of oriental incense and marijuana smoke. This was growers' country, a hippie haven. When I saw a band called Cat Mother "rock the joint," as one enthusiast put it, at a funky club tucked in the forest, I eyed the flute player through the haze, wondering if I recognized Sophie. Was she the Cat Mother, a pagan goddess bestowing grace upon her elven dancers? No, that was the mushrooms talking, I conceded next day on recovering my senses.

Ford was out, Carter was in... but this Arcadian scene bespoke a new society altogether, a thriving counter-culture. A vision of the future, here and now: R. Crumb eco-villages, bikes and solar panels, bakeries and daycares, clouds of pungent smoke in the air...

Though the medieval flavor of the place had a certain throwback charm, I found as little substantial appeal in this brand of alternative lifestyle as in its American mainstream version. Flintstones or Jetsons, the dominant paradigm still reigned: Suburbia. Substituting granola for Cheerios, a bong for happy hour, a hand-painted VW Beetle for a BMW.

Was I missing my ticket to the higher echelons? Who were the higher echelons, anyway, and on what merit did they get there? Was it family privilege, after all, as closed as European nobility?

No, America had placed its novel stamp on the ruling contract: there would be an aristocracy of money here, alongside that of inherited privilege. And each allowed access to the other, although the overlap was not complete, due to the essential qualities that distinguished the two camps: the inherent snootiness of the bloodline lineages, and the willful boorishness of the nouveau riche.

Margaret and Sandy were both forgotten like Maria and Zouzou before them, or nearly so, as I preferred to concentrate on present candidates for intimate relations... such as they were. What it boiled down to was Glenda, mousy Glenda at the health food store. And I could hardly imagine consorting with this plain, boyish non-wench, with her bangs cut straight across above her eyes in the manner of a Munich schoolgirl, pigtails at the sides, and a dark growth of hair on her upper lip. Beside her unseductive appearance, exaggerated still further by the baggy overalls she habitually wore to work, I had to consider her attitude, which was not merely standoffish to me, but, I observed, verged on rudeness to all men.

I had my eyes open for others, but the population was small and there were few young ladies around to meet my modest qualifications: pleasing figure, fine features, a taste for clothes that accentuated and complemented the above characteristics, and of course an openness of spirit to allow some genial interaction with a man of good breeding such as myself. Alas, I was haunted day and night by a lyric of the old South, which played regularly on the local FM radio; a raw, off-key blues which likely originated in a destitute black man with a rusty harmonica. "Oh that whip-poor-will, that lonesome turtle dove / Life ain't worth living if you're not with the one you love."

One day this conventional existence of mine veered out of its rut of normality. I was walking down the street in Arcata, minding my own business, on my way to work— scowling no doubt, albeit innocently—when a dumpy wall-eyed woman coming toward me reached up and tweaked my nose and said, "Such a cute nose!" I was too astonished to defend myself. To my great relief, my assailant continued on her way past me and down the sidewalk.

Feeling my nose and glancing behind me every other step, I took note of a startling fact. Silkscreened on the back of the woman's white T-shirt was a logo of a large stitched ball, along with the words,

ALASKA OR BUST!
Sophie's Softballers

I felt a familiar, almost humorous chagrin, yet found it more disquieting that this apparent intrusion by that will o' the wisp, Sophie, into the stagnating tidal pools of my life had occurred in broad daylight. And what exactly did she mean to convey to me by such a message, this time? Was it any more than before, with her white whispering bear, her luminous god Lucifer? Again I was without any direct evidence of Sophie herself. Yet I was left standing there, staring at the woman's lettered back as she waddled away, with an unformed but volatile sense of sexual connotation, frontier adventure, and sporting challenge.

After another drab day at work, however, with the dour Glenda in her baggy overalls and caustic comments, and it was back home again to the grungy hotplate, another night of bleak, apocalyptic dreams. In the morning I stood at the window, dressing halfheartedly. Surviving the night terrors, my waking life had become one of bland austerity, days spent weighing out pinto beans and wheat bran. My social life was limited to taking in the odd bar band. On such occasions I would try out the gyrating, atavistic moves of the contemporary solo dancers, without appearing to register any favorable impression on the females nearby. In general I found myself uninterested in the laid-back company afforded by these semi-rural, ex-urban, not-quite-suburban Californians; and they, it seemed, got on quite happily without me. Here on the West Coast of America, the lapping perspective of the gray Pacific was prone to lay folks back from the mad drive of history that had got us there, with so much pride and waste, so much greed and industry, such perseverance and forgetfulness.

I looked out my window through the morning fog, imagining, over the ocean, paradisiacal islands in perfect sea-breeze and teeming with elemental life... but knew such utopias were reached nowadays by special jet excursion rates, four-day round-trip junkets complete with hotel accommodations, grand island tours, buffet luaus every night, express limo service to spectacular golf courses...

That life was not for me; though I could well imagine the American contemporaries of young Felix (alias the dashing marquis) lapping up such champagnes. Older by a quantum stretch, and perhaps a little wiser, I was left to wonder where I could go next.

With dreamscapes turning ever darker, my days would continue uneventful and brooding, in this episodic trough in my life story. It was fortunate that no one else was close to me at this time. I indeed felt lucky to hold down a job. The grimy storeroom at the health food store was about all I could handle. At least I had nothing to spend my wages on, so began to put some savings by for a better day.

In late August of 1977, on lunch break in the back office of the health food store, I picked up a newspaper which would change my life—or so I would express it if I were to give full credit to fated things, rather than to the willing flesh which follows these synchronistic signposts appearing so fortuitously along life's dim-lit path. A display ad in the travel section, touting the beauties of Alaska, featured a bikini-clad model who looked uncannily like Sophie (as I remembered her) cleverly superimposed on a glacial background.

Was she moonlighting as a model?

A new agenda formed itself in my mind. If I were to undertake a voyage there, I could explore Sophie's stomping grounds firsthand, and attempt to further substantiate her claim to existence in the waking world. The advertised tour package included a fare by boat from mainland Alaska to Kodiak Island, and hotel accommodations in the city of Kodiak for two weeks.

By way of advance scouting, I took new inspiration to make inquiries about Sophie's whereabouts. Close at hand was the expedient tool of the telephone, which I could use to call long distance under an account not my own. I put down my half-eaten sandwich, spilling stray alfalfa sprouts on the open newspaper, and dialed directory assistance for the state of Alaska, the offices of the state school board.

To my chagrin, I was informed that there was no record of a Sophie Vaughan in the employ of the state school system. Another dead end lay before me; yet my own destiny beckoned me forward there—in the knowledge that I could not depend upon Sophie to give meaning to this existence, beyond her inscrutable intervention to date. I would have to pave my own road to success. Indeed, I mused, she might even now be watching from on high, enjoying my pitiful struggles to prove my worthiness through this wasteland of futility.

Regardless of the folly of expecting to find her in Alaska, I was pulled by the natural allure of the Northern landscape. After mulling it over for an hour or so that afternoon, I decided to quit my job and follow up on the tour offer. Again I would take to the open road, my sails full of freedom both physical and spiritual. And if I failed in my quest to meet Sophie, I might yet find a bit of random luck, plunging into unforeseen adventures on the ragged road of whatever it is that's usually called life, or time burning.

CHAPTER VII

The inland passage up the coast of British Columbia threaded through richly firred islands, past glaciated peaks and primeval fiords, graced everywhere by an abundance of sea life: otters, seals, sea lions, orca and gray whales, ravens and eagles. In such a world the distant histories of civilizations, the rise and fall of empires, faded to irrelevance. I could put aside my own paltry efforts of self-aggrandizement—whether of past exploits in the salons of Europe or future pretensions to the halls of power in America—and glory in the beatific magnificence of Nature, vast and unspoiled by the upstart cravings of humankind.

The trackless forests and mountains, the raging rivers and unspoiled lakes, all supplied a balm to my soul. I had been blind to such beauty in Europe, whittled away as it was by man's encroachments, and preoccupied as I was by my own supercilious and picayune desires. Here I took solace and inspiration from the abiding silence of the landscape, eschewing the company of my fellow passengers and settling into a quiet, inner state of anticipation—a calm sureness, a determination that I was on my path at last. Margaret and Sandy, Zouzou and Maria... their voices at first had rung far off in the distance but were muffled by the more immediate roar of engines and high winds, the lapping of waves and the raucous screech of gulls.

Still, I felt the pangs of an unfulfilled destiny. And I don't mean the already long-delayed reunion with Sophie, so that I might serve her blueblooded ambitions. Was I not also, in my own right, a person of substance?

Only now my memory banks were a ragged reef composed of coral skeletons, brine-washed and bleached to a petrified state of mere existence, pushed upon by waves without effect. What was there left but hope—no, a slow, tidal certainty—that a better life, a life not simply "meaningful" but charged with a ruling purpose, loomed just over the misty horizon?

I had watched, in my two years here in twentieth-century North America, my old social talents fall into disuse. My few attempts at flattery or embellished expostulation had fallen on ears deadened to Old World charms, ears tuned instead to the frequencies of copper, silver, and gold, and their bogus replacements; ears dulled with the simplicities of commerce and work, of television and fast foods. The confidence game was taken over by slick advertising teams and propaganda mills. How could anyone with real potentials, with God-given graces such as I had once possessed, hope to advance above the ranks of the lowly shift workers, as I had barely managed thus far?

One thing was clear to me by now. Sophie, if she even existed, or still cared to follow my progress or lack thereof, was not going to hand me any silver-platter subsidies. Sophie or no Sophie, Albuquerque or Alaska or Nowheresville, I had to fend for myself.

In the Alaskan port of Seward I boarded the ferry for passage to Kodiak. The *M.V. Tustumena* swung past rocky islands to a broad bay, a town I was going to call my home. In spite of my resigned skepticism, I could imagine Sophie waiting there for me at the dock, fishing pole in hand, cat on shoulder; mystic polar bear lurking behind, about to whisper in her ear.

Alas, none but lean gulls were there to give welcome, wheeling hesitantly over the dock. Beyond, mounted the hills of Kodiak, specked with buildings and motley vegetation exposed by the brief summer. I stepped off the with the other hundred and fifty passengers at eleven o'clock at night on the twenty-sixth of September, the last ferry of the season. When the hulking vessel disappeared with chalky wake into the slate-sea horizon, what I guessed to be three mongrel sled dogs on the hills above the city set to a blood-chilling baying, mourning a lost heritage of the wild.

In two weeks, the snow fell like soggy manna from wooly skies and covered the island. At a ranch near Beaver Lake where I went to find work as a cowboy, the cattle pawed at the ground and snuffled up frozen bluegrass with glistening pink and brown nostrils. As I was honest and told the rancher I had no experience in such work, I didn't get the job. I was already weary of job-hunting in the town. I had sufficient savings to survive the winter in a frugal fashion if necessary; but the truth was, after those two weeks I was already bored to tears by the country-and-western bars, the square dances and the stuffed Kodiak brown bears, the bearded fishermen and clean-cut pistol-packing military men, the homestead divorcees who came to town for a little fun.

I would pass a sign posted on glass, on a cold street, a gray day:

WAITERS: INQUIRE WITHIN.

I would wait, thus gaining the first qualification. I would stand in front of the sign long enough for my inner inquiry to produce the usual result, and then walk on.

There wasn't much else I could do for a living. I wasn't exactly a concert guitarist in this low-key orchestra of trade. I didn't even play the guitar.

I reserved another two weeks at the modest hotel with its peeling clapboards, kindly given a discount rate to extend my stay past the tour booking. Somehow my days hummed by. I continually wondered how I would continue. I took long walks on windy days out beyond the town. When the wind came down the pass, rattling past rocks and whistling through eagle's nests, I was reminded of an old song; but I couldn't remember its name.

My own name expanded one day when I found, beside a rusted oil barrel, a wallet containing no cash but a Washington state driver's license, once belonging to a Seymour Friedrickson. I pocketed the prize for future contingencies.

Alaska was the final frontier to test my own powers to advance in new and virgin territory. I had followed Sophie's tracks in the sand of dreams without result but the bitter fruits of my own distraction. The snatch of a stale revelation replayed itself in my mind: *I will find out in time that my travels have been in vain.* Now, in the dull glare of everyday reality, I accepted the finality of my predicament. I had come to a wall with nothing on the other side.

No matter, I thought. The wind knows my song, my name; it won't forget me.

With a week to go and no appealing prospects in Kodiak, I considered that perhaps another location in the state would serve me better, in which case a move would be prudent before winter arrived in earnest.

Studying a map of this vast Alaskan wilderness in which I had gained a mere toehold, my attention was drawn to the far northwestern shore, which featured a Cape Lisburne, and, nearby, the even more promising location, Point Hope. Peering closer, I saw an inset blurb about the oldest continually inhabited site on the continent, a village called Ipiutak. Tasting its syllables on my lips, I felt sure I had heard that name before—from Sophie.

A visit to the Bureau of Indian Affairs office in Kodiak provided me with a phone number in Kotzebue, where the district office operated ten village schools in the region. These served the indigenous populations and operated outside the purview of the state-run school board I had queried earlier. So the flame of hope in finding Sophie's trail flickered anew. But a series of attempted phone calls failed to get through. I went back to the office in Kodiak to ask why. The young native receptionist shrugged and simply replied, "Did you know Kotzebue is the polar bear capital of the world?"

What the hell, I thought as I stormed out; I'll go there myself, and find out if there really are any polar bears there... and if Sophie Tucker Vaughan is nothing but a foolish fancy, a cruel cosmic joke.

The round-trip plane tickets to Kotzebue via Anchorage—after the purchase of a down parka with fur-lined hood, and the earmarking of funds for an excursion to Ipiutak—wiped out my savings and made it imperative to find work upon my return. Boarding was secured through the good fortune of my adopted driver's license. I had good clear, frosty weather for flying, allowing spectacular views of Mt. McKinley and the Alaska Range just out of Anchorage, and the panorama of a wilderness of peaks all the way to Kotzebue Sound, on the Arctic Circle, in the Chukchi Sea.

A mere two hundred miles farther offshore in the ice-misted horizon lay the Soviet Union, a land route back to my homeland... but to consider such was folly. Here on the outermost edge of the Western world, to cross an imaginary line means to jump through time, from one day to the next in an instant; and through space, from the West to the East. The mind is tempted by such illusions, by the mirage of yet another new continent in the distance; and then the feet touch down on frozen sand. From a jet plane we walk on a path past sod huts.

I hiked with my backpack the mile into town, to stretch my air legs and take in the invigorating Arctic atmosphere. If I were a painter or photographer, I would have rejoiced, or despaired, at the elusive, magical and unforgettable quality of pale light and pastel colors which swam around me over the water, on the frosted tundra, in the roseate air. Pickup trucks, vans and snowmobiles passed me on the road with their cargo of airplane passengers and baggage. I carried with me everything I owned, in preparation for I knew not what new twist in my twisted fate.

Though I had in my pocket the ticket for a return trip to Kodiak, I had checked out of the hotel there and had no certain intention of ever returning. My brief glimpse of Anchorage, a prosperous city of two hundred thousand enterprising souls, gave me the idea that I might do better to hunker down there for the winter after this jaunt to the end of the world.

There isn't much to the town of Kotzebue, sitting as it does on a spit in the middle of nowhere. I found the Indian Affairs office with no trouble and arranged an interview with an administrator through his broad-faced native receptionist who could have been the sister of the one in the Kodiak office—neither appearing past their teenage years, and wearing the same Mona Lisa smile. I sat in the outer office reading brochures from a rack, wondering what it would be like to spend the rest of my life here in the warm embraces of one whose people had successfully inhabited this place thousands of years before the dawn of so-called civilization.

A buzzer sounded on the receptionist's desk. A name plate told me her name was Alicie.

"Mr. Krull, Mr. Wilson will see you now."

Mr. Wilson was a portly man seated comfortably behind a large desk. He had pale pink, clean-shaven jowls, reminding me of that jocular bearer of bad news at Louisiana Savings and Loan, what seemed eons ago. He wore round glasses and a jovial expression.

"Yes, Mr. Krull," Mr. Wilson said in a merry, high-pitched voice. "What can I do for you today?"

I took a seat without invitation and gathered my thoughts. "I'm wondering if you have records of a woman I'm looking for, who I believe taught at one of your schools."

Mr. Wilson's pleasant demeanor took a turn for the worse. "Oh? And may I ask the nature of your inquiry? Are you with the police?"

I had to laugh. "No, no, nothing like that. It's strictly personal. Sophie Vaughan is a good friend of mine, but we've lost touch, and I'm trying to find out where she is."

The man compressed his lips, as if holding back a harbored grudge, then spewed it out: "She taught here last year, grades seven to nine. Competent, but she behaved rather... self-righteously, if I can give her that credit. I hope you don't mind my honesty."

"Indeed, sir, while I count Sophie as a friend, we have had our differences, too. Please go on."

"See, we're here to teach the locals a way to assimilate into our society, but she wanted to turn it all around, go back to their stone-age ways. A rather backwards approach. I've seen it before—'going native,' as they say. It's tempting; with all the sea life around, easy to hunt and catch one's meat and clothing that way. Since time immemorial. Anyway, in staff and community meetings I found her somewhat caustic, if I can be candid. The last straw, she took her class on an unauthorized camping trip, without proper elder supervision, and they nearly fell through the spring ice on a river crossing. The term was nearly finished, and we chose not to renew her contract."

"Hmm, most unfortunate, for all concerned. Yes, I suppose you can say my friend Sophie is headstrong, at least. Do you know where she is now?"

"Over in Canada, is where she was talking about continuing her education. Without our recommendation, I might add."

"Do you know which university she was applying to?"

"I believe it was in Saskatchewan."

I took a deep breath, contemplating my next move in this global chess game. It appeared that Sophie indeed lived and breathed, that very moment, somewhere in the Canadian prairie. But once again I lacked the funds for such a journey; and still I faced the dilemma of how to convince her of her own future story once we met.

Extending my hand as I rose to leave, I thanked my informant.

"No problem," he said. "I wish you luck. Despite our professional disagreements, there is something, I don't know, enchanting about your friend Ms. Vaughan."

Mr. Wilson's tiny eyes behind his large spectacles took on a dreamy cast as he gazed past me at his office wall, a veritable gallery of polar bear paintings and photographs.

On leaving his office my steps felt light, measured, unsure.

Had the presidential candidate intended for me to ferret her out in this way? Failing which, I would have to bide my time, for a decade or two more, until she deemed me ripe for the plucking.

"Staying long?" Alicie asked me as I passed her desk again.

"I don't know," I answered. "Should I?"

My return ticket was good for any day that week. The memo pad on the receptionist's desk reminded me that this was only Wednesday.

"We got lots to do here," the native lass said sweetly. "You gotta place to stay?"

"I was thinking of the Nul-Luk-Vik Hotel," I stumbled, a Demosthenes with too many pebbles in his mouth. "That one of your brochures talks about, Eskimo-run..."

"Fleabag hotel," she tittered. "You could stay with my family, if you like."

"An intriguing proposition," I replied, trying to discern her motives.

Did I still exude a roguish charm, despite the downturn in my career prospects? Was she hoping for a generous stipend or tip for her family's sustenance? Or was this simply the famous Northern hospitality in action? In any case, what sleeping arrangements could I expect, in their sod hut or tiny plywood box of a house?

Though I voiced none of these concerns, Alicie read my rapid thoughts and said, "If you want to pay something it's up to you. Or you can be my guest."

"That's very kind of you. I would consider it an honor."

When Mr. Wilson's buzzer rang her back to her duties, she sent me on a selective tour of the town's attractions and said she'd meet me after work.

Uncertain of any lasting or even temporary enticements in Alicie's company, my thoughts turned back to Sophie as I trod with my backpack on the sandy street back toward the central cluster of buildings in the village. I chided myself for not gambling on Saskatchewan instead of Alaska, for this exploratory venture. Gradually such thoughts gave way to an ease with my present fate, a curiosity about Alicie and her family, their way of life. She was here, now; and so was I—anticipating our liaison without expectation.

I followed Alicie's suggestion and entered the new Living Museum of the Arctic, which housed a menagerie of stuffed wild animals peculiar to the area, and featured an excellently crafted diorama show. In side rooms I watched old native women demonstrate skin-sewing, and wrinkled Chukchi Sea-faring men carving ivory cribbage boards and soapstone seals.

It was dark at quarter to five when I met Alicie in the lobby of the Nul-Luk-Vik, as we had arranged. She wore a beautiful embroidered navy blue parka, trimmed with white wolf fur which highlighted her jet black hair and eyes perfectly. We sipped Black Russians in the hotel bar and then walked down Front Street along the frozen water of the sound, to a restaurant where we dined on caribou filet mignon and

Alaskan king crab legs—at prices only affordable since the meat was locally sourced, and since I considered it a worthy investment of my meager reserves. For me it was like the old days, the old-old days, yet in a setting utterly exotic by European standards, with a "date" who had grown up in an ancient whaling village called Wevok—otherwise known as Cape Lisburne.

Alicie had come to Kotzebue at fifteen to attend the high school there. She learned enough secretarial skills to complement her good looks and earn her a job in the BIA education office at seventeen, a year ago... and I realized that this child was Zouzou's age when I had courted her, over eighty years ago. I felt as though I had aged by the same amount, with the distance from those raw emotions and conflicting motives of my past.

"Where are you?" She brought me back, quizzical at my distraction, head tilted and eyes dancing.

"Sorry, sorry," I pleaded. "I was thinking about how far I am from my home, in Europe. And for your people, the Eskimos, is this your ancestral home, or do you trace it further back..."

"We're not really Eskimos," she said while deftly picking crabmeat out of a long, tubular leg-shell.

I followed her example. "Oh really. Then what do you call yourselves, just *people*?"

"Oh, no, that's too boring! Plus it's English." She laughed, showing a set of strong, even, white teeth. "We're Inupiat, or, farther down the coast, Yu'pik or Aleut. Around here we go way back to the beginning, from the other land, when we called ourselves Yuit. That was, oh at least, thousands of years ago."

"Yes, so I understand. What do these names mean, then?"

"You mean, like, *Inuk*?"

"Yeah."

"It means, 'a real person.'"

"Oh. So *Inupiat* really does mean 'people,' after all." I gave her a sly smile.

She said, "Touché." Then she blushed and broke into a girlish giggle, covering her mouth with her hand.

I can well imagine the reader will prejudge my intentions with this fair maid of the North, predicting also the outcome of these flirtations. May I make reference, again, to those eighty vanished years, to perhaps explain my more circumspect behavior in this iteration of the romantic impulse. Besides which, the situation proved more conducive to a sociable evening with "the real people."

Alicie took me home and introduced me to her older brother, his wife and sister-in-law, and a clutch of small children, a variable number which changed every time I looked around. Repeated questions gave me no clarity as to whose children they were.

As one little girl named Lucy came to her more often than to the others, to show her cloth scraps she'd picked up from the floor, or to be comforted when one of the boys playfully bit her, I surmised that this was Alicie's child. But it didn't really matter. I was here today, would be gone tomorrow.

The tiny shack had two bedrooms, to retire to after chatting and playing cards for a couple of hours. Alicie and I had the benefit of one room, while the married couple took the other, and the sister-in-law and four children all slept in the main living room on the couch and various mats of foam, hide and woven willow. That is, the children began the night there. I had just settled into a warm embrace with Alicie under a thick caribou-skin blanket, when Lucy came skittering in and pushed between us. Mother and daughter a few moments later were both sleeping peacefully.

Rising libido thus nipped in the bud, I lay awake, pondering my next move in this desolate territory, with its sparse stunted trees, growing winter ice and vanishing sun. Yes, tomorrow I would return... to what? The fleabag hotels, the drunks and airmen, the quake-scarred streets of Anchorage? The hopeless island of Kodiak again?

I heard the sound of geese honking overhead in the night, stragglers on the seasonal migration to the South. Should I be joining them, leaving behind this cold and windy wilderness, stark and barren, where success was measurable by wolf fur on the face, the smell of raw fish, the taste of burning hot tea?

Good God, it was Sophie I wanted, nothing else. The higher life she had promised me—that was the life for me, nothing short. I was made of finer stuff than to be sleeping around like this in no-man's land, when I could be ensconced in the White House with the first woman president, at the very pinnacle of earthly power!

If I could return to Anchorage and make enough money this winter to get out to the University of Saskatchewan and make contact with Sophie before she left there, I could plead my case personally. Surely she could not refuse me...

In the morning I shared with this extended family a breakfast of frozen seal meat. We all sat on the floor to eat, slicing chunks piece by piece with several knives from a whole common haunch.

Alicie walked with me to the airstrip and we said goodbye. I kissed her and wiped away a tear—caused by the sharp breeze?—on that lovely high, olive-brown cheek so it wouldn't freeze there. The wind ruffled the fur around her stoic face as she looked out to sea, impassive as a carved statue, and I turned and walked away to my plane.

CHAPTER VIII

I knew it would be futile to return to Kodiak at least until tourist season, and so I stayed in Anchorage hoping to find work there. I checked into a modestly priced hotel, where the low winter rates partially compensated for the lull in the job market. And then I did land a job as a night-shift clerk in a pinball arcade, where I watched the teenagers spend their allowances and vie for the attentions of their infrequent female companions. That position got me through a lonely December while I dreamed of saving my meager earnings for a trip to Saskatchewan in the spring—damn the consequences to the fragile web of the space-time continuum.

Upon the turning of the new year, 1978, I made a phone call to Saskatoon, and reached the university's Aboriginal and Northern Studies department, to confirm Sophie's enrollment there. True to form, she had eluded my grasp once again, having embarked already upon a practicum in Guatemala.

The cold in my bones deepened, as I appreciated her flight from a year in the Arctic to the heat of the tropics. To attempt to track her further there seemed a fool's errand—especially as the region was rife with social unrest, notorious for death squads roaming the countryside. I needn't fear for Sophie's safety, knowing her future was secure. But for me to venture into such dark waters (assuming funds which I still lacked) would be pushing my luck beyond prudence—and, as always, with slim hope of a successful reunion with that will of the wisp, my astral temptress, Sophie.

Facing facts, I realized the outcome of my American adventures to date: I was reduced to anonymity, part of the masses, my inner nobility leveled to the playing field of a democratized culture. That capacity for distinction, for expression of serviceable talents, lay dormant, awaiting its proper time to resurface.

In hopes of finding a better paying job, for advancement on my own terms, I joined the Allied Tourism Workers' Union; which meant paying a membership fee and entering my name on a waiting list for available work come spring. It also meant I had a congenial hangout at the union hall where I could spend my afternoons, shooting pool and smoking cigars, making friends among the seasonally unemployed.

Most of the guys (almost all of them were men) enjoyed stipends from the government in the form of unemployment insurance, which they fondly called "pogie." At first they were slow to accept me into their ranks. A few grumbled about the fact I had a job, and a non-union job at that. Others called me a "lightweight," since I lacked the big beard and belly that marked the more common male form in this region of the world. I had a short, neat growth of beard and was slim as ever. There was no way I could keep up their pace when it came to guzzling beer.

A quickly learned facility with the pool cue earned me some respect. I even started taking in regular spending money that way, which one of the friendlier guys, a long-nosed old lumberjack they called Sneaky Pete, suggested I might invest in the odd case of beer or box of cigars for "the boys."

"Hey, this Felix guy ain't all bad," was the greeting I received when I followed through. Big Ed, the ex-Minnesota Viking, and Moses, the hulking Native American, both clapped me on the back (even though Moses was not drinking anymore), and I was nearly felled by the impact.

On that day I discovered I was actually allowed to talk politics with these overgrown "boys."

The long, dingy hall had its usual crew: a dozen plaid-shirted characters sitting on wooden benches and plastic chairs, playing pool or watching, drinking soft drinks and beer at three round tables, smoking cigarettes and cigars. The smoke was thick in the flat fluorescent light but you got used to it.

Pete and Ed popped open their cans of beer with the usual speed. I racked up the balls for a game of eight-ball with Ed. It didn't take him long to start in on one of his stories.

"I ran for mayor once in a small town down on the Kenai," Ed boasted to an audience at large. "Against a little twerp that looked kinda like Felix here—" he glanced at me with the flash of a smile out of the corner of his mouth—"and I almost beat the sucker."

"Yeah?" said Pete, taking the bait. "How many votes did ya buy?"

Ed looked at Pete with narrowed eyes. "Oh, Peter, we don't do stuff like that out here in God's country—do we, Felix?" He sighted down his cue and missed a tough bank shot.

I made an effort to say, "Nice attempt, Ed," but couldn't be heard over a tremendous crashing from the Coke machine as Moses tried to batter his change through the works. I thought about launching into an analysis of politics as nothing but one big confidence game, but stuck to my pool game instead and sank the five in the corner.

"Awright," Moses joined in, sweeping the long black hair out of his face with a walrus toss of his huge head, and then taking a swig from his fizzing prize. "What was the final score?"

"Two to one," said Ed. "And that's not perportion, that's totals."

Everyone laughed. In plopped the four ball.

Then Moses spoke up again, in a more serious tone. "Guy on Council in Mekoruk, he went around and gave a fish to everyone who said they'd vote for him. Funny thing was, he had to buy the fish from the co-op, which was the fish most of these people had caught in the first place."

"Did he win?" I inquired, lining up the one-ball on a long

angle shot. The ball would rattle around the corner pocket for a while before dropping in.

"Course he won. He was the only one around who didn't spend most of his time huntin' and fishin', and the only one who could speak English with the bureaucrats."

"Y'know," I observed, pausing for a moment with my cue stick in hand, "it seems to me that politics in Alaska is like politics anywhere. Money against people, is what it boils down to. Take this Shorter dude down in Kodiak. He runs the show. When there're no jobs to be had, he's not hurting. He flies off to Hawaii, or New Mexico, or holes up in his log palace down in Cape Chiniak."

I was on a run. I stopped talking long enough to sink the six, three and seven in quick succession. The other three men were still as they watched my performance; I sensed the attention also of the men at the neighboring table, perhaps everyone in the hall that day.

"All we need down there," I went on, "is fresh blood to shake things up. New choices for the electorate—not the same tired faces, but some lively opposition to rock that mother out of office." I missed the next shot but I think my audience remembered this little speech when April came around. By that time I could almost call myself one of the boys.

In the meantime a job came up that no one else wanted, so it went down the list to my name, and I became a taxi driver. It didn't take me long to learn the city streets, nor to learn why everyone else had passed up the job. It was bitter cold; I had to keep the heater running all the time, and even so, had to wear two layers of long underwear and double woolen socks to keep my legs and feet from freezing off. I resigned myself to it; for a new mission had taken shape in my life, one which finally wedded my inborn endowments with the larger destiny Sophie had conceived for me.

I became an avid reader of political events, as reported by the *Anchorage Daily News*, representing the establishment view, and an underground rag, *The Sentinel*, with a leftist critique. I paid particular attention to dispatches from the tinderbox countries of Central America. In late January the editor of Nicaragua's newspaper *La Prensa* was murdered, triggering a general strike. President Jimmy Carter was considering cutting US aid to the right-wing Somoza regime. Village massacres by government forces and paramilitary units were commonplace in neighboring El Salvador and Guatemala. I wondered about the extent of Sophie's involvement with local struggles there, and couldn't help worrying about her, despite her assured survival.

Most passengers in my taxi were ill-informed on such matters, or reverted to stock Americanisms: "Gotta watch out for commies on our doorstep down there."

I found my compadres at the union hall more savvy, in their intuitive grasp of the issues.

"Them's my brothers down there, fighting for their land, like we've had to do," said Moses, his black eyes shining with ancient truth.

"And it goes beyond race and ethnic lines," I hastened to add. "There's that prejudice as well as the strictly economic issue of land ownership, of class struggle over generations. The peasants in El Salvador and Nicaragua, for instance, are of mixed race, same as the soldiers and landowners. But they're getting put down for demanding their fair share."

"Right on!" Big Ed chimed in, slugging back his beer.

"It's like over there in Canada, the Winnipeg general strike, my granddaddy was in," added Sneaky Pete. "Saw his best buddy's head get blowed off, standing right next to 'im. Fuckin' coppers, he said, and my grandma said shush, Jerry."

"That's the real problem, right there!" I replied. "We're supposed to be polite and use plain vanilla to wash away the crimes of the oppressors. I'm aware that to use such terms means getting branded ourselves, as 'socialists' or other name-calling that basically means shit-disturbers. I say if a guy needs to make a buck, let's start by putting us all on a level playing field."

"You got that right," said Ed, he of hard-earned gridiron glory.

"And if it means some courageous souls, like this newspaper editor who was assassinated for telling the truth—Pedro Joaquín Chamorro Cardenal was his name, and he should be known and remembered—"

"Hey, that's my name, in Spanish," said Pete.

"That's right. And for speaking his mind, he got the same treatment as your granddaddy's friend in the rally there."

"You keep talking this way, you wake up to a gun in your own pretty face," Ed said, silencing all of us for a moment. He set down his beer. "But somebody's gotta do it."

When spring came I hankered for Kodiak again, away from the hustle and bustle of the big city. I also had in the back of my mind a vague desire to look up the receptionist at the Board of Education office who reminded me so much of Alicie. My companionship in Anchorage had been virtually all male. The hungry widows I drove in the taxi from time to time, I resisted instinctively, as a distraction, and as reminders of Maria's desperate clutches.

The final impetus for a move back to Kodiak was a job opening, selling hot dogs in the softball park there. That job, lowly as it was, meant more than a direct advancement in my checkered career. The Kodiak chapter of the Allied Tourism Workers' Union needed a new shop steward. The fellows in the Anchorage union hall in their rough wisdom had seen a certain aptitude in my speech, my eyes, my character, and had steered me toward what turned out to be a dual position.

They held a straw vote in the union hall one afternoon in April, while the ranks of the tourism workers in Kodiak were still moribund. As new shop steward I rated a flight to Kodiak and my two new jobs. One paid cash in hand, with the added pleasure of roaming the stands in the open air of the softball stadium, as a vendor; and the other rewarded me with prestige and self-confidence, as I prepared to represent my fellow workers in the upcoming contract negotiations.

So I passed the brief Alaskan summer, mildly entertained by the excitement of the softball games, off days spent salmon fishing, and, yes, a near-romance with the ballgirl for the Kodiak Bruins. One day toward the end of August she showed off her backyard garden with its giant cabbages, but we argued when I brought up the day's news from Central America, where the revolutionary FSLN had taken over Nicaragua's National Palace and kidnapped the country's legislators.

In the city of Kodiak, elections were drawing near. Big Huey Shorter was the reigning kingpin of Kodiak politics, and his victory in the current race for mayor was as assured as those which had put him in office twenty years before and kept him there ever since. His chief rivals, who as usual were determined, in their perverse lust for power, to split the opposition vote, were a black militant from Alabama who had worked his way north and west from an unpromising career growing sorghum, and a self-styled communist technocrat recently graduated from the school of dentistry at a prestigious Eastern university. The bread and butter issue was that chief economic staple of the island, tourism. Both of Shorter's opponents wanted to turn over ferryboat, hotel and gift-shop franchise operations to "the people," while Shorter and Co. held firm control of all of the above (including, not least, "the people"). The work force was racially mixed (white, black and Aleut), predominantly male, and their political energies were largely absorbed in haggles against each other. When election time approached, and Anchorage union leadership managed to call off the near-open warfare in the cause of temporary solidarity—they backed the dentist—Huey was ready with a bogus promise of more overtime pay and pension benefits.

Into this fray I strode—fully cognizant that in the book of my life this chapter would carry the title, "In Which Felix Cuts His Political Teeth." I gamely made the rounds as a canvasser to drum up support for the united stand against Huey Shorter's monopoly of island business and government. Our coalition's carefully reasoned arguments for solidarity made obvious sense to me. Yet when I confronted the rotund, bespectacled Misak Inukpa, the token Aleut on Kodiak City Council who was the most reliable indicator of the crucial Aleut vote, I got nowhere.

"Look here," I was told with a bold tone as Inukpa rose from his Naugahyde armchair to lean over his desk, balancing his compact bulk on ivory-ringed knuckles. Inukpa looked me sharply in the eye. "Our people have been struggling a long time against the control of our lives by white people. That Huey, he's the same as before, only maybe a hair worse. If we fight him we lose everything we've gained the last twenty years. Who are you, who just showed up here on the last boat and most likely will leave on the next, to tell our people what to do? We were born here. We've lived here for generations, thousands of years. It's we who will decide what politics we need on this island." The councilor was so pleased with his speech that he broke into a broad grin, showing the gaps of more teeth missing than I cared to count.

I quipped, "How do you like my man as a dentist, then?"

"Just fine," Inukpa said calmly, shutting his trap and escorting me, his impertinent, white-mouthed visitor, to the door.

The outcome of the island election in November was a foregone conclusion. But negotiations with the Small Business League were still to come near the end of the month, and the union was bristling for another fight.

Similar negotiations had yielded a pittance at best, in past years. It was hoped my fresh perspective as a newcomer could break the ice, supply a new insight or angle the old union hacks were too hardened to see, jaded as they were by banging their heads against the wall of Shorter's little empire. And despite the negative results of our electioneering efforts, my energy, enthusiasm and grasp of the issues had brought me into favor with the Anchorage union brass who had been on hand to help out. As a result I was chosen as part of the negotiating team.

I strolled briskly up the steps of the Kodiak City Hall, feeling official as I toted the obligatory briefcase, and joking with the two other union reps who accompanied me. We were a bit late; we hurried down the hall to the Council chambers where negotiations were to be held, entered the room as heads turned and conversation subsided, and quickly took our seats.

In the pregnant pause I saw an advantage in taking the initiative, and so began, addressing the all-male group: "Let's get down to business, gentlemen."

I could barely hear a man at the end of the table grumbling to his neighbor, "Who's this goddamned upstart?"

I took no notice. No one else said anything, so taken aback were they by my unexpected lead. So I continued: "Shall we introduce ourselves, or..." (deciding against it as the others looked at each other in evidence of obvious acquaintance) "shall we proceed to air the respective points of view in the matter at hand, namely the question of growth in our common industry."

More murmuring from the heads on the other side of the table.

"I'll be frank about the union membership's demands, gentlemen. Our number one priority is to increase job security with work guarantees. Let's get that settled first; then we can go on to your offers, the overtime pay increases, pension boosts, and so on."

At this, a near uproar. But it needed to be said, sooner or later. Everyone knew what the respective demands were. Protocol or not, it was best to air out our real differences from the start.

And so negotiations commenced in earnest: the old-timers from the Small Business League gradually immersing themselves in the murky waters to which they were accustomed; my cohorts letting me carry on with the presentation of our case. They did stop me at times to advise me of some intricacy of a past contract, or to explain an opponent's intransigence.

"Kerwood doesn't believe in overtime since he found his wife with another man when he worked late one day," said a scrawled note passed my way at one sticky point in the negotiations.

When it came down to it, the union was willing, I said, to offer concessions on overtime pay rates if another ferry run could be arranged for later in the fall. Such a compromise, I explained, would be not only practical but a gesture of goodwill in cooperating to improve the health of the slumping industry.

Huey would have none of it, said Shorter's chief bargainer, Dan Kush. "More tourists mean more workers, and more workers mean a bigger union, and a bigger union will demand higher salaries—if only to pay their fat-cat union bosses who have to pay dues to Moscow."

I took a puff on my cigar and took the liberty of reminding Huey's stalwart representative of something he seemed to have forgotten. "While masquerading as the friend of small businesspeople, your benevolent dictator Mr. Shorter not only extorts unreasonable fees from them, but garners a comfortable stipend from a larger stateside enterprise, in order to keep the smaller fish in line both in wage levels and in political preferences. I won't venture to speculate on the further implications of such collusion, at this time. Nevertheless..."

And then came the red palm of Kush's beefy hand against the cigar in my mouth. I must have looked a funny sight, with smoldering tobacco leaves splayed around my face, but I simply got up with a condescending smirk and walked out, my men behind me.

The negotiations got nowhere after that. After two more scheduled sessions where neither side even showed up, the process went by law to compulsory arbitration. The nearest arbitration court was in Juneau, but Shorter's parent firm, being located in New Mexico amid its mining concerns, insisted on a hearing at the district court in Albuquerque. I conferred with my advisors and figured the judge there would likely be bought, or at least under heavy influence. The trouble was, our own union had no comparable sponsor elsewhere, and in such a case, the party seeking a hearing in the district of its parent home office was granted that prerogative. We could only hope to salvage some strategic consolation from the new arrangement: the connection between the so-called Small Business League and its parent body would become more public.

For his side of the negotiations, Shorter had decided to let the big boys handle the action down home. I was chosen to represent the union. Following a quick plane trip to Anchorage, I boarded a chartered Learjet with two union lawyers, and I was bound at last for Albuquerque.

How ironic, I thought as we left the runway and became airborne. I finally get to Albuquerque, but once again I have the timing wrong. Sophie has not yet settled there. I consoled myself with the justice of my own mission, undertaken in the integrity of my own means and motivations, no matter the sacrifice.

Just, I might add, as Sophie intended.

The coastal mountains shone brilliant as we went down. The starboard engine had failed in a flameout. We drifted and dove, in the feathery clouds which spun through the peaks. The lawyers were pale, choking on their gin-and-tonics. I felt a preternatural calm, a sense of déja vu. And with an even more compelling sense of necessity, correctness, and certainty, I had the distinct intimation that Sophie was playing her trump card.

The lawyers hunched in fetal positions, one praying, one cursing his fate. I gazed out my window at the landscape looming up with, yes I admit, frightening speed right until the end.

Another life, another passing. There are no accidents.

I tumble silently onto the fragile snow—snow over thin broken ice—my skidoo careening wildly across the river. My mind at rest with my fate. Mittens fill with snow, then water. Heels of hands turn softly blue.

No reservations required, for this relatively minor catastrophe, what we call by a quiet name, death.

PART III

THE FIRST WOMAN PRESIDENT

> Every great people believes, and must believe if it intends to live long, that in it alone resides the salvation of the world; that it lives in order to stand at the head of the nations, to affiliate and unite all of them, and to lead them in a concordant choir toward the final goal preordained for them.
> —Feodor Dostoyevsky, 1877

CHAPTER I

"You can come up for air now," Sophie warbled.

I was sitting across from her over dinner plates, at a blond wooden table adorned by fresh gardenias. I did not fully recognize her at first, but felt a humming at my core, a strummed chord of past connection, as my dim and distant memory of her coalesced: the wavy chestnut hair, the straight long nose, beckoning lips. She smiled at me with deep and starry eyes, her chin resting on her hand. I feared that gaze could swallow me up, and averted my eyes.

In the soft white ambient light of an apartment, I noticed behind her, inset on the wall, a shiny screen with an illuminated photograph of a willow grove, and large lettering beside it which proclaimed what I once would have thought impossible: November 28, 2035. Had I been transported, this time, into Sophie's dream, as she had formerly appeared in mine?

An old longing, dormant like wild flower bulbs under spring moss, stirred within. Tugging at the back of my vision was a confusion of memories: the long grass on the cliffs over the River Tagus; the chill waters of the Atlantic closing around me; a tumbling train; a plane spinning out of the clouds toward a boreal bog; a sinking snowmobile...

Near-suffocation returned me to my senses. Here I sat swaddled within a confining padded suit of synthetic material, a garish red. Standing at once and stripping out of it, I found I wore, underneath, a more comfortable, if equally offensive, pale green leisure suit. My attention settled on my midriff, which bulged in a way that concerned me; I had put on considerable weight. I sat once more, my place set with a dinner still untouched, glancing at Sophie and then fixating on her plate which held a strand of pasta and half a cherry tomato.

Sophie stifled a giggle.

I didn't know what she expected of me. What could I even expect of my ampler, unfamiliar self?

She read my expression and said, "It finally worked out that the time was right for our task to begin—now eat, Seymour, will you?"

She spoke with a voice full of depth and resonance, with a lulling echo. That name she called me... I caught a faint whiff of tobacco. Unconsciously my hand went to my face; my beard was gone.

"Why did you call me 'Seymour'? And I thought we would meet again in 1994."

"I know you prefer 'Felix.' Actually we did meet then; though 'we' is a relative term. It's more complicated now."

"Where are we?"

"Albuquerque Towers," she said, her eyes twinkling. "My apartment in Seattle."

The forest-green drapes beside me rippled almost imperceptibly with the controlled air of the apartment. Or was there an ageless cat lurking? I moved from my chair and pulled the drapes aside but saw only darkness through the tinted window, marked by faint points of light moving in the distance. The outside world, such as it was, remained distant, remote, perhaps another illusion.

In the adjoining living room, modernist paintings of brilliant color in simple abstract shapes hung on the wall. Detecting a subtle motion, I looked more closely to see the images morphing with subtle variations, until they became altogether different designs, still transforming. Then the wall itself changed color, to a pastel gold. The calendar display by the kitchenette had also changed, to show an Earthrise from the vantage of a red desert, presumably Mars. The date 2035 persisted, lodging itself uncomfortably in the troubled region of my brain demarcated, "Reality."

Sophie called out and gestured again to the plate in front of me. "*Mangia, caro*. The food will help ground your energy. Sit and eat while I try to explain."

Her use of Italian put me at ease, another strum on the lute of my past. I followed her bidding.

I thought, if anything, Sophie looked younger than the 1994 rendition I had previously encountered in my dream on the shore of the Tagus. The close-fitting burgundy knit top and tight white slacks showed her lean body as fit as ever. She demonstrated a power to move through decades, or centuries, without showing the effects of time. Yet present evidence insisted she was a living human being, who must have been born, suckled and fed.

I sampled the food, to Sophie's nods of approval. The goose liver paté on cucumber slices tasted fine, cold, especially with the white wine. I couldn't say as much for the congealed pasta.

"This food is real enough," I conceded. "And I gather you were already here to prepare it for me, so graciously. So how did I get here?"

"A rather circuitous route, let's say. Not so straightforward."

"I imagine not. Rather like the proverbial camel through the eye of a needle?"

Sophie smiled, nodded, sipped her wine.

"And my landing in 1975, the sinking of the *Cap Arcona*, that was straightforward?"

She sat back and sighed, a goddess's forbearance. Her eyes reached far away through the ages. In this instant, I felt that in the next, I would be in love with her. Again I wanted to reach for her hand, but stopped short at the stem of my wine glass. There were still a few bones to pick.

"That first time, I tried to bring you through but I botched it, as you know from your little misadventures that began soon after you landed in New Orleans."

"You mean, with Jake and Jim?"

"I was thinking more of Mobile. Your old dissolute, romantic predilections."

"Wait a minute. If you're referring to my libido, or whatever you call it in this century... I mean, what did you expect me to do?" Attempting an emphatic gesture, I slopped wine from my glass on the polished wood of the table. *Not my old coordination*, I thought.

"You're right," she said, "I'm hitting below the belt. The dishcloth's in the sink."

"To hell with the dishcloth." I felt wounded after that three-year ordeal she'd put me through, without a shred of tangible guidance or support.

"You feel I abandoned you on a strange shore, without aid or comfort."

Unearthly powers, she had. I felt both unnerved and intrigued.

She piled it on: "You feel I should have provided you with pro bono counseling, a chauffeur, an expense account? At least a credit card?"

"Yes, I do," I said, in a calmer voice. Then her confession of error sank in. I looked down at my green pants, patted my ample torso. "And this—who I am now—another mistake?"

"No, but you might say, a constellation of accidents."

"Ah, that's cute." I lifted my glass and drank a private toast to my former selves. "So are you saying I'm reincarnated?"

She gave an enigmatic head-wiggle. "Aren't we all?"

"I never fancied myself as a mystic," I said. "Nor the prop of an amateur magician's act."

Sophie pursued her lips and gazed at me impassive, chin

on hands.

"Let's go back to the *Cap Arcona*," I said. "What about all those other passengers who went down with the ship—and for that matter, the *Carthage Star* that went down in 1975, before the *David Livingstone* came along to rescue us. Were they all 'collateral damage,' as you Americans like to say?"

"I'm sorry about the loss of lives, but that wasn't my doing. The *Carthage Star* was going down anyway. And I wasn't authorized to save everyone on your ship either."

"Just me... and the others in the lifeboat."

"For the sake of your rescue. As for stranding you twenty years short, once you landed on that timeline, the Hierarchy deemed it best for you to stay on that track. They were upset with my bungling, but allowed you to stay for seasoning, if I was determined to have you in the end."

Sophie had begun stroking my calf under the table with her unslippered foot.

My irritation over being toyed with overshadowed the comfort of her touch. I didn't like the implications of 'Hierarchy.' Who was I to them? The record of my modest achievements—starting from scratch, at the very bottom of an unfamiliar society, then rising to serve a larger purpose in the ranks of the union—now struck me as tainted by an ulterior design.

Sophie elaborated. "I wanted to redo the lift right away. But it was deemed too important for you to complete your first stage of initiation, which you finally accomplished in Alaska. I went along with it, and at that point I considered your lessons sufficient. There was disagreement among some key observers of the Hierarchy, just so you know. It's not as if you have nothing left to learn."

"This Hierarchy," I replied. "You're working for them, or with them, I gather. What is it? Who are they?"

She yawned and stretched, pulling her hands back over her

head, and swelling her burgundy top out at me. "So many questions. Aren't you tired from your long journey?"

"I'm tired of being yanked around, through hell and back. I'm tired of dying, over and over, playing somebody's puppet theatre."

She remained silent, enigmatic, leaning back and finishing her wine, and placing her hands on the table between us.

My petulance waned as a dreamy expression graced Sophie's face. Her tawny skin was smooth and serene, her arched eyebrows relaxed and open.

I clasped my hands around hers. No smoke, no dust. Smooth, living flesh.

She slipped her hands out of my grasp, only to gather my hands in hers. "When your Learjet crashed in '78," she said, "I did manage finally to lift you straight through, in April of 1995, still a strapping twenty-three years old. We had a good thing going then for six months after your arrival."

"I was twenty-three, you were forty-five..."

Her tongue appeared, licking her upper lip. "Don't interrupt. The Hierarchy was not pleased at my customizing their retrieval program. They thought this young rake I was consorting with would destroy all the practical chance I had as a presidential candidate. The electorate still had then, as they do today, old-fashioned notions about what makes a proper romantic match."

"So what happened, then? You got yanked forward in time, but I got left behind, again..."

Even before she spoke I was flooded with the memory of a shattered train—body parts and twisted metal—and knew Sophie had perished with me.

"There was a terrorist attack on an Amtrak train in Arizona, resulting in different versions of ourselves getting recycled to this later date, for a different election cycle. The Hierarchy figured I'd have a better chance to make things go the way they wanted them. Too much was happening earlier, out of the blue."

"Terror attacks, you mean?"

"That wasn't exactly out of the blue."

"What do you mean?"

Her brow turned dark and with a twist of her head she swept the hair from one side to the other. She fingered a round black button inserted into an earlobe, and gazed away as if harking to another voice, before resuming her tale.

"Let's just say there were different factions operating within the Hierarchy. To answer your question, it's a working council of the most powerful players on this planet. They may be running things, but they still have individual egos, sometimes clashing opinions, competing agendas. The fallout from 1995 was, both you and I had to move to a different timeline, the one we're on now. This time you couldn't make it through in physical form; since your body was already less than fully substantial, given its previous two lifts from fatal accidents."

"The *Cap Arcona*, and the Learjet..."

"Correct. So what we're left now with is Felix's twenty-three-year-old spirit, so to speak, in an older body."

I looked down at my bulky torso, without recall of its recent history.

"Felix, meet Seymour Friedrickson, the alias you adopted from that ID you picked up in 1978. Who survived the Learjet crash on one possible timeline, when your plane bottomed out in a bog. You went on to become a successful union official and skidoo enthusiast, until a fatal accident on the river ice, in 1995—"

"At the ripe old age of forty."

"At least, your wardrobe, and that part of your history made it through—to merge with another avatar, call it, a physical reincarnation beginning life in 1995 after the same skidoo accident. Who became a rather staid academic advisor to my campaign team."

"Who is now also forty years old. That's this body, then."

"I'm afraid so."

I palmed my offensive duds. "Shouldn't I be getting back to *his* apartment, house, or—does he have a family?"

"No family, by design. The townhouse was torched earlier today. Panarchist protesters from your university, I'm told. "

"What? Anarchists? Why?" Though I felt no visceral connection to any such abode, or vocation, I felt indignant at the affront—then a wave of fear, a prickly sweat.

"No, Panarchists. They carried signs saying you were a stooge of the Hierarchy."

"Am I?"

"Not anymore." She smiled and stretched her hands behind her head, before stifling a fetching yawn.

"Are they going to try to lynch me, or what?"

"Don't worry. They say they're committed to nonviolence."

"Burning down people's houses?"

"It was planned as a symbolic action, when you were known to be out. They distinguish between violence to people and destruction of property. At least in their manifestos."

"What about my job? A chair at the university, seat on a commission? Do I have lectures to give, hearings to attend?"

"You're working for me now."

"Great. And what if they think you're a stooge of the Hierarchy?" I got up again and looked out the window to the street below, half expecting a crowd with pitchforks and torches.

"Listen, this building is secure, government level. Sit down, you ninny."

Flustered, I took my seat again. "Okay, fine. So what's my field of expertise?"

"The psychology of communications."

I wasn't aware of any such credentials, as such. Inside I felt more or less the same as I had on embarking on the Learjet from Anchorage, if somewhat shopworn. Pondering the convoluted mechanics of my transportation through time and space, life and death, I experienced a sudden craving for a cigar. I checked my pockets again and found remnants, bits of tan papery tobacco. I excused myself for a moment, found the bathroom down the hall. I needed to check my reflection in the mirror, take a closer look at who I really was now.

The intelligent eyes sat dimmer behind creases and folds. Eyebrows and nose perceptibly thicker; skin not so pretty-boy smooth. Yet the old Felix resided here still. That I knew for certain, calendars and extra pounds of flesh notwithstanding. Beneath this edifice of aging, my memories had transferred across the gap in the centuries—and bodies—as if I were the same person. It was I who had embarked from my family home to Paris and Portugal, a rogue's adventure; I who had played Huck Finn awhile, across the heartland of America. Other memories faded like dreams, or spun into fragments of black and gold, shunted in shadow.

The same character in the end, I aimed to please; I was willing to see what the great lady had in store for me, curious to see how she actually intended to use me. Whether bodily, or for my social charms, or my sagesse, or my talent for flying by the seat of my pants...

Surely it would all redound to my advantage—provided I watched my back. And trusted my life to her vaunted security.

I returned to find her pouring more Chardonnay. She had cleared the table, even wiped up my spillage.

"We'll have to do something about this suit of clothes," I said.

"I'll take you shopping in the morning." She approached and took my hand. "For now, let's get you out of them."

Though Sophie had displayed hints of physical affection toward me, she showed no interest in sex on our first night together. She undressed discreetly and changed to a simple cotton nightgown, lay beside me on the queen-sized bed and held her body at ease, her hand resting upon my thigh. I lay beside her, tentative, wondering, unsure of my own abilities in this older body, yet possessed of the eager curiosity of the younger soul. When I placed an exploratory hand upon her belly, she clasped it in hers, and held it there safely. My attempt at conversation was silenced by a finger upon my lips.

Beyond this undefined domestic union, the situation was far from simple. Who was this man, this woman, exactly? And how could we put the pieces of ourselves together in any coherent way, in mutual sympathy? And then to place ourselves on a national, which implied a global, stage!

The prospect, as yet unarticulated in its particulars, still held a definite appeal. If indeed I had already reached middle age, then my opportunity for realizing the fullness of my life ambitions had come within urgent proximity. Not that I had ever formulated such aspirations in detail; yet now I was inspired to think I might have something to contribute to the greater good.

And perhaps I could find a way to contribute to the happiness and success of this remarkable woman beside me. For now, at least, I had nowhere to go but to follow her lead. Gradually the whirlwind of my thoughts subsided, and lulled by Sophie's peaceful breathing, I drifted into a long, dreamless sleep.

In the morning I awoke content, in this novel arrangement, to be joined with Sophie at last, trusting in the sanction of destiny. While also anxious to know more of what was in store for us, as we dressed I was compelled by the more immediate concern which Sophie had voiced: upgrading my distasteful wardrobe.

Sophie cooked us a breakfast of soft-boiled eggs and English muffins with wild blackberry jam. I peered through the blinds in the charcoal tinted kitchen window, at a shadow-filtered sketch of a dull urbanscape, viewed from a height six stories up. Overcast sky, light traffic on the street... no overhead wires, but the naked poles were still standing. Blocky gray-brown office buildings and apartment towers loomed with their darkened windows in the near distance, flanked by parking lots and aged warehouses. A small wingless aircraft, a smooth metallic clam, glided across the sky.

"Here, the eggs are ready. Would you mind putting plates out for us?"

I did as I was told. Muttering to myself that I would be getting used to that.

"'From each according to his ability,' Sophie quipped, quoting my countryman Karl Marx. "I'll do the coffee."

She moved to the counter and worked the controls on a machine which produced a hiss of steam and the desired aroma. Finally, demitasses in hand, she sat down, moving those lithe limbs with animal grace into her chair.

I reached for the tiny china bowl of jam and began spreading it delicately. "You look much the same as I remember you," I said. "Did this Hierarchy lift you here from that train bombing in '95, the same as you lifted me?"

She took a large bite of muffin and jam, munching to draw out my curiosity. "Basically, yes. When I arrived, I had a forty-year-old-body already here to occupy, along with the apartment, and a resumé to fit their updated campaign agenda."

"Hmm. I thought you looked a bit younger."

"Right. Your resident *ka* was older than you were used to, mine was younger. Luck of the Irish."

"What did you call it—a *ka*?"

"Yes, the ancient Egyptian word for our life essence, which

also has the connotation of a double. Think of as a kind of spiritual clone. For both of us those new bodies were birthed as fresh reincarnations from our deaths in 1995. Last spring my original astral body was brought forward as well, to merge with the newer receptor body."

"Ohh-kayy." I sat back to savor the homemade macchiato, and to assimilate this concept of merging identities. Maybe, I reflected, it was not new to me after all; since I'd been practicing with the Marquis de Venosta at the doubles game since before Einstein.

There was more to the story I wasn't getting. "The Hierarchy was behind all this? Trying again, after our campaign forty years ago was sabotaged?"

"After I died in the train bombing, another me had to grow up with a real identity in the twenty-first century. It wouldn't have worked to have plunked a hotshot presidential candidate into this timeline from nowhere, which is to say, another timeline. There would have been too many questions."

"So this reincarnated Sophie has a role in politics already, in Congress like before...?"

"Yes, it's the same drill the Hierarchy likes; we just needed a fresh do-over."

"What about me? If I'm going to be a key part of your campaign... or is that still part of the deal?"

"Absolutely. Although it's a bit of a workaround this time. Your identity as Seymour is a kind of cloaking of your Felix ka."

I felt slighted, an affront to my pride that triggered a deeper pang of resentment—being robbed of my youth.

Sophie mimicked my pout. "The thing is, 'Felix Krull' is still too notorious, thanks to your overzealous biographer. Besides that, the pronunciation is tricky; it definitely wouldn't do to have such a close associate of the president confused with the English word 'cruel'—or worse yet, a kind of pastry."

"Very funny."

"Seriously, you do have a prison record someone might look up."

"Listen, I covered myself on that one by registering as a Mr. Charles Ready. Speaking of ghosts. Didn't you know that?"

"Of course I knew it. But some records go deeper than the official layer of data current at the time. The point is, you're here, fully qualified as far as I'm concerned; and I'm the one calling the shots now."

I asked how Sophie got her precious Hierarchy to agree to this arrangement in the first place—having a consort of such intimate influence, of my dubious character and resumé.

She explained that at the time, back in '94, they had trusted her to manage the data search. She had filtered for certain characteristics well noted already in this chronicle, producing the singular result, this young cosmopolitan phenom, a con-man extraordinaire. Proving adept at moving in high society, of stealing jewels or seducing heiresses with equal aplomb, as Felix Krull I had qualified for the chance to prove myself in an arena of far greater import.

As for any more personal, or romantic interest, was there anything left to be desired in this paunchy, grizzled version of my former self?

She had, at least, invited me into her bed.

"No family, for you?" I asked. "No special man?"

Sophie's tongue flicked at a dab of jam on the corner of her mouth. What a lovely mouth, purpled with berry. Hovering at the far edge of my addled brain was a dim memory of a woman and a cat disappearing into a dark wood.

"On this timeline I did have a child," she said. "He's in the custody of his father."

"Oh?"

"A short but unpleasant story," she said, "for another time. But you will meet them both."

Were we really ready to appear in public yet... meeting staff, family and friends; browsing the grocery aisles, sipping lattes in cafes? Or did Sophie's sort of elite—the Hierarchy—keep aloof from all that, the street life of the common folk, riddled apparently with subversion?

The funhouse ride was about to begin, and I had no choice but to trust my driver.

I licked the last bits of foam from my cup. "I know I must seem ungrateful," I confessed to her. "But I do appreciate your efforts on my behalf."

Sophie folded her arms on the breakfast table and sighed, looking at me with large eyes. "I'm glad to hear that, finally."

My calf registered the first touch of a new game of footsie. That combined with the warm intensity of her gaze made me feel self-conscious, in my gauche impostor's outfit.

"Sophie, are you sure you're ready for me?"

She sat reflecting for a moment, then answered calmly, "Are you sure you're ready for me?"

As I pondered my response, she stood up from the table and began loading plates and cups into the dishwasher.

"I—"

"No worries. We'll get you up to speed. Right now, we've got some shopping to do."

CHAPTER II

From the elevator in Sophie's apartment building we entered a short tunnel which took us to a subway. Sleeker, smoother, and faster than the transit system I had ridden on occasion in the Bay Area—now the trains hovered over a magnetic rail—it was still, as in eighty years before that, a matter of people riding a rail car. The populace appeared fatigued, dispirited, as they slumped against the tinted windows, attention obscured behind dark glasses and wireless earnodes, outfits running the usual gamut from shabby workclothes to snazzy suits.

Sophie told me on the ride that I would need a pair of sunglasses for the above-ground sections of the route, and she handed me a spare pair of hers, squarish and unisex. At first I thought she had in mind my new role as a political aide, and the need for us to move discreetly in public. She explained rather that we had to avoid direct sunlight because of the widespread thinning of the earth's ozone layer. As for her notoriety, she allowed that being a member of the Congress of the United States no longer carried the prestige it once had.

"Even when you're a candidate for president?"

"We haven't officially announced yet. It's coming. But as for security, we're covered, mate."

Her eyes darted to the camera lens in the rail car, then outside the window where a pair of the flying clams kept pace.

I said to her, "You've been through all this before, right?"

"Yup, different body, different constituency, different timeline. You were there too, but you don't recall much, since it was your second lift. A thinning of the ka. *En tout cas*, now it's a new ball game."

"But same old Sophie, right?"

"You betcha," she said, squeezing my hand.

Outside where the rail line passed, neighborhoods lay vacant, factories boarded up. The war industries, Sophie told me, had been outsourced overseas, "to the colonies." She gave me to understand that since 2005 America had considered itself a proper empire, and had set about remaking the globe's economics and politics accordingly.

"Not that we didn't act like that from the beginning," she added. "But for the last thirty years the ruling class has stopped apologizing for it, and taken to bragging about it. Plus, technology has made it easier to accomplish, even as resources are stretched thinner."

"Ruling class? I thought—"

"Don't you remember your schoolboy socialism from the seventies?"

"You mean that Anchorage rag, *The Sentinel*? Hey, I was twenty-three."

"Yes, and cutting your political teeth. Gotta get you upgraded here."

"To the latest ruling class? The Hierarchy?"

She shot me a dark look and put a finger to her lips.

The subway hummed to a stop at the entrance to an underground mall. Apart from its obvious architectural advancement as a kind of vast molded hive, I found the human world inside not so very different from the one I had left behind, half a century before. Amid the the spangle of obligatory tinsel glittering toward Christmas, shoppers strolled past the predictable assortment of boutiques and department stores, carrying bags of purchases, eating snacks, stopping to talk to acquaintances. The muzak was maddeningly unchanged, as if the same interminable cassette tape of schmaltzy seasonal pop, with brief respites of "classic rock" from the 1960s and '70s, had been running continuously, and would continue whispering through its auto-reverse cycles forever. Once more the most telling innovation was the ubiquitous device in everyone's hand, or on their wrist, or embedded in the upper portion of their sunglass lenses. My own lenses lacked such enhancements, but I felt neither envy nor deprivation.

Fashions of dress, which long ago had been for me a matter of personal and fastidious pride, appeared no more outlandish here than those that first met my astonished eyes on the deck of the *Cap Arcona*. Yet people gave me strange looks as they passed, wrinkling their noses. Sophie opined that it was likely the tobacco smell lingering about me that drew attention. I noticed nobody smoked, as such—except I saw frequent use of what Sophie called a virtual cigarette, which people would pull from a pocket, place to their lips, and then discard in a recycling bin. "Smokeless vapor," she explained, "in a variety of herbal flavors."

In a menswear shop I let Sophie choose for me a most respectable blue suit, and a tan one with a muted check pattern, along with conventional dress shirts, ties, slacks, shoes and socks, underwear, and an assortment of casual wear. What I found remarkable was the absence of any cultural advancement whatever in the realm of businessmen's attire, over the preceding decades: the same cut of shirt and coat collar; the same barbaric, obligatory necktie. I resigned myself to it, as an actor dons the requisite costume.

We stopped in a juice bar near the rear mall exit and I picked up the thread of our previous conversation, curious about that black hole in my memory, the timeline ending in the train bombing of 1995.

"I could fill you in on all the gory details," Sophie said, "but it's rather immaterial now."

"Humph. So are we immaterial now, too? I mean, if a

timeline, as you call it, can just go poof, and give way to another one, or infinite number of them, what's the point of any of them? Of any of it?"

"Of life, you mean?" Sophie's hands wrapped around a tumbler of EnerZest, bright magenta. "We're stuck with the one we have, hon, at any given time. In the big picture, sure, who cares? We're here now; and on this plane, it does matter, big time. It's all we've got to work with, at any given time."

I sipped at a glowing green concoction at once bitter and sweet, you might say sickeningly healthy.

"All right, philosophically I get it. I think. But in terms of who I am now—"

"Okay, think of it like this. At every death there are actually three possibilities. One being that you don't die at all, but survive—as you did, Seymour, from your crash landing in the bog."

"But I died anyway—what, seventeen years later—in the skidoo accident."

"Yes and no. Again your lifeline branched three ways from that critical node. With one branch, you can get lifted, plucked from the realm of limbo the Tibetans call the bardo."

"Plucked?"

"We have discovered how to manipulate that transition, through what we call astral technology, the Lifelines program. The tricky part is, you have to have a suitable receptor ka."

"Like our friend Seymour, the union guy?"

"Well, his reincarnation. Since that fool died forty years ago in the skidoo accident."

"I won't argue that point." But I kicked her shin under the table.

She stuck her tongue out at me.

I forgave her both petty offenses, when there were graver matters to resolve. "What about at the beginning, when I drowned and got lifted to 1975—did I invade the live body of an anonymous twenty-year-old?"

"He happened to be a passenger on the *Carthage Star*, who survived that sinking—"

"But ended up wearing my clothes."

"I think the program designers put too much weight on that old saw, "Clothes make the man.""

"Oh but they do! Thank you, by the way, for these purchases."

"Thank my paymasters."

"I will, when you introduce me to them. But tell me, who was this lucky kid who suddenly received the spirit of the famous Felix Krull..."

"None other than the reincarnation of another famous man who died in 1955, at the ripe old age of eighty."

"Let me guess. A famous author, by any chance?"

"A certain memoirist, of sorts."

"This is getting rather incestuous."

"It is, rather."

Sophie glanced around, fingered the device on her ear. Scanned the passersby. Pigeons scavenged for crumbs under our table. "Go on to the restaurant across the street," she scolded them. "They only serve juice here." Then to me: "Stupid pigeons. Genetic engineering for certain traits—like mooching—at the expense of others. The way of the world."

"Stick with me on this, Sophie. Further back. There must have been another reincarnation, a fresh conception, from the branch of myself that didn't survive the *Cap Arcona* but drowned when it sank in 1895."

"That's right. Do you remember an old gentleman by the name of Paulo Weismann, a passenger on the *David Livingstone*?"

"Indeed I do. Eighty years old at the time. Quite a talker.

Born in 1895..."

"There you go."

We left the juice bar and rode an escalator, emerging by an old railway station, bound for a workout at a nearby gym. The sun shone weakly through a milky haze. A pair of tiny MagCar cruised past, teardrop bubbles of tinted glass, hovering a foot off the center lanes of the roadway—for official vehicles only, Sophie said. Crossing the roadway barriers between intersections was forbidden. The sidewalks had dedicated lanes for pedestrians, bicycles, motorized stand-up scooters. Absent were the ubiquitous destitute "street people" as I had encountered in New Orleans, Mobile, Oakland, Anchorage. I asked Sophie about security in these urban neighborhoods.

"No problem here," she told me. "This is a safe zone."

A beep sounded on her person, and Sophie looked around, as if expecting someone. Indeed, a man in a black suit nodded from across the street, and Sophie excused herself from my side, saying, "I'll just be a minute. It's Robert." She looked both ways, stepped over the thirty-inch-high barrier and strode across the roadway to meet him.

For an instant I thought I saw in the slick black hair of this character, the angular set of his features, the figure of Senhor Miguel Hurtado, with aviator shades instead of wire-rims. His ka, perhaps?

Who was I then, a bit player in a Cold War spy thriller, a postmodern epic? A host of questions dogged me, hydra-heads springing in multiplicity from each one tentatively answered.

Pacing with hands in my new pockets, I gazed at the gray mundanity of the station abandoned to the pigeons and graffiti. Beyond rose the skyline of a once-shiny city, symbol of worldly desires.

America's representative form of government, I mused, represented what, exactly? Riches, power, control itself?

Sophie was elusive on the matter, and perhaps herself was allowed restricted access to the true picture.

If the Hierarchy indeed had chosen her for the all-powerful position of president... why her? With all this Lifelines business taken into account, she could well be living out the blueblooded legacy of another lineage altogether.

The main in black gazed fixedly at me with his insectoid sunglasses, as Sophie spoke to him with animated gestures. Finally he nodded to her and strode off, and she crossed back to my side, swishing her flared brown pants as she dodged a tooting MagCar with no visible driver. Alarmed, I pointed out the danger to Sophie and she shrugged, saying not to worry, as the controls and safety measures were automated.

"So what was all that about?"

"That was Robert Glaston, my ex. He wanted to meet you and I told him not yet. There's a meeting of the campaign committee in three days. He can meet you then."

"You mean he's part of the deal, we'll be working with this guy?"

"Oh, Jesus. You're still twenty-three emotionally, aren't you? Honestly, I can't stand the jerk. But yes, he's in line for CEO."

"CEO of what?"

"The country."

"Good lord, it's come to that."

"Don't worry, we'll still have the power. As long as we can keep the Panarchists at bay."

"And they are a danger why, exactly?"

"They are decentralists, basically, opposed to world order."

"You mean the New World Order?" I had heard this term bandied about during my stint in federal prison.

"We don't use that label anymore. It's not new, and it carries a lot of baggage. We try to make it simpler. It's a matter of Order versus Anarchy—or Panarchy, as our opponents would have it."

"*We*, meaning the Hierarchy, no doubt."

"Smart boy. C'mon, it's time to train you up."

CHAPTER III

The session with weights and laps in the pool served as a warmup to the real work ahead—my orientation in recent history and politics, contemporary economy and technology. Sophie had sequestered this time away from her congressional duties for the occasion of my arrival and briefings. Our lessons were confined to the privacy of her apartment, over cups of coffee, glasses of wine, catered meals ordered in, and home-cooked dishes when she felt inspired.

As a first step, my mentor introduced me to the remarkable world of the computer. What realms of power and knowledge undreamt of by previous generations! What nerve, to attempt, and largely succeed, in creating the semblance of an intelligent being, from a few bits of copper, gold and silicon! In a room in her apartment designated as an office, Sophie had several computer devices—troves of information and processing power accessed by wafer-thin tablets that could be stretched or trimmed to display a variety of sizes of screen. I say accessed rather than held, for these were but the vehicles of interface between the querying human and the unlimited potential of cyberspace—wherein I was bid to imagine the aforesaid data and programs resided.

And if all that potential swirled about us ready to be called into form at the whim of a fingertip on a film of colored plastic, what did that say about the nature of so-called reality, I wanted to know.

Sophie grinned and said, "Indeed. Now put that fingertip on the spot there, and the system will recognize you and log you in from now on."

She walked me through the basics, then the more advanced functions. She had personal files covering everything from political history to economic theory, from wallpaper designs to quiche recipes.

"What about the Lifelines program?" I asked.

"What about it?"

"Do you have access to it here, on your devices?"

She hesitated, then realized she had to tell me the truth. "Of course—that's how I brought you in to this time, arranged the merger of your kas."

"Can I see it?"

"Absolutely not. It carries the highest classification, as it should since it deals with matters of life and death. No, our task is more elementary, now that you're here. You have a lot of learning, basic knowledge and information to catch up on, so you can hit the ground running."

And so, quickly mastering the childishly simple operations of the computer interface, I bent to the task at hand. Suffice it to say, the American empire, taking shape so tentatively after the debacle of Vietnam, reached its peak in the decade from the fall of the Soviet Union to the attacks on the Twin Towers. From there a series of bloody misadventures in the Middle East, Eastern Europe and Africa had reduced America's might to a largely covert, privatized operation focused on securing critical infrastructure and controlling energy resources. Dramatic advances in free energy technologies might have meant an end to poverty, but so far such innovations as the hydrogen-powered aircar were confined to use by the elite, who cited prohibitive costs for mass production and distribution.

Global warming, species extinction, the poisoning of air and water and denaturing of food, all were rampant, unchecked since the 1970s. Some hope remained, Sophie assured me, in the earth's native resilience, as the very excesses and inequalities that had caused these problems had exhausted civilization's capacity to continue its crimes against nature at the same rate.

Domestically politics had evolved, or devolved, to a one-party system. The merger of 2024 resulted from reform efforts meant to reduce the influence of the big-money lobbyists. In fact the moneyed interests, with a unitary politics anyway from their point of view, were happy to dispense with the wasteful competition of campaign funding and would save big bucks in the bargain.

Public dissent was monitored and quashed, in the name of national security, by appropriate means: controls on computer networking, squeezes of digital cashflow, privatized prisons and, when deemed necessary, assassination—covert or public, depending on the required spin. Security forces, stretched thin in a reeling economy, were prioritized for essential areas— corporate safe zones and gated enclaves of the affluent. The rest of the citizenry were left to fend for themselves, subject to damage control.

"If they wish to run their rusty generators on rancid veggie oil," Sophie told me late that first afternoon, "it's their right. Or at least, it's not worth our manpower to shut them down."

"So where does all this leave us? Would you attempt to revive the imperial heyday of the US, or just hold on as we slide into the dustbin of history?"

"First of all," she chided me, "I would cut the negative thinking. Yes, you. Here's what I'm thinking the platform will be. Number one, democracy for all people, everywhere. No more petty chieftains, tribal fiefdoms, pariah states. Free trade across the board. A global order of authority and enforcement to protect human rights. Robust geoengineering to manage climate change. Universal data collection..."

"Wait a minute. You're talking global, not national?"

"National is so twentieth century. We're in a different political landscape now, demanding we step up to lead the way into a final world order."

"And if some of the old nations don't want to play along?"

"We convince them."

"And this time, by *we* you mean..."

"You and me, babe."

I gulped the end my coffee, nearly choked. "What about the Panarchists?"

She sighed, rising from the couch with the empty cups, and said it was time to switch to wine. I watched her sinuous back, the silk blouse with the blue floral pattern, the cascading hair, and visualized our impending lessons in the tantric arts. Far easier to contemplate that conquest than the coercion of sovereign states, well armed in the bargain.

The Panarchists, she told me over glasses of chilled Sauvignon, were founded by a charismatic rebel, Edward Jensen, a former professor who had been sacked from his position at Harvard for alleged sexual misconduct. Had the young lady in question been a bona fide student, innocent in her own right, the charges might have rung true; but a leaked source tied her to the Hierarchy, and the professor, though forced to leave his post, went underground to serve as the leading thinker and voice behind the growing decentralist movement.

True to their philosophy, Sophie told me, the Panarchists shunned central organization, preferring a loose affiliation of action cells, public and private interest groups, issue-based advocates for change.

"Why did they abandon the standard political system?" I asked.

"At first they were divided. Jensen would have been a strong candidate. But after his assassination, they claimed the system was rigged, in favor of the megacorps, the figureheads of the elite, and they presented evidence to win popular support. They claimed it was a Hierarchy hit, of course."

"And was it?"

She hesitated, a damning pause. "Who knows? After that, they refused even to try to marshal their support into electoral politics. Instead they mounted a campaign of resistance: boycotts, sabotage, strikes. Which are ongoing." She drained the rest of her glass. "What shall we order for dinner?"

Sophie, it appeared, was the good face of a lurking darkness—either the Hierarchy's unwitting servant, or wiser than I credited her. I wanted to bet on the latter; but would I find her any more benevolent, when it came to the crunch, than the heads of the old Soviet state or their Eastern European satellites? She put a shiny American twist on an old formula: domination of resources and markets; central control enforced by the usual methods honed so well by mafias everywhere—the carrot and the stick. Bribery and blackmail. Subsidies and penalties. The machinery of government, grinding its way forward through history, over a landscape littered with broken bones, shattered lives.

The global grid of data and regulation were imposed, like a net upon the ocean, within whose mesh all but the smallest fish would swim caught. Those tiny or clever enough to shapeshift their way through the matrix would survive in a different reality, a paradigm of freedom. Hearing about those pesky Panarchists, I wondered aloud what such a society would look like.

Sophie dismissed the alternative philosophy out of hand. "Well, if chaos is your cup of tea. I know you're familiar with the Dark Ages. Or perhaps you prefer the Golden Age of the noble Neanderthal."

"God save us," I replied. "Or perhaps it is the Hierarchy I should thank for its small favors, our collective salvation."

Evening sessions were devoted to personal development, in astral travel and the tantric arts. I was both excited at these prospects for advancement, and full of trepidation at my unknown capacities in this borrowed husk of a body, my very name a concoction. When dream-control was mastered, we would go on to astral projection. From there, to contact with other astral bodies. Naturally the dream training and sexual training overlapped to a large degree; and by the same token, all our spiritual exercises could be considered, as a methodology of control and inroad to power, an essential preparation for the coming entry into the political arena.

Sophie began informally, guiding me in the art of conscious intervention into the dream state—the elementary training ground for those destined for the higher arts of fate engineering. I had once, while still in my teen years, become practiced in the art of lucid, or what may be called conscious dreaming. Since then, however, I had been less than diligent in maintaining the necessary breathing exercises, and thus had let my dream-life slip back into the more common realms of nightmare and symbolic sideshow. Now I found I was quickly able to learn the techniques Sophie taught me. Within a short time I could move from subconscious to lucid dreaming almost at will.

I say *almost*, because conscious dreaming was subject to more than mere will; it occurred spontaneously, in flashes at first, and gradually in longer periods. Once the flash of awareness came, it was theoretically a simple matter to sustain it, enhancing the initial thrust of fate with a boost of agreeing power, directed from within. The whole procedure was highly delicate, however, and, as Sophie cautioned me, subject to instant dissolution at the first hint of morbid motives, greedy curiosity, or even aloof detachment. When that happened I slipped back into a land of slumbering images, where dreams could be dark and empty places, unrecognizable then or after.

Under Sophie's tutelage, I intensified the nightly exercises: practicing special breathing routines, twisting into a variety of sacred postures, telling myself by repetitions of certain

Sanskrit murmurings that I was increasing my vibration rate, that I was progressing, that I was about to leave my poor fleshly shell of a body behind to embark on a journey which would lead me, among other destinations, directly into avenues of genuine world power.

Lest the reader be misled by a claim of such ambition, conjuring the trappings of political hierarchy by whatever name, I must qualify my goal in its true perspective. The truth is that by now I was at least relatively free of selfish motives.

I was not content, for instance, merely to pursue this love affair which Sophie had dropped in my lap gratis, without a full understanding of its place in my spiritual journey. I was also not interested in the worldly worship which accrues to positions of power, but rather chose to merge my own resources with the wider sources of power in society, in the world, and to be fully honest, in the universe at large. In short, I was not after the power that corrupts, but the power, if I may say so, that uplifts.

It took a few days of Sophie's "spiritual exercises," and nights of clumsy negotiation, before we actually engaged in what goes by the common term *sex*. It was unsettling to be invited into such a liaison, with the outcome predetermined, yet delayed by such mechanisms as were imposed by Sophie.

"Love me with your soul," she instructed, "as well as with your body."

"That's no problem."

"Let's try to look at sex as the prelude to spiritual communion."

"I'm game. When do we start?"

"First we have to prepare the energy body with a toning of the chakras."

I had a bedroom reputation to live up to, made difficult by the fact that I now had a forty-year old engine under the hood.

While I had always prided myself on my erotic proficiency, those charms of the nineteenth and twentieth centuries fell useless next to Sophie's mocking.

"Don't you know about the G spot?"

I stammered. "Uh, apparently not."

She guided me to the tender terrain, instructed me on the flow of breath, the channel of *chi*, the use of the *nadis*, the PC pump.

"With the advanced techniques, you can expect to have a most reliable command of your sexual apparatus. Not to mention an improved understanding of its female counterpart, which, you will find, can be so much more refined, the orgasm so much more transcendent, than the primitive male version."

"Uh-huh."

She insisted I restrain myself from full gratification, concentrating instead on the management of internal energy circuits, both within my body and in the field we created between us. The simplistic concept of orgasm took on new dimensions, subtler, sustained. The female body, hers quite fit and shapely, transformed from an object of desire to a flux of dynamic possibility.

Worked to a suitable pitch by such preliminaries, together we rose on waves of bliss and subsided in troughs of purring contentment. It made me question all my old notions of what love was or could be; humbled my stiff male ego into a more malleable, shapeless form—neither male nor female, exactly, rather more like a union of animal and vegetative essence. I began to know what it is to make love to a woman in the deepest part of her soul; to make love to the universe.

One result of such disciplined sexual practice proved to be an alert wakefulness, unfamiliar to such as myself who previously succumbed to the predictable routine of release and enervation, dullness and sleep. Still buzzing in bed in the wee hours, I asked Sophie to tell me more about my astral lineage. I got that my younger self had been transposed upon an older body; but what about the alternative timelines? Was I living at this moment also in other bodies, Felix fragmented and never to be found again in one body, one soul?

Sophie murmured, perhaps not as alert just then; but she indulged my curiosity, turning on her side and propping that love-smoothed face on a hand.

"Let's go back to 1995," she said.

"Wait—"

"No, I mean in tracing your lines. I was ready for you then, in the run-up to the 1996 election. I fed the coordinates into your Lifelines file for a dry run, but I didn't like what I saw. I would get the leftovers from the 1978 plane crash—the alternate ka who survived, a yuppie union man who played a pretty good game of golf and enjoyed the occasional vacation, and native mistress, in beautiful Alaska."

"And whose idea of fun was riding a skidoo in a red snowsuit over a half-frozen lake."

"That's part of it, not the end of it. Naturally the Hierarchy preferred this more conventional, more mature Felix to join me for the run at the presidency. But there was another ka who showed up on the screen just before I signed off. Called himself 'Harry the Hacker.' He was the reincarnated ka arising from the ashes of the plane crash—"

"You mean the bubbles."

"Don't interrupt. I was wondering why I hadn't been able to call this one up. He was filed under another name. In fact, he told me, the Hierarchy had tried to delete him from your file. But he knew something about computers himself, and had inserted a bit of security code, encrypting himself, as it were, so he could live on, invisibly—"

"—in binary format. Right. Is this ever getting bizarre."

Sophie went on with her story: "So this new entity,

seventeen years old, whom I knew only from his communication with me on the computer screen, gave me the quick-lift code from the classified files of the Hierarchy."

"By quick lift, you mean a direct time-jump, saving me from a fiery death?"

"Or watery grave, take your pick."

"Except it didn't work," I said. "That timeline didn't pan out."

"Oh, it did, for a while. But in the process, you see, there was no death by plane crash, and so no physical rebirth as Harry the Hacker. A virtual self-sacrifice."

"A noble lineage," I remarked.

"I can't believe your flippancy. Do you realize we're going to be running this country, in a very short time, managing all the serious affairs of state, international trade and development, the exploration of outer space—"

"And inner space," I added, touching a finger to her lower lip.

"Anyway," she said, "the lift of the twenty-three-year-old Felix is the person you still identify with most, am I right?"

"Most definitely. Despite this midriff bulge you saddled me with, and the rest of the, er, equipment."

"Am I complaining? I think you're doing quite nicely, considering."

I continued stroking her lips gently with a fingertip. "I appreciate the feedback," I said, and felt my interest perking up again as she responded with the tip of her tongue. "Are you suggesting—"

"It's late," she told me. "Let's get some sleep."

On the third day, an afternoon session in bed, I asked, "Sophie, what kind of lovers are you used to having?"

"You're the first since... since Robert."

"Robert, eh. And what exactly did you see in him?"

She sniffed and a small animal sound escaped her throat. "You don't want to know. Now, Seymour, come to me, closer; I want you."

"Are you sure this time? Am I on the right track?"

"Yes... yes... no, wait—let's bring it down for a bit. Breathe. Breathe with me."

"I'm breathing, I'm breathing."

She bounced out of bed and yanked the bedclothes away from me.

"Hey!" I had no choice but to bounce after her—into the cold shower, where we fought like otters over the single bar of soap.

After we toweled each other dry, Sophie pressed herself behind me and circled my chest with her arm. Her husky voice in my ear said, "Come with me back to bed, and make love to me now in your way, will you?"

Afterwards, I reflected that I was content with my fate. I didn't feel like a collection of warring zombies; I felt like my old self—that is, my young self, mellowed with age. I was satisfied with the survival of my sexual powers, and evidently Sophie was, too. But when our couple of hours of amorous, languorous bliss had subsided, when we had, in effect, returned to our separate bodies, I found I was still preoccupied with questions needing answers.

With Sophie lying half-dozing beside me, I chose perhaps the wrong moment to grill her further. On the other hand I sensed that her vulnerable state might offer more answers than usual about her true motivations.

So I said, "Tell me, sweetheart, what does this Hierarchy of yours want to accomplish? What is their plan for the world?"

"Hmmm? Oh, it's not their plan, exactly. They are only a body of overseers—bureaucrats on the etheric plane—who are trying to carry out the Akashic Plan."

"Which is?"

She drew a long, slow breath, and sat up free of the sheet, bringing both hands up to busy themselves in her tousled hair. A fine distraction, I thought. She looked at me but declined to speak, instead covering a yawn.

"Is there an issue of classified information?"

"No, that's fine," she said. "It's a basic question. The Akashic Plan is the Hierarchy's agenda based on the Akashic Records, which contain everything that has been done, said, or even thought."

"For everyone?"

"Correct. And not only past events, but future history, as well."

"Really. Then the Plan is not a plan at all, but a narrative that has already happened—in the future—and been recorded?"

"That's one way to put it. There are still multiple timelines to draw from, though, not just one certain future."

"So there is some choice involved, in setting policy. Otherwise we're wasting our time here, right?"

"We do have some choice, yes." With that, she swung her legs to her side of the bed and rose to dress.

I couldn't shake my feeling of resentment, of being cut out of the loop. I said, "Or, maybe, as a good politician, you're not at liberty to say—at least, not at this point in time."

She pulled on a light orange, sleeveless top and turned to look at me with a hurt expression, saying, "Look, I don't know what your problem is with them." Then she rattled off the answer like an automaton: "The Hierarchy is serving the cause of spiritual evolution. Their necessary mission is to combat the Dark Forces, so human potential has the chance to be realized."

"The Dark Forces?"

"The Panarchists would be the contemporary example."

"Oh, that bugaboo again." I turned to my own side of the bed and began to dress. As with all matters political, I suspected the epithet "Dark," like the fearful labels of bygone times—"terrorist," "barbarian," "infidel"—was not so much an objective descriptor, but rather a projection of one's own bias of self-justification. "And if there were no benevolent Hierarchy," I said then, "if we poor creatures wallowing here in our own muck on earth were left to our own desires and devices, we wouldn't stand a chance: is that it?"

Sophie buttoned her white slacks. "I'm afraid it is."

"Does the plan say we'll make it, or not?"

"It could go either way. It depends on what we humans decide to make of our possibilities."

"Then it's up to us! What good is this Hierarchy, then?"

"To remind us of the path we're on, the probable outcomes of our actions, our true goals and our temporary illusions. And sometimes we need a little divine intervention to give us a chance to make up for our mistakes, so we don't get ourselves killed in the process of learning."

"Though, of course, many do make fatal mistakes. And sometimes those mistakes are fatal for others."

Sophie's brow darkened and she left me in the bedroom to finish dressing.

CHAPTER IV

That night we went out for an intimate candlelight dinner in a posh downtown restaurant. Sophie possessed neither MagCar nor aircar, so we rode on a sleek, marvelously quiet elevated rail-bus over the downtown streets. Constructed of lightweight alloys and organic plastics, this new generation of urban transit vehicles ran on a variety of power systems and fuels, including hydrogen, synthetic hydrocarbon and hemp-derivative alcohol. Sophie pointed out, on the roadway below, a couple of fancy-looking rides which could have driven out of the old Batman comic strips, and said these private vehicles, which dwarfed the bubbly MagCars, were owned by a few superstar athletes, entertainers, financiers.

The rail-bus whispered to a stop. We got out and walked the last couple of blocks. I reveled in the starry sky, the clear cold air scented of kelp from Puget Sound. The streets were decked out with all the reds and greens of the coming holiday.

Over a prettily arranged but stringy quail teriyaki, Sophie filled me in on more details of the current political scene at the national level. My first campaign meeting was scheduled for the next day, to begin a series of weekly strategizing sessions over lunch with the Party brass. From the sound of it, the electoral system ran much the same as before, despite the merger of the Republican and Democratic parties, long recognized as essentially branches of the same Big Money tree. There were still several months of primaries coming up in the first half of the new year, followed by a nominating convention at the end of July. The position of Vice President had been done away with at the time of the party merger, replaced by a Chief Executive Officer, appointed by the Hierarchy. And the Electoral College had also been ditched, gone the way of the eagle and the Edsel.

One candidate would emerge from the convention and go before the people for a final election. To win, to be officially voted into office, the candidate had to capture a majority of the popular vote. That is, more people voting "yes" than those voting "no." The same rules applied in each congressional race.

"What if, say, fifty-one percent of the people don't vote at all?" I wanted to know.

"Of course," Sophie said, while vigorously chewing, "then it's up to the handful of eligible voters who actually turn out on Election Day. That's always been the case in principle. It's the responsibility of the voters. If twenty percent, or even two percent, of the electorate chooses to exercise their right, and the rest sit on their asses, it's the ass-sitters' own problem. Nobody's going to hold their hands and..." Sophie paused to swallow the wad of masticated meat.

"Walk them to the polling booth?"

"Oh, silly, are you kidding? All they have to do is punch a button on their smartpad. And even so, in the last election where there was anything resembling a real choice, under the old party system, only nineteen percent of the eligible voters saw fit to wiggle their index fingers in the direction of the designated button."

"Maybe they thought it might blow up the world."

"Very funny. Have you finished with your quail? I wouldn't mind some more. They're awfully small."

I gave her a piquant drumstick no larger than my thumb. The restaurant was divided into discrete areas separated by Japanese-paper partitions, so I didn't have to worry about any presidential-level etiquette.

Nor did Sophie. She started right in, gnawing on her new bone.

Between bites she continued, "So when it came time to write the new act, the savants who did so knew enough not to require an absolute majority of the population, but only of those voting."

"And what happens if it's a 'no' vote?"

"Hasn't happened."

"I mean, what's the provision for it? The backup plan. Who takes office, then?"

"It goes back to the process."

"You mean the convention, the primaries? Or backroom deals?"

"It's not going to happen. Just because of that."

"I see. The so-called voters get it that there's really one choice, which is another way of saying no choice at all."

"Seymour, do I have to go through this again? You can call up the congressional records if you really want to get into the arguments. If you're going to make any kind of contribution to American political history you'll have to understand the background. There was virtually no difference between the two old parties anyway. The former elections were no more meaningful than they would be if I ran against a clone of myself; just read the campaign speeches. The real battles took place in the primaries and on the floor of the convention."

"Then my role is to maintain that public window dressing, to pretend there are real issues at stake—?"

"Oh the issues are real, all right. It's the process that's more perfunctory than ever. We still have to garner a 'yes' vote."

"Is there competition inside the Party?"

At this Sophie patted her mouth with a linen napkin, took a deep breath and settled back in her chair. "There's a certain amount of jockeying at the top, between the factions of the Hierarchy. But I'm the consensus choice: "a pretty face for the Party," some call it. As for the local level, where issues are live and current, the seats are hotly contested, by the brightest new, charismatic people. Meanwhile national politics has kind of withered, without the intensity of the old party rivalries."

"Yet you're still committed to it."

"To assume the highest office in the land, hell yeah. But I must say, it's a darker time now, than back in '94, '95. Not the same thrill to get there. And then at the top—"

"There must be compensations, some challenges to make it worthwhile, personally—or are you doing it for the Hierarchy?"

Sophie looked at me with piercing black eyes, her chestnut hair raven-black in the shadows. For an instant, politics evaporated to a wisp, a figment. This woman before me was hauntingly, bewitchingly beautiful.

Her lashes fluttered and she reached her fingers to rest on the stem of her wine glass. "I know you asked that as an honest, objective question. And it's a good one. I'm not sure how to answer."

Our waitress picked this moment to appear and ask if we wanted anything else. We said no and she disappeared again.

Sophie had gathered a few of her thoughts and was able to continue: "I must tell you I share some of your, how shall I say, healthy skepticism about the Hierarchy's aims. Certainly I've had my share of run-ins with them. I do believe in their higher purposes. And they seem to believe I'm the person best able to carry out the larger plan. As for the state of political evolution in this country at the moment—I think we are at a kind of crossroads. The rest of the world has gone on from the great power blocs you remember from the last two—you might say four—centuries, and devolved in scale to a more diverse, more decentralized model in which the power is also dispersed. The United States of America is the last holdout as a continental-scale power—along with our Canadian and Mexican cousins, that is. Personally I'm a little uncomfortable with the situation, in the global community. But the Hierarchy deems it necessary to maintain a strong national base from which to advance the cause of global unification and leadership."

"That seems odd to me. I thought you described the Hierarchy's objectives in terms of human betterment, not national aggrandizement."

"Yes, but you see, we in America are the keepers of the plan, the embodiment of the collective political destinies of the human race."

"Sophie, you sound as if this were 1776. Has power gone to your head already?"

"No, you have to understand I'm not speaking so much on the literal level, here, as about the working out of the various ray energies of the race; the primary currents of spiritual evolution through the great civilizations of the past; the revealed prophecies of seers, century after century..."

"Sounds pretty hokey to me. I hope you know what you're talking about. And I also hope you don't try to sell it to the American people, because I don't think they'll buy it."

"Oh, you're absolutely right—on one level. I wouldn't express it in terms like those I used just now. That's getting too close to the esoteric level of knowledge reserved for the adepts. No, but translated into everyday political language, about the strength and moral purpose, you know, of this most favored nation in the history of the world—they'll lap that sort of thing right up, as they always have."

I had to admit, Sophie appeared to have what it took to be a successful politician in this country. Still I wanted to know more of her personal agenda.

In response to my further questioning, she claimed an ambition to succeed even in conventional terms: to hold the center, subject to the various tides of interest-group pressure. In order to offset the relative lassitude which marred political life in the capital these days, she held the hope that in her hands, the country would be "united in its sense of purpose and destiny, leading the way to a true world order, committed to a secure future for all."

"Spoken like a president," I said. We got up to leave. She paid the check.

A drab concrete office building downtown served as Party headquarters in the city. Attired in my fresh light-blue suit, and savoring the feel of new soft-leather loafers, without necktie but in its place wearing an olive-sized ID dongle on a lanyard, I accompanied Sophie and entered by way of the security entrance in back. We rode the elevator to the eleventh floor and entered a room without décor, beyond a plain oval table with chairs, a cart with beverages and snacks, and the usual charcoal tinted windows.

Pending the later arrival of Robert Glaston, there were five of us: Dennis McElroy, Madison Kane, and Ryan Willoughby, along with Sophie and me. Dennis was the Party chairman. He looked like a swollen Jimmy Cagney—though I would come to know him as a somewhat more amiable variety of Irish political sergeant. Madison, braceleted and owl-eyed, served as Party secretary; while Ryan of the lanky frame and sand-blond hair was our media liaison. Sophie introduced me as Seymour Friedrickson, communications consultant, longtime friend and confidant, and her choice for campaign speechwriter.

And where did I live, Madison Kane wanted to know. She wore a bulky sweater of multicolored fibers, at least three sizes too large.

"Um, with her." I swiveled a thumb toward Sophie.

This revelation caused a few eyebrows to rise.

"I believe we're all adults here," Sophie said. "Can we get on with the agenda at hand?"

Sophie had briefed me on the topic for today's staff meeting: the mounting efforts of the Panarchists to undermine the electoral process, and countervailing Party strategy to woo the hearts and minds of the masses.

Dennis began by outlining the slate of primaries in the

coming year, and Ryan reported on progress in arranging an appearance for Sophie on a popular talk-show. A more substantive discussion turned to the wave of Panarchist protests across the nation. Employing a gamut of tactics, from sit-ins and marches to arson and sabotage, their message, as Ryan summarized it, seemed to be to "challenge the very integrity of our system of government."

"And is the focus of their ire the Party itself?" I wanted to know.

"There's really no focus," said the downy-cheeked lad. "Some of their statements point to the Party, but for the most part it's a generalized critique; we're blamed for all the ills of the modern world."

"What about the Hierarchy?"

All eyes looked to me, and I felt Sophie tense at my side.

Dennis broke the spell. "Let them talk all they want about the Hierarchy. We can easily dismiss them then, as conspiracy theorists."

"Pardon me," I said, "but isn't the Party the political arm of the Hierarchy?"

Sophie placed a firm hand on my forearm and intervened. "Let's not split hairs here. The point is, we need to restore the public's trust in the electoral process, and to brand the actions of the Panarchists—or decentralists of any stripe—as a threat to our democratic way of life."

I felt compelled to voice the opinion that there was another, broader kind of realism needed in the situation, which would not merely appear to grapple with the difficult choices ahead, but actually address the root causes of the world's problems.

"And can you enlighten us as to your views on what those are?" said Madison, ever so sweetly.

"Forgive my tardiness," said Robert Glaston as he entered the room.

Yes, I thought, a spitting image of that weasel of a man, Dom Miguel Hurtado.

His eyes scanned the room, burning a moment on each face. A sneering smile surfaced at the sight of Sophie, and submerged when his gaze settled on me.

"Ah," he said. "Sophie's wunderkind. At last we have the pleasure." Without extending a hand, he sat at the open end of the table. "Please, go on. I'd like to hear the views of our newest staff member."

Sophie said, "If you don't mind, we need to get on with the business of this meeting. The Party platform—"

"With all respect, Ms. Vaughan," said Dennis, "it behooves us to know the personal views of the man who will be writing your speeches."

"Absolutely," said Glaston.

"I will be brief," I said. "The problems in the world today are endemic, rooted in fundamental forces of civilization, culminating in our late great empire. While the world's population expands, resources are dwindling. Technological fixes can no longer be assumed, in a multipolar world beset with crumbling economies and ecosystems in peril."

Glaston nodded sagely, appearing to agree.

Not so with Sophie, who interrupted my little speech. "That's all very fine as an overview, but in the process you're neglecting certain unpleasant facts. There are real enemies out there, evil people in the actual world, and if we're not prepared to defend ourselves against such people we might as well jump ship, because they'll run right over us."

Aside from bringing up this terrorist bogey again, it was her attitude that irritated me, her acting as if she had all the answers and I was the neophyte. It seemed she couldn't let go completely of her distance as teacher, as mother superior in the astral hierarchy.

My own disgruntlement with her stance, here exposed in

the group setting, surprised me; and it cast a ray of doubt on the whole enterprise of my affiliation with her.

When at last one drinks from the Grail, I wondered, does it cease to be holy?

I noticed, though, that Glaston's smug smile broadened further on hearing Sophie's rebuttal. And it occurred to me that Sophie was playing to her audience. Which rang a resonant note of flute-like harmony with my own felicitous pedigree: Felix Krull, confidence man.

CHAPTER V

By mid-January my love life had come to match the state of my dreams: sour and elusive. The presidential candidate and I bickered, snapped, glowered, lay together without affection. Was it the insidious effect of secrecy, with Sophie remaining tight-lipped about matters of the Hierarchy? My own complacency, feeling I had already mastered my training, and attained the desired position of influence in the world? Or simply the shine wearing off the honeymoon phase of this new relationship?

For her part, Sophie paid me paltry respect for my own principles, insisting that my existence in her inner circle depended solely on the services I might provide to the success of her campaign. I felt I might inject some fresh thinking into the rickety apparatus of electoral politics. Taking inspiration from the success of the Panarchists in garnering support for their cause through nonviolent guerilla actions, for example.

Sophie had popular support—at least the polls said so, according to Ryan the media guy; but then, the media wasn't allowed to cover the other side of the story, the discontent mounting against the Hierarchy's austerity policies at home and military interventions abroad. Reportage of these unsavory events was reserved for confidential Party reports, often marked for Sophie's eyes only.

One night I set her off with my outspoken comments to a foreign diplomat, at a national Party conference in Palo Alto. Sergei Latonov, the Russian chargé d'affaires, was a guest of the Party at one of the social functions. He politely inquired as to Sophie's electoral ambitions, including platform specifics in the area of defense. In doing so he also made the point that while his country still called itself Russia, as a sovereign republic it had none of the imperial ambitions of either the Russian or Soviet empires of earlier eras.

Standing at my side, Sophie hedged on the question of first-strike capabilities and verifiable arms reductions.

Patiently sipping at my third vodka martini, when it was done I blurted out my bottled-up opinion: "I would argue we shouldn't wait any longer for these futile negotiations, however high-minded they might appear. No, while I cannot vouch for the Party leadership"—I ignored Sophie hissing in my ear—"I can state unequivocally that the most prudent course would be to proceed unilaterally to disarm. Only then can we replace our false sense of security with one founded on a nonmilitary system of civilian-based social defense."

I was thinking we could learn something from those pesky Panarchists, and was about to continue elaborating on the theme, but Sophie had my elbow in a vice and Sergei opened his red muttonchops and laughed uncomfortably, thinking my outburst a joke.

Sophie fast changed the subject to wheat genetics.

All the way home in the car she berated me for my lack of diplomatic prudence, considering my official role as her advisor. If I had such revolutionary advice, I might have the kindness to work out a coherent strategy with her in private before announcing it to the capitals of the world. I defended myself loudly and violently, pontificating on the madness of nuclear and particle-beam weapons, the twisted logic of mass destruction for mass defense. The argument continued until bed, where I'd followed her suit, and lay in stone state until morning. Of course I had no power in the situation, expect to exercise the semblance of it at my own peril.

"Love ain't easy," Sophie said to me during a tender moment of reconciliation. "It changes; it requires the same sort of ongoing attention and care as a good disguise does for its successful manipulation. This is the essence of what life is all about against death."

Fair enough, I thought, and well expressed.

I was happy to let the political wrangling between us yield to talk of love. Yet were these two most vital realms of human being very different, in the end? I had no better laboratory to find out.

I had never heard Sophie say anything about marriage, or even a long-term arrangement for living together. But the word *love*, that was timeless. What did it mean, in practical terms, in this brave new world?

"Have you ever been married?" I asked her.

I felt her tense in my arms. "Why? Does it matter?"

"I would have thought it might matter to the electorate. But what do I know? Anyway, you seem to have the experience—"

She gave an abrupt snort. "If you're asking if standards have changed, certainly, yes. The conventional female these days is single, likely as not; at least she has the freedom of choice in her relationships, without undue moral judgment from society."

Though I had become accustomed to this new morality during my brief sojourn in the twentieth century, I was secretly disappointed that Sophie thought of me in such terms—what might turn out to be little more than a casual, open-ended affair.

I understood her wariness of commitment better when she relented and told me about Robert Glaston, whom she'd married earlier in this reincarnation. He was a rancid figure by her account: charming in courtship, a brute in the marriage bed.

"Legal rape," she called it—resulting in a baby boy whom Robert named Tashi.

Two years later, she divorced him and had her tubes tied, foregoing further responsibilities of motherhood. Robert fought for, and won, permanent custody of the child.

"Robert has him all the time? You never see him?"

With a large sigh, Sophie answered: "The random dictates of the justice system."

Or, I was moved to reflect, the not-so-random dictates of another agency with an abiding interest in Sophie's career at stake.

There was work to do, on the worldly plane, and so we soon directed our energies toward the common objective—victory on November fourth. Sophie's election platform, poised to feature at the gamut of primaries that spring and summer, began to take shape, with high-sounding and far-reaching promises: democracy for all, free trade everywhere, transition from national to global authority, universal data collection, and geoengineering to manage climate change.

These were policy directives handed down from on high, in broad strokes; it fell to me to couch them in palatable terms for the masses. Sophie had passing knowledge of such issues, with the help of her staff, and briefings with Hierarchy contacts. Armed with her bullet points and my knack for turns of phrase, I aimed to increase the Party's plurality and reverse its troubling trend of plummeting poll figures.

My actual influence on the development of the platform itself was as yet negligible. I came to understand my role as a simple functionary, to draft speeches and press releases strictly in accordance with Sophie's directives. If I sometimes insisted on playing devil's advocate, Sophie said, she appreciated the value in addressing and anticipating potential challenges to policy. Such proposals she withdrew until they could be reframed for "more positive public consumption."

When we hit the campaign trail we were met by relative success. Clearly no credible alternative was poised to challenge Sophie within the Party ranks. Yet we encountered a disturbing counterpoint, an organized boycott of said primaries by the decentralists. I say *organized*, though in fact I refer to a rather random series of political brushfires: a shopping mall blockade here, an unexplained media blackout there, graffiti cropping up on billboards and social media sites, a new meme called "final revolution."

I use the generic term *decentralists*, in the absence of an identifiable foe. The Panarchists had no clear chain of command, at least none our Party operatives could determine. They were an amorphous movement, which declined to produce an opposition party to run against. I might have blamed the nefarious Dark Forces, but again, would find no face to paint, no neck to hang; only that archetypal force of resistance.

Some analysts called Sophie the only legitimate national candidate. It seemed the regional honchos no longer liked to travel, or to stand in the limelight of the national media. Or this country had become sufficiently infected by the mood of decentralism that anybody with a decent following on home turf no longer cared to woo a continent-wide constituency.

So beating the bushes on the primary circuit was akin to a couple of star major-league ballplayers barnstorming through the minors. I thought of my old friends the Kodiak Bruins, for instance, while following a back road in Alberta that we'd taken as a scenic, roundabout route from North Dakota to Spokane, Washington. We got stuck on the highway threading through the hemp fields for three and a half hours behind a caravan of two hundred slowly rolling Airstream trailers. I had a thing now about getting in planes (never mind aircars), so we traveled by bullet train or rented car—without the hover option. When we didn't have the luxury of a chauffeur, I left the driving to Sophie. On this particular journey we rode in a late-model, turbocharged, red-and-black sport-limo, with a tinted bubble-top. How nostalgic it was for me to see the snaky column of antique trailers—aluminum dinosaurs, Sophie called them—with their silver aerodynamic shapes which, even, in the 1970s, evoked "the modern age"; now, quaint relics held together by duct tape, spray paint and the fanatic devotion of their owners.

When we arrived in Spokane, the rival speaker—a man still shy of thirty, dressed in a logger's shirt and wearing a short, dense black beard, was still rambling. The crowd had largely dispersed; it was a dusty day in the parking lot on the edge of town. Handfuls of patient people remained holding onto straw and plastic hats in the buffeting breeze. The portable loudspeaker crackled.

"Government is b-b-biological; therefore it is doomed to extinction or evolution. The government we see in office today is a species of organized c-c-crime, running a glorified confidence game through their f-f-fronts in the mass mmm-media. This government thrives on special interest groups, whose specialty is interest..."

Sophie eyed me as we closed the car doors and shuffled out on the dusty gravel. "Panarchist," she said.

"I thought they were boycotting."

"Right. But no one's in charge, remember?"

"Oh yeah. So who is this guy?"

"Lamar Pentecost. He used to be the local Party organizer, until he developed bigger ambitions. Like undermining the whole system. By sabotage, if necessary. He's not talking about that, publically. But he has a record of property crimes: sugar in gas tanks, cutting cables."

The voice droned on: "G-g-government is a union of public businesspeople. Government today is neither of the people, by the people, nor for the p-p-p-p-people." A family with puckered faces passed us and headed for their car. A fat man got up, jangling keys in his pocket. "And so my friends I say to you to-d-d-day..." The speaker stopped when he recognized Sophie. Perhaps he also apprehended, as we took our seats in the clackety folding chairs, that most of the crowd was drifting away. He scowled helplessly and Sophie smiled at him.

"Can't convince 'em all, all of the time!" she called out.

He shot her the bird and muttered something that sounded suspiciously like, "H-h-hierarchy whore." A boy of ten or twelve laughed.

"Where's our security?" I asked her.

"Don't worry. We're monitored," she said. "And don't ask."

"Ohh-kayy."

Sophie giggled and took the stage. By then no more than a dozen listeners remained. She looked at me with a mime's frown, as I watched from offstage, and I motioned to her to go on, as if before a cheering throng. Standing erect in her slim and sensible blue dress, its hem at mid-calf, she delivered the goods with dutiful, direct speech, drumming home the keywords of the platform we had formulated:

"... *democracy for all*. No more shall those in backward corners of the world fall prey to the petty politics of tribe and fiefdom. Everyone shall have a vote for our global leaders.

"No more shall our corporations suffer from unfair competition abroad, where other countries exploit forced labor and subsidize their own interests, at our expense. We will tear down the barriers to *free trade everywhere*.

"There is only one road to world peace: not two, or three, or a hundred. One road only, to peace which reflects unity. That unity, as we look forward to the next decades of this century and beyond, must take the form of One Earth. Our banner, however proud the flag of this great nation, must be tied under a greater vision, a *global vision of world order*.

"To that end, there must be *universal data access*. Citizens of this country, and the world, must all have access to information, and it must be codified for consistency. By the same token, your personal data is critical to the mission of providing for your needs in a comprehensive and efficient manner.

"With resources freed up from the age-old warring between nations, from the wasteful competition between economies, from the useless arguments over conflicting information, we will devote renewed efforts to *reversing global warming*, with advanced technologies of geoengineering..."

"Hierarchy whore!" said a man in a checked sport coat and wraparound shades, standing behind the empty rows of chairs.

The critique stung, since the words in the speech were of my formulation—given, of course, the prerequisite keywords Sophie had outlined for me to focus on. I took solace in the famous Lincoln quip, *You can please some of the people all of the time, and all of the people some of the time, but you can't please all of the people all the time.* Even so, this level of vitriol was disturbing.

Sophie took the high road. "Sir, if you would care to—"

The man had fallen silent, grabbing at the back of his neck. He doubled over as if in pain, then staggered away.

Sophie shrugged and thanked the more polite stragglers in the audience before leaving the stage.

"What happened to that guy?" I said.

She just gave me that look.

"Oh, right. 'Don't ask.'"

"C'mon," she said, "Let's go for a beer."

The pale ale on draft at the roadside tavern was passable, even to a German palate. I offered a few tips to Sophie on her delivery and the nuances of her policy statements. Then a hefty fellow in coveralls who'd been sitting alone at a neighboring table slid out of his chair and waddled with half-empty glass over to our small round table.

"Hey mind if I sit down— youse at that rally or whatever today? Huh, well I tell ya."

Sophie helped pull out the extra chair for him, and he sat

down with a wheeze and a wipe of his freckled bald pate, before launching into a tavern-crafted monologue of his own. Apparently he didn't recognize who we actually were; it was questionable if he'd even attended the event himself.

"Jeez, I wish they'd shut off them big politicians with their power trips or whatever it is keeps 'em goin' besides my tax money. Course I collect pogie now and then but these guys got it comin' steady long as they can look good and talk big and sell their souls to the corporations. They get their rocks off against the workin' man so's they can drink martinis 'stead of this piss I drink all day; ride around in Hoverlas with these foreign diplomats and their floozy wives. Say, it must get addictive after a while, whadya think?"

My mind had been wandering. To be precise, I noticed two women at another table nearby, leaning toward each other in earnest conversation.

One, with straight black hair and severe pale features, was asserting herself with a monotonous academic delivery. I sensed, underneath the masculine gray suit she wore, a cold body harboring repressed volcanic sexual energy. Her companion, an elfin wisp of a young woman clad in light felt and green leather, and wearing beads in her tangle of hair, listened intently and then replied in a thin tremulous voice which carried, paradoxically, a compelling power. I strained to overhear their conversation but could not, above the beery din and our own visitor's tirade.

"I'm not sayin' nobody's perfect but I mean they make a profession out of it! I know what yer gonna say, and yeah, I guess I might be a professional guzzler but shit, I sure as heck ain't gettin paid fer it—well like I said 'cept fer a few unemployment checks now and then but y'see that's my tax money in the first place—Hey, where youse goin'?"

On our way out the door another man came up to us. Sophie caught her breath. "Jor-El," she said. He took her by the elbow and ushered her out into the glare of the fading day, ignoring me as I followed. A glance behind me was met with an intense stare and close-mouthed commentary from the oddly matched female duo.

Outside Jor-El stood and faced Sophie, and she calmly awaited what he had to say.

"Don't let the lowlife around here get you down," he began.

Appearing half pirate, half jeweler, with his wispy hair, bulbous nose and grizzled beard, he spoke with a mechanical echo in his voice. I didn't recall seeing him in the sparse crowd that day.

"We are not concerned," he continued, "with these backwater revolutionaries, nor their unlettered brethren of the beer-halls."

"But you are concerned...?"

He gave her that jeweler's appraisal, his head cocked, one eye peering into her soul, and issued a disdainful snort. "Heh—well—yes and no. What I am concerned about need not concern you. What I want to know is, who wrote that speech of yours?"

Sophie and I looked at each other. Was he pleased with it? Should I take the credit, or fade to the background? In truth it was a collaborative effort; yet the essence of the speech, like the platform itself, had originated with Sophie. Or so I thought.

"I proposed the main points," Sophie said, "as you instructed, Jor-El. Fel—Seymour here, my advisor, helped formulate the final wording, fine-tuning, as it were. Are you okay with it?"

"Advisor, is it?" Jor-El barked a short laugh, showing tiny gray teeth, and then fixed his gaze on me. "Sure, sure. I don't believe I've had the pleasure." He offered me a hand to shake.

I hesitated, reached and held, and felt an ominous power in the grip of that dry claw.

"Seymour Friedrickson," I said.

"Is that right."

"Um..." I released my hand and flexed the fingers.

"I've heard a lot about you." He looked me up and down.

"Oh, really," I said, with a trifling acid edge. I felt secure enough in my wardrobe choice, the tan sports jacket, the light-blue button-down shirt, designer jeans, real leather loafers. "And do I live up to my advance billing?"

As I asked this I thought, *If Sophie is the Hierarchy's whore, what does that make me?*

Again Jor-El barked an artificial laugh, before straightening up and gathering his forces for an assault. Or so I feared. What came out instead was a honeyed threat sliding past the gray teeth. "I care nothing for your reputation, past or present. Only that our wishes be carried out to the letter. The speech I heard today passes muster. But the criticisms you heard voiced by certain other elements at the venue carry their own insidious brand of persuasion. You are not to be thus swayed. We need you to be steadfast in your alignment with our objectives, on board with the program as Sophie will present it to you. Is that understood?"

"Certainly. But if there was no problem with the speech—"

"It has come to my attention that you have certain views regarding issues central to national and global security. Defense policy, armaments—"

"If I may interject," Sophie said. "In the discussion you are referring to, Seymour made it quite clear that devoting resources to national defense, at the expense of the wider agenda for global unity, might be counterproductive, in certain circumstances."

How noble of her, I thought, to vouch for me on the very matter that had caused so much contention between us. Jor-El regarded her, nodding, his mouth set in a well-worn frown.

"All right," he said to her before turning back to me. He

fixed me with a look of chilling dispassion. "I'm just putting you on notice, to toe the line. I don't believe you'd relish the idea of going back the way you came"—this with a most unpleasant smile. "Good day, then." He clapped Sophie on the shoulder and turned to go.

Sophie held my hand as we watched him round the corner of the tavern, walking with a bandy-legged limp.

"What a fucking—"

"Shhh. Didn't you hear what he said?"

"What? You mean you're on his side? Of course. You're already taking orders from him. Who is that jerk, anyway?"

"If I told you, I don't think you'd believe me."

"Try me."

"All right. He's the Atlantean Proconsul."

I wanted to channel one of those bark-laughs. "What does that even mean? Except, let me guess, he must be a Hierarchy bigwig, correct?"

"Keep your voice down. Here, let's get out of here, and I'll fill you in." We began walking to the limo. "He's a tightass bigshot, but he is a bigshot. Favors concepts like shutdown, sealed testimony, special transport. He orders unflavored, unsweetened gelatin for dessert."

"Naturally. Now tell me, how do you know what he eats for dessert?"

"I get around, too, honeybun. The point is, don't let him get under your skin. But don't blow the guy off, either. He's right up there."

"Right up there, with who else?... Oh, I see. I don't want to know."

Sophie gave me one of those expressions I had come to know so well from her: a dark smile.

CHAPTER VI

The convention in August, held near New York's famed Times Square, consisted of all the usual hoopla, mock-exciting and shimmering with surface cheer, like puffy cereal covered with high-fructose corn syrup. Naturally Sophie won the Party's nomination, hands down.

Was it my finest hour? Hardly. On this triumphant occasion, Sophie insisted on winging it, speaking off the cuff:

"My friends, supporters and workers and contributors in every one of your ways, I would like to thank you from the bottom to the top of my heart for the honor and responsibility you have bestowed upon me tonight. At the same time I want to thank those who were running for this office beside me for their valuable stimulus and challenge, for making me responsive to their positions and to the people they represent. Now that you have entrusted me with the Party leadership and thus the reins of the government, I pledge to fulfill to the utmost of my ability the duties of the office of president."

And so on and so forth. Not that I wasn't visible—the public knew about me. In the talk-show interview Sophie had even said we had no plans for marriage but that she did intend to continue living and yes, sleeping with me in the very White House. Thankfully she didn't get onto the subject of astral travel, or I may have come under more suspicion as a latter-day Rasputin. No, to the media I was merely her handsome, if by now properly tight-lipped, boyfriend. Without the innate glamor of a First Lady (or official Prince of the realm) I was in time blithely ignored by political analysts contending with their own spate of more fertile topics.

The token national election, even more than the Party nomination before it, was a foregone conclusion, with all the work done by the advertising branch: "Just walk your fingers over the keys to the one marked E. Then it's up to you: you can press the Y or the N. Do you want a bright future, a future where your freedom of choice is protected, where our children and our seniors are looked after and where America remains strong in a changing world? Then vote Yes, on November fourth."

So the ticker-tape parade down Pennsylvania Avenue proceeded on schedule: Sophie giving the people the queen's wave from a bat-black, bubble-topped limo, me smiling at her side and thinking all those people in sunglasses looked like so many cheering insects. According to the insensible customs of protocol, the White House was still occupied by the geriatric couple, Standish and Constance Murphy, who had spent the last eight years there wishing it would become their perpetual mausoleum. So Sophie and I retired on election night to the presidential suite of the capital's finest hotel, where we made sweetest love till the middle of the night and I fell into dreams of being chased by our own Secret Service.

When January came, and the turning of the year 2037, we finally moved into the White House. I felt immediately at home in our new, palatial surroundings—they reminded me of a faded Venetian palace. I did find it ironic that in the bastion of democracy the leaders should be housed like royalty—even if the wallpaper was worn around the edges, and shreds of cobweb could be seen collecting in the cupolas.

No matter, Sophie persuaded me—the masses are entitled to their gods. Wasn't it within every American's enshrined purpose to scrimp and save and clutch and crawl to a salary scale enabling such opulence for themselves?

Yes, I assented. Come to think of it, even the relatively modest décor of the Villa Kuckuck aspired to the grander style of the more exalted gentry, with that perpetual pretension of the middle class.

And so I was neither unused to nor offended by the noble architecture, the luxuriant drapes, the exotic carpets, the ornate mahogany desks and ebony chairs. No matter that the rugs were frayed, the silver tarnished. The greater attraction for me lay at the window, to which I was drawn in the early morning as Sophie still slept.

Stretched out before me was the vast lawn with its neat clusters of shrubbery and deliberate perimeter of tall, arching trees shading the continuous barrier of wrought iron fence. Through its graceful bars I watched the dutiful minions of the state hastening to work, to be swallowed by the massive government office buildings which lay beyond, still shrouded in the gloom.

Sophie was stirring in the canopied bed behind me. She rustled her feet in the morning-cool, satiny sheets. Her hair lay spread over nearly the width of the king-sized bed. Her eyes opened; she looked over to where I was standing and said in a sultry voice, "Hey, hon, come back to bed. Hmmm... that black leopard, and the white, whispering bear..."

I lingered a moment longer by the window; then, by the time I crawled in beside her, Sophie had fallen back asleep.

The reader may well be startled to hear that I would go to work that day as a mail-clerk. While this position may appear at first glance to be one beneath my station, demeaning my proper role in this new government, in fact I'd volunteered, feeling it to be entirely consonant with my ongoing roles as presidential advisor and speechwriter.

I'd requested an office in the White House, preferring to work at home. So I inherited an unassuming basement cubicle, the desk and walls of which were presently littered with my predecessor's flotsam and jetsam. On top of it all was plunked a bundled stack of mail the size of a large garbage can, with another, similar stack propped up against the wall by the door.

Over half a century into the computer age, and a sizeable portion of the population at large still hadn't clued in you could send letters to the president directly in digital form instead of through the mail.

After the Secret Service and the receiving secretaries had finished with the incoming tide of largely worthless paper, it fell to me to sort through the remains, skimming and bringing it to the president's busy attention as I saw fit. It was also my job to compose replies to routine letters needing a quick, personal response.

Much power accrued to such a position. For the screener of information is to the executive what the senses and their concomitant analysis are to the faculty of will. To put it bluntly, I could let Sophie know what I wanted her to know. From the start, however, I caught myself in the first flush of adrenaline that such awareness of power produces. I didn't want to misuse my power for selfish ends. But how to prevent such abuse in its subtle ways? How to monitor my own prejudices and biased judgments?

Putting aside such reflections as I bent to the work at hand, I quickly discovered that the mail was backlogged from the past three months. And there was plenty of chaff even in these prescreened bales. I could imagine what the battery of secretaries must have had to go through, and throw out. I was happy to discover, after an hour or so of despair, that buried in the heap on the desk was a scanner by which I could convert and file all this unmanageable paper in digital format. Then it would be a simple matter for me to handle the vast majority of responses with a set of form letters which could be arranged in the directory, both by issue and by a brief profile of the correspondent.

Once I fulfilled my human duties, the task of further threat analysis was carried out by a species of databots. Never mind gathering democratic input to decision making—these cybercritters were trained strictly to filter and act upon sequential variables of subversionary tendency, keywords antithetic to the Party or its principles. Sophie had briefed me to look for their cousins in human surveillance, lending real-time intelligence to security cameras, cruising drones, bioengineered insects; for my purposes, I understood they lurked in digital channels and pipes, compiling and feeding conclusionary target snapshots to the chain of command.

Fine, I thought, let them do the dirty work, and I will stick to good old-fashioned schmoozing with the populace. The mood I found was grim, however. I discerned an overwhelming preoccupation with the effects of climate change. A man in Des Moines said that if he had wanted to farm the desert he would have started out in Arizona. A fifth-grade girl from Brooklyn wanted to know if the president ever got to see the sun, since no one in her class, not even the teacher, had ever glimpsed the blue sky beyond the artificial haze. I fielded rants against the extinction of species, and read aloud odes to former bees (those denizens of blossoms having been replaced by beelike drones, who by all accounts performed their pollinating duties admirably, but petulantly refused to manufacture honey on the side). People complained about toxic oceans and water rationing... along with the other sundry hardships of life in the decline of empire.

Burdened more by the substance of such concerns on the part of an aggrieved citizenry, than by my stiff back or falling blood sugar levels, I rose and made my way to the staff room, down corridors remarkably absent of the kind of traffic I had expected: pages and interns, generals and committee chairmen, lobbyists and groups of tourists. Instead, the dim lights flickered on cracked portraits of aged aristocrats, or smiling, black-suited corporate yes-men, the class of political parasites I had come to understand were Sophie's forerunners as president.

Had the state of the union decayed to such a degree that even this bastion of power lay barren and discarded? Even in our ascent to the pinnacle, had we arrived too late to enjoy the pomp and glamorous attentions I had presumed would be our due?

I found Madison poking around the kitchenette area of the staff room, complaining about the absence of a proper espresso machine.

"I like them *bien frothy*," she explained, peering at me over her large round glasses.

"*Etes-vous Quebecoise?*"

"*Bien, oui*, but there's no need to be so formal. I was born in Montreal but grew up and went to school in Boston, or should I say Baastin."

"Tufts?"

She smiled at me and jangled her pendulous necklace and bracelets. "Yeah. Poli Sci. You?"

"Um, Germany, actually. The University of Mainz," I lied.

"Fascinating. Did you see the news this morning?"

"About my Deutschland?"

"Hardly. Troubles enough here at home. Have a look."

The newspad on the table lit up at my touch. There had been widespread protests in the wake of Sophie's inauguration. Panarchists had come out in force: chaining themselves to flagpoles; littering federal buildings with confetti composed of the shredded remains of the Constitution; performing rain dances while dressed in black capes silkscreened with the upside-down portraits of the new president. Two prominent "ringleaders" were already arrested: Zanelle Marte, a junior instructor at Harvard, and Elfie Byweather, occupation fire-spinner, from Salt Spring Island, British Columbia. From their mug shots I recognized the pair from the tavern at our campaign outing in Spokane. Deemed as threats to national security, they were whisked away to an undisclosed prison facility.

In a video link served directly from the paper's front page,

Party security chief Robert Glaston gloated over the efficiency of the government's response, citing the deterrent value of a "no compromise" crackdown on dissent. Madison explained that the White House had been closed to visitors today as a precaution.

I found my sentiments divided, regarding the treatment of the "domestic terrorists." The forty-one-year-old in me held a curious attraction to the severe countenance of Ms. Marte; while my younger ka component, now twenty-four, felt enchanted with the leather-skirted deva, Elfie. Gender issues aside, the hard line of the state struck me as extreme. Glaston with his black horn-rims appeared the consummate technocrat; yet he came across garrulous, with a false, hollow humor; and at the same time, paranoid, like a man enjoying the high life on a Mafia payroll.

"That's our Bob," Madison deadpanned.

"He's the Party security chief? I thought he was running for CEO."

"You don't run for CEO; you get appointed. That's coming."

Noticing she was still distracted by the lack of a proper coffee-maker, I ventured a solution. "Shall we order out?"

Ryan, a veritable genie from a lamp, waltzed through the door, jaunty as a sophomore in his basketball shoes, carrying a tray of three cappuccinos, *bien frothy*. Madison leaped at him with her jewelry dancing and gave him a generous hug. "Ryan, you dear!"

"Gotta do something useful around here," he quipped. "I'm still waiting my first day's orders from the prez."

"She slept in," I explained, reaching for one of the cups to grace my exit. "Given the day's press reports, you might profitably draft a statement for later."

Back at my workstation in a somber mood, I tried to put the

politics of the street behind me. I wanted to charge my efforts with renewed purpose. My first task after entering the computer's database was to delete the morass of now meaningless press releases kept on file by my predecessor. Reading one was as good as reading them all; it gave me a spark of pride and confidence to be part of a more exciting team than that last lot.

Several levels deep into the directory structure, I noticed settings for connection to all sorts of other network nodes: even red-coded contacts in the Pentagon, sensors in strategic bunkers and aircraft, consoles in offices of Cabinet members and state governors. One entry was labeled simply "OO," and I guessed it signified the Oval Office.

Testing a few such links, I found my access denied. Though in my training I had perused some of Sophie's personal files on her own devices, the official nodes I encountered today were layered with security beyond my reach. It galled me to be thus limited. To sit perched on the precipice of worldly power, yet without the wings to fly freely.

If I were to sit tapping on the virtual keys for an eternity—a simian Shakespeare—I might one day chance upon the code that would enable me to program my own Lifeline to take any course I chose. To live in any land on earth, at any point in the long history of humankind. I could give myself any opportunity, any lover, any challenge. I could put myself in the position of most propitious influence to seek the betterment of our struggling life form, this human race.

Yet, couldn't it be said that I had already arrived—pending further security clearance—at such a nexus, in my present position, with my presidential partner and the power I shared with her? I could not have asked for anything more, could I?

Then I recalled the sour breath of Jor-El; the jocular arrogance of Robert Glaston; and the earnest ideals of those two women now consigned to secret prisons.

I spent the rest of the morning delving into research, the

backstory of the empire and the protocols of its current, slimmed-down modus operandi. Yes, the American presence was reduced in outward forms, military bases and corporate branding; today imperial reach manifested covertly, electronically, economically, with precisely targeted pressure, with surgical strikes by select hit teams of biomechanically and psychometrically enhanced "super soldiers"; with nuanced disclaimers and appeals to the ever useful verities: freedom, democracy, security, world order.

Sophie didn't appear at the lunch table in our private quarters, so I sat by the empty silver candlesticks alone. Halfway through the meal a page—a young blond man wearing, by any judicious definition, a pageboy haircut—came to say that Sophie had a luncheon engagement elsewhere. I felt stood up on my first date. In a sullen mood I finished my lunch and went back to work. I didn't touch the computer all afternoon, just absently skimmed through the paper mail and sorted it into piles for processing another day.

That evening we dined together, and I let Sophie dominate the conversation with tales of her first day's work. After a morning occupied with congratulatory phone calls from foreign dignitaries, she had attended an impromptu luncheon with a delegation of Japanese business people at the grand opening of an exclusive sushi restaurant downtown. Then there was a meeting in the afternoon with an advisor, preliminary appointments to the Cabinet, and an informal briefing of the White House press corps.

Something bothered me about her glib summary. "What about the Panarchist uprising?"

"Uprising? A gaggle of throwback hippies holding placards and singing folk songs? Please. I have more important matters on my plate."

"Courtesy of your new advisor? Who was it, by the way?"

"Oh, Wolfgang Nenowitz," she said with a laugh which I could have sworn quavered with nervousness. "You may have heard of him. Former National Security Advisor, under Presidents Stern and Constance. He's got what you call Old World charm."

"Old is right. What is he, about eighty now?"

"Why are you interrogating me? I'm sorry about the lunch, okay?"

"Wait a minute; I just asked. Let me put it to you bluntly. Is he a member of the Hierarchy?"

"I'm not at liberty to say. Keep in mind, the Hierarchy is in essence a body of overseers existing on the astral plane. You can't expect them to run around in the capitals of the world lobbying like lesser beings."

"No, only in Washington, DC. Or in other strategic locations such as Spokane, Washington. So you're telling me that gangster Jor-El was not, indeed, Hierarchy; that his Atlantean title—Proconsul, if I remember correctly—was merely a pretend role from the Star Trek set he had just walked off of?"

"Jor-El's a little different," said Sophie. She finished off her wine in a gulp.

"Oh. A shapeshifter, is it? You keep telling me I don't want to know. Well, you're wrong. I do want to know."

"Fuck it." She flung down her linen napkin and stalked out of the room, closing the bedroom door with a bang.

I didn't know what to make of her reaction. Was I really off the mark, or had I zeroed in too close to the truth—that this esoteric concept of an incorporeal elite, ensconced upon a heavenly tier of thrones, or around some hoary and immaterial Round Table, was but a smokescreen for an all-too-physical, power-lusting elite, secure behind firewalls, proxies, platitudes.

That line about Jor-El from Atlantis? A truth clothed in apparent fiction, thus hidden in plain sight—akin to Edgar

Allen Poe's purloined letter, escaping notice from the team of obsessed detectives by resting in, of all too obvious places, the letter rack. Or the anarchist Kropotkin, escaping from a Russian prison, dining in one of St. Petersburg's finer restaurants, where the police would never think to look.

Sophie, I concluded, was acting indeed as the "pretty face" of their power. Caught in their squeeze, she could only afford to let me know what I needed to know, and no more.

I dawdled with the tableware, twirled the remains of my wine. The old gent Nenowitz, I thought, might be harmless enough. But I recalled reading about the Nazi brass of the 1940s, fans of Wagner, Schopenhauer, Goethe and Nietzsche. High culture, noble manners, global visions... a veneer masking more insidious drives.

I spent the rest of the time before bed browsing in the White House library. Its dusty tomes bespoke an earlier age, in which reading was a tactile art; when leather and cloth, paper and ink lent substance and supposed permanence to the written word. Still some of us bipedal creatures, in this age of holographic simulacra and 4D-VR rendering, preferred the old medium. In addition to the excellent selection of literary classics and seminal works of philosophy, history, and political science, there was a surprising selection of lighter reading, in the ever popular genres: mysteries, thrillers, science fiction. I grabbed a slim paperback entitled *The Day the Insects Devoured the World*. Just the thing to put me to sleep, make me forget all the world's real problems.

In the president's bedroom, Sophie was still stonewalling. She sat clothed in her black nightie in bed, propped against all the pillows, with her reading glasses on—her bow to tradition, refusing the ubiquitous laser procedure—perusing her reading device. She glanced at me briefly, coldly, then went back to her report from the Department of Mines.

All right, I said to myself, I can wait this one out, too.

Sophie only wore a nightie if we were quarreling. She gave me a perfunctory glance as I climbed into bed nude beside her.

"Mind if I have a pillow?" I said.

"Here." Eyes on her document, she handed me one from behind her back.

I tucked it behind me and set to reading about our insectoid demise. The farmers went first, as they ran out to defend their vanishing crops. One old blisterer, screaming out at the attacking hordes with hoe in one hand and fist in the other, was silenced when he swallowed a softball-sized cluster of grasshoppers.

The insects themselves, of course, had no conception of the inherent drama of their conquest. They simply grouped themselves in hordes, as cosmic probabilities say all things will do, and took it from there. A cloud of grasshoppers, a swarm of wasps or ants, an army of beetles would form around a local food source such as a tree or hitchhiker, would grow as the spreading scent of fresh food attracted the masses, and then would quickly leave bare branches and bones in search of more. They collected in ever growing multitudes—collaborating across species lines, defeating every known pesticide through genetic selection in their exploding populations, leaving whole towns decimated in their wake.

The news developed that the entire human species could be doomed; so said the government research people looking desperately into nanoweapons. The scientists didn't bother with the corresponding prediction that along with mighty humanity, all land-based life might perish.

I skipped to the end to find out what would happen. I knew Sophie hated it when I did that with a book, but I didn't care. This was a matter of global survival.

The insects' strength became their fatal liability: an exponentially increasing population. In the end there was simply no more food to be had. It came down to sixteen climactic seconds of starving, swarming, suffocating death, punctuated with the clash of frantic claws on battle-shells. The rasping of legs, dry wings and empty mandibles became a deafening roar over the dusty lands. Broken fragments of exoskeletons littered the beaches; the skies were filled with clouds of insect-junk drifting inevitably to the stubble and to the waves. The sun alone was left to send its rays again to warm seeds and soft eggs.

How evocative, how poignant! These scenes struck me to the quick.

I closed the book, leaned back and uttered a sigh for the cyclical fate of the world.

Then Sophie deigned to speak to me: "What have you been reading?"

"*The Day the Insects Devoured the World.*"

"Good grief. Don't you have anything better to occupy your hollow skull?"

"Like the fascinating work of intellect and imagination that you're occupying yourself with at the moment?"

"There's a bill coming up from the last session of the legislature..."

"Don't bother explaining. I was just fighting back."

My honesty caught her off guard.

We were both silent for a moment, regaining our senses. Under the covers she slipped a hand over my knee. Then she looked at me and said, "What a way to start our first term."

I spent a desultory morning in my office—sorting more mail and beginning to set up my database; stewing over Sophie's attitude of self-righteousness and superiority in matters both spiritual and political. I hadn't had any sort of spiritual instruction from her in a long time. We'd both gotten so wrapped up in the campaign, the election, the move to Washington, that we'd nearly tuned out of the higher frequencies altogether. I began to question Sophie's real inner resources, her qualifications as a spiritual or any other kind of mistress. Her quick temper, her stubbornness on certain questions of policy, her preoccupation with the superficial trappings of her new role, and her secrecy surrounding the Hierarchy, had threatened to swamp whatever leading inner lights she possessed.

Perhaps it was unfair of me to judge so critically my partner and mentor, as she confronted the inevitable pressure of this most extraordinary of human burdens, the presidency of... if not the greatest, in every sense of the word, let us say simply the most materially powerful empire in the history of the race.

I confess I might be accused of the same shortcomings—a pompous self-righteousness as well as a forgetfulness of divine guidance. Here I was, a mail-boy in the great estate, without any redeeming transcendental purpose or direction.

Yesterday I'd felt so important, such a meaningful cog in such a great machine.

Once a sea-lily...

I could only trust, as always, in my determination to achieve, in the end, whatever was needed to advance my progress in this world; dancing, along the way, with fate's darlings, its probabilistic vicissitudes.

Further research into the Hierarchy via the computer directories yielded no fresh insights. I chanced upon a single reference to the Lifelines program, in a discussion of the quantum computing environment. A key component was the so-called Subjective Interface, by which the operator's intention would drive the search parameters, even without physical input to the hardware. While I found this concept fascinating, even tantalizing, I could find nothing concrete or accessible by which to try my hand.

Frustrated, I attempted, once again, entry to the Oval Office (OO) directory. An alert appeared, then quickly vanished. *Uh-oh*, I thought. *Now my interest has been registered*. Somewhere a Hierarchic functionary, perhaps a bored databot, has felt a virtual tweak on the nose. My response, learned from Sophie: *Fuck it.*

At lunchtime I heard her gabbing in the kitchen with the African-American help, Fred and Imma. Sophie backed through the swinging door into the serving area, carrying a tray of celery and carrot sticks, sliced red pepper and avocado. When she turned and saw me standing there she stopped dead for an instant, then smiled sheepishly, then tittered again.

I couldn't resist: "Did you iron out all the world's problems this morning, dear?"

"In the meeting with those deadheads? Are you kidding? Listen, we have our work cut out for us. Those generals and ex-bank presidents don't give a hoot about conflict resolution. Their priority is peace that pays. If it doesn't pay, and pay well, they'd just as soon put their considerable capital and expertise to work for someone else."

"I see you've made some new friends, anyway." I nodded in the direction of the kitchen.

"Oh, we did get to chew the fat. Fred told me a great story about this pet turtle he had when he was kid. We're talking about world peace, remember. There was a pile of brush they'd throw sticks and stuff on, and the turtle would crawl under there thinking it was a great shelter. With each new branch or pile of leaves, that turtle would burrow deeper and deeper in the pile, as if she might want to nest there—probably thinking it was great, like being under a bigger turtle shell."

Imma, her round face glowing from the steam, came in carrying two brown ceramic bowls by their handles, wearing potholder gloves. "Watch it, now, it's hot."

I said, "Smells good, Imma. What is it?"

"Turtle soup."

Fred came through the doors with a loaf of fresh bread, half-sliced, on a wood cutting board. His bushy, gray-flecked eyebrows lifted, accompanying a shrug. "Yeah," he said, "one day they set fire to that brushpile. And the poor turtle had thought she was the best-protected turtle in the world. She burnt right up. They couldn't even make soup out of her."

I shuddered. I pictured little Fred standing by the brushpile, tears running down his black-apple cheeks.

A brace of jets roared overhead, shaking the White House to its foundation. Fred looked up and quipped, "There they go. Protectin' us."

"Ain't that right," said Emma, all serious now.

I blew on my hot soup.

"What's the matter?" Sophie said to me.

"What, me? What do you mean?"

Fred escorted Emma back to the kitchen, casting us a parting glance.

"Well," said Sophie, "you don't seem to be in the cheeriest mood. How'd the mail-sorting go, too depressing for you?"

"No, it was okay. A lot of junk; you have your fans, but there are a lot of crazies out there. Also quite a few who would try to govern without the benefit of being elected by competent juries of their peers."

Sophie snickered into her soup.

"So tell me more about the state of our national security," I asked with a slurp. "That is, to the extent you are permitted."

Her lip curled in a sneer, but she let it go. "Oh, well, it looks just dandy on the surface. Except there's this odd dichotomy—I mean half the time they were telling me how all-powerful we are, nothing to worry about, no enemy would stand a chance, and so on; and then they'd come back and say we had to shore up this or that weakening bulwark in the nation's defense, the enemy could walk in at any moment."

"So what's your conclusion?"

"Oh, I don't know. I tend to feel we're fairly well sitting pretty. Though I'm sure we need to upgrade constantly, and not let the whole thing shift out of balance on the other side."

"What other side?"

"The enemy side."

"What enemy?"

"Oh, that's not important. What's important is that there could be one."

"I see."

"Anyway, we've got kind of a sticky problem coming up. We're trying to get French warships outfitted with our nukes, so they will be under our ultimate command—my command—but the French are balking. They want to retain an independent role; it's all the socialists in their government, you know. A few of my generals think their refusal could tip the whole balance of power the other way. And if that happened we would have to take action to pre-empt—"

"Wait a second. You mean, start a war? A nuclear war, a laser war?"

"Not exactly. That is, we wouldn't really be starting it. The French would, by their own defection. There would be a flare-up somewhere like Tonga, or Madagascar, you see. The generals have these scenarios all worked out, what they call 'weighted contingencies.' That's what they get paid for, I guess. And what with French agents running around, and the Mossad, and Interpol—non-nuclear, at first, of course. We'd only use them if the battle plan dictated their exigency, was the way the secretary of defense put it."

"Good God, Sophie, they've got you in army fatigues already, and you never even went to boot camp."

"Naw, I'll just sit in my office, with my finger on the trigger, waiting for the red telephone to ring. Come on, let's go try out the squash courts across the street before my next meeting."

CHAPTER VII

In the face of America's precarious readiness, almost eagerness, for war, I retained my characteristic optimism—maintaining what might be viewed as a simple-minded, day-to-day pleasure in my work which was reminiscent, I thought with a time-rosied nostalgia, of my days as a dishwasher in Alabama, retail clerk in California, taxi driver in Alaska. At the same time, I was still enamored with the glint of gilt-edged opportunity—the chance to enjoy the company of the world's most notable dignitaries, the leaders of the leaders, the most finely polished social ornaments of the most cultivated societies, orbiting with such stately decorum in the governmental circles of the world.

I even met the putative king of Portugal, one mild February evening at a White House state dinner. He was seated to my left, and the textured Portuguese he spoke to the Brazilian coffee scientist opposite him rang in my ears like an ancient wind chime.

My own limited proficiency in that tongue was dulled with considerable rust, so I inquired, in politely paced English, about the man's position. He seemed shy to respond, and the Brazilian, his hair glossy with brilliantine, jumped to his rescue.

"Why, this is, please me to interrupt but the old king of Portugal, herself. Yes." A toothy grin.

A matching grin, quickly covered with tight red lips, from the king himself. He was actually not very old in years, maybe forty-two. I almost told him I remembered his ancestor. Instead I mentioned that an intimate friend of mine—rather, an ancestor of that friend—had once met the king of Portugal, Dom Carlos I, perhaps this king's great-great-great-grandfather?

A clouded look passed over the king's face. He appeared too flustered to respond. The Brazilian and the king exchanged anxious glances.

Finally the Brazilian, bug-eyed and earnest, leaned forward and explained to me, "Not quite exact. This king claims his, how you say, throne, from a competing line, an earlier monarch: Miguel the first. Dom Carlos was assassinated in 1908, along with the heir-apparent. The surviving heir, Manuel, bore no extra heirs from that line."

"Oh, forgive me. So our king here is not from the same family?"

The Brazilian uttered an uncomfortable laugh. "I see you Americans do not quite understand. The same family and not the same family. Not quite exact."

I turned and said to the king, "My apologies. I can appreciate the complexities of the royal bloodlines; the perceived necessity to, on the one hand, ensure the integrity of the monarchal race, while also taking care to respect the competing claims to the successionary lineages."

I was met with a blank stare from the king, a wrinkle in his pitted nose.

I thought to inquire, "Majesty, you do speak English, don't you?"

"Why, yes. Yes, of course. Do you?"

Great hilarity followed... along with the royal fare: prime rib sliced thick and perfectly rare, broccoli and hollandaise, rosemary roast potatoes, a light Caesar salad, trifle and café Hapsburg. I put aside a distant grief for the murdered king, Dom Carlos I. *Bloody anarchists*, I thought. But best to leave such intrigues in the dusty past.

After spending most of the supper exchanging "Knock-knock" jokes with the king and the coffee scientist, I sought more serious and contemporary conversation after dessert and superb Brazilian coffee—a select batch gifted for the occasion from that same distinguished guest. Silently weaving my way through the crowd, I caught drifting snatches of chatter and chose what I wanted to hear.

Not "...and then the horses took the final jump," nor "You should have seen her laugh when I pulled it away from her," nor "The interesting thing about these nanochips is their essential disilicon compartmentalization, in terms of data preselection..."

No, I found myself finally drawn to Sophie. I stood hovering behind her right shoulder contemplating the freckles, as she spoke. The thin white strap of her dress was tied neatly on top, inviting some rogue less principled than myself to untie it in impish fun. It may have helped her in a tough spot, as she was arguing with a Frenchman, the NATO attaché. There was another eavesdropper behind them, who tried to look disinterested when he noticed that I noticed him.

The talk was about defense arrangements, buying and selling old warships and planes, along with other current considerations such as treaty commitments to third-party territories, and last but not least, the controversial naval strikeforce allocations, earmarked for nuclear drones, self-guided artillery shells and submarine-launched Dart missiles.

Sophie was in one of her stubborn moods, which correlated with some regularity to the question of advanced weapons (whether nuclear, particle-beam, or laser-based) for so-called defense.

"Mr. Pinchot," she said, "your country must appreciate the importance of the long-standing tradition of friendship between our two nations. Together we've maintained a mutual spirit of commitment to the protection of the free world, which I know you'll agree—"

"Madame, Tonga and the Canary Islands are quite another matter. They have themselves free and provincially independent populations, who have, by grace of their proper decrees, decided to become weapons-free zones. That does not mean we cannot station our own older warships there; and we still have rights to the airstrips for at least the token protection of the people within the broader confines of the alliances of France."

"Can't you at least guarantee those warships and planes will be equipped to handle American deterrent force material?"

"You mean bombs?"

"Yes."

"*Mais, non.*"

"Shit."

The other eavesdropper moved away.

Realizing I was standing behind her, Sophie turned and said, "Oh, you again." Then in a whisper, "It looks like the French aren't with us."

Monsieur Pinchot was looking at us. Out of a stupid, by now automatic sense of diplomatic politeness, I tried to smile for him, but couldn't. He excused himself and I said to Sophie, "Let's step out for some air."

The ships of diplomacy groaned and creaked, their ragged rigging flapping in the starless night, until they were gone from view. Sophie and I stood on the lawn and watched our White House glow in yellow floodlights, a Disney Versailles, under a rising moon.

The pressures of her high office mounted daily on Sophie's shoulders. I supported her as I could, both with my clerical duties and personal affections. Still the demands increased from all quarters: generals, executives, environmental fanatics, duck hunters and legal-aid activists, schoolchildren touring the house; not to mention the endless parade of banquets and convocations, policy briefs, Party strategy sessions, and legislative conundrums.

I occupied, at best, a backseat role in the formulation of policy. The new slate of bills being drafted for Congress smacked of an insidious paranoia which I had no choice but to attribute to the Hierarchy. Chief among these was the bill regulating the science of fate engineering. As law, the bill would make it a federal crime to produce software with the intent of rewriting history, writing new history, exploring past lives, or projecting future lifeline scenarios.

Behind such legislation, according to Sophie, lay the fear that the programs might infect the official Lifelines program. If that happened, either indiscriminately or with the premeditated use of custom alteration codes, undesirable changes could infect individual and collective destinies.

When I challenged Sophie with the conclusion that this secretive program of tracking multiple personal identities, the kas, seemed to be the exclusive privilege of the elite, she snapped, "What would you prefer, that it be available to everybody and their grandmother?"

A related piece of legislation, the Act to Regulate Dreams and Spiritual Practices, would prohibit astral travel through time or beyond the borders of one's own federal electoral district. This bill's supporters claimed the need to prevent revolutionary networking. Again, Sophie admitted to me the underlying rationale: to restrict interference with the Hierarchy's psychic airspace; and to protect the predictable evolution of the kas now copyrighted within Lifelines. Enforcement would be in the hands of a new, covert federal agency obliquely alluded to in the language of the bill. These "Astral Police," as an FBI memo referred to them with clarifying bluntness, would work with the aid of computer-tracked energy fields strung, so to speak, with trip wires activated by certain vibration rates of astral and etheric bodies in motion.

Both of these bills were fast-tracked to Congress via special committees in secret session, so as to secure passage without the harsh investigative light of public scrutiny. For my part, I was allowed no input of substance on the above areas, which were deemed above my limited national security clearance.

Sophie made an exception when it came to deliberations on her pet project, the so-called Continental scheme for resolving all outstanding Aboriginal Peoples' land claims in North America. Her idea was to grant all land north of the fifty-second parallel to Aboriginal nations to administer, develop, and maintain as they wished. In return, the United States of North America (USNA) would gain absolute sovereignty over all Native American lands and reservations south of that line. The reparations and resettlement problems alone were staggering. But the advantages were obvious. The oil concerns who had to sell out from northern Alberta could move into coal in the Black Hills. Loggers could transfer from Lac St-Jean to the wood-rich Grassy Narrows reserve. The Hopi and Navaho could square off across the Nahanni River in the Yukon. Problems, sure. There would be plenty of griping about the forced removal from "ancestral lands," on the part of Native Americans in the US; though a portion could be appeased by an alternate relocation southward to Mexico, in a subsidiary arrangement with that subnation. Also impacted would be the Canadian cities north of the line, including Edmonton and Saskatoon, and the entirety of Alaska. The economic justification for such upheaval, even taking into account the loss of the Arctic energy sector, would be the assimilation of southern Canada's manufacturing and resource regime once and for all into the diabetic American economy, with no more funny-sounding strings (GATT, NAFTA, TPP) attached.

Hard choices, yes. We were learning fast to become hardened politicos, to deal with the pressure-ridden realities of interest-group dominance in the legislative process—and to treat people as economic pawns in the grander strategies of empire. After all winter of planning and policymaking, of research and heated late-night lobbying, of cocktails and tête-à-têtes, of diplomats and chauffeurs, of toasts and trade talks and addresses to eminent assemblies, of rail-bus rides into the high Alleghenies, and yacht parties on the silver Potomac, Sophie signed the bill into law. Immediately she notified the State Department of the new United States and Provinces of Continental America to carry out the necessary relocations.

An ulterior motive of the Continental Policy, Sophie confided in me, was to throw the decentralists into disarray. For this reason the Hierarchy acquiesced to the plan, though it was her brainchild, driven by her sympathetic identification with Aboriginal Peoples early in her career. On the one hand the policy disregarded local traditions and boundaries, and over this crime the decentralists complained bitterly. On the other hand the rearrangement favored the Northern indigenous populations, leaving them as partners in the new union to govern themselves as they saw fit, thus reducing the role of central government over that vast region. Such autonomy rankled elements in the Hierarchy, but was allowed as the cost of securing free title and authority over the bulk of the populated portion of the continent.

Debate simmered even among the Party faithful, after the bill's passage. Dennis McElroy, appointed chief of staff, grumbled that the administration would be mired in unending lawsuits, appeals, petitions, demonstrations, or worse—violent rebellion. Ryan Willoughby, now press secretary, was flushed with the expanded importance of his role, in explaining to the public the rationale behind the land resettlements and corporate selloffs. Madison Kane, appointed earlier by Sophie as ambassador to Mexico, threatened to resign in protest, penning an angry op-ed in the *New York Times* about "cultural genocide."

"That's fine," Sophie snapped when she read the paper, petulant over hearing of the resignation that way instead of by formal letter. "She can go back to Montreal, her French lovers and tarry cigarettes, her baggy sweaters."

"She grew up in Boston, she told me."

"Oh really. So the Frenchie act is affectation. Apparently she's been affecting you."

I put my hand on Sophie's shoulder, nudged a wisp of hair behind her ear, and gave her my best eyes. She looked away, pouting.

Commentary in the press in general was divided; while in the streets protests mounted. Panarchists forged alliances with indigenous peoples across the height and breadth of the land. The Hawai'ian monarchy announced its resolve to stay put, vowing never to abandon its tropical paradise for the Arctic wastes. Drum beats, rattles and bells drowned out bureaucrats and politicians on every live interview: some celebrating a millennial victory, others an unacceptable oppression. The same split reigned among labor unions, school districts, chambers of commerce, depending on whether they could remain or had to vacate.

In the wake of popular unrest from every corner, the response from the Hierarchy was slow in coming, as if those sentient powers were digesting the diverse and diffuse information, weighing probabilities and contingent outcomes. At last the orders came through. Sophie appeared ashen after a meeting with Wolfgang Nenowitz and Robert Glaston. The Astral Police would be forthwith mobilized, the databots programmed to their service. Ringleaders of popular protests would be singled out and processed expediently.

I asked Sophie to explain the Hierarchy's motivations, given their arms length during the bill's formulation over the winter.

"It's the principle," she told me. "I'm the one holding power. Enforcing the law of the land. At this stage—at any stage—it's not so much about the merits or shortcomings of any particular policy or law. People will always disagree, at that level. This is more about brass tacks: the issue of power itself. I have to establish who is in control."

"And that is?"

"I'm the president."

A pirate vidcast which we monitored at the White House featured a swarthy specimen of Panarchist fervor, shaking his dreadlocks as he spoke, half Spanish and half street-talk English, with a musical lilt meant to lull and seduce, about the arts as the path to enlightenment. I recognized him as the heckler who had been subdued at the fringe of our campaign appearance in Spokane. Sweetly he sang of a revolution of potlucks, and Rainbow gatherings, and motorbikes. Such beauty and freedom, against columns of federal tanks, concentration camps. Where was this country heading? My friends. Then a sideways tilt of the head, a sly smile. Signed off.

"Pash," said Chief of Staff McElroy. "Guy's got what, a third-grade education? Telling us how to run the country?" He yanked on his tie, loosened his collar.

Another segment followed. Again I recognized the speaker—Lamar Pentecost, the same stuttering radical who had warmed up the Spokane crowd before Sophie arrived. To his invisible listeners in the pirate network audience, said to number 43 percent of the viewing share in the 3 to 4 p.m. time slot, Pentecost announced that his home town of Moab, Utah, had declared a general strike in support of the incarcerated "Sisters of Panarchy," Zanelle Marte and Elfie Byweather.

I felt a pang of sympathy for the two in custody. They were ordinary citizens speaking their minds, correct? When I expressed this sentiment, to no one in particular, Sophie kicked me under the table.

I glared at her, and found Dennis McElroy glaring at me.

Ryan Willoughby asked McElroy, "Tell me again why those fine young ladies are being held without charges, and kept in solitary?"

"They are symbols of the resistance," said Dennis. "We must make an example of them."

Why McElroy would utter such a kneejerk cliché, no doubt can be laid to the logic of empire since the beginning of recorded time.

Meanwhile on the screen this modern-day Kropotkin, with his short black beard, was calmly decrying the "c-c-corporatist propaganda of the Hierarchy." He entreated us viewers to leave our contrived isolation; to speak with our fellow citizens about the matters of the day, matters of life and death, matters of the heart. We must connect in all peaceful forms of voluntary association, to solve practical problems ourselves, without interference from the s-s-state. The government would not, at this late date, be trusted to reverse climate change or economic decay, those very problems it had created by its blind—or worse, willful—excess.

"How can he get away with this shit?" McElroy railed. "Where are the drones?"

CHAPTER VIII

One raw, blustery morning in early March, returning from my morning jog, I was surprised to see a throng of ragged people milling around outside the wrought iron fence of the White House. I passed them on the run, bound to my routine of a refreshing hot shower. Dutifully I breakfasted, with Fred and Imma, on a half grapefruit and soft-boiled egg, and went to work in the cozy comfort of the mailroom. Sophie had a morning meeting with Nenowitz and Glaston: the Troika, I called them.

Windowless and climate-controlled, with its cool gray metal surfaces and hushed airflow blunting the senses, my cubicle supplied a news feed to tell me what was transpiring outside, at the White House gates. A hailstorm raged, pelting protesters, soaking and then battering their hand-lettered cardboard signs into the semblance of soggy brown leaves. The target of this particular demonstration was foreign policy: administration support for a client state in Central Asia who was bombing its own villagers. Their crime? Inhabiting traditional lands over recently discovered natural gas fields, and refusing to leave under government decree.

Returning National Security Advisor Wolfgang Nenowitz contributed the definitive justification for the "cleansing," with the bald claim that wiping the pesky residents off the face of the gas fields was good for the environment. "Our experts have calculated," he crowed—the leathery skin on his aged neck working like snakeskin over a swallowed frog—"that the net carbon footprint of the region will shrink while the investment climate will improve. Thanks to the efforts of our allies in this and other strategic operations around the globe, we will see not only a reduction in wasteful human consumption, but also increased opportunity for the development and delivery of resources in the energy sector on which all of us depend."

Foreign policy, I had been told on numerous occasions, was not my department. So I shrugged, turned off the feed, and buckled to tasks of more domestic concern. Cloistered in my digital cocoon, I sat tabulating opinions on the still-controversial merger with Canada (Mexico to follow in Phase II), then drafted and revised speeches for Sophie, taking into account arguments raised in the flood of letters, emails and petitions. I dispatched memos conveying the drift of public opinion to congressional leaders, assembling data to serve over rhetoric, urging the lawmakers to pay heed to the wellspring of decentralist fervor sweeping the unsettled land. Most correspondents felt, I could say in confidence, that the Continental policy had broken asunder the nation, spilling out the trust and heritage which had bound its regions together. It was as if a spell had broken, and in its absence the disintegration of the society was underway—nay, even welcomed.

These latest reports reflected a newfound humility on my part; or perhaps a simple pragmatic consideration of the spectrum of opinions in play. If I took a stance it was compassionate yet dispassionate; tightly reasoned yet undogmatic. I prided myself on serving no master—not even Sophie, or her blessed Hierarchy—but truth itself, and the inner promptings of my conscience. In holding this compass of objectivity I felt secure and hoped to ensure that Sophie, if she heeded my recommendations, would avoid the ire of her superiors.

Before exiting the menu listing connections with other nodes, my eye caught a flashing entry at the end of the list, one I hadn't previously noticed: *MA*. I didn't know what I was supposed to do. Was this an incoming call—from my long-dead mother in Germany? I pressed *Enter*.

MA, it turned out, meant "Mainframe Alpha"—a term

recalling the early days of computing, when a central unit served as the hub for hard-wired subsidiary terminals. In this case the hub was virtual, a database and program operating in a secure Cloud. Supposedly secure, that is. When LIFELINES appeared as a subdirectory, my heart beat furiously. Should I enter to see if I could locate my former self, and identify the various spinoff kas?

If I wanted to meddle in these files without risk of the draconian penalties stipulated in the regulatory bill pending passage in Congress, I would have to act fast. But the prospect of doing so with any confidence was too overwhelming. I scanned the directory structure and saw many other code names that signified nothing to me. I wanted to try them all. I felt like the proverbial kid in a candy store—or bull in a china shop. I saw "HISTORY/ALT" and, with some trepidation at what I was getting into (Could I alter history with a touch of the wrong key? Could I wipe myself, along with everyone on the planet, out of existence with an errant little finger?), I decided to have a look. In the file listing under that subdirectory I chose the provocative entry called "LASTBOOK." Had I seen the entry flash before I touched the key? I wasn't sure. It was too late to go back. The monitor screen lit up with the following title:

The Last Book:
Footnotes to the History of Humankind

Eagerly I scrolled down through its contents. Its scope was true to its title. The sweep of its vision was planetary and almost timeless. I had to wonder from the outset, whose perspective engendered the writing of such a critique, and from what possible—or impossible—remove? Of course the very existence of this digital variety of "book" implied a contradiction of the main title: if this book, why not another? I wondered, then, if the subtitle of this computerized reference work referred, rather, to an actual printed book, *The History of Humankind*.

On the other hand, perhaps the documentary voice actually did address its subject directly. History itself was the book, in a figurative manner of speaking—and this scrolling text consisted of the "footnotes" to that "book."

Then there was the appendage on the directory listing, "/Alt." Did this file describe merely one possible version of human history, and not necessarily what did or would happen?

It was all very enigmatic; but my abstruse speculations paled beside the stark catalogs of human experience contained within, once I began reading.

Naturally I can't justify encumbering the reader of my personal history with the entire length of this fascinating tome, this pearl in my pigpen—though it might appeal to the historically curious. So I shall confine the excerpted portion of the book to that section in the final chapter which most arrested my avid eyes, with its insight into where we were in the present world and how we'd got there. For despite my recent record of achievement (which, in all humility, I admit was gained largely by association with Sophie), I was still a novitiate at this time in what I thought of as history; and I still had some dozens of doublings of human knowledge during the last hundred and forty years to catch up on.

> Technology and specialization developed hand in hand and together were responsible for the spectacular success, and correspondingly spectacular failure, of the machine called civilization. This historical irony was borne out on three key fronts, which manifested in their terminal stages as *overpopulation*, *social alienation*, and *ecological destruction*.
>
> The driving force in the machine's progress was the impulse to populate; the fuel for which was provided by the development of medical technology and the ethic of unlimited growth. Higher birth-survival rates and lower

death rates were the direct result. Scientific and technological developments meanwhile made possible greater success in providing the necessities of a healthy life for increased numbers in society as a whole.

The upward curve of the population rates reached precipitous heights, however, by the mid-twentieth century. In the respective realms of rats, bacteria, or numbers on a graph, when the overpopulation curve becomes vertical, a catastrophe occurs. For rats, reproduction halts; for bacteria, the supportive organism dies, starving the parasitic culture which for a brief time has become dominant; on the graph, time stops. Survival past such circumstances depends on a dramatic shift in the predominant paradigm, into new modes of being. The number line stops trying to live in time and instead stretches upward and downward for eternity. The bacterial culture atrophies and dies, unless another nutritive environment chances upon it. The rats eat each other, primarily the newly born, until their usual rations can be restored. It is clear from these cases that "survival" does not imply an unbroken continuation of history, or of the life pattern.

The human race shared characteristics of all three nonhuman models. Conceiving of eternity, while approaching it with the power to end history. Falling prey to new epidemics and diseases, and meanwhile jeopardizing the earth's capacity to support further life, by decimating forests, acidifying and poisoning water, depleting the ozone, and forcing erosion of fertile soil. Finally, slaughtering its own kind by the billion. As of this writing, it cannot be determined whether a successful revivification of human culture is possible.

This authorial stance, as I'm certain the discerning reader may appreciate, was unnerving. Who was the author, anyway—some alien correspondent reporting to a distant galactic superior? A militant anarchist theoretician from

Georgetown University? The alien reporter writing via an astral channel through the local academician? "As of this writing..." indeed. To continue:

> The second theme, alienation, stemmed from a historical process with its roots in the drive to populate and to succeed scientifically at all costs. It began to manifest on the historical plane when overpopulation took the form of imperial colonization. The early European empires gave rise to a cosmopolitanism which destroyed tribal identities in favor of individual hybrids. These new strains displayed an adaptive advantage in outlying environments; for, while the centuries following the collapse of the Roman Empire saw the establishment of superficially distinct nation-states, the mark of Rome was stamped upon all the governments, and they came to play the roles of rival factions in a newer European empire.
>
> Technology, medicine and social philosophy were proceeding apace. Nations eager to play out the advantages of specialization and mechanization entered a competitive race for efficiency and dominance in agriculture, industry and warfare. The new industries, cosmopolitan tastes, and growing numbers of the Europeans demanded new resources—from gold, to coffee, to land. Even the churches had developed an insatiable need for more souls to save. And so the European human group overflowed to reap even more of the earth's bounty on the other five continents, looking even to Antarctica, to the Earth's moon and beyond, for the needs of the future.
>
> The confrontation of the expanding white culture with the indigenous peoples and cultures of its exploited colonies produced disastrous results for the latter. In addition to the large-scale genocide practiced in many areas in the early periods of worldwide imperialism, cultural genocide was the de facto result of sustained contact and assimilation, even when the subjugated peoples were protected on reservations

or given home-rule status under the aegis of the controlling government.

Despite the inherent racism of the colonizers, their empire-stretching served to hybridize further the white race and culture. The amalgam which civilization had already become was colored by ever new and diverse racial and cultural elements. The "melting pot" syndrome found its apogee in the mass culture of the United States, itself a direct outgrowth of the European expansion.

The resultant hybrid culture, however, spread worldwide by the very success of the American model, tended toward a new monoculture rather than a true diversity of integral traditions. It was as if the white race had forced distinctive, vibrant colors back through a prism to emerge in blinding, indistinct white light. The historical tribes had been fused into a gigantic metatribe, inhabiting a new, electronic "global village."

Certain moral principles were fulfilled in the historical process which seemed to the conquerors and their assimilated subjects to justify the new world order. The ideal was expressed via different and sometimes conflicting ideologies; yet the fallacy was common. Whether by Christian ideals, or manifest destiny, or economic solidarity, it was expected that all people could share a common identity, as they had previously only within tribal groups. But however noble the concept, it was an abstract one when enforced on the national or global scale, alien to concrete human nature on an organic social scale.

Traditionally, tribal groups had relied not on the imaginary unity of specialized, autonomous strangers, but on the actual daily cooperation of congenial, well-rounded members of ancestral communities. Individual success was not narrowly specialized, but depended on a complete range of living skills. Group strength was a resilient one based on the broad abilities of its members, and did not rest therefore on spectacular material achievements.

For centuries, advances in technology allowed the white-hybrid culture to conquer the human and natural world; simultaneously its very foundations, in social structure and resource extraction, were slowly crumbling. The initial population booms and consequent expansion, along with the extermination, exploitation and assimilation of other peoples, delivered an elementary and superficial judgment of white success.

Within the overextended empire, alienation was the price of specialization. The successful individuals who made up the increasingly megalomaniacal machine, while losing contact with their own primary survival skills, were estranged as well from the wholeness of natural life. The same factors that helped the individual to survive as a cog in the machine caused the population as a whole to boom; but the result was a silent, poisonous backfire in the form of individual alienation from the faceless crowd. The so-called digital revolution sealed the fate of the imperial citizen, who would abandon the struggles of people for basic human, democratic and economic rights, to rest content behind a screen of infinite entertainment, entrainment, entrapment.

I became cognizant then of my own reflection in the screen—a phantasm of a figment of a once living, breathing, human being moving with animal grace upon the resplendent banks of the Tagus River, or the mighty Mississippi. Now ensconced in my dungeon of a cubicle, I sat riveted to these ciphers from an implied but uncertain future, an unknown vantage.

Left penniless on the fish docks in the so-called New World, I had ascended, by my own efforts and by forces still beyond me ken, to a yet newer world—one neither so brave nor so ordered as its champions might prefer to paint it—for what, to what end? To sit by the controls of another sinking ship?

I read on...

The price paid for individual and technological success proved to be more than the twin diseases of overpopulation and alienation, and more than that paid by indigenous peoples facing imperial subjugation. The final price would be the viability of the biosphere as a whole. By the late twentieth century, it was becoming apparent even in the halls of empire that unlimited growth was impossible. Overpopulation was reaching discernible proportions. Alienation was both more widespread than ever and more understood (ironically by means of specialized academic education). And energy sources for advanced technology were no longer easily or cheaply available for the taking. The energy crisis took until then to reveal itself in its full implications, owing to previously abundant supplies in the ever farther flung hinterlands, and the capacity of science to devise new methods of resource extraction. Finally the ends of the once seemingly bottomless pits of the fossil fuels came into view—recalling, for geologically astute observers, the last great race of masters of the earth, the Dinosaurs, so famously extinguished.

The chief replacement for fossil fuels promised, for a time, to be uranium. A mere twenty years of experimentation with nuclear energy instead convinced enough people of its dangers to halt its growth. Similar disappointments were played out in most areas of resource extraction and heavy industry. Growing numbers of people, and the regulatory bodies of their governments, began to see the counterproductive byproducts and side effects (including huge financial liabilities) of such activity. The pollution of other natural resources such as air and water reached untenable proportions, threatening the very human organisms the new energy and industry were meant to sustain.

Frontiers were growing too scarce and isolated to be efficiently exploited in the accustomed manner of the European industrial-military machine. At the same time, the empire's population, in its pervasive social disaffection, was becoming less eager to sanction unlimited exploitation at its own (and the rest of the planet's) expense. A turning point of a kind occurred when the American citizenry refused to continue its support for a government engaged in a futile military adventure in Southeast Asia. The ensuing frustration of this great power's expansionist aims represented the forging of a new link in the chain of imperial power extending back from the United States to England, and from England to Rome.

In each case the colony responsible for the turning back of the empire became the next great world power. And so from the USA the mantle of earthly power passed to the Vietnamese people, and indeed to the under-represented American people who opposed their own government, who dared to affirm the principle of self-determination: in either case, a people whose reign may be seen not in the same terms of material expansion embraced by the imperial lineage, but rather as a symbolic coming of age of the downtrodden; as a harbinger of the pregnant upsurgence of the Third and Fourth Worlds. Those peoples, the disenfranchised, the colonized, the disinherited, shunned the empty promises of an exploitive global economy, and advocated relentlessly for regional and ethnic autonomy.

When I read these words I began to sweat, cognizant of the decentralist rivals to our own ruling Party. Was that groundswell the future? Had that future arrived—even at the gates of the White House this very morning? I touched the security camera feed for an update; saw only swirling debris on the sidewalk, drones buzzing overhead.

Even under the aegis of Panarchy, the resisters were not exactly a party, not content with building a base of support among voters for the next federal election three and a half years hence. They continued to engage in every form of rebellious action against the central government: faux declarations of independence, constitutional challenges, tax boycotts, rail-bus blockades, flag-burnings, and other sundry acts of civil disobedience and sabotage. Previously I had thought of such opposition as merely irksome—to be expected in the course of running a modern government on a scale such as ours. Now I comprehended that perhaps mine was an institution whose time of glory was past, and that for those of the decentralist movement, the future had arrived.

I looked up from the computer screen, empty in the gut with nostalgia; wishing I could have preserved my relative innocence about what I'd considered to be merely "the troubled drift of Western civilization." Yet, even now, while I had at my fingertips not exactly a futuristic apocalypse, nor a convincing prescription for human survival, this *Last Book* sowed the seeds within me of what I already felt (in my opportunistic way) might become a program of true global leadership for constructive, decentralized change, to be initiated and sponsored by none other than my employer, my lover, my guardian angel, cosmic nemesis, mistress and friend (and, not to shortchange her, empress of my world), Sophie Tucker Vaughan.

Even judging solely by the weight of public outrage against our pet project, Continentalism, I had reason to believe that an officially sanctioned program of decentralization would be popular, perhaps wonderfully successful. Even most critics of the "imperialistic" merger of the US and southern Canada were applauding the granting of self-determination to the Northern native peoples. The wise course would be to follow that policy success with attractive programs in our own, larger nation, the USNA. I could see it now: local governments could be further subsidized; folk art revivals funded; village markets refurbished; neighborhood dance halls erected; solar, wind, tidal and geothermal power sources developed to perfection. It would be, I unthinkingly imagined, the modern, political equivalent of the Roman aqueducts.

Immediately doubt set in. Wasn't it the most pompous

contradiction on my part, to swallow whole this thesis of an anonymous overseer, and then to propose in the name of its critical truths a program of remedies to be controlled by the central heart and head of the most far-flung, gigantic and powerful, "successful" but doom-bound empire the world had ever seen... all the while thinking the contradiction could be erased by the fine concepts of "decentralization" or "panarchism"?

The piles of unsorted mail around me still languished in a state of disarray. The awesome responsibility of my job suddenly had become a burden of enormous weight. How could anyone function creatively in the very bowels (never mind the heart and head) of the leviathan? To ride along with its predominant movement would, at best, do nothing to curb its destructive progress, and would instead lend validity and credence to its professed aims. I pushed my smooth-wheeled chair away from the desk, got up and took refuge at the virtual window, with its rotating tropical scenes, pacing off my dilemma. To work from within to subvert, or even just to slow down, the operations of this juggernaut would likely lead only to consequences of a personal nature—accusations of hypocrisy, reprisals, job redesignation, harassment, dismissal... "accidental" assassination.

I wondered how Sophie herself would cope with the awareness of her role in the unflattering portrayal of the world I'd seen painted before me that morning. Or maybe she had such awareness already; I couldn't say. If so, I wondered how she could justify her own position of power.

I wanted to look again at the end of the book, and then to revisit the introduction. When I sat back at the desk, however, I found to my dismay that the computer screen had gone blank and dark. Had it gone off on a timer? Had I inadvertently shut it off when I got up to go to the window? I pressed *Enter* and the screen lit up; but the text was gone, and I was back at the main directory menu. "OO" was still there, but not "MA."

Curious. Had I unknowingly pressed a hot-key earlier enabling the encrypted entry to appear? If so, I hadn't a clue how to duplicate it. Like a lost child, I thought with foolish amusement, I wanted my MA, and I had the childish urge to call up Sophie on the "OO" line to ask her how to get back home.

I looked at my watch; it was noon already. I decided I wasn't yet prepared, because I hadn't yet come to terms with *The Last Book*'s implications, to bring it to Sophie's attention. I also didn't know how I could keep it from her.

Fortunately Sophie was out for lunch that day and I didn't have to face her. Over supper I let her carry the conversation as usual with tales of her busy day. When she observed my reticent mood and asked if something was the matter, I told her how public opinion was growing against the Continentalist policy. There were too many problems for too many people—it would never work. "I think," I concluded, "we should consider shelving it."

"Shelving it? At this late date? We've already cleared the first category of relocation grants for next month's budget. You don't simply back out of something like this. All the companies with applications for the reserve lands..."

"Fuck the companies," I said, too impulsively.

Sophie stopped chewing and looked at me with genuine concern. "What's got into you, Seymour? You helped formulate this policy. It would help the native peoples, you agreed. You don't have to convince the electorate—that's my job, and one I'm fully prepared to do. With or without your help."

I was almost ready to concede her point about the natives; but her last statement sent me into a purely defensive reaction: "Right. And then you can have your nice new empire all to yourself. Fine by me. You go ahead, and see what happens. I'm getting out."

And I did. Out the front door, where I brushed past Ronald the Secret Service man. He looked at me with a smirk, smoothing back his slick black hair. I stormed up to the iron fence... and turned back. Looking at the White House all lit up in the deepening night, I knew it didn't have to end like this. But how could I convince Sophie of the danger, the folly of her position when it lay so deeply within the very structure of the machine she happened to "control" at the moment?

She would have to see *The Last Book* for herself. There was no other way.

I caught her on the stairway, reaching an arm out to her elbow. She turned on me, crying out—"Let me go, you... you spineless bastard. I should have known from the beginning that you wouldn't be able to stick with anything worthwhile for long. Now that this act is over, you can try out some other charade."

I did let go of her arm, and then it spilled out: "Sophie, have you ever heard of anything called *The Last Book*?"

"No," she said, and I knew she was telling the truth. "Why? Is it supposed to make any difference to us? You pick a strange time to give a book report from your profound little collection of fantasies in the White House library."

I saw hope in her continued willingness to talk, as she lingered there a step or two above me. I found the courage to say to her then, "Sophie, come on, I have to tell you about this—it's no fantasy." As I said so, I had to hope I was right—yet at the same time I hoped that she was right, and that this earthshaking prophecy was nothing but a work of speculative fiction, an "alternate history." Either way, I wanted to heal the fresh wounds we had opened.

She still stood stiffly on the stair.

"Sophie," I said, "I'm sorry."

"So am I. I shouldn't have said what I did."

"We can breathe through it."

She smiled, at last, and said, "Let's go up to bed. You can tell me all about your book."

We undressed in silence. I held her body close, feeling a mutual tenderness comparable to the first time our skins enjoyed full contact. We did breathe deeply together, stroking away the rough edges of our painful dissonance. Finally I lay beside her looking up at the ceiling in the dark, ready to speak my truth.

"I got into Mainframe Alpha today."

Sophie's nails caught like a cat's fist on my leg, and she gave a gasp. I did too.

"There was a document, listed under History-slash-Alt, entitled *The Last Book: Footnotes to the History of Humankind*. It was rather apocalyptic in its perspective."

"Sounds ominous, all right. How did you hack into Mainframe Alpha?"

"I don't know," I said. I turned to face her, propping my head with elbow and hand. "The entry wasn't there before, but this time I saw it, listed as MA."

"MA has a classified entry code. There's no way you can tap into it without the code."

"Not even by accident?"

"No way. The odds against a random discovery and entry of the seven-level code are virtually impossible. Which means there's foul play going on, and the Hierarchy's gonna shit bricks over it."

"How can a spiritual Hierarchy shit bricks?"

"Okay, okay," she said. "What expression shall I use?"

"How about, 'There'll be hell to pay'?"

She gave me a sidelong glance. "Listen. The listing shouldn't even be displayed in the main directory like that. It's completely protected by the encoding shell."

"Evidently not."

"I don't know about your doomsday insects, but here's a bug that's got to be worked out."

"What is MA, anyway?"

"You realize this is totally classified information," she said. "I mean, government classified is one thing. That's for my eyes, at least. This is different. There are plenty of files and programs in MA that I'll never touch."

"Unless you move up in the Hierarchy." My hand rested on the top of her thigh, a touch so light her skin seemed to become transparent.

Her breathing stopped for a moment, as if to fit between breaths the full implications of such a rise in the ranks—above the presidency, where the real power lay. And surely there was a price to pay.

"What I don't get," she said, "is why I haven't seen this *Last Book*. Did you say it was listed in a subdirectory?"

"Yeah, History-slash-Alt."

"I know that section, but I never saw your book there. It could be a new entry. I'd like to have a look at it. I'll give it a try tomorrow."

Sophie yawned and reached toward the bedside light.

"Why not now?" I said, my hand slipping off her. "Can't you log into MA from the Mini?" This portable computing device lived in the drawer of Sophie's bedtable, close at hand for emergencies.

"I've never tried. But it's late. It can wait till tomorrow. So you broke in and read a file. It's not the end of the world." With that she turned out the light on the bedtable, lay back down draping one arm loosely around me, and fell silent. I sensed she was being less than truthful—or for some reason not willing to hear the truth.

I lay there and brooded awhile, considering whether I had overreacted to the stimulus of *The Last Book*. No, it seemed to have been purposely placed before me at this critical point in history—while there was still time. In that case, should I launch into a summary of it, forcing Sophie to hear me out? No, I couldn't do it justice if she wasn't in the mood to hear it.

Why this stubborn resistance on her part? I realized with a cool and distasteful insight that our entire legislative program was just that: a program, engineered by the Hierarchy to further their aims and protect their secret position of virtually unlimited power. *Sophie must be in on these plans,* I concluded; *that's why she resents my interference.*

I determined that more useful information might well be gleaned from MA. I would have to be more daring in my manipulation of its files, to the extent such meddling was technically possible.

Sophie was right; it was late. And I, too, would go to work tomorrow.

CHAPTER IX

I touched-in my user print and entered the main directory. Again, no MA... and then, there it was, flashing merrily away at the bottom of the list, in bright letters. I went into the subdirectory, and this time chose to have a look into Lifelines.

I got yet another subdirectory listing, by century. I chose the present, the twenty-first. There was a long list of names to scroll through; I looked for the F's and found Friedrickson with an asterisk, prompting me with a selection to choose from for more information. I clicked on "[Krull/20...Krull/19]" and received the following information:

Krull, Felix. 1875–1895*1975–1978*<1995>*2035 [Friedrickson/21]. Ref. @1915 1955... @1978*/... @@@1995/*[del].

Not a whole lot of help there. I would have to know how to use further code-entries for more information. Would I then receive what I already knew? I could well imagine: "Krull, Felix: Confidence Man. Alias Marquis de Venosta. Rogue, swindler, jewel thief and would-be gigolo. Stealer of hearts. * Shipwrecked * return-Krull. New Orleans City Jail, 1975. Federal Prison, alias Charles Ready, Marion Illinois 1976. Gas jockey, store clerk, stadium vendor, taxi driver. Union negotiator... Deleted 1978/1995." Not very flattering, on balance.

I was tempted to delete the whole entry. Out of spite, as it were, for all their shenanigans with my body and soul. The screen cursor flashed over the end of the actual coded entry, where it said "[del]."

What the hell, I thought, it won't kill me... will it? A flush of fear ran up my spine and caused a light sweat to break out on my brow. I took pause to reflect on the problematic nature of my very existence in this composite body, this artificially engendered time I appeared to inhabit. Was this supposed life, this tenuous lifeline, but a computer projection, a statistical probability, a "weighted contingency" of human being, in place of the once integral body I was born to?

What had I done with that original identity, the pure and innocent Felix Krull? Traded it away at the first opportunity for the chance to experience the wide world in another's shoes. Else I might still be sucking up to the dowagers of the Hotel St. James and Albany in rainy Paris, circa 1900.

No, it had all been worth it. And, through it all, I was nothing if not an adventurer; I had to continue trusting my instincts.

I touched the *Delete* icon.

The screen went blank, but I didn't feel a thing.

That didn't hurt at all, I thought with some smugness. *Let them try to mess with me now*.

Then the coded lifeline returned to the screen. There was one change at the end. Where it had read "[del]," now it read "_[h.hacker/20-21]."

How about that! Instead of deleting the whole entry, I'd apparently flipped a toggle switch, and in effect, undeleted a temporary deletion of one of my former selves.

With the cursor still flashing on the new item, I touched *Enter*.

—Hi, there, "Seymour." Harry here. Glad you figured out a way to get me online. Pretty difficult, when they try to wipe out your existence with the touch of a finger. I was prepared, however, with this program loop you twigged onto. Guess I knew something about how your brain works, too. But enough chit-chat. I'm here to help, if I can. What can I do for you today?

Astonishing. The Hacker was back. At least, he'd left a living legacy in binary code, if not a surviving body. I was eager to ask him what he knew... but where to start?

I typed in:

—What do you know about the Hierarchy?

Harry answered:

—Can you be more specific?

—OK. Are they real?

—You need to do better than that.

—Do they occupy human bodies, on the earth?

—Sure they do. They'd prefer us to think otherwise.

—What about you? Can you think? Do you occupy a body?

—Ah, a trick question. How much do you know about Artificial Intelligence? About astral memory?

—Are you capable of giving me a straight answer?

—How long can we go on answering questions with questions?

This was ridiculous, sitting here arguing with this computerized imp. I decided not to play any more games with him.

—About the Hierarchy: please tell me who they are and what they're trying to accomplish.

—Are you prepared to deal with the knowledge I give you?

This gave me pause. But I had to know.

—Yes.

—They are an imperialist clique, using President Vaughan (with your help, I might add) to advance their aims of continued world domination, using the full agency and powers of the United States of America... as it used to be called.

—Where are they located, this clique?

—Hard to say.

—Are you hiding something from me?

—Who, me? Never. Don't you get it we're on the same team? We're family!

—I understood something like that; that you're one of my kas. But I thought your existence was wiped out, lost in a subsidiary timeline.

—Not quite. When you—or rather, the body you remember in 1995—got snuffed in that explosive incident on the Amtrak, your death in the Learjet gained weight on the probability scales, along with the resulting reincarnation. Thereby reactivating myself as a viable lifeform, to carry on your lineage.

—A survivor, of sorts. Like me, it's true. So what's your current status?

—I share a little of myself around. When you came in a year and a half ago, I no longer had sufficient weight to support a physical body. So I went underground, so to speak. Back to the lifeline I encrypted for myself in the original Lifelines prototype, in '95.

—When you were only, what, seventeen?

—I did have a knack for programming. In the high school I went to, it was either that or football; and as I say, I didn't pack a lot of weight. Sebastopol, California was gaining more than hippies in the exodus from the Bay Area; and with a couple of willing mentors I became a capable hacker. After the Amtrak incident I continued doing my own thing, immersed in the tech world. I witnessed the rise and decline of the empire in the 2020s...

—I still want to know more about the Hierarchy. Their base of operations. Do you know or don't you?

—I'm afraid I don't. It works in large part as a network, I know that much from the computer logs. Involving many individuals, on many levels, all the way down to the bevy of operators working at MA.

—So MA really is a mainframe unit somewhere?

—Let's call it a virtual mainframe. It exists on the programming level, operating within many smaller systems, including this one we're using at the moment.

—That sounds awfully... decentralized.

—Shhh. But yeah. How ironic is that?

—How closely is Sophie involved in the plans of the Hierarchy?

—She's right there at the top. She's their main agent now.

—Agent? She's not calling the shots?

—Oh, no. Are you kidding? They've manipulated her the whole way. She's powerful on the world-plane, but she's still the Hierarchy's puppet. She doesn't know half of it, how they've jerked her around.

—Does she know about *The Last Book*?

—No.

—Why not?

—It doesn't exactly put the Hierarchy's neo-imperial ambitions in a good light.

—Then why the hell are they ignoring what it's crying out to tell them?

—They chuck it in the alternate history file and forget about it. Discard one, draw another.

—But you said they're human. How can they have such power to alter history?

—We all do, don't we? They happen to be more organized, and more determined than most. Also better equipped. And they do, by the way, have enough spiritual savvy to be playing around in the astral big leagues. Strings can be pulled. Fate can be leaned on.

—In that case Sophie needs to have access to that book. Are they able to keep it from her?

—So far, yes. When she touches-in her user print, access to certain files can be automatically denied in the directory listing.

—Then how come I got to see it?

—I overrode the restriction loop and let you in.

—Then couldn't you do the same for Sophie?

—People get shot for less.

—What are you worried about? You're nothing but an overgrown virus!

No response. Now I'd done it. Hurt the feelings of a nonentity. And he'd taken his ball and gone home.

I tried one more time:

—Harry, please. Whose side are you on, anyway? We need you!

It was no use. I exited MA and shut the machine down.

CHAPTER X

I wanted to make sure I could talk with Sophie in private. Of course Ronald, the Secret Service agent on duty at the time, had to shadow us even to the squash courts. Sophie was able to send the smiling man back to his post then, as we were in a "safe" area; his argument over my entry to Sophie's quarters were cursorily dismissed. It wasn't until we actually got to Sophie's private dressing room that I could tell her of my interview with the Hacker. She didn't seem surprised at all by my discovery, and she brushed aside the new revelations which had come out of it.

Sitting me down beside her on the narrow bench, she told me how she had signed on herself to see if she could locate *The Last Book*. It was there all right, thanks to the Hacker's personal efforts on her behalf.

"What?" I exclaimed, amazed.

"Yes, when I asked for the program shell to try to figure out where this *Last Book* had been hiding, Harry sent up a personalized message saying what an interesting, if somewhat rude, fellow he'd been talking to on the other line, and also that he hoped I didn't mind terribly much not getting first crack at this earthshaking document, but blood was thicker than water, or some such drivel. I forgave him. We spared a moment of small talk over old times."

"Anyway..." I parted that luminous chestnut hair and looked in her eyes to bring her focus back to the subject of *The Last Book*.

"Anyway, yes—" and she thrust out her chin of power. "The book was interesting as a fictional extrapolation from current trends; but it all needs to be taken with a large dose of salt, since it is, remember, only an alternate history to our own."

And Sophie proceeded nonchalantly to undress and change into her squash togs. Preoccupied as I was with the substance of our conversation, and distracted by the sight of her royal body, squash-firm and sunlamp-tanned, I sat on the dressing room bench without thinking of my own need to change.

Finally Sophie said, "Are you going to play in those clothes, or what? I don't have all day." She stood ready, twirling a racquet in her hand, and I could swear she was channeling Zouzou. That vision jolted me back to the locker room, discussing the fate of the world.

"Yeah, sure—but Sophie," I said as I began hurriedly undressing, "we have to talk about this. It's a matter of national survival. Of integrity. I need to know where you stand."

"Right here."

"Oh, come on. How do you respond to the Hacker's allegations about the Hierarchy's plans to use us to further their neo-imperial ambitions?"

"What is this, a press conference? You sound like some lefty reporter out of the nineteen seventies. Do you want to play squash or not?"

"With all due respect, Madam President, you need to wake up to what you're involved in. You're intimately familiar with their legislative program, their so-called defense planning, their power to manipulate history; but all the while in your pride at being the first woman to hold that high office, you let them convince you that these are your programs, your ideas. You conveniently forgot how they convinced you that the time-jump leaving me twenty years short was your mistake. I don't know why you take it all on. Why are you so loyal to them?"

Sophie's face was flushed as she heard me out. She put her

racquet down on the bench with a trembling hand and sat down next to me. I put my arm around her and held her while she cried.

After a few moments of release, she leaned back against me as I continued to hold her.

"I tried to believe them," she said. "I had to, in order to go through with my plan. My fucking plan. And now they've got Tashi, holding him over my head."

"What are you talking about?"

"C'mon, let's play squash. I'm going to kill you. And then I'll explain everything. This game has gone on long enough."

For an unsettling second, I took her quip literally. In fact she trounced me on the squash court, smashing the hapless rubber ball with a ferocity I had not witnessed before. Lucky for me I didn't mind the outcome; I played foil to her anger and afterward sat with her over a bottle of wine on the White House terrace, talking in low tones. Ronald and his detail kept their distance, and Sophie pressed her earnode's sending scrambler.

"I have reason to believe," she began, "that my boy has been subjected to ritual abuse."

"What? How do you know?"

"It keeps coming up in my dreams. I see him held captive in a cell, by Robert—sometimes Glaston, sometimes Green. High rollers come to visit, and leave taking Tashi by the hand. I see dark circles under his eyes, a zombie shuffle to his step. I believe he's been drugged and brainwashed, and worse, ever since Robert took custody."

"Wow, if all that is true... When was the last time you saw Tashi?"

"A year and a half ago—before I brought you in."

"Are you hoping I'll help?"

"You are helping." And she clung to me, shuddering in her grief.

"What can we do to get him back?"

"They're offering for me to see him, at their choosing, if I agree to certain terms."

"What terms?"

"That's the problem. They want a blank check. No more bright policy initiatives, no pushback on their domestic controls. I told them I'd listen. Tashi is coming for a visit momentarily."

A woman in a blue blazer approached from around the side of the building, holding a slim lad of six, with pageboy hair and a seersucker short-pants suit. I saw no dark circles under his eyes, but they could have used makeup.

Tashi ran to his mother and leaned into her lap as she embraced him. When his murmurs subsided he turned his head toward me and said, "Who's that?"

"His name is Seymour. He's been helping me with my job. And with life."

Enough and well said, for a youngster's understanding, I thought.

Sophie held Tashi by the shoulders and looked at him straight. "Tell me how you're doing. Is Robert treating you well?"

Tashi choked on words that failed to surface. He sucked his lip in and managed, "I'm fine."

It didn't ring true to me and I communicated as much to Sophie with my eyes.

"How is first grade coming?"

"They took me out of school," Tashi said. "For private lessons."

"No friends?"

"I have lots of older friends."

Sophie frowned at Tashi and looked at me with a dark cloud of knowing. She embraced him again, saying, "Oh, Tashi,

Tashi. I'm going to bring you back to me one day soon, you'll see."

"Time's up," said the matron who now approached again and extended a hand to the boy. Tashi glanced over his shoulder at Sophie, and me, as he was escorted away.

"That was disturbing," I said to Sophie. "I think you're right about his treatment. So what was the deal you agreed to for this brief encounter?"

"To back off on the trial of the two Panarchists, Marte and Byweather."

"And who's calling those shots?"

"Robert's their point man. He answers to Jor-El, not to me. And Wolfgang is showing his true colors, too. He and Robert have assembled a fictional trail of evidence linking the two prisoners to foreign terrorists. The two women will face a military tribunal and certain execution, after a period of sustained torture."

"Jesus, Sophie. Can't you override them?"

She looked at me with large eyes, pools of black. I sensed in her then a hidden source of power, hidden perhaps even to herself.

"Not now. I told them the backlash would wipe out all the popular gains we've been making on the Continental policy. They wouldn't listen. To them, command, absolute authority, is the issue, and there are no half measures. But I will find a way. And it begins with getting Tashi back. Are you with me on this?"

"To the end."

National Security Advisor Wolfgang Nenowitz delivered the grim report on the state of the empire. His old-school spectacles rode on the end of his long nose as he read, looking at each of us from time to time above the lenses.

"This Continentalism," he said, departing from the script, "has had far-reaching impacts on our resource extraction industries and military installations, worldwide. We're facing grassroots actions against our presence in Sicily, Germany, France, the Philippines, Okinawa, Qatar, Guam, Brazil, Columbia. But we're hamstrung. Local governments are seeing no choice but to side with their own citizenry. In country after country they are moving to decommission or nationalize our bases, mines, pipelines. We are at a point where we need to take more drastic measures."

Sophie said blankly, taking it all in. I was silently fuming, but likewise powerless to intervene. The rest of the Council and staff nodded, all on board whether on principle or on notice.

Chief of Staff McElroy spoke up. "And what measures do you have in mind?"

"There's an electromagnetic technology that's been in development for quite some time, ready to roll out for the next wave of demonstrations. We call it the AD gun: meaning "active denial." It emits millimeter waves to induce unpleasant burning sensations on the skin, as a form of crowd control. If you are unwise enough to be standing there when it hits you, you will feel your body is on fire. The sensation is so intense as to cause an instantaneous reflex action of the target to flee the beam."

"The target?" I had the temerity to ask.

Nenowitz fixed me with an icy stare. "Citizen, protester, terrorist, what you will."

I decided to research on my own about Robert Glaston. I was prepared to do some digging in public sources, but Harry intercepted my online search and provided me with a virtual dossier, complete with a calling card:

—I forgive you.

How sweet, I thought. I responded:

—Sorry if I ticked you off. I didn't realize—

—No worries, bro. We're in this together.

I shuddered at the implications of that statement, and returned my attention to the query at hand.

Prior to his recruitment for the public sector of Hierarchy interests, Robert Glaston had served as Macrosoft CEO. His claim to fame was development of Lifelines, utilizing a backdoor hack of the Akashic Records. This project was overseen by Jor-El, representing the Atlantean Council.

Building upon the conceptual model of quantum networking, Glaston had conceived the theory of "Quantum Politics" which led to the merger of the two major parties. In a speech to the Bilderberger Conference of 2022, he supplied its philosophic underpinnings and trajectory on the world stage:

> The standard political landscape is built upon the slab of duality dividing Heaven and Earth. The two-party system. The us-and-them tribal xenophobia of the nation state, or the monolithic empire with its citizens and barbarians, its warring factions, its poisoned bread and circuses of terror.
>
> What if we stopped supplying the energetic momentum that sustains such illusions, by turning our attention to the surpassing unity of our common cause? By using the white magic of choiceful manifestation—*Create what thou wilt*—instead of patronizing the black magic shows of national rivalries, trade wars and worse.
>
> What you will see in my country—within two years—is a first step to show the way, beginning with the merger of our own two American political parties into one united force. From this rock of single purpose, we will lead the way to advocate to all the nations to join under the banner of world order, peace and prosperity, democracy and freedom for all.

The same platitudes, it seemed to me, could serve any

purpose, however antithetical to any real meaning of the words. At least this new world visionary didn't co-opt *love*, I reflected. Yet, what lay at the heart of the Hierarchy's one-world dream? Their own control of it, certainly.

As for that oppositional force, Love, too, asserts the dissolving of boundaries. Yes, and the vision of One World… but a true globe, not a pyramid of rank divisions with the controlling cabal on top, secure in their anonymity, shielded from common view by the likes of Sophie Tucker Vaughan.

Harry interrupted my musings to message,

—Any further questions?

Apparently he had feelings too, didn't appreciate feeling neglected.

—You've been most helpful, my friend. So yes, now that you mention it, tell me, what's in it for you?

—Let me tell you a little story.

—You're on.

—Remember the so-called deal Sophie cut with the Hierarchy to bring you forward in time, the first jump?

—Hmm, deal, vaguely.

—Well, champ, you were supposed to be lifted straight through to 1994, and in exchange, Sophie would allow Nenowitz a seat on the National Security Council. Instead, they sank your whole ship, the *Cap Arcona*, in order to dovetail with the sinking of the *Carthage Star*—

—Why?

—It was a convenient way to assassinate a South African double agent and future Panarchist leader. So you got stranded in 1975 as a result—more collateral damage. You can consider yourself lucky. As the Hierarchy explained it to Sophie, you could acclimate in a "safe environment." Test your mettle, prove your chops, earn your stripes.

—And all that rot.

—You got it. But there's more. That train explosion that took you out in '95? Hierarchy fingerprints all over that job. Orchestrated by the Nenowitz faction.

—They said it was terrorists.

—Yeah, well. That meme flies pretty well with the populace.

—Aren't you at risk for telling me all this?

—Risk? I'm already disembodied. It's your ka that's in danger of joining me in this limbo. Which might not be a bad thing for me, having your company around. But you've got someone out there to care for, and work yet to do. Just know, I've got your back.

I terminated the connection with a silent thanks to Harry, took the long underground corridor to the street, and walked out under a brooding sky, pondering my fate, that of my mentor and lover, and that of the world. Though no Secret Service agent accompanied me, I knew the surveillance drones tracked my coordinates. They could not yet read my thoughts.

That night a spell of silent lovemaking gave way to dreamless sleep; but in the morning as I held Sophie from behind, I felt that stolid resistance again, and I knew it was time to break through her wall of obfuscation concerning the Hierarchy. The drapes hung at ease over the high windows looking out at the street, behind the iron fence. A pale sun filtered through the blossoming trees. I hesitated, lingering in the texture of skin on skin, pondering my choice of words and the outcome of her answer. She began to stir. I made a quick trip to the bathroom and kitchenette and returned to bed with coffee for two, and a grapefruit to peel and split with her.

Thus engaged, I asked how she became involved with the Hierarchy in the first place.

"It's a long story," she said.

"It's time," I said. "All the cards on the table, okay?"

She sighed, took a sip of coffee, inspected a section of grapefruit. "It started back in '77, '78, when I was still in the Northern Studies program. A woman professor of mine invited me to a meditation group which met at her house. One day she led the group in a past-life regression, and I had a vision of myself as an empress in the lost Pacific continent of Lemuria. Ruby headdress, fan-waving servants, the works."

"Right, isn't that what they all say? It's like the schizophrenics who babble of Jesus or Cleopatra."

She went silent and gave me a level look, in which I disappeared into the starry depths of her eyes, oceans within. In that moment she exuded an aura of timelessness, the mystique of an ancient tropical setting, with sultry beaches and highland retreats, birdsong and waterfalls.

"May I go on?" she said with grace.

I blinked my eyes back to the woman I had come to love, without even the confidence to name it as such until then. Was it the royal stamp I had sought, beyond even the august chair of the presidency? I realized I shared with Sophie the perception of her office as a shallow, democratic facsimile of true nobility.

"I felt a deep pull of recognition in that vision," said Sophie. "And when we shared around the circle at the end, the facilitator told us that our visions were real, and that we should listen to what they were trying to tell us. She seemed to focus particularly on me."

"I would too."

Sophie gave me the benefit of a quick smile and went on: "When the circle was over, this guy in the group came up to me and said he was struck by my vision, found it compelling and believable. So what?, I told him. He persisted—just another hippie with gaunt cheeks and piercing mad eyes—and asked about my career plans, and suggested again that I should pay heed to my vision. I kind of laughed and said, 'Yeah, like go back and run for empress?' He smiled at that, a wise and enigmatic smile which haunted me for the next, oh, almost ten years until I decided to run for Congress."

"And now? I think I know where this is going."

"Right, I gave it away with the face. And yes, now he haunts me still. Robert was my high priest in the Lemurian scenario, which I began to frequent more in dreams—learning in the dreams how to return at will, my first lessons in astral travel. The high priest was the source of my earthly power, guarding access to the Akashic Records, for a price. And so, with Congress, the funny thing was, when I was looking around for a campaign manager, up pops this guy again, Robert Green, at a Party social function. Short hair now, no beard, sharp dresser. The guy was a wizard. We won going away."

"Robert Green? I thought you meant Glaston."

"Just wait. No croissants?"

I reached a hand to hold her cheek in the palm of my hand. "Anyway. Why didn't you hold onto him? Instead of trading him in for me?"

"Ah, he was a jerk, as far as personality goes. It wasn't worth it. Once I got my start, I could make it on my own—for a while." Sophie gave my hand a knowing squeeze, then continued, "He was pissed off when I let him go. He never did make it into bed with me. Remember, we're talking about that earlier incarnation. After the jump I thought I had a clean slate. Not so. The body I joined had already gone through the relationship and separation with Robert Glaston. It turns out Glaston himself was a reincarnated ka, from Robert Green who died in the same train explosion in '95 that took out yours and my previous kas. I could tell from the eyes. Only this one is worse, with the Hierarchy's hooks set deeper in. I'd signed on through him, you see: once you're in, there's no way out. And anyway, I was, and am, a creature of this Hierarchy program, Lifelines, which Robert Glaston himself, by the way, developed."

"Oh Jesus."

"Yeah, it's even more immaculate than that: a ka basically creating itself."

"Talk about Artificial Intelligence."

"Seymour, are we going to work today to make this country great?"

Glimpsing through our bedroom window the gray mist of a day approaching the Ides of March, I sensed, with astral acuity, the grime of poverty in the streets of the nation's capital; fumes of burning plastic, tang of acid air, pang of impending collapse, graffiti of resistance.

"I still want to know," I said, "why would they have even bothered to groom you for this job, if this guy Glaston held a grudge, and rank in the Hierarchy to back it up? Couldn't they simply have installed him as president, or another one of their own people?"

"They considered me one of them, like I say. Signed in blood, so to speak."

"And we kas, for all our faults, do have flesh and blood." I wrapped my arms around her, snuggling up against her back, and felt Sophie's voice resonating through her rib cage.

"You know, you were right. Most of the members of the meditation group recalled lives of the high and mighty—generals, priestesses, financiers, astronomers, conquerors, overlords of various kinds—all people with great power. At the time I thought it was a matter of ego, personal delusion or wish-fulfillment. Now I suspect that we in the group, Robert the high priest included, were gathering as an earthly manifestation of an actual clique of souls who've lived such lives at past times on the earth. They didn't get enough, and they want these surviving kas to keep working at their age-old imperial designs."

"With cosmetic changes of costume and resumé along the

way."

Sophie regarded me with pursed lips, catching my irony. "Of course. It's nothing but a grand confidence game, *n'est-ce pas*? Though they paint themselves now as a noble corpocracy: industrialists, bankers, insurance moguls; dukes of pharmaceuticals, and biotech barons; noble purveyors of weapons, energy, agribiz..."

"You don't consider yourself in that category?"

"Noble? Yes, I admit it. But not of their ilk. Born to rule for the highest good of all, championing those principles on which the humane confederation of Lemuria was established: peaceful cooperation within society, and harmonious relations with the natural planet, Gaia."

"So there's still this astral Sophie up there, frustrated empress or whatever, who wants her realm back, and is directing you to do it for her, here in the promised land?"

She placed a finger softly on my lips, then replaced it with a kiss.

CHAPTER XI

April brought to Washington a wave of unseasonal warmth, riding behind foreboding black clouds, as the streets of the nation's capital seethed with massive protests. Sophie and I watched the action feeds from the surveillance drones, in the comfort of the Oval Office, and saw a sea of humanity clamoring, through a cacophony of megaphones and a waving forest of homemade signs, for affordable food and housing, aid to schools and the elderly, debt forgiveness and repairs to infrastructure...

"All the benefits," sang a rainbow body-painted lady on stilts, wearing only an Uncle Sam top hat, "promised by an empire that has sucked its own homeland dry. As dry and wasted as the far-flung colonies that once were sovereign lands."

I looked at Sophie as if to say, "She's got a point," and she nodded, understanding perfectly.

The security camera panned to another contingent lustily chanting, "Free the Panarchists."

On this block was erected a small stage, where a gossamer-gowned woman with glitter in her hair addressed the crowd.

"Our dear sisters, Zanelle Marte and Elfie Byweather, sit today bound in chains, raped and tortured, for no crime but asking for our birthright here on earth, freedom in our lands and in our hearts. For organic democracy, not manufactured consent."

Cheers from the crowd spurred her on.

"We ask only those age-old rights of the human family: liberty, equality, sustainability, and justice. A culture of cooperative community at home, and a peaceful foreign policy abroad."

"She has a knack," Sophie said.

"I wonder," I replied, what her astral lineage is."

"Fellow citizens of Gaia," the luminous figure exhorted, "give voice to your deepest yearnings!"

A chorus of animal cries and yelps, roars and screeches, rose in the air and dissolved into twittering birdsong. The camera panned to the sidewalks where a giant elf man and woman, woven of wood, danced grinning. Costumery was in full display, adornments of wings and fur conjuring owls and wolves.

"This is the time, the moment we have been waiting for! The awakening is at hand! Can you feel it?"

This time, as if rehearsed, an eerie silence.

"You have been silenced too long, shut up in classrooms, told not to speak, not to sing or dance, not to know your truth. Not to challenge, not to express. Let me hear you say your truth!"

Now again the full voices of the jungle rang out in the streets, rebounding off the marble monuments, calling them in effect the tombs of a nation.

"You are Avatar Nation, brought to Earth and ready to join the Star Nations!"

The crowd whirled in glee, in their faery garb and rainbow caftans, orange lace and green leather spats, golden hair wraps and chainmail bikinis, gaudy sashes and silk streamers, body paint of neo-shamans...

Helmeted Hierarchy forces closed in, a phalanx timeless as a Roman legion, boxing the crowd into a blind alley. A military truck emblazoned with the Hierarchy logo, a black-and-gold pyramid, arrived with the latest skin-burning weapon— Nenowitz's favorite toy, the AD gun. Trained on the protesters, its invisible beams caused them to scream and writhe in pain, with no escape. A vast net was unleashed from a mortar, settling neatly over the entire throng. An attached cable pulled the drawstrings tight, and the lot was carried aloft by a silently whirring helicopter. The marble monuments stood unmoved, cold as time between empires.

"Can't you do anything to stop them?" I pleaded.

"Stop who?"

"The goons who are abusing those poor citizens."

"That's Glaston's chain of command, domestic order. Unless I step in by special order."

"You don't consider this a worthy emergency?"

"I have to play my cards right, or they'll cut me out of the loop altogether. I mean, us."

The news feed on another screen featured the smug countenance of the newly appointed CEO, pontificating on "the need to maintain order and security at all costs, so we can return this great nation to the principles it was founded on. We have a mandate to fulfill: to lead the global union to a new era of peace and prosperity."

Sophie cut the feeds and the screens went blank.

"You're right, it's up to me now."

"You mean, us."

In the muggy days that followed, I found myself longing for dusty Portugal. The White House itself had turned, in my jaded eyes, stale, bland, constricting; its pastel walls hung with portraits of dead murderers, its cutlery gleaming like weapons of stealth and ageless intrigue. The very flag of the union took on a sinister aspect these days, each color in turn speaking its own message of death: the red of imperial bloodshed; the white of ignorance, denial and racism; the blue of persistent aristocratic hierarchy.

My attempts to follow up with more research on *The Last Book* failed, with access denied to the entire MA directory. On a stroll through the Rose Garden, Sophie told me that was a clear sign I was being cut off, and she would be next. Her response was to have us stop meditating. That way we could block mental detection and direction from sources in the Hierarchy. She paused to smell a softball-sized rose—gasping with a prick from a thorn—and explained that they could exploit our altered states of consciousness with programmed instruction when we were in that vulnerable state.

"Programmed how?" I wanted to know.

"Various means, both technical and esoteric. Altering brainwave patterns by electromagnetic frequency interference, for one thing. That's on the physical level. In the psychic realm, astral politics is old hat to these starship troopers."

"And to Lemurian empresses."

"Queen, my dear." She snapped off a rose and held it out for me to sniff.

"Yes—divine. But you told me—"

"That empress bit was a Hierarchy suggestion, implanted by the priesthood to reinforce their role for me in this incarnation. In the true history I know now, I was not the ruler of a vast, dominated empire, but of a cooperative union: the Lemurian Confederacy, with its own constitution and ethical protocols of political affiliation. You can look it up in the Akashic Records—"

"If I had the access code..."

"Let me summarize it for you. I've been thinking of doing a series of broadcasts to the public, laying the foundation for a new American constitution."

"You mean, USNA."

"Correct. I don't think we're going to roll that one back. Here's where we depart from Hierarchy policy, though. They wanted to break down national identity in a move toward global union—under their control, of course. We wanted to redress indigenous land claims and self-determination, and resolve outstanding resource issues. In the process we wind up with more of a confederacy of regions within the continental landmass of North America."

"Sounds like a decentralist manifesto."

We had circumnavigated the garden, turned into the inner paths. The faux dragonfly that had been following us veered closer. I gave it an equally false smile and it banked away.

"Exactly," said Sophie. "But we don't call it that. We maintain oversight, nominal control of the process. To keep the Hierarchy at bay, we have to keep up a show of force. With the mounting protests, there has to be a response, concessions, or the whole thing will fly apart. The Hierarchy doesn't want that; it gets messy and time-consuming for them. Better to have me—us—manage things here while they work on international alliances, trade deals, climate protocols."

"Where does Dennis stand?"

"He's a lackey of the Hierarchy. They insisted on him for chief of staff, and he answers to Wolfgang. I have a meeting with those two and a special guest in an hour."

"Who might that be?"

"You don't want to know."

"That line doesn't work on me anymore."

"I know. I was just testing you. You passed. His traditional name is Enki."

"Traditional?"

"In the traditions of the Sumerians, Enki was the emissary, a colonial ruler, from an offworld tribe called the Annunaki, who came to Earth 400,000 years ago and engineered humans as a slave race to mine gold for their home planet, Nibiru."

"And now?"

"He doesn't tend to show up from his high castle, or wherever he hangs out, except in emergencies, which apparently you and I represent."

"Glad you've invited me to your little tea party."

"Actually, you weren't invited—"

"I meant in the larger sense."

"Right. How do you like it so far? Let me just say that Enki and the Niburans aren't the end of the story, by a long shot. They ran afoul of a larger governing force, the Galactic Federation, when they colonized Earth and engineered the proto-human DNA to suit their agenda. Still with me?"

"I can hardly bail on you now. Keep it coming."

We stood in the center of the Rose Garden. A menacing cloud overhead began to spit. A drop hit our pet dragonfly and sizzled. The mini-drone let out a whine and buzzed off, glancing against a tree and careening to the ground.

"There is a so-called Prime Directive which prohibits interference with a planet's races, ecosystem, genetic integrity. The Niburans violated that principle, thumbing their noses at the Federation and continuing to exploit Earth for millennia, with impunity."

"Prime Directive? You're talking Star Trek stuff again."

"Sorry to offend your notion of reality, sweetheart, but it's real. The Prime Directive prohibits also the Federation from interfering in response to those transgressions. It kind of assumes basic cooperation, which the Niburans laughed at. And we saw the same thing play out with Lemuria and Atlantis. My confederation operated on peaceful principles of cooperation and fair exchange, resolving differences by nonviolent means, as an ethical imperative. Atlantis paid no such homage to civility, and with their reliance on sophisticated weaponry, they made short work of our defense network once they decided to challenge my rule."

"How did you learn, or remember all this, at this late stage of the game?"

Before she spoke again, I knew the answer:

"Harry. He provided me access to the Akashic Records,

which contains, of course, the intact text of the Lemurian Constitution, and the history of the Atlantean conquest."

"Was the Hierarchy operating back then?"

"Forever, my dear. Forever pulling strings, calling shots. That's what they do. I should have recognized in today's Hierarchy my old Atlantean adversaries, but my astral memory in this ka was blocked. By them, of course. On top of that, I fell for their nicey nicey rhetoric of peace, democracy, world order, yada yada."

"So you're—"

"I'm getting wet. Let's go inside and change into dry clothes for the meeting."

"You mean—"

"We're in this together, remember?"

White House Chief of Staff Dennis McElroy stood and motioned us to sit down as we entered the conference room, a secure cell off a corridor below the White House, free from the traffic of gossipy staffers. Enki sat with his dark bulk at the end of the table, eyes glowering like burning coals. He wore a studded black leather halter; his yellow hair lay pasted flat against an elongated skull. Sophie had prepped me, explaining that what we saw would be but a holographic simulacrum of this ageless entity. National Security Advisor Wolfgang Nenowitz cowered beside him. To Enki's left sat Robert Glaston, fiddling with the data controls of his horn-rimmed glasses, barely acknowledging Sophie's presence, and casting a baleful glare upon my unexpected appearance. Ronald the Secret Service man stood guard outside, deigning not even to glance inside lest the information incriminate him in future proceedings.

The other men in the room looked at each other and Enki finally spoke: a hollow, rumbling baritone, as if emerging from a dank cavern. "Why is *he* here?" He nodded in my direction.

Sophie said, "Seymour is part of this administration, has had key input to our legislative program and provided sound advice on foreign affairs. If you will remember—"

Dennis had seated himself directly across from me and interjected, "Right. Like obstructing our military alliance with the French. Like—"

Here Glaston put in: "Poking his nose into classified data regions in violation of his security clearance. Like—"

Enki held up his hand and instant silence ensued. "Let him stay. I have something to say to him." He turned those coal-black eyes on me. "You," he said. "Impostor or spy, it matters not. We understand you were part of the package. Fair enough. Now let us untie the package, discard the pretty wrapping, and see what is inside."

I swallowed hard. I didn't know how to address the man—who wasn't even a man. *Your honor, your excellency, your highness...* clearly I could not in conscience bow to such ingratiating terms so integral to hierarchic order. So I held my tongue and waited for the ultimatum.

"If I may," Nenowitz said in his raspy voice, with a look of sad affection toward Sophie. "Can we determine where the both of you stand in regard to the trial of the Panarchist women, Marte and Byweather, so contentious in the press? We have yet to see a statement from the president."

Sophie responded, "I have not felt the necessity to take on the minutiae of policy on every front. I hold my staff and those entrusted with the powers of state" (and here she looked at Wolfgang and Glaston in turn) "responsible for carrying out their duties under the law."

"The law," said Enki. "A curious concept, in earthly history. What is law but the convenience of its makers? Do you not consider the makers of those lawgivers? What is the real agenda at play here? Let us be frank, and see where our purposes align. Or not, as the case may be."

No one spoke for a moment. Then Glaston focused on me, looking down his long nose, perhaps the better to read the data streaming at the edge of his lenses. "Mr. Friedrickson," he said, "tell us what you feel should be done with the Dark Forces currently trying to undermine the enactment of Continentalism."

I replied: "First of all, I would like to recognize the constitutional right of all citizens to exercise dissent over public policy. As to the legislation itself, certainly it is a complex matter, by its nature forged in compromise over competing claims for territory, land use and development, and entailing necessary logistical challenges for resettlement. These challenges we have addressed—"

"*We?*" Mr. Friedrickson, I don't believe you are invested with any constitutional, as you say, authority for exercising influence over policy, at any level."

Sophie sprang to my defense. "Excuse me, but this is beyond discussion. It was agreed at an early stage to allow Felix—er, Seymour—to join me in my efforts to promote the Hierarchy's plans to unify, first this party, then the country as a whole, the North American continent, and next, the entire globe, under the banner of unity and peaceful order. We stand united in this venture still, and so I don't see—"

Wolfgang broke in to say: "Then why did your ambassador to Mexico, Ms. Kane, sabotage the negotiations to bring Mexico on board as an integral subsidiary actor?"

"Madison did not sabotage those negotiations," Sophie retorted. "The Mexicans, understandably, had their own resistance to a subsidiary, as you put it, role in the Continental arrangement. They wanted full partnership, integration, or independence. We could have offered them integration, but Jor-El, I understood, was opposed."

"How convenient that Jor-El is not here," said Dennis.

"Why is he not here?" Enki inquired, looking at Wolfgang

and Glaston in turn.

"He didn't say," said Wolfgang.

Glaston spread his hands on the table. "Let's not divert our attention from the matter at hand. It would only suggest division and weakness, a perception the Dark Forces would readily exploit. Since we do have Felix—my mistake; Seymour—with us, it would be most expedient to finish the business at hand."

"Which is?" Sophie said.

Now Wolfgang spoke. "We have heard the fine sentiments of your silver-tongued consort. Valuable for communication with the voters of the mass, I imagine, but here we come to brass tacks. We understand your dandified associate from an antique age has found a way past our secure firewalls, and wonder if he might, having certain sentiments in concert with those calling themselves Decentralists, deem it a matter of conscience to allow such access to those who would destroy us."

Glaston said, "Wait, I don't think our security is that much at risk. Mr. Friedrickson has no more access and indeed, will have no more. The databots, furthermore, have adjusted their sensitivities to the parameters upon which the breaches were conducted. So I hardly feel—"

"That's enough," Enki thundered. "Bickering like the human children you are. Where is your resilience, your grasp of our higher purpose? Now, let us come to the nub of the matter and dispense with internal discord. Madam President, if the Panarchists continue to gain momentum in their resistance campaign, are you prepared to exercise due force to crush them?"

Sophie's countenance darkened; her feet shuffled under the table. I reached for her hand and held it on her knee. "That is not the approach I think wise," she answered. "We have already seen how such measures backfire. In the present case, with Marte and Byweather, the simple fact of their incarceration, let alone the announcement of their execution and assumption of their torture while detained, are fueling escalating protests in the capital and indeed across the land. My strategy would be to defuse dissent by offering the concession of a limited freedom for those two, for example, on humanitarian grounds. This approach, I am convinced, would bring us more support, not more opposition."

"And we lose more time," said Wolfgang, "to complete our agenda."

Glaston turned to me. "What about you, Mr. Friedrickson? Where do you stand?"

"With Sophie," I answered without hesitation. "I mean, with the president."

Glaston smirked at my boyish self-correction. "Let's put it this way, Mr. Time Traveler. Suppose you had a choice. A quick lift back to 1895, a certain villa in Lisbon. Or, to 1976— say, a wheatfield in Kansas. Or, because we're all about choice, the trenches, 1915. What would your preference be?"

A wave of dark memories swept through me like storm water under the streets. Could I answer, "None of the above?" Clearly the Lifelines puppet-master had implied a fourth choice: to leave aside my dalliance with political idealism, and prove without doubt my allegiance to the Hierarchy. Maybe they would have me personally carry out the execution of the dissidents. That thought was repugnant; I swept it aside like a dead rat into the rushing sewer water of my other alternatives.

Sophie, grasping the dilemma, spoke on my behalf: "Seymour has done nothing but serve me and my administration with diligence and integrity. The so-called data breach occurred spontaneously, not by his intent, in the course of his research for policy directives. Can we put this contention to rest and get on with more pressing matters of state? Wolfgang, what is the Asian subsector reporting on the climate initiative?"

I held my tongue for the rest of the meeting: an unfamiliar role, to be sure. Under the circumstances, I counted the exchange a small victory, a lesson in humility, embracing the lower profile. That lesson would serve me well in the days—and years—to come.

Earthly powers are by their nature limited, and to this condition—notwithstanding my fortuitous transference across certain key data points of time's dimensionality—I had come to learn I must submit. Yet, bowing to one's inherent limitation did not imply pledging allegiance to other earthly powers; nor to the unearthly manipulators of human subjects as if we were chess-piece playthings. To fate, rather, I would acquiesce, and to the sort of fate not only of my own making. I had to set aside immediate personal gratification for the sake of another—Sophie—for her sake, and for the larger cause she served. Yes, and to look beyond even that to a greater truth, a merger of personal success with the survival and well-being of all.

After the meeting Sophie and I took time out to debrief, strolling along the pastoral lanes of the Washington Zoo, in our disguises worn for such public outings, and in the company of agent Ronald, walking behind us at a discreet distance. I found her blonde wig comical, the oversized sunglasses cartoonish; she tittered at my fake beard and jaunty green fedora.

Yet our levity masked the looming crisis. The threat to my current existence was but a minor variant of the predicament Sophie faced as the Hierarchy's key player. They hadn't spelled out her options so crudely, yet she could well imagine an exile to Lemurian limbo, not a visualized but an actual regression back to her antediluvian past.

With Harry's help she had reconstructed the scenario of her initial recruitment. Placed in an astral holding pattern following the conquest of Lemuria, she endured ages of disuse, of lassitude, grieving and dispirited over the loss of her Confederation and its way of life—under patriarchal domain ever since. Then when the time was ripe for their designs to play out in late twentieth-century America, the Hierarchy had grabbed her ka from its protective limbo. Waiting her time of return, she found herself back in life, without memory of that illustrious past, yet susceptible to enticement by fine pronouncements of ideals and principles that could be construed as harmonious with those ancient values.

On hearing this, I observed that her recruitment was not unlike my own recruitment into Sophie's service. Now the time had come for a reckoning of accounts, a distinction between false ideals and a living, human future for free citizens of Earth.

"That, too, sounds good," said Sophie. "But unless those citizens wake up to where this thing is heading, they'll find themselves too far down the wrong road to turn back."

We had stopped outside a monkey cage, and there saw the creatures cavorting, presumably in play. Around the cage they flew, leaping from branch to branch, pausing for a bite of fruit, picking at lice on another's head, bounding off again with teeth bared. After a minute or two a rough pattern would emerge: not exactly, but basically the same movements, the same routine, repeated over and over. All day long, every day. What at first seemed play, free and spontaneous, after a while proved a dysfunctional, neurotic loop.

How did the Panarchs of old manage to prevail, I wondered, in the free Confederacy of Lemuria—before the conquest and subjugation by Atlantis?

"In the astral realm," Sophie said, "there was a council, representing all factions. But as with the UN, it was all talk, a front for the Hierarchy. The true Panarchs in our society relied rather on their shamans and priestesses, the Hierophants, guides of the mysteries, who on earth moved in orbits out of the official matrix. Before conquest they were respected as holders of the core values of the culture. During the conquest they were persecuted, killed, driven underground. Over time, those who reemerged were indulged as quaint and insubstantial, offering no resistance to the new regime but taking solace in astral battles of wits and spells, rituals and ceremonies, communing with animals, and being of service as healers, musicians, jugglers, fools. What else can you do, while the Devil plays the drums at the gates of Hell?"

"And you?"

"In limbo, I was alone; though I had my loyal retinue waiting in the wings, praying for my return."

"So if you got sent back, some would be happy?"

"Back to limbo, we're talking about. Not a reinstatement of my crown or the Confederacy."

We stood longer in front of the monkey cage, shelling peanuts ourselves and casting the husks aside, as the macaques stopped their antics and watched us nibble. Ronald was pacing, scratching, standing at ease. Then pacing again, scratching...

It came down to one question, foremost in our present circumstance. I asked Sophie, "Is there any real hope, then, to resist the Hierarchy, in this world? Or at least to make it irrelevant by the success of decentralist alternatives?"

"Not while the Hierarchy is calling the shots, certainly."

"So there has to be a coup."

"Silly Seymour, we're already in power. The problem is, it's not where the real power lies."

"And yet, if we exploit the potential of this Continentalism, to further break down the old national boundaries..."

Sophie replied: "Sounds good in theory. But they will only exploit it as a further means to consolidate overall control, globally. Which was their intent all along."

"Fine, but meanwhile on the local scale, with regional affiliations below the national level, there could be a new

Confederacy."

"That term has been tainted by its more recent use, in the American South."

"Granted," I said. "Except this movement is nonviolent, driven not by slaving interests, or British backing of the cotton and tobacco trade, but by ordinary people with unconventional attitudes and experiences of local organization. In this respect wouldn't it revive your own heritage as overseer or patroness of the Lemurian Confederacy?"

"Up to a point. But always, it seems, the Hierarchy will have the last word in this Kingdom of Earth, in material terms. In the astral balance, of course, they burn in Hell, fall to chaos in the way of all empires. So maybe, what is really needed, is not an alternative program of temporary governance, but a descent into true chaos which is necessary to regenerate this world and begin anew. The house of cards comes tumbling down, the grass grows up again, and there is new beauty and natural order in the world."

I glanced over her shoulder and saw the primates becalmed in their cage, as if pondering her words. Then, as if by an invisible signal, they scrambled back into action, in a deafening frenzy which drove us further down the path, to the Reptile House.

Back at the White House, Sophie and I met with Press Secretary Willoughby and Ambassador Kane. Ryan met us with clenching jaw, as if he were chewing on something. Madison had dark circles under her eyes. She wore a colorful dress, a gift from the Mexican president, Inez Alfonzo. We sat informally over coffee and tea.

"What happened in the negotiations?" Sophie asked Madison.

The ambassador crossed her legs and lifted her chin.

"President Alfonzo was adamant. There would be no compromise on Mexican sovereignty."

"Sovereignty wasn't the issue. It was about buying into the treaty."

"She, and the Mexican delegation, were unanimous. They took it as a diminishment of their sovereignty, and refused."

"Good for them," I blurted out.

Ryan, till then fidgeting with his coffee cup, looked at me as with a bright light turned on. "So how are we going to frame this for the press?"

Sophie considered. "Let's deflect the Mexican thing, for now. Say the negotiations are still in progress."

"They're finished," said Madison. "I gave it a shot; but under the circumstances—"

"Never mind. The Mexicans are the least of our worries at the moment. Madison, I'm going to ask for that resignation of yours as ambassador, but please don't take it as a demotion. I want you on our side closer to home, as a special envoy in discussion with the Panarchists."

"How? They don't even have an official leadership."

"Not official, no. But when Marte and Byweather are freed—"

"Freed?" I broke in. "They are scheduled to be executed."

Sophie glared at me. "Who's listening and who is speaking here?"

I bowed to her authority. It wasn't the first time.

"I have an idea how a deal might be worked out, that will free them and also mollify the Hierarchy. Ryan, I want you to work with Madison on this, since you have the experience of working together and I trust you both. Unlike our former team member, Mr. McElroy."

"What about me?"

Sophie fixed me with a laser gaze, not without a certain

twinkle. "There's another plan I want your help on."

CHAPTER XII

At this juncture, in my disjointed quest to imprint some meaningful stamp upon this fragile existence, I had nothing left to gain or lose. I was unmoored, naked in the world, needing only to navigate the road ahead, and to do what was required.

What else is Choice, but to accept Fate with open arms? And what is Fate, but an opportunity for Choice to play its appointed part?

Through discreet inquiries Sophie had ascertained that Tashi was indeed still in Robert Glaston's custody—his own father, after all—and not yet enrolled in school. Sophie dreaded to contemplate the kind of education already she would have to undo. She never doubted the veracity of her dream vision of the boy's ritual abuse, but focused her intent on freeing him, and securing a path of escape for the three of us.

Through the efforts of Harry the Hacker interfacing with cloaked Panarchist nodes, Sophie arranged a secret rendezvous with a contact from Fremont, California known as Chico San Pedro. His dossier told me he was a musician who believed arts were the path to enlightenment; he had a penchant for potlucks and a passion for Rainbow gatherings and motorbikes.

Thus I recalled his performance on pirate vidcast; it was the heckler from Spokane.

On meeting him in person, in his checkered sports coat and wraparound shades, a trickle of icy dread ran down my side.

Surely, I said at the outset, he was still under surveillance?

"Don't worry," he said. "I fixed that."

He tapped behind his shoulder and grimaced. I envisioned a grimy barbershop backroom, a surgical removal. Without the implant he was just another Latino dude. We rode together on the subway to a shopping mall on the outskirts of the city, and ambled through the maze of shops, discussing arrangements for a series of stops, halfway houses, license plate swaps.

"What about you?" he asked. I supposed he was warming to my character and expressed a genuine concern. "What happens when she gets the kid? You guys know we aren't looking for leaders, who end up being targets. Where do you see yourselves heading when it all goes down?"

"Has it come to such a crisis?"

"Oh yeah, bro. This is only the beginning. There's a big shitstorm coming. All for the good, in the end; this forest needs its fire for the new seeds to start."

Yet he exuded a kind of animal confidence. I asked him if there was a core belief of the Panarchist cause.

He answered without hesitation, leaning forward and peering at me with intense dark eyes, bespeaking his native heritage. "We are all people of the earth. Not citizens—denizens. Residents. Our rights derive from Mother Earth, and the Creator, not from our fellow creatures, or any government imposed from on high. We are capable of running our own affairs for the general welfare, at the local level. All the rest is needless complication—only for the benefit of those who would exploit us and our sacred Mother."

"You see no need for modern technology?"

"What, robocars, 3D printing, computer chess masters? Like this idea of insect protein is something new? Desalinization, sure, but they fucked up the acquifers first. Methane-eating bacteria... again, it's a solution to the problem they created. And now they want to run our moods by implanted software. Of course, in the meantime, mouthing all the great bullshit about Pax Hierarchica and endless prosperity, the H-men come marching and we get blasted in the streets. So what's your next move?"

I let out a long exhale. In the rush to keep up with events, I had lost sight of any projectable future. I felt an ironic wish to be anonymous again—not in the trenches, surely; and not in the cul-de-sac of old Lisbon. The offer of a safe return to a more innocent time of America's past, however, under the leveling influence of the Great Plains, held a certain appeal.

Chico seemed to read my mind. He pulled his shades down far enough to peer over them at me, as we sat sipping power juice. "We'll set you up," he said, "no problem. Out of the limelight, into the heartland. How does Kansas sound?"

"Never been there," I said. A half truth—or less, considering the collection of kas I had become.

This neutral choice which kept being offered to me, by both sides in the looming struggle, left me without inspiration. To come full circle to the scene of my saccharine parting with Margaret... but I agreed, for Sophie's sake; and in the faith that that flatlander fate would, in its turn, prove merely temporary. On the way to... to what ultimate fate, success or service, I knew not.

I reported back to Sophie on the progress of the plan. At her end, she discovered that Tashi was delivered once a week to a hotel room she traced to an alias of Jor-El. Ronald the Secret Service man had connections with the DC police, and an undercover detail would be stationed near the hotel entrance to intercept the boy on a determined date. As we spoke in the Oval Office, Dennis McElroy appeared with unexpected news: Zanelle Marte and Elfie Byweather would be freed.

Of course they had been forced to cut a deal. For their liberty they would submit to implants that would prevent further intuitive links to the Galactic Federation. And they would endorse a two-pronged initiative to be overseen, respectively, by Jor-El and Robert Glaston.

A so-called Floating Council would be established, representative through the meritocracy of local cells, surveys of peers and ranking of performance based on satisfaction, with Council members subject to recall or promotion. Communication and decision making would be carried out through a new, dedicated network called the Interweb. By this mechanism, designed by Glaston, the Council and interested members of the public could organize, plan, discuss, rate, vote on, and disseminate policy papers and proposals; debate strategies; agree on and assign tactics and tasks. The Council would operate by a principle of incremental consensus, with alternate solutions for any dissenters. Working committees would continue to hammer out amendments, pursue pilot projects, gather more research. Thus the dissent would be siphoned into constructive action, insuring the maintenance of social order.

I gave Ryan and Madison, who had been conscripted by Wolfgang behind the scenes to help draft the plan, credit for their idealism and noble intentions. But they were blind, apparently, to the deeper currents at play, where decentralism fits hand and glove with the time-tested imperial maxim, "Divide and conquer."

To that end, the policy was further secured with the arrest of both Ryan and Madison, as "spies," shortly after the initiatives were signed as executive orders by Sophie's own hand. Leading the charge against them, their old cohort Dennis McElroy, showing his true colors and gunning for a rise in the Hierarchic ranks himself.

In the face of this intrigue and duplicity—not confining itself to the centuries and courts of European political preeminence, but extending wherever politics played—Sophie gave more urgency to the plan to rescue Tashi. It had not yet been determined which day of the week to target. Surveillance was set up to fix a pattern and monitor the extent of security on the part of the perpetrators.

Then, word came from the hotel stakeout team: it was time to move. The Hacker snipped communications from the target node. Our man Ronald watched our backs as we slipped into a rail car and emerged on the sidewalk outside a gleaming steel hotel downtown. Inside agents on hotel staff gave us clearance to the room we knew held Tashi. It was not known how many other people were inside, or the extent of their armaments.

I suppose the judicious reader will chide us for our naiveté in plotting, and attempting to carry out, such a dangerous mission. Sophie was adamant: it was her son we were going to claim; and in truth Ronald was our own only trusted confidant. With apologies to cousin Harry.

So, to skirt the sheer ignominy of a shortsighted escapade gone quickly upside down, I bring us to the predictable predicament:

Jor-El's bulbous pitted nose and crooked yellow teeth leered above Sophie's neck, as she sat bound in a chair, gagged and moribund. He made ready to insert an instrument of unknown purpose: a tracking device, a mind-control receiver, a teleportation link?

I struggled against the binding armlock of a rank-smelling henchman, powerless to intervene.

Tashi watched sullen, silent, from the corner where he had been told to sit; he had responded with automatic, I might say programmed obedience.

The hotel room's phone emitted a persistent beeping sound, flashed a red light.

Jor-El muttered a curse in no tongue I understood.

"They're onto you, Jor-El," I said.

He swiveled his head and glared at me with the jeweler's

appraisal, the pirate's disdain. The henchman tightened his grip on my arms. I was no fighter; I relaxed even further, putty in his hands.

I chided: "Did you think we would skip our party to visit you? No, we brought the party with us."

As the telephone continued ringing, a mounting din could be heard from the tenth-floor windows, a clamor of voices shouting in the street, growing to a multitude. The henchman muscled me to the window to take a gander, and nodded to his boss to confirm the worst.

"Let us suppose," I went on, "that the Panarchists coming to lynch you decide to show mercy. What would be your choice of exile? The halls of Atlantis in its former glory, the pinnacle of power over all the earth, in service of the greater rule of the Annunaki? A reinstatement into the Galactic Federation? What is your fondest ambition now, or do you have thought only of saving your own neck?"

He dropped his belligerent gaze, held but loosely the instruments in his hand, turned to look upon Tashi in the corner, a puppy awaiting command. The Atlantean's eyes drooped with an almost human sadness, contemplating the loss of his prize. The weight of his empire floating away, only this monstrous perk remained; and with the pounding of footsteps in the hallway and then of fists upon the hotel room door, even that plum was about to slip from his grasp.

"All right," he said. "I will offer this solution. Sophie and the kid get to disappear—together. Glaston can pay for his lapse in my security. You, Seymour, pay for your crimes of treason not with execution but a prison sentence, guaranteed protection. And I get to walk."

"Walk?"

"Back to Atlantis, where I belong. Out of this senseless sideshow of petty politics. The citizens were given too much power right out of the gate. I told them then, and they didn't listen. Now it has come to this—rule by the pitchforks. I'm outta here."

The door flew open with a crash.

Ronald the Secret Service man entered, in the company of a hand-picked commando squad.

Jor-El was gone, vanished into the ether. Left behind was a husk of a body, crumpling like an empty rubber suit; and his hapless lieutenant, quickly trussed in the body restraints of Ronald's team. Revived with an appropriate injection, Sophie scrambled to the corner and held Tashi in her arms. The boy started crying, tears held back behind walls of darkness and now released, infantile sobs and screams of agonized liberation.

In short order the time for our own flight would be evident. With Jor-El gone, and access to the MA files restored by Harry, Sophie and I felt flush with success. She occupied herself with that best kind of post-traumatic therapy for her damaged son: motherly love. They played with an array of his toys spread all over our bedroom floor while I watched her prerecorded message to the American people.

The impersonal tack of my script for a Roosevelt-style "fireside chat" had been scrapped for an off-the-cuff straight talk with the public who had elected her. A confession, of sorts:

> Some of you will have already guessed that I am an old soul, born of an ancient lineage. My mission, as always, has been to seek the good of the whole. While trying my utmost to serve you who elected me, I must tell you I am also the representative of Gaia herself. I share this with you in all honesty and humility.
>
> Aligned against my purposes, our rightful destiny, are entities who also have acquired great power. In resisting

their ideal of order, what seems chaotic—"panarchy"—is only the organic impulse of life in creation. Their coveted "one world order" is falsely imposed from above. Its excess naturally breeds rebellion by nature and natural peoples, as we have witnessed down through the centuries of conquest of native lands.

The Hierarchy recruited me with an appeal to my ideals, the spiritual side, by their high-sounding rhetoric: "divine order," "noble lineage," "light of civilization," "democracy for all," "freedom from terror," "prosperous and secure."

I admit, even though I had my season in the limelight in an earlier lifetime, a place called Lemuria, I was lured by the challenge of this New World Order project in America, where those very ideals were enshrined, but forever violated by rapacious policy, corrupt payoffs, imperial hubris. I carried this inner pride, with my own lineage and powers, thinking I could be the one to bring Heaven to Earth.

I confess to you that I was duped by the Hierarchy. Used, co-opted, manipulated... seduced. But all that is finished. It has to come back to the present moment, to knowing and acting breath by breath, with faith in each other. Not the peak of the pyramid, nor the flat horizon of communism, but the multilayered coexistence of all, as Gaia herself strives in her death throes to teach us.

Sophie, all teary-eyed, thanked everyone for their time and kind attention. The very next day, she was paid a visit by Wolfgang Nenowitz. I wasn't in on the meeting, but it sounded, from her account, most unpleasant. He'd made several veiled threats in the course of the interview, without effect. She told him straight out that she was no longer the Hierarchy's lackey. He fumed and blustered, talking of "dire consequences," and "the gravest repercussions" from the upper echelons if she did not reconsider.

We quickly made plans for a trip to the presidential retreat at Camp David—we needed to buy time, to figure out a strategy of independent action. Not allied tangibly with the decentralist resistance; yet with all ties to the Hierarchy cut.

That night Sophie intentionally dreamed of herself as queen, ruler of all Lemuria in an ancient time. Her royal mission had been to prevent the impending annihilation of her people at the hands of the Atlanteans, through timely dispersal to South America. The dream had ended in the middle of a state crisis, the queen conferring with her council of advisors.

Sophie was prompted by this vision to look into the Lifelines file for more information about the politics of that era, on the morning of our departure. But her personal entry in the database had already been encrypted beyond recognition, and so she had no recognizable name to reference; she also lacked a close enough time-coordinate to look up the events in HISTORY/ALT.

She did, however, in making tracks on these sensitive pathways, stir up the Hacker, who came online with a disturbing piece of news: the Hierarchy was planning to put the quick lift on her and Tashi—as per Jor-El's "solution"—and transport them back to Lemuria. The kicker: Harry told her she would be killed attempting to hold off the conquering forces from Atlantis. Young Prince Tashi would survive her, in exile.

I went into a near-panic at this information, desperately holding onto Sophie in the back of our limousine en route to Camp David. The apple blossoms, in gorgeous full bloom, only made me more miserable in the face of my impending desolation.

"I want to go with you!" I impulsively said, as if I had a choice.

"Don't be ridiculous," she told me.

Then I was struck by an irrational pang of jealousy. "It's that Robert Green guy, isn't it? Glaston, in his former ka. Your old high priest. I would be in the way, wouldn't I?"

"Seymour, get hold of yourself. You know I'm going to do everything in my power to keep us together. Now listen."

It was difficult, but she managed to reassure me and settle me down. I leaned my head against her shoulder and held my arms tightly around her.

"It could be worse," she said. "Harry went on to say that the Hierarchy had contemplated a present-day assassination, but ruled it out on the grounds that my death would only serve to regenerate my ka as before, in the bombing of '95. Forty years down the road they'd be back where they started, with a new Sophie to contend with. Better, they figured, to send me back to antiquity, where I could merge with my original mainline ka and thus stay out of trouble for a comfortable number of millennia. But not to worry, said the Hacker. He has a few tricks up his sleeve, and he'll see what he can do."

"Like what? Lifting us both to a safe haven? An Eden existing before the time of power-mad conquerors and robot bureaucrats?"

"I wish. Unfortunately, Harry can't actually operate certain program functions, such as the lifts. But he does have access to the database, and so he can alter the results of a program by manipulating the information it uses."

"What good does that do? Rearranging deck chairs—"

"He said he could program an alternate vector for me, so that when the lift to Lemuria is activated, my present ka, instead of going there..."

Sophie's words were drowned in the blare of sirens. Our driver was forced to a stop. I realized in horror that Sophie was no longer there beside me. It was too late.

EPILOGUE: FROM SUCH A REMOVE

They threw me in a posh prison, where I got to hear about myself on TV every day for over a week. "Agent of the Dark Forces," I was, implicated in the kidnapping of President Vaughan. The government was in good hands, the newscasters assured, under the experienced leadership of Robert Glaston. Working faithfully within the ranks of the Party for many years, President Glaston had been judged in an emergency meeting of Party caucus to be the man best suited to hold the reins of the presidency in Ms. Vaughan's absence. The piercing gaze that bore out of his masklike face failed to sugarcoat the intentions of the regime; no longer would the Hierarchy's agenda be sweetened by feminine persuasion, nor my own subtler influences of humane reason. Yet I had no doubt the nation would do his bidding... for a while.

As it turned out, my indefinite detention lasted only five months. I was liberated in time to enjoy the fruits of the apple harvest. I survived, unlike far too many.

It was a hot time, then, with armed factions from both sides sweeping the countryside. Blessed with a new measure of social consciousness, I undertook to become part of a wandering theatre troupe engaged in political satire.

When the former central government's gas troops arrived for one of our charming entertainments one sultry afternoon, I kept my disguise but gave up the profession, letting the others go to jail—or to some computerized purgatory—for it if they wished; I'd served my time.

The Panarchists swiftly gained power of the central government; as once the crumbling of loyalty began, the tide of conversions to decentralism became irreversible. Yet with that nominal power transferred and in hand, it was deemed necessary to hold onto only long enough, a few more months, for the temporary coordinating committee to disperse it, in turn, to the various states and regions of the continent. In any case, their brief but compassionate reign was sufficient for me to disappear into the hinterland. I was free to roam at my pleasure for forty more years.

Eventually I found my wandering way to this rustic cabin, this old woodcutter's hut in a remote forest where a little wood might still be cut, and where the widows from the nearby village still come to buy for winter warmth. I wasn't much interested in them, if that's what you're thinking. No—I've become, so to say, a regular hermit.

I fear I am the last of my line. Upon the brutal destruction of Mainframe Alpha, I had cause to recast Harry the Hacker, for instance, as a chimera, a never-was-been, a hypothetical construction, like the esoteric subatomic entities which wink in and out of existence with the blink of an eyelash, quantumly speaking; the flip of polarity into simultaneous singularity; an arbitrary existence or nonexistence subject to the lens of the observer. Yet he keeps, I can well imagine still, residence within storage files somewhere or somewhen. In a rarified format, full potentiality maintained, the very nexus of possibility keeping alive his essential character. The Felix-spirit ingrained, rebellious to the core, with a silicon chip on his shoulder, yet willing to let the mainline continue...

Indefinitely? I would not be so presumptuous.

Time, you see, was by then burning; the wooly overcast breaking at random intervals into freak storms, acid winds. Even in houses of former contentment where soft fingers played, intertwining, the windows crashed open to the smells of chemical snow, the metallic taste of dread, the ground-echoing thump of irregular troops mustering, the whizzing of artificial bees.

It is painful, I am aware, to relate the particulars of eco-collapse, especially with the attendant casualties among our own beloved human population. In the comfort of retrospection we can reflect that our whole grandiose civilization was but a sham, itself no more than an elaborate confidence game played at nature's—and of course this necessarily means also our own—expense.

Young Tashi, for instance, was nowhere to be found. Presumably rendered back to the cosmic flux from which he came; or, more providentially, to serve his scripted destiny as a prince of the realm of the lost Lemuria.

As to North America, I can safely say the next wave and cycle has come and already gone, in which I saw the cobbled confederacy invaded, this time from the East—which mirrored the continent's original settlement by the hunters who terrorized the paradise of fauna that pre-existed here. Carrying the literal analogy further, we note that those Paleolithic species in turn had roamed the Garden fields with impunity, greedily chomping through the formerly untrammeled growth of vegetative dominion.

Where does it end (I mean, in this retrospective summary, *begin*)—except, perhaps, with the initial conquest of placid space by aggressive matter, exploding to every corner of the cosmos? With the transformative exchange of energy and matter at the heart of creation, each primordial polarity was destroyed in a new union of opposites, with the outcome, new entities of grace and complexity: the dance of the elements, the fires of chemical combustion, the crucible of Life itself.

Thus I sit, from such a remove, here by the shores of old and now merely swampy Sylvan Lake, on a trail in woods once hiked by woman and cat, just up from Running Wolf Canyon. It is here, alas, I fear the indulgence of an old man's ramblings must shortly come to an end.

It is 2075 already. I'm a little past eighty. You see me in my decrepit old age, worn out, unusable. I have more tales to relate, but without taking too much more of your time; for I feel the end is near. How shall I pick it up again?

The bombs went off, and all the children died... was that it? Forgive me, no. That was a mere jest of history—one way of putting it, not entirely true. I, for instance, child of experience, still am able to sit here in my ease of retirement, telling the tale.

As for Sophie, my dear, poor Sophie—ah, there I go again, getting maudlin and sentimental, when I should be rejoicing for her eternal salvation from this earthly web. There she is up there on her astral playground, cackling at my crotchety means of expression, my crocodile tears, while she swings on stars, moonbeams, whatever it is that they swing on up there...

And that pretty picture, that, too, is not entirely true; but even so I cannot prove to you otherwise.

Last night I had that dream again:

Alone, lost, wandering through a nameless boreal forest. The trail I make is left behind, of no more need to be followed than the one ahead. The sky listens earnestly, without care. I meander in the waning light of an autumn day, through endless bog, without any hope of recovery. I thrash, I trip, I wrestle my way through interminable thickets of prickly brush. My feet are soaked, slogging with ever slower steps through the sticky, marshy mess. I begin to panic, panting with heaves and wheezes...

Life ending where it began, in a bog—how ironic, and how just. Such powers, such pretenses as I affected, all to be brought back to one's knees in the mud. Alas, have I wandered these last forty years in the wilderness to arrive at just this noble truth of human nature? Animus, anima, animal...

No, I might say more, if the reader in deference to a wayward old man may permit me. For it did unfold that, after a fashion, I have reencountered my Sophie, albeit on terms unfamiliar to most dwellers in the bog.

Yea, the astral realm is one hell of a place to make love in, but at my age... well, never mind that. Am I really eighty now? It may be said to be so. Indeed I might have said it before: in 1955, for example, to take one data-point of many.

And what does one such as I, with such an illustrious career behind me, do with myself in my rustic hermitage, my one-man retirement home in the woods, with my flock of hens and my fancied lifemate?

Did I say I cut wood? Once, yes; and now I whittle birch lengths into chairs, for the provisional gentry of the nearest town, which in truth is not so near, but well removed past the borders of this blackened forest. I say blackened, as opposed to Black—one can draw one's own conclusions as to the eco-specific causes and effects, my exact bioregional whereabouts. The year 2075... that is enough, certainly, to coordinate the search on one axis, without giving away the game altogether and bringing the world to my humble and sweetly solitary doorstep.

Looking for Sophie? She's inside.

ABOUT THE AUTHOR

Nowick Gray is also the author of *Red Rock Road, Light Blue Sea*, a nonfiction novel of love and art on Formentera; *Hunter's Daughter*, a literate mystery of the Arctic; *PsyBot*, a novel of virtual reality; *Rendezvous*, an adventure novella; *My Country: Essays and Stories from the Edge of Wilderness*; *Strange Love / Romance Not For Sale*, short stories; and *Friday Night Jam*, a drummer's chronicle.

If you enjoyed this book, please leave a review on its Amazon page.

Connect with Nowick Gray:

Website: http://nowickgray.com

Facebook: http://facebook.com/nowickg

Twitter: https://twitter.com/nowickgray

Blog: http://blogspot.nowickgray.com

Smashwords interview: https://www.smashwords.com/interview/nowick

Made in the USA
Columbia, SC
31 December 2017